Lara McKeon
based on a true story
CELEBRITY RULES

Library of Congress Number: 2007941458
Cover Photos:
©iStockphoto.com/Joellen Armstrong, Lisa Klumpp
All rights reserved.
Copyright © 2008 Lara McKeon

Cover and Interior Design by Bobby Dawson

ISBN-13: 978-1-58385-207-1
ISBN-10: 1-58385-207-7

Special thanks to the kind people
who helped me with this difficult project:

Diane B.
Jo B.
Kathy C.
Mary C.
Jeanne D.
Janet O.
Robin O.
Carrie P.
Barbara R.
Karen S.
Lorraine S.
Kelli V.

based on a true story
CELEBRITY RULES

CHAPTER ONE

Lara didn't know where she was, but she was relieved there weren't any lions in the room.

She blinked, then opened her eyes wider and remembered. She'd pulled out her favorite sheets, the denim ones that weren't from Pottery Barn but could have been. Comfort bedding, required after a difficult move, a change of states.

She lay quiet a minute, then suddenly sat up and twisted around to the window. The late-summer morning sun leaked through cracks in the blinds. No tornado. Not yet. Lara dropped back onto the pillows and squinted at the bedside table. It'd been three weeks since her move and already she'd built a little tower of books on the nightstand. At the top was a library copy of a popular novel, followed by a slim new Mother Teresa quote book, then a dream dictionary, its pages softened from use. At the base of the stack was a spiral-bound notebook with a pen clipped on one end.

She'd dreamt the lion. Its cage had been ripped open, and the zoo grounds were littered with tree limbs flung onto cars and buildings. A newspaper headline, "Lion Escapes Zoo, Wanders City," had appeared and she'd known a tornado had torn up the city, then left it stunned and quiet in that strange way of passing disasters.

A cat jumped up beside her and she stroked its head. "Should I write it down, Dinky?"

Lara reached for the notepad under the books and snatched it away fast to keep the heap from tumbling. It was thinner now since she'd ripped out a section of 20-year-old college notes. The remaining sheets were half-filled with short dated entries. She flipped to a blank page and mulled over the tornado. It likely meant chaos, true enough of her life. And wasn't there something in the Bible about a prowling lion? So maybe an old remembered verse had revisited her.

She wouldn't bother writing it down. She put the notebook back on the pile, then climbed out of bed. Soon she was dressed to go down for breakfast. But as she headed for the stairs, she paused at the bedroom door. In a far corner, a television squatted on a table like a foot-high troll ready to spew out news and movies. She paced over to it and clicked on the weather station.

—✺—

Across town, near seldom-used train tracks, a shabby man grinned as he practiced belching out the tune to "I'll Fly Away." It'd get a laugh from his friend Dave. He lounged back on the wide stone steps in front of a red sandstone mansion. Despite his smile, he had a castoff attitude, as if he'd at some point been bumped out of a gigantic round of musical chairs. He kept shuffling around the circle, but he never found his place.

The house behind him also seemed to have lost its place in the world. It jutted up from among newer short buildings and gaping empty lots, an oddity since its neighboring grand homes had fallen. Stable people had vacated this part of town, leaving it to types who knew the hours the soup kitchens served and where to find the best secondhand clothes. When the "better people" left, pieces of the old building began to disappear. The formal light fixtures and doorknobs went first, sold or stolen after the building was chopped into apartments. Then a young couple with money had driven past and taken a liking to the turret's coned roof. Soon it was capping their gazebo in a suburb of Kansas City and the house's lone tower stood with a flattened top, like an attached oatmeal box.

A man and woman dressed in fresh outfits from the mall made a wide path around the man as they passed. George paused in his song and lowered his head, then peered out from under his blue baseball cap. He'd seen the look the young woman had given him, some uppity stare. But her face wasn't familiar so he let himself look up fully at her. She was probably on her way to those warehouse flea markets. Good. He didn't need someone he knew showing up in his part of town. Much as he wanted his kids to come find him, he didn't want that kind of trouble so early this morning. Anyway, he didn't have anything to feel shame about. They knew he had his own apartment down here, and disability was disability, it didn't make him a bum. He pulled a bottle out of an inside pocket of his jacket and swallowed once to settle his nerves. Just a hair of the dog, nothing wrong with that.

At the corner, the couple passed a taller younger man. George saw Dave eye the woman up and down as if he thought he could pick up on her. Funny thing, sometimes he did get the woman. But this time she kept on talking to her man and ignored him. She thought they were bums, but she didn't know anything. George was disabled, and Dave—well, maybe Dave was a bum.

As Dave slouched along the sidewalk toward him, George could see his friend's eyes were already bloodshot. Must have had a hit earlier, which meant George didn't have to share his bottle. He took another swig to celebrate.

Dave hunched down on the step next to him.

George scratched his gray-speckled stubble and leaned forward with his elbows on his knees. He pulled a sandwich out of a plastic bag and sniffed the bread. "I got peanut butter from the Charity Brothers. What'd you find?" They were working out a system. If they went separately to the kitchens, they could figure out where the best food was, then the other could go back and get extras. Peanut butter was a bad start. Maybe Dave did better.

Dave unwrapped a sandwich then shook out the colorful paper he'd had tucked under his arm. "Mercy Place is using up that government bologna. A good day would be sausage and that thick coffee from the Polish Ministries. Good stuff. But today's not a good day." His eyes skimmed the paper as he held it up. "Shit! Dirk Durmont with some blonde." He threw the paper to the cement and kicked at it.

George's laugh was a snort. "I'd take his women for sure, even the ones he's done with."

"I wouldn't take nothing from nobody got it so easy. Could have been me, you know. In high school he wasn't nobody. I could have made it just like him, gone out to California and been a big star, famous and rich and shit. If I'd got the right breaks, I could have ..."

"I'd take his money!" George said. "With his money, I'd get any woman I wanted. Get cleaned up and get any woman I wanted." He ran a hand over his wild dirty hair, sat up straighter, and shouted out, "Come and get it, ladies! Georgey Boy is here!"

They took bites of their sandwiches and chewed a while.

"Saw him, you know." George spoke through his peanut butter.

"Yeah, but that ain't nothing." Dave shrugged. "Grocery store, library. Hell, I went out with some chick said she almost married him, half the women around here saying the same damn thing. I could still do it, get some breaks and go out and do what he did. He ain't nothing.

What I'd give to ... " He chomped a huge chunk off his sandwich and worked his jaw.

Music began throbbing from a window above them.

George laughed and looked around at the house. "We'd get *her*, up there, if we was Dirk Durmont, that's for sure. Did I tell you ... "

"Yeah, all that stuff she has on the walls. But you know the elevator in there," Dave looked sideways at George while tapping the side of his head. "It don't go all the way up." He laughed mean.

George hooted. "I don't care where it goes! I'd jump on it anytime." He stood and wiggled his hips to the beat of the music, then stopped and pointed up. Chunks of black clouds were scuttling across the sky.

Inside the house, up a black plastic runner that led to the second floor, a chipped painted door rattled in rhythm with a loud bass. Behind the door, a barely furnished room was lit only by streaks of sun that snuck around lowered window shades. A pale young woman in red panties and bra danced.

"Anyway I see it, I need you here ..."

Alice lifted her arms until her wrists crossed above her head and shuffled her feet, keeping her ankles close together as if bound. As she danced, she thrust out her breasts, large and propped forward by the push-up bra.

"At night I'm not alone when I have you near."

She moved her legs apart and sunk down into a plié, clenching her thighs and hips.

"Our future is the only place I see,
We'll dream our fantasies, only you and me ..."

She leaned back into an arc while her fingers beckoned her lover toward her. She tipped her head back and shook her hair, forcing the yellow overprocessed mass to move. Still inviting with her fingers, she slowly rose and swayed. She swung to the side, bumped her hip toward him, then moved with practiced fluidity to tip her opposite hip.

"Now you're part of me." She smiled at the tall blond man.

"Now you're part of me." She stretched up and kissed his mouth hard, then laughed and backed away quickly, the beat of the music guiding her movements.

"I know you love me, Dirk."

The man pictured in the poster taped to the wall smiled, but didn't respond.

Still she moved toward him, enticing him with her movements. The song coming from the cheap boom box repeated. Framed photos of Dirk Durmont surrounded it on the dinette table and lined the walls of the living room where she danced. Many of them were identical, a professional press photo artificially signed "Love ya, Dirk Durmont." Within the frames, cozied up to the actor's face, Alice looked out always wearing the same set smile.

The CD ended and the music stopped. Alice froze. An expression of sorrow mixed with panic appeared on her face. Suddenly, she turned to look behind her, then rushed to the dark apartment hall and peered toward her bedroom door. She slapped her hands over her ears and pressed hard, then slapped down again on the sides of her skull. She ran to the CD player and hit "start."

"Anyway I see it, I need you here ..."

She relaxed and smiled, then danced toward her companion on the wall.

———

Hours later, Lara was fed, pressed, dressed, and headed for Discount City. She parked, and as she walked toward the store her eyes went to mounds of dark clouds roiling in the distance. With effort, she forced her mind back to the list in her hand. Forget tornadoes. Number one on the day's list was to buy supplies for her new home. The store entrance caught her by surprise and she stumbled into the door. For an instant, a look of pain shot across her face, but she quickly replaced it with an expression of cool reserve. She glanced around and straightened her shoulders to walk in with dignity.

This huge store with its harsh lighting and stacks of cheap merchandise was not Lara's usual choice. But today she needed a houseful of cleaning supplies and this was the quickest way to get that chore crossed off her list. She grabbed a cart and pushed it along the aisles. Half-way through the store, she looked down into her cart. The bottom was covered with basics: dish towels, a trash can, duplicates of disinfectant, a large white dish drainer. She cringed and looked away. They could be pieces of a "starting over" kit.

Starting over. Options—like her therapist said, people who have options are lucky. Not many people could move to a new city and start over. Lara examined her cart again. Maybe the only thing that shouted "humiliated divorcee" was a large plastic tool chest; the man always kept the tools. Embarrassing, an intelligent women like her not being able to keep the tools—or a husband, for that matter. How hard could that be? But she knew by now that sometimes the intelligent and brave thing to do was to walk away from an impossible situation.

Groceries now. She pushed her cart across the wide aisle dividing the food and housewares sections of the store, then stopped to squint up at a sign hanging from the ceiling. Sugar, cake mixes, baking goods. Not today. It'd be fun, but being alone in the house with a cake wouldn't be a good thing. She'd already gone through several cans of low-fat frosting, seeing the creamy chocolate shrink to barely enough to cover a cupcake and having no one else to blame for its disappearance.

With resolve, she forced her cart away from the baking aisle and swung it around.

Years later, she would wonder why her guardian angel hadn't led her to chocolate cake. Instead, as she veered to the right, she almost hit a cart moving toward her. She corrected her direction and missed the collision, then looked up at the other shopper ...

Lara's inhalation was a gasp and her eyes widened with shock. Good grief, he looked like Dirk Durmont! The man winced and looked away, his eyes like those of a cornered animal, a creature who was accustomed to but dreaded being pursued.

She would later regret not doing the normal thing, not leaning in to the actor's beautiful face, the face so many people wanted to be near, and saying "Excuse me, do you know where they keep the cottage cheese around here?" Instead, she honored the spooked look of the hunted creature in front of her, forced her face back into its usual distant reserve, and moved past him down the aisle. As she walked on, wondering what this famous man was doing in Granville, she noticed the boy with him silently laughing. How silly she must have looked!

The actor left an eruption of excitement where he had passed. Two aisles down, a woman leaned against an end-cap, examining his body with a lascivious leer. Embarrassed, Lara averted her eyes. Other women had stopped to stare at him or had gathered to whisper. When she found the cottage cheese, people watched her as she read the cartons' expiration dates. She smiled at them and moved on.

Soon, however, she felt she was being watched by more than the groups of excitable women. At the deli, she noticed a slim young man eyeing her. She flashed her "hi neighbor" grin at him, then shopped on until she reached the frozen foods aisle. Coming toward her were Dirk, the boy, and the man who had watched her buy sliced turkey. Determined to be courteous this time, Lara looked away and stared into the glass door she was passing. She felt foolish putting on an act of being more interested in mocha swirl ice cream than in this sexy man. But with her history of ruinous relationships, right now Lara did find desserts safer and more fun than men and the havoc-creating "thang" that went with them everyplace.

As she passed them, she was startled to hear a snicker and a whispered, "Yeah, she's okay."

Strange. Why wouldn't she be okay?

Later that day, Lara sat on her porch with a notebook in her lap. Her view to the street was junked up by fallen branches left by the storm that had blown through the city that afternoon. No tornado, thank God, and the zoo was okay. A familiar unease made her shiver and she steered her thoughts to other matters.

She looked down at the notebook and read what she'd written.

Sept-22-98
Journal,

I ran into Dirk Durmont at Discount City. It wasn't someone who simply resembled him; he looked exactly like he does in movies and pictures. And he had this look in his eyes like a hunted animal, so it must have been him. I walked past without speaking.

I keep thinking about how much he has accomplished. I envy him that.

I have two possible computer programming jobs pending. I had to take aptitude tests for one company last week. The tests were hard —math story problems, then questions like on the test I took to get into grad school. I wish I'd studied more.

I'm reading a book about perfectionism now and it's hitting home.

I'm feeling better, now that I'm moved in. More at peace. Will this feeling last?

Lara couldn't shake the sense of failure that had clung to her since the divorce. But today she'd seen Dirk Durmont and then learned from her sister that he had lived in Granville and his family was still here. Just like her. Well, if a man from Granville had gone off and become a movie star, surely she could get a life going for herself! She had goals and she was going to make them happen. A beautiful home, check. A good job, almost. A man? Not yet. Worry lines appeared between her eyebrows and she reached up and pressed them away.

Now snug in a wicker chair with its back and arms around her like a scratchy hug, Lara smiled at her hunch that something was waiting for her here in Granville. Maybe she *would* find a good man. Stranger things had happened. It had been a rough year, but among her losses was a miserable marriage. She was just astounded that a loss which was a gain could cause so much pain. But now she was resting on a porch that she—she alone—owned and no one could take away from her. Things had to get better now. She'd been raised an army brat with a lifetime of having her roots yanked up and it was time to make a home-town for herself. Much of her family had settled here, so Granville it would be. She would no longer have to hesitate when people asked where she was from.

She looked out to the quiet street lined with deep-rooted oaks and houses. She'd changed into fresh jeans and a favorite sweater—company clothes. She wasn't expecting any visitors, but she wanted to make a good impression on her new neighbors; she had 40 years to go until she was 80-something and she intended to live those years here.

Lara pulled out a blank sheet of paper and started a new list. Cleaning supplies, check. Decorating, in process. Her rooms were already set up the way she wanted; before the moving van arrived at "the old house", the lost house, she'd drafted out the floor plan and made tiny templates of the furniture she was taking with her. She'd resisted the urge to cut out a paper family and play at walking them through the flat little rooms. Instead, Lara acted the grown-up, and when the crew showed up to take her life to another state, she handed them copies of the drawings and kept her dreams to herself.

Now there were other projects. This was what she had in front of her to do—fixing up her new home. This is what she would focus on, not the sad past or the scary future.

"Paint the porch floor." Number one project. The porch was orange, an unflattering color on her. Not that she intended to get her face close to the floor, but still. Do ASAP.

The list grew quickly. She finished, then stared off without focus. A man and woman led by three dogs moved along the sidewalk across the street. They stopped and waved. Lara sat up straighter and grinned, delighted. Neighbors were waving! She waved, then let herself settle back into an easy peace.

Life was going to be okay. Finally, life was going to be fine.

CHAPTER TWO

Stay 100 feet back from him, they'd said.

The L.A. police didn't like her much.

Alice pulled her car onto a gravel road off the highway. From here, she could watch for Dirk leaving his mother's house, which was set back someplace beyond that tall iron fence. She knew he was there; that's where she'd left him last night. He'd gone to dinner with people, then they shopped. Rather, his brother Dylan shopped while Dirk waited in the car. Alice knew he wanted her to come up and knock on the window, but that pesky business with the police still had her nervous. Today she'd talk to him and clear up this mess between them.

Alice waited, wondering which of his vehicles he would use this afternoon. Suddenly she glimpsed a white truck moving toward the gate. Frantic now, she dumped her purse out onto the seat beside her and grabbed a can of hairspray. She spritzed and fluffed her hair fuller, squirted a cloud of perfume toward her body, then smeared on red lipstick. Her trembling hands dotted red on the end of her nose, making her look like a confused clown. She peered at her reflection in the rearview mirror and cursed, then wiped at the spot with her fingers.

Dirk's truck pulled onto the blacktop highway and she lurched her car out onto the road. She wasn't the only one who reacted. Several cars popped out of side roads to follow him and he ran them through the city until he'd lost most of them. Alice was almost left behind with the others, but she spied his truck as it turned onto High Street and rushed to catch up.

"Those others are gone, Sweetheart. Now it's just the two of us." Alice laughed and turned her radio up louder. "Wait'll you hear what those pricks pulled in L.A.!"

It was her father who'd told her what the police said. That was after they picked her up, after that silly misunderstanding. Dad and her brother took her home to Kansas City and talked about "stabilizing", and then they visited a doctor and the pharmacy. She ended up with a zip-up red silk bag that rattled from the pills in their orange plastic bottles.

She hated the pills. They made her sick. She went from being full of ideas about her life with the man she loved, to being a deadened thing, growing fat and slow. And worse, she was lonely. It seemed as if Dirk had abandoned her, and she even missed the bitch voice, the hateful thing that watched her. She'd never felt so alone. So for awhile she swallowed the capsules on schedule, but when the state gave her back her driver's license she figured she was doing just fine and was done choking down strange stuff. Those pills were for sick people and she was not sick until she took them.

She didn't understand the fuss about the dog. If she could talk to Dirk, she knew he'd clear it up. He must have fired that housekeeper by now, the one who called the police. And Alice didn't keep the stupid dog. She only took care of it awhile, figuring he'd want it with her instead of that witch who was watching his house. She'd explained it in her letters, but he was acting like they'd gotten lost in the mail. She'd have to talk to him to clear it up.

"Dirk!" Alice shouted out the window. She squeezed her car closer to his bumper as they moved. "He can't hear me. When he sees me back here, he'll stop."

She drove along, keeping TV-cop close to the white truck in front of her. When it suddenly slowed, she had to stomp her brake pedal to avoid hitting it.

"Watch out for that Laura Bitch," a voice from the back seat warned.

Alice pressed one hand over her ear, but otherwise ignored the comment. She slowed more to stare at the blond woman walking the large golden retriever along the sidewalk. She looked familiar …

"Laura Starbright!" Dirk's former fiancée, the actress! "What's she doing here? He dumped her, didn't he? He dumped her after I wrote him the truth about her."

"Some bitches never get it," said the voice from the back.

She stared at Lara. "Her hair's a little darker now. Still cut the same, to the shoulders." Alice looked up at her own hair, visible in the rearview mirror. The color was similar to the actress' pale blond. "She's a little shorter in person, too, but cameras will do that."

Confusion. She didn't want to lose Dirk's truck, but she needed to make sure Laura knew she'd better stay away. Was she ignoring Alice's letters, her warnings? Not smart. She pulled over into a cross street as the woman neared it.

Moments earlier, Lara had had the street to herself as she trekked through the neighborhood with Buckley, her super-sized golden retriever.

It was a treat, having this gorgeous place to walk, these streets of well-kept older homes and huge oak trees now tipped in dusky fall colors. Today, the two paced along quickly, but slowed at every house with a porch so Lara could study the floorboards. It'd been a good day; Saturday usually was. She'd found a job, so she could cross "make a living" off her to-do list. She'd found a health club. "Work out," check. This morning, she'd visited home improvement stores and collected paint cards in shades of gray, green, and brown. Soon she'd paint her porch floor, before winter got any closer.

"Dammit!" She suddenly tripped and landed with a thud onto the grass. Buckley stopped ahead on the sidewalk, then stepped back to stand beside her. Embarrassed, she looked to see if anyone had witnessed her clumsy tumble. No cars, no people with dogs, no people with people. Just her big dog. When she'd first seen him two years earlier, the dog's size had scared her. But he needed a home so Lara welcomed him into the little family she was building around her. She now used Buckley for support and pulled herself up to a stand, then walked on. The new pain in her ankle made her wince, but she fought the urge to limp. If she ignored the pain, it would go away.

She stopped at the next corner and waited for two approaching vehicles to pass. The white truck looked familiar; the last time she'd seen it, Dirk Durmont was behind the wheel.

"Oh look, Buckley! Our famous guy." The dog lifted his ears and watched the street. Lara wasn't surprised to see the truck; Dirk sometimes showed up in her neighborhood. She thought it likely he had family in one of the larger houses or owned one himself, and that having extra mansions must be nice.

But as the vehicles passed, she saw that behind the actor's truck a red sports car trailed, only feet away—crazily close. Lara had already seen a little of how the locals reacted to this man, their intense interest in him. And she'd read stories about psychotics endangering celebrities' lives. Whether this woman in the red car was a clueless "fan" or outright insane, if she was chasing an unwilling victim she was a criminal. A wave of compassion washed over Lara. What kind of life could Dirk have, being hounded constantly? And it was his success that had brought this on. How unfair and sad.

Buckley strained against the leash, eager to cross the road, and Lara stepped toward the curb. But suddenly the red car turned the corner onto the street beside her and stopped. She peered into the car and a woman with frizzy yellow hair stared back.

Strange. What was she doing?

Then Lara had an idea.

"Whoa, puppy. Let's wait." She stood still, staring down the woman behind the wheel. "Looks like we've distracted this one. If she's chasing Dirk, he can make a getaway if he hustles." The white truck was moving farther down the street. But as Lara watched, it slowed and then stopped.

Why wasn't he leaving? She glanced toward the car pulled up near her then back at the truck. Did he know this woman in the car? Then she sensed a wave of something nasty and a thought came to her.

How dangerous *were* these stalkers?

The last thing she wanted was to cause some incident. "Let's go, puppy dog," and she let Buckley pull her forward into the road.

Alice watched Lara walk away and reversed back onto the street. She peered down the road, then saw that the white truck had stopped. It now jerked forward and took off.

"I'm hurrying, Baby!" She watched him turn at the corner and sped to follow him.

A whisper came from behind her. "You know that Laura is doing him no good in this town. He'll want you to take care of that."

⟨⟨⟨⟩⟩⟩

"Whoo-hoo! Too fat!" Michelle leaned back and laughed along with the three girls crammed into her small turquoise car. They rode around the Granville downtown square, shouting "too fat" out the window at anyone standing on the sidewalk.

Her car was part of a procession, the vehicles running out like rats from the streets set between tall old buildings. Michelle Hamlin didn't like what she was seeing. Women were everywhere. Women with hair color too close to her own purchased Fantasy Blond, which was rumored to be Dirk's favorite shade. A dark blue car was crammed with five women in yellow topknots and red halter tops. The old brown and rust SUV held four slicked-straight shiny-haired blondes and the newer beige sports car carried a trio of lemon-streaked bobs. Michelle and her friends were the only cool people, with their long yellow hair combed over bare shoulders and silver tube tops.

These other women probably thought they were going to meet Dirk. No way, not if Michelle could help it. They had rounded the square for the fourth time when she turned the steering wheel sharp left. Brittany, Stacy, and Delta were tossed toward the car doors.

"Britt, cell phone! Call Connie again," Michelle ordered. She'd had it with this cruising. They were going in circles here while Dirk was out there someplace else. "Delta, did you bring one of your Dad's bottles?"

"He was in his room all day; I couldn't get near the case," Delta replied in a small voice.

"Hell, give me one of your cigarettes then!"

Brit waved the purple phone. "They can trace this when they find it missing." She dialed the memorized number.

Michelle quick made up a story. "Someone gave me that phone, a hot guy who never wanted to lose touch with me. Here, give me that." She grabbed it after Brittany dialed, then shouted into it, "Girl, what's happening!" She nodded, then shrieked. The three girls in the car shrieked in response, not needing a reason for their screams. She threw the phone back over her shoulder and turned the car down a side street.

"Dirk's in a white truck down on Lincoln Avenue, near the University!" Michelle raced her car down narrow streets, barely missing parked vehicles. Soon they were again part of a caravan.

"Connie!" Stacy shouted and waved out the window at a small white four-door. "Phone!" Someone tossed it to her. She tapped into it, then spoke. "Hey! Where is Dirk in all this?" She listened for a minute, then shouted "No way!" and laughed. "Where does she live?"

A minute later she snapped the phone shut and handed it blind toward the back seat. Brittany reached out her hand with its long multicolored fingernails and took it.

"You will not believe this!" Stacy shouted, squealed, then pressed her mouth shut and grinned.

"So where is he? Tell us!" Michelle mentally cursed Stacy's pain-in-the-butt smug attitude. "Does he have friends around here?"

"Oh, right now it looks like he went on to his mother's house."

Michelle grit her teeth. "Lost him! What an f-ing waste of time."

"We could try there, his mother's," Delta said.

"Hell, no." Michelle snarled. "Connie said someone said we have to stay away from his family. Unless he has a big movie star party there, then I am getting an invitation no matter what I have to do!"

Stacy spoke up. "But you will never believe what Connie told me!" She grinned again at the others, looking like she had a secret.

Michelle tried to ignore her, but after a few seconds spat out the words, "What, dammit!"

"He has a *girl* friend around here!"

"No way!" The others shouted.

"Yes! She has a house along one of these streets. Someone saw her. And … ," Stacy paused.

"What, you whore!" Michelle shouted.

"And … her name is 'Laura'! Isn't that romantic?"

Brittany gasped. "Just like Laura Starbright! I can't believe it! Laura Starbright broke his heart, and he's lost without her, so he found another Laura!" She sank back into her seat with a sigh. "It's like a movie!"

"Too bad we didn't bring a camera," Stacy said.

"Where does she live?" Michelle didn't like the sound of this. A real girlfriend here in Granville?

"Around here someplace. We're not sure. She's blond, of course, and has a big dog. A blond dog!"

Brittany sighed dramatically and said, "She even looks like the real Laura. It's so romantic!"

"This we need to look into," Michelle said, and drove toward Connie's house.

—◆◆◆—

Something strange was happening in this town.

Lara let herself in through her back door, leaving Buckley curling up near his doghouse. The cat Dinky and her new pound kitty Mick followed her into the living room where she gave the front door a tug to make sure it was locked. She sat to take off her walking shoes.

Today the streets had started out empty, but soon were busy with speeding cars. Occasionally a vehicle had slowed near her, then accelerated when she glanced toward it. And early on that one woman, the one following Dirk so close, had outright stopped next to her. Too strange.

Lately, bizarre things were happening around her everyplace she went. At Discount City and the home improvement stores, people stopped in the aisles to stare at her. They must think she was someone else. Who? She'd asked her sister if she looked like some local TV personality. No, she'd told her, not anyone in Granville.

Then, one night at the health club last week, a man had pointed her out to his friend. "That woman," he'd said. She'd heard this before, "That's the woman" along with pointed fingers and head nods. But then this man had followed the comment with, "Dirk can sure pick them."

Dirk Durmont? Why were they looking at *her*? She laughed. Were some of these people mistaking her for Laura Starbright? Dirk had been engaged to her, hadn't he? She might have visited Granville. The actress was younger, taller, and prettier, but was there enough of a resemblance to confuse people? And Dirk—did he see it? If so, judging from the number of times he'd shown up around her in the weeks she'd lived there, Lara had a hunch he missed his former girlfriend. Sad.

That might explain the stares. However, there was something else.

The comments. "Dirk can sure pick them." Not everyone was confusing her with Laura Starbright.

It seemed they thought she, Lara McKeon, was dating Dirk Durmont.

Well. Lara stood and looked out the front window. They'd soon see that she wasn't Laura Starbright, and that Dirk Durmont was never with her, and then it would all blow over and she could get on with her normal life.

As she watched, a small turquoise car crowded with yellow heads slowed in front of her house, then sped away.

A worry line appeared between Lara's eyebrows. From habit, she reached up to press it away.

She would stay busy, that's what she'd do. She had plenty of things to distract her. All this was just silly.

She'd stay busy and it would soon blow over.

Alice leaned into the screen of the computer in her bedroom. Behind her on the bed, several tabloid papers lay open exposing photo spreads of Dirk Durmont and a blond woman. On the floor next to her, computer printouts of stories and pictures formed a messy pile under a pair of scissors. She glanced up at a page torn from a magazine and taped to the wall, a photo of Dirk posed shirtless with his arms folded over his chest. He looked down at her as she typed.

Subj: Dirk news, Laura back?
Date: 10/11/1998 3:09:34 AM Central Daylight Time
From: WonderOne@mail.com (Alice)
To: DirkDolls (group)

Did Laura Starbright move to Granville? Can't she take a hint? I mean, Dirk dumped her when everyone told him about her and Manley Upphart. Is she desperate or what?

I really saw her, I am not imagining it. She was walking down High Street with a big dog.

Days later, the official local Dirk Durmont newsletter came to her, one of the many fans on its email address list.

Subj: DirkLetter
Date: 10/15/1998 4:28:54 PM Central Daylight Time
From: HotGirl11@mail.com (Karen)
To: DirkDolls (group)

Dirk Dolls, do we have news!
Our worldwide AND Granville stud muffin has an official local thing going on. We have it from a good source that an old (like years older than him) Dirkfriend Lara McKeon has moved into a house on High Street in Granville. We knew he liked cruising that neighborhood. And we thought it was because of the cool houses! Not so. Check out 1049 High. A blond Laura Starbright type woman lives alone there, except when she has a certain visitor.

And are things ever lucky for us! She works at General Insurance, which is in the same building where TeleSales is. This you know is where the newsletter editors (me and Angela) work. We have someone at Gen Ins trying to get into personnel to get the details. We'll keep up on all her outfits for you, and she weighs herself on the scale in the second floor copier room, so we have our peepers looking out for numbers. She's hard to catch, moves real fast, but we know she weighs over 100 and not 150. We do know she's a computer programmer (geek) and works out evenings at Brandt's Gym, the downtown one. Yep, the same place where Dirk goes when he's in town! Convenient.

If you have any news, keep it coming! I'm attaching our list of cell phone numbers so we can call around when we see her. We have to get to the bottom of this, how this woman thinks she can move into town and into the pants of OUR MAN! And if she'll share!

His truly,
Editor Karen

Chapter Three

In the hills south of Granville near the town of Rockton, a chalky blue mobile home squatted, shrouded in fog. A hacking cough sounded from a room at one end. The noise woke Delta seconds before she heard the beep of an alarm come muffled through her bedroom wall. She lay still, listening. The blare of the clock stopped. Mark had squeezed it off, Delta knew that. She heard a thud and giggled, picturing him rolling off the edge of the mattress onto the living room floor. The coughing stifled.

She heard a match scratch, then the heavy scrape of a mattress being pulled up and dragged to its place up against the hall windows, across from her bedroom. He always made his bed in the morning, and did it in one big motion. Strong for a skinny guy. Delta was proud of her big brother.

She heard him moving in the living room and knew he was getting a cigarette for her, like always. His footsteps came back in her direction and stopped at her door. He knocked softly with one knuckle. He was hitting the nose on the poster of Dirk Durmont taped there. He always teased her like that.

"Delta!" he whispered.

She didn't answer, but pulled the rose-covered sheet over her head to hide her grinning. He opened the door. Inside the tiny room, she had pushed her bed—low, it being only a mattress, like people had in Japan—into one corner. She lay still. Cool air tickled one leg, but she kept it hanging out so he wouldn't know she was awake.

"Delta!" He moved to the bed, grabbed a corner of the floral sheet like a bouquet, and gave it a quick yank. It flew off, exposing her wearing only panties, sprawled on her back across the bed.

She popped her eyes open and laughed. Mark stood in his red bikini underwear. If she looked at him right, his messy black hair seemed like it almost touched the ceiling. The sight made her giggle. "Mark, your hair all up like that, you look like some creature in Gramma's Bible pictures!" She lay still a minute and watched him stare at her naked boobs. It was bad of him, but she knew he liked it.

"Look!" She pointed to the lump growing against his red bikinis. "Ma will shoot you if she sees that!"

"Screw you!" He laughed, still staring at her bare breasts.

"Ma would shoot you twice for that!" She laughed and pulled the sheet over her body.

Mark smiled, then squinted at her and snarled. "Shit, Delta, what'd you do to your hair?"

She rubbed her face into her pillow, then propped herself up on her arms, blinking. She studied her brother's face. He was lighting a second cigarette from the one clenched in his teeth, looking as if he was working on something important like when he counted out his bags of pills to sell. He seemed in a good mood. He'd been cranky lately, so she was having to watch him. She was never his target, but when the meanness came over him she sorely missed him being his usual self.

She wrapped the sheet around her and crawled to the end of the bed, reaching up for the extra cigarette. After she had surrounded herself with the smoky halo of two drags, she pulled a long strand of hair around in front of her. What had been a soft ash blond was now a solid crayon yellow.

"It's Fantasy Blond. Do you like it? Michelle had us do it so we can meet Dirk Durmont."

Mark smirked. "Dirk Durmont, the movie star."

"Yeah, he's in Granville again. And Michelle says he likes blondes."

"Well, before you meet any movie stars, you have school to get to."

Delta flopped back on her bed and groaned. "I don't wanna go."

"It's this or the GED, and take it from me, the GED's a bitch."

"I can't go, Mark." She paused, then asked, "What if I'm flunking out?"

"You're going to go, so get your butt moving. I'll make coffee." He walked back to the kitchen, then shouted back. "Yeah, your hair's okay."

Delta lay back and gnawed on a fingernail while she peered up at the little holes in her ceiling tiles. When she was little, she used to pretend she could climb up and hide in those holes. Today she wished she could disappear for real. What was she going to do about school, that English paper and those math problems? And after this year, there was a whole other year before she'd graduate.

Think sunshine thoughts, like Gramma told her. Mark liked her hair. Maybe Dirk Durmont would, too. She crawled out of the sheets, pulled off her panties, and walked naked down the hall to the bathroom.

—⁓—

In Rockton, a yellow-haired teen stared up at a hand-held mirror. Her eyes were hard as she examined the glass which reflected another mirror, which reflected her Fantasy Blond hair.

"Gorgeous!" She lowered her voice to bass. "Michelle, you are hotter than any chick anywhere."

She turned to face the bathroom mirror and practiced a careful half-smile, parting her lips and dropping her jaw to show teeth. Her eyes scowled. Not enough cheekbone. She sucked in her cheeks, picked up a makeup brush, and dusted a line of rose across each side of her face.

"Shit. Dirk'll never see past these fat cheeks." She'd had a breakfast bar already today. Maybe if she took something, one of those white pills, she'd burn it off fast.

"Shelly, let's get to school. Hurry now."

A chunky graying woman stood in the bathroom doorway.

"It's *Michelle*, Mom, *Michelle*."

"What's that on your face? Those pink stripes." She didn't say anything about the new hair color. The hair battles were over long ago, Michelle's win.

Whatever. "Dirk Durmont loves high cheekbones."

"Oh, Shelly, stop with the movie star crap, would you?" Norma Hamlin looked her daughter over as she spoke. "He is not going to notice some girl from Rockton. Didn't that Jason call you last night? He seems nice. And how do you know what Dirk Durmont likes, anyway?"

"Everybody around here knows what Dirk likes! Hell, half the town of Granville is after him. That's chicks and fags, both." Michelle laughed and stroked blue eye shadow onto one lid.

"Well they may be after him, but they can forget about catching him!" Norma said.

Michelle glared at her mother a minute, then began her other eyelid. "He hangs with women around here. You'll see. Some hot young thing like me will show up and he won't know what hit him."

Her mother laughed. "Oh, hell, Shelly! You are such a kid!" Her eyes narrowed in anger. "But you *are* old enough to face reality. You are never going to get with some movie star who will take you away to Hollywood." She spoke slowly, her tone harsh. "You'd best be looking around here for someone to settle down with. Some of the single guys at work want to go out with you."

Michelle picked up a mascara wand and stood silent, sweeping black onto her lashes. She could hear her mother breathing harder and knew she was getting mad that she was being ignored. What the hell. She would not answer her, no way ever. Who did her mother think she was, talking up factory losers, thinking she was that desperate? She swept on more mascara and after a minute her mother snorted and walked away. Michelle snorted back and rolled her eyes as she rubbed the sides of her face to blend the pink. She had much bigger plans than to settle for some local jerk. She was going to be rich, rich, rich, and when she got with Dirk she'd be famous, too.

Still looking into the mirror, she grabbed the sides of her bra and forced her smallish breasts toward the center. A hint of cleavage appeared. Not enough. One day she'd have big tits, bigger than anyone. Hell, that jerk from Granville had bought her that car. How much more could tits cost?

"Shelly!" Her mother shouted from downstairs.

She rolled her eyes and strutted to her bedroom in high-heeled slides, then pulled a knit top over her head. A new leather purse rested on a chair near the door. She clipped off the price tag and twirled it around by its handle. She'd tell everyone her rich lover—he moved to France so no one knew him—had shipped it to her. Maybe no one had seen the bag in that little shop in Granville. But if they had, they'd know it cost a fortune. That is, if anyone was brainless enough to pay for it.

She grabbed a backpack, then walked out to her car.

In the driveway, her mother revved the engine of a gray compact speckled with peeling paint. When she saw Michelle, she rolled down the window.

"Those jeans are too low! Look, if you sit wrong, you're going to show the whole world your business. I swear, Shelly, you've worn me out."

Michelle ignored her and got into her own car, which her mother thought was paid for with money from a summer job she never had. She now faked a big smile and waved at Norma, who drove off without looking.

She sat a minute looking across the patchy grass to the brown and beige boxy house in its row of look-alike buildings. Boring. She deserved better than this. Her sister and two brothers were gone now, so she had the place to herself. Except for her mother, but she was easy to ignore. Years ago, her father had run off with her mother's makeup lady and never made it back. Good riddance.

Her car started after two tries, and Michelle drove on toward Rockton High School. She waved at a young man in jeans and a t-shirt who stared out from under the hood of a black Trans Am. Charlie. Not too bright. Maybe he'd buy her new tits.

"You think we can meet Dirk Durmont, like face to face?!"

"Yeah! Here's the plan." Michelle leaned in and lowered her voice so the boring going-to-college crowd sitting nearby wouldn't hear. She and her three yellow-haired friends sat at their usual lunch table at the edge of the school cafeteria. Now the others were silent and staring at Michelle, waiting for her next words. She paused to suck up the admiration, then spoke. "He's still in Granville, that we know. We can stay at Connie's folks' place this weekend." Michelle slurped her diet soda and tried to hide her excitement. "We've had someone on him all the time he's been in town. Dirk usually hits a health club, and if he goes to the usual one we can get in there through the side door."

"Dirk Durmont! I can't believe we're for real going to get in with him!" Stacy said.

Michelle peered at her face. She didn't know why she let Stacy hang with her. Not pretty. Too fat.

At the mention of the movie star's name, the girls at the next table had stopped eating and grew quiet.

"Let's get real, girl-gang. He's not married, he likes hot young chicks and ... that is *us*!" Michelle paused, her fingertips resting on her chest. "And ... he likes blondes, and that again, thanks to your most-cool leader myself, is us again! We know he's around town; we almost saw him last weekend."

She looked around at her three friends. The four of them had a look that would have been totally cool in a music video. Their straight hair was the same color as most of the TV actresses, all eight eyes were topped with bright blue eye shadow, and each wore a black t-shirt and jeans worn tight and low. Mr. Simmons, the history teacher turned lunch monitor, stood nearby, peering down and hoping for a cheap thrill if their jeans slid any lower.

Delta was staring at her with an annoying clueless look. "It'd be so cool to meet Dirk."

But Stacy said, "Like you think we're gonna get with him for real? Us? We're gonna be standing in the longest line in Granville, that's for sure! But he does date Granville girls, doesn't he, 'cause I heard it from Miranda that he went out with that one at the university and even wanted to marry her, or at least that's what she was telling everyone." She laughed and rolled her eyes. "But still, you think there's a way for us to go out with him?"

The girls at the other table looked at each other and grinned. One of them whispered something and the others laughed.

Michelle pressed her lips into a thin line and glared at Stacy. She really pissed her off. Lately she'd started talking about how after graduation her parents were going to make her go to Mountain College to study nursing. Boring.

She looked at Brittany and saw that she was waiting with her eyebrows raised. The expression had barely changed her face; Michelle knew she was being careful not to crease her forehead to keep from getting wrinkles. She hated to admit to herself that Brittany looked more like a magazine picture than the others did. She was the tallest, and then she wore those high heels so she could tower over Michelle. Her face got second and third looks—from men and women both—with those wide blue eyes and straight nose that could be a model for someone on that plastic surgery show. She was smart besides. She didn't talk about college, but she wanted to own a chain of beauty spas in Los Angeles and already knew how to do fake nails. In spite of all that, Michelle didn't think she was much competition. Dirk would see that Michelle was the hottest girl around and these others were her hangers-on. She'd keep Brittany as a friend; she was handy, what with her slick ways with Internet searches. Useful.

Stacy burst out laughing and leaned in. She nodded toward a table of boys in dark t-shirts. "Did you hear that? Jesse is screwing Sandy while Dot's at his mom's place with the new baby! Ha!" She looked at Michelle and widened her eyes. "So, anyway, you don't think Dirk would go out with us for real, do you? And what about his new girlfriend?"

Michelle clenched her teeth. "That girlfriend story is crap. You saw her! He wouldn't be with someone like her when he can have someone like me. And I didn't say anything about 'us' going out with him."

"What's 'a theme'?" Delta broke in.

Stacy went on. "All I'm saying is he doesn't go around with under-agers or we would have heard about it, right?" She was sucking up now. "Talk about stories! If he'd been messing with …"

"As if he asks for ID. Like, 'You're hot, let's hook up. Uh … I'll need three photo IDs proving you're not jail bait.' I'm sure!" Michelle spat the words out, then turned to Delta. "Delta, you got an English paper due?" She was glad to change the subject. She would ignore Stacy; she was determined to get into the celebrity's circle. She wasn't going to hang around Rockton, doing something boring like going to Mountain College or working at the parts factory. One day she'd be so famous her name would be in the tabloids.

"Yeah. Mrs. Carlson wants us to write about the theme of some story," Delta said.

"Brittany," Michelle whispered. "Get that assignment from Delta. Not now!" She glanced at Mr. Simmons. Her sudden movement made him peer at the back of her jeans. Michelle turned back to the girls. "After school, get it and work it up for her. Delta, you gotta get through this year. If you flunk out, we'll *all* look stupid."

Delta looked down at the soda can in front of her and said nothing.

"Okay," Michelle continued. "Saturday night we'll hang around the bars downtown—Dirk might be there. So it's fake ID time. We need those silver tube tops again and the red ones, and white capris. Delta, did you get that red tube like ours?"

Delta shook her head, still looking down.

Michelle continued. "Okay, after school tomorrow we'll hit Discount City and grab one. I'll let you use my ripper I got from Kendra. Gets those f-ing plastic shoplifting things off."

"So we're going to meet Dirk Durmont." Brittany's voice was coming out breathless, like a game show player close to winning the big prize. She usually went along with stuff and didn't say much—like Delta did—but Michelle knew her wheels were always turning. Maybe that wasn't such a good thing. Brittany sometimes looked at her like she was figuring her out, judging her, not like she was trying to think up words like Delta had to do.

Michelle sat up straighter and looked around at her friends. "We, our sexy little selves, are soon going to meet and hook up with the great, and famous, and so fine, and not to mention filthy rich, Dirk Durmont!" Michelle shouted out the last half of her sentence and jumped up, raising a soda can in one hand. The others jumped up and shouted. Mr. Simmons stared at their butts while the bitchy rich girls at the next table giggled. Well, they could miss out, like they always did.

The loud command of a bell sounded and everyone rose and rushed to fill the halls.

Ten years earlier, Rockton had been barely breathing, like an old dog resting beside the two-lane blacktop that curved by on its way around the lakes. In the middle of town near the one stoplight, a two-level native stone schoolhouse contained one story of students and an upper floor of boarded windows. Along the sides of the highway were ragged recycled buildings trying to bait and hook the passing fisherman traffic with the simplest of logos. A huge wooden coffee cup signaled a restaurant, a monster plastic ice cream cone marked a snack shop, and an old row boat captained by a mannequin floated on the roof of a bait and tackle shop. The only sign that required literacy read "Antiques" in curlicue letters. The logo next to the word was a big carton of milk, peeling and out-of-date, left from the former grocery store. Off the main road, the factory that had spewed out the founding population had shrunk to a skinny skeleton, leaving the local economy hungry for the tourists who cruised through during "the season."

But if there had been a Rockton Chamber of Commerce, today its report would have been newsy and optimistic. The old engine factory was expanding after being swallowed up by a healthier parts company in Granville, 45 miles distant. And last year, Discount City had opened its new-concept, multi-service, Regional Super Store. It was becoming the hub of social activity, replacing the bingo hall next to Calvary Church.

The next afternoon, Delta and her friends marched into Discount City like a little army in pink tank tops and capri pants. She loved this store with its bright lights and piles and piles of cool stuff, all the people jamming through the aisles with their carts loaded up. It was like a big shopping circus. Michelle led them, followed by the usual lineup of

Stacy and Brittany, then Delta. They matched each other with their Fantasy Blond heads and outfits that copied Shari Rocket on the cover of "With It" magazine last month. They looked just like her.

Men walking past leered at their bodies. They seemed to know that Delta and her friends didn't wear a stitch of underwear. Men liked that, no underwear. Women didn't look so close; their gaze passed through them as if they weren't there. Delta was used to that. Most men liked them and most women didn't and that's the way it was.

Stacy was whispering a blue streak about Buzz and Danny and them getting arrested, but Michelle had always told them to shut up during an "operation", so Delta kept it zipped. They moved to the clothes department, where Michelle glanced around, then turned and looked at their faces. She frowned and whispered, "You guys look like you're in some spy movie. Chill out!"

Delta relaxed her jaw and let her mouth hang open, trying to get her face right. Michelle glared at her and rolled her eyes. She was mean a lot.

The rack of shiny tube tops stood out like broken glass in a parking lot, the fabric glittering in shades of red, blue, and silver. They were going-out clothes, fancy outfits, but it looked like no one in Rockton was buying them; the rack was jammed full. Delta didn't see why not, they were so pretty. She could think of all sorts of places to wear a shiny tube top.

The girls circled the rack and made the hangers screech as they moved them.

Michelle whispered to Delta, "You need to pull this off yourself. Show us you got the stuff."

Delta looked back at her, feeling sad and spiteful at the same time. In Delta's family, bills were covered by her father's disabled checks, her mother's tips from the bar, and Mark's pay from the factory. They gave Delta spending money, and she liked that fine. She didn't have to be a criminal to get stuff. But Michelle wanted her to steal one of these tops so she'd look cool. Well, she didn't want to steal anything. It was wrong. Stacy had just bought one last week and pretended she stole it, but lying wasn't right either. Delta knew she had to swipe the thing to make it right with Michelle.

Michelle turned and walked toward a rack of denim skirts. All the girls followed, but she twirled around fast and grabbed Delta's shoulders.

"You get the tube! Okay? Here, you'll need this." She shoved a strange tool into Delta's hand and turned her around.

Delta felt her cheeks grow hot. Feeling shameful, she looked down at the unfamiliar metal tool in her hand. She moved around the tube tops, feeling like she had misery painted across her face. Somehow this metal thing was supposed to get the shoplifting bar off, the big beige plastic tattletale that was hanging from all the clothes. She fit the stealing tool onto the bar of her chosen piece, then tugged. It stuck. She tugged again.

As she worked at loosening the plastic pain in the butt, a woman about Ma's age but fatter started sneaking up, looking over the racks at the girls. Suddenly the woman broke away from the jacket display and hurried toward Delta. Everything started happening real fast. Stacy jumped back and shouted, "Ew! What was that!" Michelle slid past behind Delta and grabbed the metal tool from her hand and a tube top from farther down the rack. The woman was staring at Stacy now, likely trying to see what she was in a fret about. Michelle disappeared.

Stacy shouted to the woman, "I thought I saw a turd! Sorry!" and squealed her laughter. She rushed away following Brittany, and grabbed Delta by the arm to pull her to the front entrance. They ran laughing across the lot to Michelle's car, where she was standing tapping her foot.

"Where were you guys?" she said. She tugged at some red fabric in her purse, pulling the tube top half out. "Delta, why were you holding the ripper upside down? How stupid *are* you?"

Stacy laughed, but Brittany shot eye-daggers at Michelle and walked around to the other side of the car. Delta blinked hard so's not to cry, then opened her mouth and forced out a laugh.

Michelle's car careened through the hills and the four girls squealed each time it skidded on a curve. Stacy leaned back in the small seat next to Delta and hooked one foot out the passenger window next to Brittany. They passed a long flat building with a tall sign that read "Guns Boats Liquor," then turned onto a dirt road. Half a mile up, they stopped in a cloud of dust at the beginning of a clearing. At the far edge of a circle of dirty rocks, rusted vehicles, and lanky brown dogs was a gray-tinged blue mobile home. Delta climbed out.

"Don't forget 'your' tube." Michelle shouted and dangled the stolen piece out the window. "Or maybe it's mine, but you can borrow it."

She laughed.

Delta took it, careful not to meet her eyes.

Michelle continued. "I'll be here Friday. Seven." She spun her wheels in the dirt and drove away from the cloud she created.

Delta turned toward her home. It huddled back near the hill, looking as if it had tumbled down on the way to someplace better, sitting on wheel rims as if it was packed and ready to roll away. On its right, a path ended at the doorway of an old native stone cottage, the original McNought homestead where Gramma lived as a girl. What remained of the building were four walls with holes for windows and a doorway. The little house skeleton now served as a small motel for Ma and her male friends, an office for Mark and his drug dealing, and lately a meeting place for Delta and her boyfriends.

Next to it was a rust-freckled metal "T"-post with a plastic clothesline sagging toward the trailer. When they were little, Mark had urged Delta to climb to the top of the pole. She still remembered how good it felt when she made him proud and hung by her knees from the cross bar. Now, messy straw bundles from birds' nests stuck out from each end as if the old pole had grown too much hair in its ears. Would climbing it still make her proud, when she couldn't even steal to be cool with her friends and getting through high school was iffy?

Walking up now, Delta's nerves took a start when she noticed her father sitting out on the stack of gray cement blocks that was the front porch. She peered at his face, trying to judge his mood. Two brown hounds lay near his feet, one whacking the ground with his tail at the sight of the girl shuffling toward him. That was a good sign; if her father was in a bad temper he would have kicked the dogs away. Near him, a grill perched on wobbly legs smoked from burning charcoal and catalog pages. One lone piece of meat sizzled.

"Hi, Pa." Delta's voice and expression were flat.

He looked up, bleary-eyed and confused. "Oh. Delta," and he nodded once in recognition, then swallowed big from the brown bottle in his hand. He hacked up some spit and shot it out the side of his mouth toward a sofa that leaned back against the trailer wall.

When Ma got some whiskey in her, she'd get chatty about her marrying Silas when she was fourteen and pregnant. They were like most Rockton couples in other ways, too—early on, he started in beating her. So she'd found a career—waitressing—to keep her busy and away from home. For awhile, Gramma showed up to babysit Mark and Delta, but when she learned that their mother was serving drinks in bars and imbibing too, she preached God and poison until Ma fired her from babysitting. After that, Ma left her babies with their guardian angels and went on out anyway.

So Silas turned his temper to his little boy. Seems her brother spent most of his young years bruised, like a dropped apple. Now grown up, there was no warning when Mark had a fit coming on. He was like a shaken-up soda can. Some incident would flip open the tab-top and he would explode. He never did hit Ma or Delta, though. His anger showed up in the battered trailer with its dented walls and kicked-in doors. Outside, Delta knew to walk wide around where he smashed bottles against the rocks or pounded them into sand with a chunk of cement.

And so they lived, like lots of families, as if they were all in the same old rerun movie every day. Then one night, Silas tripped drunk in the yard and chipped a piece off his backbone, a small part, but his back never forgot the pain. It was like Christmas that first time he leaned forward to slap at Ma and instead suddenly arched back as if someone had landed a karate chop to the middle of his spine. He pretended an accident at work to get disability checks and quit his job to spend most of his days where it hurt him least—in bed, lying on his side. He became a ghost who sometimes moved from the back bedroom to sit out in front of the trailer. Everyone thought he'd eventually drink himself to death; Ma kept his case of whiskey full.

Tonight, Delta moved in a circle around him as if he was a mad dog on an unreliable chain. He seemed like some stranger who'd dropped by to use their grill, although no "company" treatment was given him. He was blocking the door, so she detoured to sit on the sofa. It was covered with a brown floral fabric and she remembered when she used to sit on it with her baby doll and imagine the printed flowers were a garden. Now as she sat tense, the dog with the wagging tail walked over and jumped up to lay next to her.

Silas stood and Delta stiffened, but he limped unsteadily to an old broken toilet and unzipped his fly. Delta got up fast and snuck through the door. Inside, Mark and her mother were sitting at the kitchen table surrounded by warm grease smells.

Ma waved a deep-fried chicken piece and nodded toward a pile of tater tots spread on a paper towel in front of her. "Come on over here and have some of these. Mark brought 'em home."

Delta sat in the one remaining chair. There were only three chairs to the dinette set and that had been all they needed. They never included Silas and they never brought people home, at least not into the trailer. She grabbed the ketchup and squeezed red out over the tater tots. She popped one into her mouth and talked around it. "Michelle and us are going to Granville this weekend, hunting up Dirk Durmont. She says those stories about his having a girlfriend on that street are crap." She chewed a while, then asked her Ma, "Do you work tonight?"

"Always, baby."

Mark and Delta never let on that they knew their mother didn't work every day. She left every evening, and if not working she was likely spending time shopping in Granville or seeing men.

They ate silently but companionably. Not like strangers, but like people who had no need to say anything to anyone.

"Hey!"

The rough shout came from outside. Everyone ignored it.

CHAPTER FOUR

Crush, just a crush.

A song was stuck in Lara's head and she tapped her fingers on the kitchen table. As her annoyance grew she drummed harder, then realized she was pounding Dirk Durmont's face. She jerked her hand up. Spread in front of her was a full-page feature of the actor's life, including a large photo of him as a wholesome-looking teenager with carefully styled hair. It was a harmless article, but its companion piece disturbed her. A reporter had interviewed the actor's friends, asking them outright about Dirk's rumored infatuation with a local woman. The friends had refused comment, except for one, who replied that he should be allowed to pursue a woman in private.

Over the last couple of months, the song had blasted from her car radio over and over. *Just a Crush.* The overheard comments, the stares, the cars slowing near her as she walked—could this really be about her? How big was this story getting? The *newspaper* now?

Lara knew about crushes. She'd had several and had been the target of as many. They were like rainbows—mystical, heavenly, and sometimes spectacular, but then gone, faded away. And in the long run, they didn't matter.

But only one person knew the truth about the "infatuation", and he wasn't talking to her about it. So the gossips could leave it alone and it would run its course, like normal. If they'd let Dirk have some normalcy! Leave him alone, leave him alone, leave him alone! Tears of frustration filled Lara's eyes. So many words, so much talk, and here she was, isolated in the middle of it. And if the story spread any further, would any local man want to go out with her? How could she stop this? What could she do?

She took a deep breath.

Okay. Lara could continue to ignore the rumors. She had projects to take care of. She would work on the task in front of her. Today she'd buy Christmas lights. Icicle lights were popular this year and were strung across porches all over town. At first Lara thought them too bright, like stage lights for a "home for the holidays" production going on at each house. But they'd grown on her. Why not a little kitsch, some glitter, for the season? The Sunday sale flyers directed her to Home Store. She could look at holiday decorations and wall glazing kits at the same time. Fun.

Lara pulled on her coat then drove a distance to a store on the edge of town. Maybe nothing strange would happen if she shopped so far from her neighborhood. But as she pulled into the parking lot, she was alarmed to see a large white truck moving in front of her. It resembled the one she'd seen Dirk driving, but she refused to dwell on it, on him, or on the problem that was growing around her. She had a life to live, things to do.

Once inside the store, she toured through the kitchen and flooring departments, looked at unfinished furniture, then settled in front of the paint display. As she examined shades of stone and coral, she felt a movement at her right. Startled, she glanced over and saw a man wearing glasses facing her, staring.

She stepped back and motioned to the display. "Do you need in here?" she asked.

He eyed her, then shook his head and walked off to rejoin his group. He whispered something to the others and they turned to look at her. Irritated, Lara snatched one more paint card, then wheeled her cart away.

The holiday section was large, colorful, and easy to find. Lara headed for the wall dedicated to Christmas lights, passing a man with a long ponytail and another man with a baseball cap pulled down low on his forehead. They remained silent as she stood in front of the icicle lights, studying each package. How long was each strand, how wide was her porch, why hadn't she measured ...

"Dad!"

A child called out, his tone urgent. Fear? Lara whirled around. A young boy standing close behind her beamed an excited smile up at her. He didn't seem to be in trouble, so Lara smiled back, curious. She studied his face a moment; he looked so familiar. Suddenly she knew, and she tried to suppress her grin. She was looking at a miniature Dirk Durmont! The same eyes, the same cheekbones. And maybe the same face as that man with the long ponytail who had been standing with his back to her and had now turned.

She stood a minute. The men didn't move and remained silent.

Had she created an awkward situation? She went back to studying the lighting display to ease the tension. After a moment, she turned around. The boy had soundlessly disappeared. The man with the ponytail stood in the same place, motionless, his back to her. Focusing on her cart, she walked as gracefully as she could out of the Christmas section, then out of the store.

—⁓—

The holidays passed as typical for most people in Granville and Rockton.

Lara hung her lights across her porch while a man in a small sports car parked a house away and watched her. She spent Christmas Day at her sister's, where eleven family members exchanged gifts and stockings and ate from four homemade pies, three frosted cakes, two types of fudge, and a turkey stuffed with bread cube dressing.

Delta sat with her Ma and brother over a complete ham dinner Mark brought home from the grocery store. They ate and smoked and didn't talk about Gramma, who was serving dinner at church like always, or Silas, who was in the back room with a bottle like always. Mark gave them both earrings from Goldberg's in Granville. Ma bought him a red t-shirt with Santa on a sled pulled by big-boobed women in deer outfits, and presented to her daughter a little red teddy trimmed with white fuzzy fur. Delta gave her brother and mother cartons of cigarettes, and bought a fresh bottle for Silas.

At Michelle's, her mother announced for the eighth year running that she was too pooped from making Christmas dinner all those years when the kids were at home and maybe the two of them could eat out. She then gave Michelle two twenty-dollar bills, which her daughter expected and enjoyed.

Alice was nervous Christmas Day. She didn't understand where everyone had gone. Dirk was in town, but stayed in the house all day. All her new friends, the Dirk Dolls, were holed up someplace, too. So she drove around a while, then went to her apartment and watched TV while her answering machine repeated the familiar message "Alice, this is Mom. Just trying to reach you. Merry Christmas! Hope you're okay. Call me."

Lara met the new year at First Night events in downtown Granville, then the next day pulled out her journal. She liked to get organized the first day of the year. It was a good time to set goals and make lists, to review the previous year and put it away in some orderly place. It'd be especially helpful this year, when an unfamiliar type of chaos was leaking into the new life she'd planned.

> *January 1999*
> *Happy New Year!*
> *This year, I feel empowered! Finally, there's no bad marriage to hold me back.*
> *Resolutions for 1999:*
> *Work out at the gym four times a week.*
> *Overcome shyness. Reach out, <u>talk</u> to people. Learn to think before I speak so to be more tactful!*
> *Control diet and achieve 127 lbs. and hold.*
> *Learn to trust God that my needs will be met.*
>
> *What I <u>want</u>, wishes:*
> *To have a relationship with a man that's loving and sexual and exclusive.*
> *To be beautiful.*
> *To accomplish something, something meaningful.*
> *To have children in my life in some loving nurturing relationship. Foster parenting, adoption?*

She put the journal away, then looked out the window at the ice storm which had her housebound. She'd come far in the past year. A new town, a new house, a new job—scary but positive changes. There was no way 1999 wouldn't be a good year. She'd make it so! Whatever happened, she was determined to have an incredible year.

—⁓—

"I dunno 'bout no hillbillies."

Michelle glared at the big-boned blonde who sat in front of her. She sucked hard on the proffered joint and held her breath a minute, then replied. "If we *were* hillbillies, maybe that'd be a problem." Her voice was low and serious as she looked a challenge at Blair. Big Butt

Blair, that's what she'd call her behind her back.

The smoke haze gave an air of a séance to the scene. Seven women, all with similar yellow hair, sat in a circle on the floor of Blair's apartment. Three rested their backs against a worn green sofa; the others hunched over their crossed legs. Michelle looked around the living room, which was bare except for a few pieces of mismatched furniture. She'd thought strippers made good money, but Blair sure wasn't spending it on her surroundings.

Blair stood and strutted to the uncurtained patio door then back to stand in front of them. Michelle grit her teeth and watched as all heads turned to follow her movements. This beefy bitch was stealing the show! Well, she wasn't going to get away with it. Michelle dug into her purse and pulled out a gold roach clip, then pinched a new joint. She held it up until all the women were watching her. She spoke loudly, almost shouting. "Isn't this clip great? A man from Dallas gave it to me; said I was like finding gold in the hills. He's in oil." She faked a smile around at the group and saw them give her admiring looks. They had forgotten Blair, who sat down with a plop on the floor.

Stacy held her hand out. "Looks like I'm next for that, Shel, I mean Michelle. Remember when Saul Jameson stuck a knife in that tourist who said he was out snapping pictures of hillbillies? You should've seen it, all that blood! That was before he went to jail for beating up Jesse for getting Suzie pregnant. He was so mad about Suzie and Jesse, he went nuts and whacked him with a tire iron. Remember that …"

Michelle coughed and glared at her. Out in the car, she had told her to keep her flapping lips laying still. Stacy stopped and snapped her lips shut.

Blair looked from one to the other, then said, "Well, at least you got good weed." She took a hit and passed it to the next girl.

"So … what's your names again?" Blair was looking at her.

"I'm Michelle. This is Stacy, Brittany, and that's Delta."

The other three girls smiled, and Stacy piped up. "Hi! We're from Rockton, like we said, but Delta actually lives out in the country, on her family estate …" Michelle scowled and Stacy stopped abruptly.

"You seem pretty cool, most of you anyway, and Connie says you are. I seen you around here when Dirk's in town. We might let you in. Got a computer?"

"Shit, yeah. You think we're way off in the sticks or something?"

Michelle was sick of this woman thinking she could interview her. But this Blair was famous among the Granville girls for actually screwing Dirk Durmont. Or for saying she did, although Michelle was doubting anything like that ever happened. Moosey thing, she was, big all over.

"Cool. I'll get you in the email group. That's cool shit. We got this chick at General Insurance tracking that Lara's outfits every day."

"Whose outfits is that?" Michelle knew who she was talking about, but no way would she sound interested in the girlfriend.

Blair laughed. "Surely, you've heard of Lara McKeon, like where have you been!" Michelle tightened her jaw and moved her head in a slow nod. Blair continued. "*That* one. She's easy to dog, so we got her covered most of the time. We got it figured out that for some ungodly reason Dirk shows up where she is."

"Why?"

"They both don't say so, but you know they're screwing. We just ain't caught 'em yet. Look at that house he bought her! And she moved to town right after he and the real Laura broke up. Pretty slick."

"So why don't they go around together?"

"Some game they play to freak us out, I guess. I dunno! I do know he is the hottest hunk and I don't want to share him. We need to find out how serious this Lara thing is. My friend Levi is trying to get the first picture of them together; has a whole pile of photos of her already. He'll be filthy rich when he gets it!"

"Yeah, whatever." Michelle hated it, but she knew she had to put up with this oversized airhead to get in with the inner circle of the Dirk Dolls. She looked around. People's eyes were getting that spaced pothead look and soon it'd be hopeless trying to find out anything. "So how do I meet Dirk? Can you introduce me? I know he'd want to meet a hot chick who likes to party!"

Blair stared a minute, then said, "I dunno what he would want with you all, unless he has a group screw in mind. You in on that?"

Michelle hesitated. She had higher ambitions than getting lost in some group grope with a bunch of whores and bodyguards. But she needed a break.

"Yeah, sure, we're in." She didn't look at her three friends. She knew they'd do what she said.

She didn't see the surprise on Stacy's face, the disgust on Brittany's, and the confusion on Delta's.

—*w*—

If she winked one eye closed, then the other, the little white house seemed to hop back and forth. Delta grinned, then remembered the reason for her visit and grew sad again. Coming here was the only thing she could think of that would save her. Would it work?

She crept along the side of the cottage, peeking in the windows. They were covered tight so she got no clues. Finally, she tried the door in the back. It opened.

"Hi Gramma!" Delta stepped into the bright kitchen and stopped at the sight of the gray-haired woman in a thin floral dress bent over the open oven door. She hated the worn out old dresses her grandmother bought at the thrift store but couldn't convince her to shop with her at Discount City. Marianne McNought told her the old-fashioned dresses made her think about simpler times, like when her parents were important business owners in Rockton and they lived in the best house in town. Sweet dresses and bright colors made her think sweet bright thoughts. But Delta still hated the frumpy old things on her otherwise attractive slim grandmother.

The older woman now stood up with a cookie sheet loaded with mini loaf pans in her oven-mittened hands. Delta inhaled the smell of baking, and for a minute her insides felt so happy it was like she was as warm as the oven that now made Gramma's face pink.

"Delta, Baby!" Gramma smiled. She set the tray down on the stovetop and wrapped her arms around her granddaughter. "Just in time to taste these for me! I'm making them for the church bake sale, but you take some home."

She led Delta from the kitchen into the dark parlor, helped her off with her jacket, and sat her into a rose-colored upholstered chair next to an old wood stove. She turned back to the kitchen.

Gramma liked to say her little cottage was "original", and that people who bought antiques would like it. The wallpaper here in the parlor was a garden of huge roses in pinks and plums which grew darker near where the stove smoked. The sofa and easy chairs were matching pieces from back when Gramma was born, and were now fashionably "tea-stained" from years of living. Heavy red velvet draperies kept sunlight out. Gramma had told her that she was lucky that she could be poor and her home grew styleful around her. Some people made their things look old on purpose, but she never had to do that. Lucky.

A plate rattled in the kitchen. Delta called out, "Gramma, I can't eat anything. I'll get fat."

Gramma came out with a small platter covered with slices from a tiny loaf.

"Banana nut! You like that, don't you, Baby? Eat! Look at you, skinny girl." She put the plate down on a small table next to the chair. Delta pulled a cigarette out of her purse and lit it. Her grandmother stood looking down at her. Delta hated it when people did that, looked at her hard. They usually then up and said something that she didn't understand. But her grandmother never did anything that made her feel sad or bad. So she made herself think about how she would explain why she'd come by.

"Delta," Gramma said, breaking into her thoughts. "You know how you feed those squirrels out by that tree next to the trailer?"

Delta nodded. The squirrels and rabbits were always good to her. "Except when the dogs run up!" Delta answered and laughed.

Gramma continued. "Well, sometimes I feel like my family is a bunch of wild squirrels I used to feed and now they've run off as if the dogs have chased them, and they don't even know me. So it's always good to see you. You come by anytime, okay? Even if there's no reason."

Delta put her cigarette to her mouth and nodded.

"How's Mark? I worry about the kinds of trouble that boy can get into," Gramma said, still looking hard at Delta.

"Fine, Gramma. Keeping his job at the factory. Stays real busy." She didn't mention how the sheriff had come out to search for something in the hills around the trailer. The lawman had told Delta not to tell anyone, so she'd only told Mark.

"And your mother?"

"Real good. Works a lot."

"Your Pa?"

"Fine. Sleeps a lot."

"I guess when he's asleep he's a pretty good father. What a sad waste these men are." Gramma sighed. She sunk into a chair that matched the one Delta perched on.

Delta looked around for an ashtray and her grandmother pushed an empty candy dish toward her. She tapped her ashes into it. Neither spoke for a minute. Delta stared down at the carpet. She eyed a snagged flower in the rug and thought it was funny that Gramma hadn't fixed it. She was always fixing something or other.

"So, Baby, how's school?"

She sucked hard on her cigarette, then pushed her words out fast. "Gramma I'm not making it." There. It was out.

"Making it?"

"I'm not going to graduate."

"Are you sure?"

"No."

Gramma took a deep breath. Delta watched her eyes lose that hard stare and get a look like when that sick kitten took a bad turn, before Gramma found a home for it on a nice farm someplace. A sad face. "Well. Okay, how can we find out?"

"What do you mean?" Delta asked.

"How can we find out how you're really doing in school? Have you talked to your mother?"

Delta felt miserable. She pulled the last drag from the cigarette and smashed it into the dish. "No," she answered in a small voice. How could she tell her Ma she was stupid?

"Can I talk to your teachers?"

She sat a minute, then nodded silently.

"We can fix this. I'm going to call your teachers tomorrow and then we'll see where the problem is. Okay?" Delta nodded. "Can you stay after school to work extra?"

"No!" What would Michelle and her friends think of her then?

"Good heavens, girl, why not? Sometimes a person just needs extra help on something. Then she gets it, and she learns."

"They'll call me stupid!" There, the ugly word was out. Delta felt her throat close against the shame, and tears floated in a little pool in her eyes, feeling like they'd pour over if she moved.

"Who will call you stupid? Never mind, Baby. I know how people can be. So. Will you bring your books here and let me help you after school?"

Delta nodded slowly, finally relaxing.

"There you go!" Gramma sat up straight. "We'll get this figured out yet!" But even as she put on that happy voice, she had a worry frown all over her face.

CHAPTER FIVE

He certainly got around, didn't he.

Lara parked her car and looked again at what seemed a familiar face in the truck in front of her. Months had passed since she'd last seen him in the white truck, and things had only gotten worse for her. Strange people continued to react to her, but she kept up her dogged determination to ignore them. The man's expression had caught her attention. He looked away fast, then scanned the parking lot, stressed. Men often looked at Lara, but few got anxious at the sight of her. She smiled in his direction, but he didn't meet her eyes.

No problem. She was in a Friday mood, happy thinking about a big bowl of popcorn, a wine spritzer, and a rented movie. Strange sights wouldn't bother her tonight. She pulled a comb through her hair then stepped out into the cool spring air. As she walked toward the row of stores, she noticed that cars now crowded the aisles that had been empty minutes earlier. She entered the grocery store and a woman walked up to her and said hello. Lara smiled in response and greeted her, impressed by her friendliness.

After yanking a cart away from its metal nest, she pulled out a grocery list. Bananas, grapes, carrots. She picked up a tub of low-fat veggie dip and read the label. As she turned with the dip in her hand, she was startled to see a woman standing close and staring down at Lara's groceries. Lara caught her breath, tense now. She recognized trouble; the woman was too close, and had too much interest in Lara and what she was buying. She pushed the cart away from the stranger's eyes, then hurried through the next aisles.

Sugarless hot cocoa. Coffee? No, not unless it was on sale. She looked down at her list again. Potluck at work Monday. Okay. She'd make chocolate chip cookies, usually a hit with coworkers. The chocolate chips were back a few aisles. She spun her cart around ... and bumped into a woman following close behind her.

"Oh, excuse me!" Lara couldn't hide her surprise.

The woman scrutinized her face with a cold expression, then looked into Lara's cart. She didn't have any groceries herself. Was she even shopping? Lara rolled away quickly to backtrack up the aisle and was startled to see the carts that were lined up behind her. The women all stared at her face as she passed. At the top of the aisle, she looked back and saw they had all turned to watch her. Had this string of women been following her? There was no one ahead of the spot where she had been standing; she'd been leading the line.

Odd. But Granville was always odd anymore.

Lara moved faster now; the atmosphere had grown strange. She would leave the cookie ingredients for another day. She needed cottage cheese, one of her staples. She found the dairy case and squatted down to grab two cartons. But as she stood and turned to her cart, she was shocked to see she was surrounded by women! They had formed a human fence around her.

"Excuse me," Lara said from between clenched teeth. She winced. Had her words come out sounding like a growl? She struggled to stay calm and shoved at her cart. One of the women blocking it moved aside. Forcing herself to breathe evenly, Lara rushed to the checkout area.

What were they *doing*? The women of Granville needed hobbies if they had time to follow some woman through a grocery store!

She hurried home, still agitated, and pulled out her journal. But she couldn't write down her real thoughts, her greatest problem. How could she explain something that she didn't understand? People were staring at her and passing along some rumor about Lara and this beautiful, famous, younger man. She would not give the story any more life by giving it words, either written or verbal. She'd focus on positive things instead.

April 1999
Journal,

I went to a Divorce Recovery Workshop. Uplifting.

I've been having strange dreams. As usual. Last night, a car backed into a big store window and broke it. My dream book says that great changes will occur soon.

Ellen and John across the street are moving to Chicago, so I'm having a porch party for them. I finished the flyers, then Ruth and I sat out on my porch steps. My porch is quite lovely. It's becoming more a place to sit and visit. My sister Patty came to town and I had the family over, then after dinner we all sat out on the steps.

Nice, like a picture.

Where's my gratitude journal? Wasn't I using that blue cloth book?

Grateful for:
A good job
That my master's is done
A good house with a porch
Friends—Nicole, Emma, Ruth, Sara

She recapped her pen and closed the notebook. She had written, but she hadn't. Just as when she spoke, she didn't. Her friends asked how she was and she answered "fine" and chatted about her job, her house, the neighborhood. Increasingly, though, as she spoke, the strange people who crowded her in Granville showed up at the edges of her mind. When would she tell people the unreasonable truth?

See no evil, speak no evil. Where had she learned that bad events and feelings should be left unspoken, that if she ignored them they never happened? The Catholic schools? Possibly—the nuns had reacted to Lara's inquisitive questions about God with fear and suspicion, even emotional abuse. Or did she learn silence from a family system that tiptoed around and never acknowledged the sad facts of money trouble, a missing parent, sickness, and even death?

Whatever. It didn't matter now.

What mattered was that this silly mess about Dirk Durmont would soon blow over and she could get on with her normal life. She didn't have to talk about it.

Right now, she had a party to plan.

"Is Dirk gonna stay at his Mom's all night? What about us?" Michelle hated this, driving up to Granville but getting no closer to meeting Dirk.

"Wonder what he's doing?" Stacy asked. The Rockton girls sat with Connie in her mom's basement, lounging on the floor in front of the TV.

"I wonder if they play cards or games. You know, like families do." Delta had a goofy dreamy look on her face. If this was a Disney movie, there'd be cartoon butterflies floating around. Michelle rolled her eyes.

Connie spoke around the tortilla chip in her mouth. "Lara went home after the grocery store. And we already called in all our songs to the radio. What do we do now?"

"Doll WonderOne, that Alice, says she'll keep watching for Dirk. She'll call if he goes out." Michelle didn't know much about Loopy Alice, but she did know she was a hell of a stalker. Useful.

"What color polish does she use?" Brittany held her fingers out in front of her and wiggled them. Today, her nails were a medium length and painted alternating colors of plum and blue.

"Lara? She don't even use none!" Stacy rolled her eyes. "Clear, maybe. Boring."

"Then what color does the real Laura use?" Brittany asked.

"She had Passion Raspberry for Screen Awards night. I have some upstairs if we wanna do our nails." Connie said.

"Yeah, go get it and Brittany can do my nails." Michelle said. "What do you think *she's* doing?"

"I think she's filming in London. Making it with Rod Brakehart." Brittany answered.

"No, idiot! The local Lara."

Connie sat up straighter, looking smug that she had the facts on Lara. "She rented 'You Can't Take It With You' at Neighborhood Video. Looks like she sits at home and eats cottage cheese and watches movies. And drinks wine. She picked some up last week."

Stacy's face brightened. "Well, let's do that, except for the cottage cheese part. Can we find that movie, 'We Can't Make it Whatever'?"

"And my mom has some wine down here. We'll drink that!"

"Cool!" Michelle stood and directed them. "We'll go get that movie and you can open that bottle when we get back."

As the girls moved toward the door, Michelle's cell phone rang. She opened it and listened, then laughed.

"Yeah, cool." She snapped the phone shut. "I have a new plan, Dirk Dolls!" Maybe some good would come out of this evening yet.

Lara couldn't believe her ears. Someone was ridiculing *what*?

She was back out again, shopping. She'd grown more annoyed and restless after her earlier ruined trip for groceries. There were still things on her list and she would get them tonight! The women had run her out of Merker's, but she could go someplace else. But now what? Lara had turned up the wide aisle of Discount City when she was startled by the mocking chant behind her.

The voice sounded again.

"Ewww … cottage chee-eese," a woman whined.

"Well, *I'm* impressed!" Another answered.

"Now she's going to get some cottage chee-eese."

"Shhhh!"

Them again, the rude people! The "rudies," her new label for them.

Lara moved into a defense position, spinning her cart fast around a center display to face them. The three young women behind her stopped, then looked away. The one in the lead shot a hard look at Lara before she feigned interest in a nearby sign.

More of those bizarre women. There was no sense trying to shop when they were following her, publicly embarrassing her. She'd leave. She could do that again, leave and go someplace else. This town was large enough that she could store-hop until she had everything she needed. These nuts could try to keep up with her!

She moved up the aisle in the opposite direction, trying to look nonchalant. Suddenly, a man holding a cell phone to his ear hurried out of a side aisle, watching the three women as he walked. He caught Lara's eyes, stopped and stared, then turned his back to her and looked at the shelf in front of him. Was he following them while they were following her?

Lara kept pacing forward. Ahead, she noticed a tall lean man with a brown ponytail and a hat hurrying across the front of the store. For all the rushing around going on, Lara seemed to be the only one trying to buy anything. A cashier stood waiting. Lara unloaded her cart, then glanced along the front of the store. There! The man with the ponytail sat in a chair near the windows. A familiar face; a face known for great beauty wasn't easily disguised. She raised her eyebrows at him and tilted her head, trying to communicate her question, her curiosity. She had seen him around town quite a bit lately. And he seemed to be a member of the same health club. Now as she caught his eye, he looked away quickly, tapping his foot fast, then looked back at her in a steady stare.

Something brushed her left shoulder and she jerked away, then turned to see a woman leaning in to peer at her half-written check. Lara tried to be polite, but her smile tightened into a grimace. What had this woman been looking at? Her name? Her address?

Lara finished her check, grabbed her sacks, and left. When and where was she going to get the rest of her groceries this week?

—◆—

Delta watched Michelle blow a stream of smoke out the car window into the night air. She and Stacy had rushed back with her to the parking lot after Lara went to the register. Brittany wasn't with them; she'd gone with Connie to pick up the movie. She was getting busier, anyway, with her new guy Jake, so didn't come along a lot lately.

"This ain't going right." Michelle took another long drag on her cigarette and exhaled hard. She snarled as she spoke. "I got a good look at her face. I can't believe it, Dirk being with her! I'm like a million times hotter and if I could just get him to see me, he'd pick me instead!"

Delta was afraid to say anything, especially with Michelle sitting there growling like a mad dog and foaming cigarette smoke out her mouth. It was still unclear what they were supposed to be doing with that Lara. They had driven over here after Alice called to say Lara was out shopping again so Dirk might be out and around, too.

"Who was that guy with the cell phone?" Stacy looked pissed. "Like what's he doing? Following Lara around? What are all these men seeing in her? This is like some TV show or something with all these people running around getting in our way and then she leaves like that, making us look like fools. And that guy was blocking us, did you see that? What was he going to do, tackle us?"

"Yeah, who was that guy?" Delta didn't understand how this evening had gotten so complicated. When were they going to go watch that movie at Connie's?

Michelle ignored them. "I have an idea. We're going to watch awhile."

They sat while the store's automatic doors hummed open, letting out a few carts with women attached. The shoppers hurried in all directions to find their cars and Michelle and Stacy laughed and talked about how fat each one looked. Soon Lara appeared without a cart and paused, then came forward with a sack weighing down each hand. She walked to a red car in the next aisle.

"We got the car right," Stacy said. "A red ordinary car. Not even something cool. Shit, if a rich movie star was getting me a car, I'd think I'd do better than that!"

"Yeah! When my time comes, I'll be in one of those Italian Lampradinkos." Michelle dug an old receipt out of her purse. "Someone find me a pen. Can you see the license plate from here?"

Stacy read off the numbers, then watched Lara as she swung her bags into the back seat. Delta handed Michelle a tube of Crimson Love lipstick for her to write down the license. The girls were quiet a moment as they watched Lara move in her blue jeans. Delta knew the others were thinking about whether she was fat or not.

"She don't look so bad, for her age and all," Delta said.

Stacy suddenly shouted out the window. "Ooh, Baby!"

"Shhh!" Michelle's whisper was loud. "She'll hear!"

Lara stopped, still leaning into her car. She stayed that way a second, then slammed her car seat back and climbed into the driver's seat. If she'd heard Stacy at all, it didn't seem to bother her any.

"It's your big mouth that screwed us up inside the store!" Michelle went on shouting at Stacy.

While they argued, Delta stared out the window at the retreating red car. Then she saw a tall man with a long brown ponytail come out the store doors and walk toward a black SUV that had pulled up near the entrance. Two cars full of young women came to life with brightened headlights and the sounds of engines starting up.

Michelle continued. "Did you see how she turned around when you mouthed off about cottage cheese?"

"Well, we hate her, don't we?" Stacy and Delta both looked at Michelle for the answer.

"Yeah, we do! But we needed to follow her to see if Dirk showed up. And Connie wants a list of what she buys! Tonight I got shit. I'll have to make up something. Like a load of f-ing cottage cheese. And rubbers. That's what I'll say. And … a pregnancy test! That's right, I'll tell them she picked up a pregnancy test!" She let out a witch laugh that made Delta think of flying monkeys and red ruby slippers.

The black SUV pulled out of the lot and Delta watched as the two girl-filled cars followed it.

—⁓—

The next evening, Lara sat on her sofa bent over her shoe. She was determined to get a walk in today, regardless of the weird people. She looked up at Buckley, who paced in front of her, eager.

"How do you know we're going for a W-A-L-K?"

As she tied the laces, the dog rushed to the front door and turned to look back at her, then stepped across the foyer again. Lara stood, then stopped and squinted into the upper left corner of the living room.

Had a light just blinked?

"Puppy, do that again."

He sat.

"Yeah, thanks." She shook her head, then waved an arm up, watching a beige plastic box that was mounted high on the wall near the ceiling. Nothing. She walked back and stepped up the staircase, eyeing the box. At the second step, a red light glowed. "A motion sensor? What's that about?"

She moved quickly around the room to see what positions made the light blink. She'd noticed the box before and decided it was left over from an old security system. But she hadn't realized it was hooked up. Could it have a network connection?

"Well, it can blink as long as I'm not paying for it!" She bowed to the box, which flashed on and off in response. "Allow me to introduce myself. My name is Lara McKeon, newly arrived to your house and city after a life of misadventures." She lifted her arm to it. "And you are?"

Silence.

She waved and it blinked. "Ah, I see. You are an ambassador from an alien planet, come to observe life on this strange world. Well, you've come to the right city, Alien. There are many odd specimens wandering around here, that's for sure!"

She patted her thigh and her dog moved up next to her. "Come on Buckley, let's get moving before it gets any later." She attached his leash, wished Alien a good evening, and moved out the door, pulling it to lock behind her.

The night was warm, breathing spring, and the streetlights glowed through fresh baby green leaves sprouting on the trees' bare branches. It was a great night to walk. By now, Lara had covered many miles on her hikes through her picturesque neighborhood, and she enjoyed the special beauty of every season. Except for winter, which she enjoyed from her window looking out. She'd been slow to build a social life, made especially shy by the strange things that happened around her. For now she was content to keep company with her little animal family.

Tonight, Lara soon spied the vehicle that was becoming a companion to her. She had seen it her first month in town, this black SUV with its dark-tinted windows. That day, a window had gapped open to reveal a movie star blowing smoke out into the world. At the time, she had laughed, thinking that surely Dirk Durmont could smoke in his own vehicle; if it started to smell funny, he could buy a new one! Since then, she had seen it often as she walked. She still didn't know which house was his, although she had picked out a few of her favorites for him to own. The two-story brown stone with the grand porch was nice, and mysterious; she never saw any action at the large double doors. Or the huge turreted Queen Anne with the spacious grounds in the back would work for a guy with family to invite over.

Tonight, she watched the SUV approach, then politely looked away as it passed.

—∿∿—

Michelle had called the weekend a bust, but Delta thought it was fun enough. They'd watched a movie they thought Lara would like and got into Connie's mom's red wine. But now it was Sunday and a school day loomed ahead like thunderstorm clouds.

As Delta walked past the bushes lining the sidewalk on the way to Gramma's, she ran a hand along the soft green buds forming on the ends of branches. She shifted a red vinyl tote bag, heavy on her shoulder. Gramma had bought it for her when Delta was trying to convince her to get some new stylish Discount City clothes and dump the old dresses. Their final deal was that Gramma would buy some nice old lady slacks outfits if Delta would put all her books in the tote bag and take them to school and home every day.

As she walked, she sang "Row Row Row Your Boat", but the words were what Mark had taught her—"Smoke, smoke, smoke your toke, doobies not too green …."

She stopped and looked up at a tall red brick building ahead. It stood out from the surrounding smaller homes as if it was the boss of this section of town. The big overgrown yard was enclosed by an iron fence. Delta looked up at the second floor window above the entry and wiggled her fingers in a wave at an invisible little girl. It was a game Gramma and she played. Gramma had lived the last half of her childhood here after the little family moved away from the stone house near the trailer. She had liked to sit on a bench built under that upper window and watch the world. A driveway came off the main street and swept toward the front door and out the other side of the yard. When company came, the child Marianne sat and admired the dresses of the local fancy ladies as they stepped out of their cars. Now she and Delta always waved at the "ghost of little Gramma" looking out at them.

She noticed movement at the side of the house and saw the actual grown-up Gramma hurrying around to the back. When Delta got to an opening in the fence, she entered the yard and followed her.

The house hadn't belonged to the McNought family for a long time, not since Gramma's mother died and it was sold to cover bills and the burying. The new owners divided it into apartments. Gramma said its spirit had been split into pieces and then dried up, but that wouldn't stop her from haunting it. It never occurred to any of the tenants to ask who the woman was who tended the small garden in the back; the landlord must have hired her. And it never occurred to the landlord to ask which tenant was planting flowers and filling the bird feeder; it was a nice touch, but they weren't going to get a break from their rent for it, so nothing said was enough said.

Gramma saw Delta and straightened up from a stoop. "Delta! I'm running late." She held up a dirt-crusted trowel. "Doing my spring things." Her dress looked like spring, with its pattern of small red flowers on a cream background.

"Gramma, that's not one of your new outfits!" A deal was a deal. Delta didn't want her wearing those funny-looking old lady dresses around where people could see.

"I know, honey. I'll change when we get to the house. Come over here a minute."

Delta walked into a small enclosed area to join her. A metal gate was attached to the wood pickets that made up the fence; she let it hang open behind her.

"Do you see what I'm dong here, Delta?" Gramma waved her arms to take in the little garden where they stood.

"Digging." But she knew it was never that easy.

"Yes, digging now. And soon I'll plant flowers and tomatoes, then I'll come by to weed and water. Do you know why?" She bent and stuck the trowel into the earth.

Delta looked sideways at the bird feeder, suspicious. Was this a test? She remained silent.

Gramma continued. "Because it needs me to do this, that's all. I helped Mama keep it when I was a girl, and after. But then they sold the house, and you know what?"

An easy one. "No, whatty?"

"After that, no one took care of the garden. It went to weeds and trash and the fence started falling apart. So it came to me that keeping this garden up was mine to do." She put her arm in Delta's and guided her out, closing the gate behind them. "In life, there are things set in front of us that we're meant to do, and if we don't do them they don't get done. See?"

Delta nodded without understanding.

"Like right now, you're getting through high school and I'm helping you. Then we'll see about going to Mountain College and what work you want to do. There's something special out there waiting for you."

Delta tensed at the talk of college. She could barely do high school. How the hell—or dickens—was she supposed to go to college? She liked Michelle's ideas better, like hooking up with Dirk and getting rich.

But for now, she enjoyed the safety of Gramma's arm in hers as they walked.

Chapter Six

PORCH PARTY
Saturday 6-10 p.m.
Lara's house, 1049 High
Serving: soft drinks, wine, and snacks

Lara smiled as the final invitation slid out of her printer. She'd found paper bordered in gold and plum pansies. Pretty. Too bad she didn't have the same flowers in the porch planters, but it was too late to switch. She'd gone to the garden center and bought some red and white peran…, imper…, whatevers, so they'd have to do.

She straightened the little pile of flyers and carried them upstairs. Some shyness attack had gripped her when she thought about delivering them herself, so her neighbor Ruth had agreed to go along with her. Lara picked up the phone.

And maybe if Ruth was with her, no strange yellow-haired women would bother her.

Mark took the turn too sharp and rocks flew up from the tires of his motorcycle. One hit Delta's leg. She hung on to him tighter as they made their usual morning run to school on his way to the factory. Soon there'd be no more teachers, no more books. For the summer, at least. She couldn't wait.

The bike had appeared one day at the trailer, same as his car, and no one asked where it came from. Unlike the beat-up old blue tank of a car, however, the Harley was near new. They rode along for a minute, then Mark shouted above the noise of the engine. "That kegger I'm having Saturday. You and your friends can come."

"Cool!" Delta shouted back. She pulled at her denim mini skirt, which had ridden up and exposed her bare backside.

"Tell Michelle, right?"

"Sure. If she's not in Granville this weekend."

Mark turned his head to the side and nodded. Delta could see he was mad. She knew he liked Michelle and wanted her there. He'd been bothered when Delta told him about the Dirk Dolls in Granville and that woman Lara. He said it sounded bogus, the stuff about some girl-friend the actor had set up in a house. But the stories about sex parties caught his attention. He told her that any guy would screw a bunch of girls if they gave it away for free, then he'd looked at her with that "you know what I mean" face and she'd had to look away.

Delta clung to him as they rode toward town. She knew he was probably ticking off a list of party chores. He was smart that way. In her bedroom, he'd stored a case of whiskey, a box of condoms, and assorted bags of weeds, pills, and powders. He'd pick up a keg Saturday. Ma would be gone then. He or Delta would put some powder into Silas' open whiskey bottle and top it off. Mark had ways of making sure Silas was unconscious when he wanted him to be. He'd once said that the only thing keeping the old man alive was his disability check.

Mark stopped in front of the school and steadied the bike with his long blue-jeaned legs.

"This Hollywood shit." He made his words drag out slow. He did that sometimes, talking to her like she was a kid. "Will you tell me if you get invited to meet Dirk Durmont?" He craned around to look at her then went on explaining. "Or, better yet, I'll come up with something ahead of time and we'll go over it. Okay?"

Delta nodded. Strange—she never thought Mark was a Dirk fan. Did he want to meet him, too?

But he made himself clear. "If you screw a millionaire, you should be able to get a piece of the money, right? You're a good-looking girl, Delta. We oughta try to get something from that." He grinned.

———

Party day had arrived! And Lara was exhausted. She'd planned and cooked and cleaned and still worried the plans and cooking and clean-ing weren't enough. And what if no one came?

She stepped outside and studied the porch. It looked good. Color-ful rag rugs were company-special against the gray floor. Red and white blossoms topped the white planters on the railings like sprinkles on ice cream. Neighbors had come by earlier with lawn chairs which now sat open and welcoming in her front yard. She turned and faced the house. It was a simple bungalow, but extra width and height gave it elegance. Through the glass front door, cream-colored walls and graceful French doors helped create a restful scene. The original owners lived only on the main level in the 1920s, but the house had expanded like a soft balloon as the generations added attic bedrooms and a basement rec room and office. Now, in its Lara phase, it took on more formality with a seldom-used dining room lit by a crystal chandelier and a main floor bedroom that served as a library. Built-in shelves for rows of vintage books would be perfect and were planned.

A shout made her turn. Ellen and John had stepped out from a door across the street and stood waving. Lara smiled and waved and they made their way toward her, John lugging a cooler and Ellen with arms wrapped around three bottles of wine. As they neared, Lara suddenly remembered her bigger problems, and her eyes narrowed as she scanned the street. No cars, no strangers. Not yet. Surely the rude people wouldn't bother her tonight! She tightened her jaw and stood taller. She was determined to forget they existed and to enjoy her party.

"Hope you can use this wine sometime. We can't pack it anyplace." Ellen walked up the sidewalk.

"Hey! Thanks. Bring it on in," Lara answered.

With a huff, John set the cooler down on the porch and followed the women into the house. As she passed the CD player, Lara pressed a button to start sweet Celtic dulcimer music.

Half an hour later, the house was full. A man in black slacks, dress shirt, and cap moved through Lara's front door carrying a platter at head level. "Make way for meat puffs!" He swept into the dining room and placed it on the table. "Straight out of the oven."

"They smell good!" Lara said. "I don't suppose there's a recipe."

He laughed. "I can tell you what I threw in, but nothing's written down." The new arrival, Don, lived next door with his wife Georgia. On warm days, their kitchen window hung open and the smell of sautéing garlic teased Lara. Sometimes they brought a loaf of home-made bread to her.

Lara visited with more of her guests, then walked through the party for a hostess check. Tonight the rooms teemed with life. The chandelier glowed over a table crowded with food, and people helped themselves with the ease of familiarity. This wasn't their first visit; Lara had held an open house before she'd even hung pictures. For that event, she'd given in to a fear of cooking for strangers and found the name of a trendy caterer. She'd kept the caterer's name, one step in the huge task of beginning again in a new town. She needed new contacts, such as the caterer, and people to fix her car, blonde her hair, vet her pets. Starting over was exhausting and she was glad she'd never have to do it again.

Lara passed a group surrounding John. A man who lived in a two-story red brick a block away said, "So you're moving to Chicago to finish your PhD? That's great!"

"The timing is right. It's been hanging over my head, so I'm going to just finish it."

"Taste this." Ellen walked up with a tortilla rolled around a cream cheese blend. She now held in front of her husband's mouth. "This stuff is so great! Lara, recipe." She waved her hors d'oeuvre.

Lara smiled and nodded, then stepped out onto the porch. Several men had crowded chairs together on one side of the porch, circling a cooler. On the other side, the swing was heavy with women clinging to children gathered on their laps. Lara policed the food table; every bowl was full. Someone was watching the party along with her, filling up dishes as they emptied. Nice.

"This looks like a junk yard! My car is better than any of these heaps." Michelle pulled her car into a grassy space at the end of a row of parked vehicles. Beyond them, a fire lit the faces of a crowd gathered in front of Delta's trailer. "Shit, am I the only one with class around here?" She turned to Stacy. "I gotta piss."

Tonight she'd chosen Stacy to go with her to Granville. Michelle drove there almost weekly now and either went alone or with people who suited what she was doing. She brought Stacy along when she thought she might get in with Dirk and didn't want competition from Delta, whose thin body, big boobs, and that wide-eyed brainless look picked up men all over. Delta was good for when they were stalking Lara; she never questioned anything they did. Brittany was too much man-bait, too, but lately she hadn't been hanging with them as much so it wasn't hard to exclude her. Michelle was only stringing her along for her computer skills, anyway.

They each climbed out and Michelle walked into the woods. Stacy followed, talking in a constant stream about their trip to "the city." They passed a man and woman pressed together against a tree.

"Great party!" Stacy giggled. "Do you know those guys? I think that's Megan from Culstan City, isn't it? Who's she with? It's so dark, I can't see."

Michelle led them a dozen steps farther. She stopped and pushed away undergrowth with her foot, then lifted her tight black skirt and moved into a practiced squat.

"Better not be any f-ing poison ivy around here," she said as she peed.

"Yeah, I'm finding a clearer spot. I once got poison ivy on my butt, did I tell you about that? I was with Tommy Benston up that hill behind the school, and it was too dark to watch for it. Then every time I tried to scratch it in school, Mrs. Clark stared me down. So I went home at lunch and stayed there." Stacy moved a few feet away, then stopped and crouched low.

When they were done, they stepped through the branches and weeds toward a bonfire that formed the center of Mark's party. Michelle took the lead as they rounded the house. Men in blue jeans and women in tight skirts and small tops took up most of the space on railroad ties that formed a large rectangle around the fire. Groups and couples leaned against cars and trucks, drinking and laughing. Heavy rock music blared from an unseen CD player. Michelle knew Mark would have passed joints around earlier but she hoped there were a few left. In any case, she planned to get some directly from him and do a little business while she was at it.

The fire exploded and several people jerked away from its heat. The shadow of an easy chair showed dark inside the flames.

"Whoo-hoo!" Michelle shouted. "Hope no one needs that chair!"

They saw Mark across the clearing near a large metal keg. He shoved it with his foot and it bobbed up and down, close to empty. Several truck beds, however, held coolers and the fresh cold beer cans were appearing as welcomed and steady as blasts from a turning fan in summer. He looked around to do a host check and saw the two girls stepping out into the clearing. He smiled at Michelle. Stacy smiled back, but Michelle made her face bored-looking as she walked over to a bare spot on a log. Mark strode over to the nearest cooler, picked up three beers, then went to stand beside them. He handed beers down to the girls.

"Glad to see you made it," he said.

"Yeah, thanks for asking us!" Stacy said in a phony too-sweet voice.

She smiled big as she looked up at him. "We went to Granville and watched Dirk's girlfriend awhile."

Michelle glared at the flames in front of her, pissed at Stacy's big mouth and suck-up attitude. "Your idea to build a fire? It's f-ing hot over here!" She was happy to change the subject. Tonight they'd spied on Lara's party, hiding in the bushes across the street while the rich people wandered into her house carrying gourmet food and pricey wine. Michelle was determined to catch Dirk there tonight, but she never did see him. Was he wearing some disguise she didn't recognize?

"I like to burn things. Kinda a habit." Mark laughed, then got serious and shrugged his shoulders. "You were late getting here. You missed the grilled steaks."

"Yeah, right," Michelle snorted. "We had other places to go."

"Did you have steaks?" Stacy asked. "We ate in the city, but it was only burgers."

Michelle shook her head and rolled her eyes.

Mark continued. "I heard you're hanging around Granville a lot lately. Screwing movie stars."

Stacy's voice was still phony high-pitched as she said, "Dirk is making a movie. We don't screw him, though." She giggled. "Not yet! But his girlfriend Lara is having a party, too, just like you!"

"Would you keep a frigging hold on it?" Michelle snapped. She'd had enough of that uppity smart-ass Lara and her expensive house and pure-bred dog and spending three hours getting her color done. Bitch.

Mark guzzled from the can in his hand, then said, "I know all about it. You know that Delta tells me what you all do. Dirk Durmont's keeping some woman in a house in a rich neighborhood and everyone's scraping for the dirt on her. Tabloids crawling all over the place."

"And you should see her!" Michelle said. "She's old; she's 42! She's older than he is." Her anger grew. "And fat! Like maybe I'm not skinny, but neither is she!" She gulped her beer and gasped. "I hate her!"

A log in the fire fell and shot red sparks toward them. The flame grew.

"She's pretty stupid moving to Granville to flaunt her ass in your faces," Mark said.

Michelle knew he was only sucking up to her, but she replied, "I don't get it. Why her?"

"Are you sure he's screwing her?"

"What else is there?"

Mark looked toward the flames for a minute, then spoke with hatred in his voice. "I hear she lives pretty good, travels and shit, leaves town a lot. She's not dealing to him, is she?"

"Dealing?" Michelle watched Mark's face. He seemed as angry as she felt. Cool.

He bent to pick up a forgotten stick and tossed it. It landed square on the flames and ignited immediately.

Michelle stared at the red glowing line of the burning limb. "That would sure make more sense than his wanting to hang out with her and not us." Dealing drugs to Dirk! Whether it was true or not, she liked how steamed Mark was getting about it.

Mark's breath now came fast and he spat out his words. "That's so f-d up, moving in and thinking she can deal wherever she wants!"

"All I know is I hate her," Michelle snarled.

"Yeah, we hate her, *don't* we!" Stacy echoed.

The three of them stared into the fire, not noticing the heat on their faces.

"I think they'll miss Granville. It's such a homey town." Lara said. She had joined a group surrounding a woman holding a baby.

"I think they'll like Chicago," the woman said.

"Oh, they will," another added.

"They like a faster pace, believe me. Condos, traffic, they'll get into it."

"We *want* them to come back." Johns' mother's face was solemn. "But I agree. Chicago is more their style, with all that opportunity."

"Someplace fun to visit," another relative offered, her voice a stage whisper. The women's faces brightened.

Lara heard the sound of dishes clinking in the dining room. The small crystal clock on the mantel read 10:15. She rose and stepped into hostess gear, moving toward the sound of plates being gathered up.

"Can I get you some plastic wrap? Please, take some cake and cookies! Ruth, you guys will eat these, won't you?"

A spurt of new energy drove the partiers as they prepared to leave. Lara stood by the front door as the mood stirred the crowd and people left as quickly as they had come four hours earlier. Several women picked up cups and plates, walking in a circle around the party area to help clean. Recipes were promised, addresses exchanged, and finally Lara closed the door on the last group.

Then she turned to face the empty room. The CD player had been switched off at some point and the silence, after so much chaos, throbbed against her ears. She hated this moment lately when after an event, all she was, was alone.

She turned and looked up at Alien, which blinked in response to her movement.

When his mother's headlights skimmed over the crowd, Mark kicked dirt on the embers of the dying fire.

"Shit! What is it, 2?" He looked at his watch, squinting in the darkness. "Hell, Ma will want to come party, and she's probably drunk as shit already."

For a minute, Michelle thought he looked embarrassed. She pressed her watch and it lit up. "F-ing 3! I hope my mom's sleeping so she'll leave me alone." She stood up, drunk and unsteady. Stacy had left long ago with a man who said he was taking her home before her curfew. Delta was lying on the ground with her knees up over a log, passed out or sleeping.

"Delta!" Mark nudged her with his foot. "Get up! Ma's home. Watch that beaver shot." She pulled her skirt down as she got to her knees, then her feet. "Get on inside." They watched as she wove her way to the front door of the trailer. Diane was already inside and reached out to help her up the steps.

Michelle walked to her car.

"Wait a minute, Michelle. Seems we've got some unfinished business." Mark stepped beside her.

"Oh, Mark, I'll get your money for you. I just don't have it now." Mark held her as she leaned back against the car. He pressed his hands against her bare upper arms.

"I'm not letting you walk away with a bag, baby. But, since it was a small one, there are other ways to make it even." He lifted her chin and put his mouth on hers. She opened her mouth and returned his kiss; it never occurred to her not to kiss a man back. And tonight she was looking for more than a free bag of weed. She had an idea, one that would fix Lara.

"Mark, it's 3 in the f-ing morning." She spoke clearly as he ran his hands under her skirt and squeezed her naked butt.

"So a little longer won't make it much later." He kissed her forehead and mouth briefly, then rubbed his crotch against her as she pulled down his zipper.

She expertly slid her fingers into the opening of his pants. "Okay. But, Mark … ," her voice became a whine. " … I get totally messed up when I think about that Lara stealing your business. That is so wrong."

He paused a minute and looked down at her. "Don't you worry about her. There are ways to stop that." His right hand slid up between her legs.

Michelle's fingers stroked him and he gasped.

"Okay, but you better have a rubber," Michelle said, her voice cold again and unaffected by what was happening between them.

Mark grinned, grabbed her arm, and led her to the rock house.

CHAPTER SEVEN

Lara scowled. The outfit—the oversized t-shirt with leggings—was outdated. Unfortunately, she was looking at her own reflection. She turned around in front of the mirror. This had been a practical workout uniform for years, but she needed to come up with something more stylish. What with everyone staring at her as if she was some kind of show, she'd better look as good as possible.

She tied the ends of the long shirt together, leaving spandex from the waist down. Moving her legs to shoulder-width distance, she pretended a bar across her shoulders, and lowered her body until her thighs were parallel to the floor. A mirror positioned on the opposite wall in the bedroom gave her a view of her back, and she squinted to see. Good form. Her butt muscles were tensed and rounded, straining the leggings. She slowly straightened her legs and watched her gluts clench.

Her eyes popped open wide.

"Gross! I can't go around looking like that!" She shook her legs to release the tension in her muscles. She would rather look overdressed than sleazy. And here in Granville, even when she was fully dressed strange people stared at her body. She wanted to protect every inch from them if she could, so the large shirt and leggings may be frumpy, but they were her safest option.

At the thought of the people crowding her, Lara's tensed with anger. She hated that she had to protect herself from low, gossipy people, even at a gym, a place that was supposed to be about health and exercise. Their behavior was incredible! And what if she *was* dating some movie star? What business was it of theirs? In any case, she wasn't dating anyone, she was very much alone, and they would soon figure it out and the whole thing would blow over.

She checked her look one more time, combed her hair, and walked down the stairs. The light in the corner blinked. Lara had done a little research on Alien, had called the number on the sticker on her front door that read "Warning! This property is protected by A&M Security Service." A&M had never heard of her, so she was sure she wasn't accidentally connected to an alarm system. The only thing protecting her was a big dog.

But there was more, wasn't there? She owned a gun, a gift from her ex-husband. She thought a minute. Maybe she should find that pistol and learn how to use it.

Michelle bumped the car behind hers; it rocked once. "How the hell am I supposed to get my car into there? You'd think Brandt's Gym could afford a bigger parking lot, what with Dirk Durmont being a member," she snarled.

"And Lara! She's a member! Connie said she should be here today," Stacy said. "So if we're lucky we'll see her and Dirk, too."

"Oh. Great." Brittany was sitting in the front seat, sounding now like a bored drama-queen to make Michelle mad. Michelle tried not to look at her, but saw her glance back at Delta when she said, "Did everyone get their grades?"

Stacy spoke up. "I got a 'B' in English, but just a 'C' in Algebra with that jerk Mr. Bertson. But I don't think I need algebra in nursing school, so he can shove it. Then a 'B' in life sciences, and then gym was an 'A'. I think everyone got an 'A' for showing up and not messing up the shower drains like they did last year. Do you remember that time Vicky and her friends dumped that stuff down the floor drains ..."

"Delta?" Brittany broke in.

"Yeah, I remember that," Delta answered, "and Mr. Swindy had to take apart the pipes and went around and yelled at all the classes."

Michelle laughed and Brittany breathed deep, then spoke again. "And your grades? Did you get through okay?"

Delta's voice brightened. "I passed everything! My Gramma bought me a new swimsuit from Goldberg's for doing so good."

"Good job!" Brittany reached back to high-five her.

Michelle leaned away from Brittany's arm, then mocked her with, "Ew, good job." She was sick of this rah-rah party. Didn't they have better things to do? "Let's *hope* you passed! So what grades did you get?"

"Don't answer her, Delta," Brittany said and glared at Michelle.

Michelle bumped the car behind her again. "Damn!" She pulled forward, then back. The car shook. "I can't fit in this f-ing place!" She pulled out and drove around the block. Suddenly she stomped on the brake, stopping short in the middle of the street.

"Dirk alert!" she shouted.

"You're kidding!" Stacy shouted back but leaned up to peer out the front windshield.

Ahead of them, a tall lean man, his face hidden by his jacket's hood, walked away from a black SUV.

"Ohmigod, it's him!" Brittany shrieked. They all laughed and craned forward to watch as he entered a back door of the building.

"That's him alright! Call Connie," Michelle said.

Brittany palmed the phone and punched in a number. "Connie! We're at Brandt's Gym. Report!" She nodded as she listened. "And here we are! We'll get back to you." She looked around at the others, her eyes wide. "He's working out here for real! There's some private men's club in the back."

"Oh, man. How can we get in?" Stacy asked. "Can we follow him in? Someone remember what door that is, so we can find it again. If we knock hard, they'll let us …"

"We can't. They don't allow women." Brittany's voice was a whine.

"We'll see about that," Michelle said firmly. They'd let her in. They didn't know who they were messing with. Somehow she'd get in.

A car stopped behind them and a horn sounded.

"Get screwed!" Michelle shouted and flipped the driver off out her window. She drove onto a side street and pulled into a "Banking Customers Only" parking spot. "Here's what we'll do. I want to get into the men's club, so I'll scope that out. Brittany, Stacy, you sneak in the side door and go find Lara."

"Find her and what?" Brittany stared at Michelle. "Find her and do what."

"Get everything you can on her. Follow her around, see what she does. Now that Connie's getting on at TeleSales with the DirkLetter people, she wants us to get her more stuff. Delta."

Delta was staring out the window. She jerked. "Yeah?"

"You stand at the door where Dirk went in. If he leaves, come get us. Here's the phone. Call Connie if you see him. She and the others should be here soon."

The girls climbed out and hurried toward the gym in a stealthy crouch.

It was strangely busy for Saturday. Lara drove around the block a second time. Cars were jammed into parallel slots along the street in a solid line corner to corner. Was it volleyball season? She didn't remember a Saturday afternoon league listed on the bulletin board. The last thing she wanted was a big crowd.

She edged into a spot three blocks away. Slinging her gym bag over her shoulder, she climbed out and double-checked her locked car door. This was a rough part of Granville, so this gym wasn't usually busy. That made it a place where Lara could work out without socializing much and that suited her lately.

She hiked the distance to the building and walked up the wide stone steps to the front door.

Then she stopped, inhaling sharp.

Crowds of men and women in street clothes filled the lobby. Clusters of children in uniforms were gathered around them. Lara edged through them and checked in at the desk, ignoring the people whose heads followed her as she moved. She'd begun to wonder if the staring was a cultural difference, something they did in the south. Rude, where she came from, but she could try to tolerate it.

"Crowded today!" She chatted with the young man at the counter. He looked at her and smiled, but said nothing as he ran her membership card through a machine. He handed it back and she went up marble steps to the exercise room.

When she reached the glass doors at the top of the stairs, she hesitated. So many people were standing around! So the crowds weren't only for kids' sports today. She pushed the doors open and stepped in. A group of young blond women in revealing white lycra stood near the treadmills and turned toward her, gaping. Lara glanced at them, then around the room. Almost all the equipment was occupied. And at a glance, she could see over a dozen women, which was unusual for this old gym. Most of them turned to look at her.

One machine was available and she sat and counted out leg extensions. As she worked, she watched her form in a mirror on the far wall and tried to focus on her quadriceps. But she was soon distracted by the realization that the women near the treadmills had not moved. They stood and observed her soundlessly.

She finished a set and twisted around to increase the weight.

"Is that the woman?" The male voice came from the free-weights corner.

Lara froze.

Someone murmured a reply.

"She looks different than what I expected."

Lara straightened in her seat on the machine and looked in the mirror. To her left behind her, benches were set up near the dumbbells. Three men were staring at her. She turned and saw one of them eyeing her breasts. He noticed her attention and met her eyes, smiling. Lara looked away quickly, embarrassed.

The men whispered while the women near her murmured to each other. Lara paused to gather her dignity, then slid off the machine, picked up her gym bag, and walked toward the back exit. In the mirror, she saw the three men watch her as she moved.

A trainer stood near the door.

She stopped next to him. "Is it usually so busy this time Saturdays?" Lara tried to sound casual to hide her tension.

He looked at her and slowly shook his head.

"I can't find equipment to use! Think I'll try later."

He said nothing and stared ahead of him as she left.

Downstairs, the lobby was even more crowded than before. Several women turned their heads toward her as she walked. Suddenly edgy, Lara took the stairs down another level. There must be another way out of this place! Her anxiety grew. There was too much strange stuff going on, so much she didn't understand. She saw a small flight of stairs running up to a door marked "Exit" and she hurried through it.

The door led to the sidewalk beside the building. Finally, she let her tension show as she rushed to the car. When she reached it, she yanked open the door, jumped in, and pulled away. But as she drove, she passed a red truck in a large lot next to an abandoned building. When the men in the cab spied her, they sat up quickly, apparently startled. One dialed into a cell phone.

Lara sped toward her house. She just wanted to be back home. Home, where she was safe.

"Do you know who's here today?"

The little girl tried to move away, but Alice gripped her arm and bent down to her eye level. She knew the people in this lobby would want the exciting news. "Dirk Durmont! He works out in the club at the back."

The girl's mother appeared and forced a smile. "My daughter has been taught not to talk to strangers."

"Oh, that's okay. I'm not a stranger. I was her volleyball coach last year."

The woman stared, her eyes narrowing. "She didn't play volleyball last year."

"Oh, yeah. Sorry. Anyway, I was telling her about Dirk Durmont. He works out here."

The woman softened immediately. "Oh! Our Dirk? Well, I didn't know! Is he upstairs?" She looked up the steps, grinning sincerely now.

"No, he's in a private club at the back. They won't let me in. But his girlfriend's upstairs, if you want to go look at her."

"No kidding! I'll do that! What does she look like?"

"She's wearing a big black t-shirt. You'll see. Looks like Laura Starbright, but they say it isn't her, but it looks like her."

"Thanks!" The woman smiled big. "I'll run up and take a peek during the game."

CHAPTER EIGHT

The season slid into summer. In the Southern section of the Midwest, natives moved indoors to hide from the heat, while waves of tourists rolled in from cooler places to see new sights. The girls from Rockton lay out on lake beaches and got tans and invitations to nude midnight swims. Stacy's parents pulled her along with them on a tour of Mountain College and gathered brochures about nursing degrees. The four friends often traveled to Granville on missions to hunt Dirk or his stalkee stand-in, Lara.

Alice put miles on her car tracking the girls who stalked Lara, or following Dirk or Lara or bodyguards or sometimes a skinny dark-haired man in a big blue car. She danced now at Rocko's Club for Men, where she was known for the oversized breasts she had received as a bonus from her last employer.

Lara found a lotion to protect her face from the newest types of sun damage and searched for ways to save her life from the people stealing it.

So summer passed, and the Labor Day weekend arrived. Rockton High School reopened and Alice danced double-shifts for the holiday.

Lara took her annual trip to an art fair near Chicago.

9-18-99
Journal,
    I had such a great time on my trip!
    On the way to Emma's, I shopped in St. Louis. Then when I pulled up to the Sauder Farm, Paul and Em came walking hand in hand from the fields. Such a beautiful sight. E made sage and cream slipcovers for the living room chairs. It looks like Pottery Barn. She's incredible.
    We went to the Oak Brook Art Fair, then Kane County Flea Market. I bought art, a farm-implement sculpture. E is so welcoming. She says to make her house a home base and come more often.
    The next day up there I cooked a spaghetti dinner. Jackie came

over, and Carol called. Then Monday I left. Such a good time, so much love and warmth.

I am so alone here.

I must think on whatever is holy, whatever is good and pure.

I need to make a list of pleasant thoughts. I'm tending to obsess about the strange things that have been happening around me, and they're making me feel too self-important.

Better ideas to think on:

Success

Love—children, friends, working as a counselor

Exercise—lifting weights, sculpting muscle

The self-importance issue: I'm getting this extra attention, whisperings etc., mostly at the health club. But it's reminders of all the things I am NOT and it's a dangling in front of me of something I can't have. I'm trying hard to stay focused on my muscles at the gym. It helps. Working out <u>can</u> be meditative.

This must be a lesson for me to pray for protection from evil and to know God's will and to find joy in His will, not always wanting something else.

—✧—

Anybody could sneak into the gym.

The side door was always unlocked. Once in the building, all Michelle had to do was tap on the door to the Men's Club and one of the guys let her in. They liked her, and she liked the way they looked at her when she worked out. Those stupid Dirk Dolls and the men upstairs thought watching Lara was cool, but they hadn't seen nothing 'til they'd seen Michelle do the inner thigh machine in her sheer white spandex. The guys in the Men's Club loved her. The occasional blow-job helped matters, too, of course.

Twice she'd seen Dirk from across the room, but he'd left right after she got there. She was sure by now the guys were telling him how good she was at "favors." He had to figure he could get much more, being famous and all. Today she had planned to go up to him and straight out invite him to the little room she'd found under the front stairs.

But now today, this jerk in the Brandt's Gym t-shirt was standing in front of her blocking her way. She'd forgotten his name, but remembered his cock smelled like green deodorant soap, which was better than a lot of them.

"So we can't let you in there anymore," the jerk was telling her.

"Why the hell not?" Michelle was outraged. "You know the guys like me in there. And you don't want me to go away, do you?" Surely this lamebrain remembered how good she did him! She had done him, hadn't she? "Uh, … Sam." What was his name?

"It's Dan. Michelle, I have a job to do here. If you want to go out sometime, I'd like that. But I can't let you into the Men's Club anymore."

She rolled her eyes. Her going out with some gym employee jerk, like sure. She looked back at him and tried to look blank and innocent, that thing Delta did. "Why the sudden change?"

"You know Dirk Durmont works out in there."

"Well, I didn't notice, but I'm sure he can go there if he wants to."

"Give me a break, Shelly." Michelle grit her teeth when she heard the nickname. Ass. "You're not wanting to get into the Men's Club to meet some local guys. And not everyone wants you there. Too many people see what you girls are up to with Dirk, and the gym management doesn't like it. Especially with all the trouble because of that Lara woman."

Michelle tried harder to look clueless. "Lara woman? What Lara woman?"

"There's a woman who comes here, lifts weights. For real. She and Dirk are dating or something and we have this circus going on, people showing up to get a look at her. We have our hands full with that crowd without letting women go crawling around everywhere Dirk is. When he wants to see people, he goes upstairs. Just watch for him."

Michelle knew that being upstairs with Lara in the way wouldn't do her any good. She grit her teeth. "So they're dating?"

"That's what I hear. And he set her up in a nice house to keep her in Granville. Anyway, I can't let you in there."

Michelle's anger made her face hot and she said, "You're kidding!"

At that moment, the door behind them flew open and Lara strode through it. Dan nodded toward her. Lara glanced at them then walked toward the locker room. Michelle watched her, thinking the famous girlfriend looked like a nun compared to her, what with that baggy black t-shirt. How the hell did that old bitch get Dirk? Here Michelle was, younger, and … well, really much younger, and he wouldn't even unzip his pants for her. Not yet, anyway.

She only needed an opportunity.

"So, about me not going in." She leaned into his shirt. "Sa...Dam." She tilted his face up toward his.

But he backed away. "If you want to go to the janitor's closet with me, I can do that. But I can't let you into the Men's Club."

Michelle turned and marched out through the side door. Maybe outside she could run into Dirk and tell him how badly she was being treated, and how he could make her feel better. And she'd make sure Dirk knew how they all hated the L-whore. That'd fix Lara. Michelle would tell the whole world how much they hated her.

The whole world. She smiled. She had a new plan.

Saying that name sure gave her power.

Michelle was impressed by what happened when she mentioned Dirk Durmont to the tabloid paper. When she'd called their 800 number about having an exclusive story, this woman had called her right back. And here she was, sitting in the lounge of Brandt's Gym, giving the reporter an exclusive interview. Michelle Hamlin, who by the way would be the next exclusive girlfriend of Dirk with the way things were going to play out now. And the tabloid would be sending her the $500 they promised for a good story. Everyone she knew had those phone numbers ripped out and stuck in her purse, hoping for extra cash.

She was just struggling a little with some of the questions the reporter was asking.

"And how long have you known Dirk?"

The woman had introduced herself as Shirl Manier and said she was from the Dirk Camp, which must be the department that handled Dirk Durmont stories. She didn't look too awful old, not as old as Lara, but had that same boring smartass look about her. Her hair was dark brown and cut short all around, then curled to be fluffy on top. Her makeup was colorless, in beige and browns, same as her clothes. Even her eyelids were tan and her fingernails had those painted white tips, fake natural, like Lara's, but Lara's weren't painted at all, just natural. Boring.

As Michelle talked, Shirl from time to time opened a short spiral notebook and wrote in it, then closed it before Michelle could manage a peek at any words.

"How long have you known Dirk?" she repeated.

"Oh." Michelle kept her face flat as she thought up a good story.

"Oh, a couple of months now. We're getting real close, too."

"You and Lara."

"Oh, Lara and I aren't close. I mean, I know a lot about her, I know her and all, but I wouldn't call it close."

"But you called Hollywood Scoopline and told them you have a story about Lara and Dirk?"

"Well, yes. We all know around here how he bought her that house, and how he's always around where she is. They're totally into it."

"How do you know?"

"Well, she lives over in that house, and we see him over there all the time."

Shirl wrote a minute, then looked up. "You see him at the house? Are you there, too?"

"Oh." Michelle scowled, then caught herself and put on a blank face. Looking innocent would help about now. "I have friends in that neighborhood, of course, and we see him over there all the time. When I'm at my friends' house, or going to it."

Shirl wrote. Michelle spoke again. "Lara will be coming out that door any time now, like I said." Michelle had sat them at a table that looked out toward the lobby.

"And how do you know she's here and that's what she'll do?"

Michelle snorted. This Shirl Whatever was a big pain in the ass. Couldn't she just get the story and stop with the extra questions? She thought of some lines she'd read in the DirkLetter and repeated them. "Lara McKeon is a creature of habit. She comes and goes the same ways and times everywhere." There! Then she added, "Some would consider that a boring type of person."

At that moment, Lara pushed through the double doors. She paused a half-step when she saw the two women look toward her, then hurried out the front door.

Shirl had glanced at Lara, then again met Michelle's eyes. "So that's the woman."

"Yes. That's the woman that Dirk is following all over town."

"And again, how do you know that?"

Michelle inhaled deep and replied, "I have people who watch for that type of thing, or, er, Dirk's people watch out for me, or for her, or both of us actually. He likes me to know where he is, 'cause I get worried." She was worried now, as her story fell apart.

"I see. And your name is," Shirl opened her notebook again, "Michelle Hamlin. Address, phone, I'm set." She stood. "I appreciate the information, Ms. Hamlin. We in the Dirk camp appreciate any help you locals can give us. Dirk's life isn't easy around here, with so many people complicating things for him. It's nice meeting you." She reached out to shake Michelle's hand and turned and left.

Michelle stared after her. What the hell was she talking about? And when would she get her money? In any case, this would roast Lara's butt but good when it came out all over the headlines. Enough of that secret shit! Who did they think they were fooling?

—⁓—

This wasn't the same room she fell asleep in! Lara gasped.

She popped her eyes open wider, then remembered. Oh, her guest room. She was trying it out, advised by a magazine article. The first step in creating a welcoming guest bedroom was to make sure it's comfortable. She wanted to treat her first visitor right.

It was comfortable, but a little chilly. She'd open the heater vent. She'd already cleared closet space, then placed magazines, an alarm clock, and a basket of snacks on the bedside table. She still needed chocolates; she'd put them on her shopping list. And pillows. She wanted an abundance of pillows. Then, with some nice soaps, small samples of toothpaste and lotion, and a few fun toothbrushes, she'd be ready.

She had lots to do today, so rose and put on jeans and a sweatshirt. She peaked out a front window, located her newspaper, then opened the door to peer up and down the street. A car was coming toward her; she pulled back and watched it through the sidelight. It slowed in front of her house then accelerated and moved on. After another scan of the street, Lara stepped out and hurried down the sidewalk. The air was hinting of fall, but it would be another month before she'd have to wear shoes for this morning ritual.

Another car appeared on a side street, turned, and came fast toward her. Lara immediately bent over the paper on the ground, letting her hair fall around her face. If the weird people were showing up at her house, she would not let them see her without makeup. She turned while still in a crouch, then stood and moved back up the sidewalk, looking down so the shield of her hair remained in place.

Safe inside again, she made her coffee and oatmeal and sat in the kitchen with the paper spread open in front of her. The jumble word puzzle was an easy two minutes and her horoscope predicted "You will meet with challenges but your natural buoyancy will be an inspiration."

"I'd better get another cup of 'buoyancy'." Lara refilled her coffee mug.

Mick lay in the bay window, enjoying the big uncovered view of the backyard. One of her project lists carried measurements for custom shades, but maybe she wouldn't bother; she liked the view, too. She walked over to the cat and tickled him between his ears, then sighed and looked out. To her right, she could see Buckley asleep in another hole he'd dug. To the left, two squirrels ran up a tree, across a branch, then onto her roof out of sight.

Lara looked ahead. Suddenly alert, she narrowed her eyes into a squint.

Was that man looking back at her?

Across her back yard and beyond the house behind her, Lincoln Avenue was visible. And on Lincoln, a truck had stopped in the middle of the street. Lara focused and stared. It was a big white truck, like Dirk Durmont's. As she caught the eye of the driver, he accelerated and drove on.

Lara quickly pushed her back against the cabinets, hiding from the exposure of the window.

She looked around the kitchen. Had he been watching her?

For how long?

She crept along the edge of the kitchen table, the round pine table she'd hand-rubbed with oil so many years earlier. She lowered herself into the matching ladder-back chair and looked out the window from this seat she frequently filled. Past her yard, between the houses on Lincoln, she was visible from the street.

How long had she been watched from *this* point? As she sat, she clung to the table as more of what was familiar and safe shifted away.

Michelle got up from the floor and dug through the bedding. "Where the hell are my cigarettes?"

Stacy pulled a thin blanket tight over her head. "Ew! Who farted!"

"Well, what do you expect, bitch, with all that crap beer around last night."

"You finished your smokes off, remember, then copped all mine," Stacy replied. "You owe me a bunch by now."

Delta's voice came from under a floral-printed sheet. "I have mine around here someplace, but I don't know where."

Connie looked up from the sofa. "You can't smoke in here. Go out back and hope my mom doesn't see you."

"You're kidding! Why? Does your mom steal people's cigarettes cause she's too cheap to buy her own? I guess she bought that crap beer, too," Michelle snarled.

Brittany raised her head from a pillow on the floor. "You'd better get a cigarette quick and fix your bitch self before the mom and Connie kick you out." She sat up and stared. "Ugh! What did you put on your hair? Hope no one sees you out there." She flopped down on her side and pulled a blanket over her head.

Who did Brittany Bitch think she was, mouthing off all the time anymore? Michelle pushed her stiff hair down at the sides with open palms. An overload of sprays and smoke, molded by hard sleeping, had sculpted it into something that felt like yellow wings. "Whatever. So, Connie, sorry about the cheap beer and all. You got a cigarette by any chance?"

Connie reached down to her purse on the floor and handed her pack to Michelle.

Brittany looked over at Connie. "So how's the job? TeleSales."

"Oh, fine." She answered and sat up. "It's a pain in the butt having to get up and go in every morning, but it's a good paycheck. I'll be getting an apartment with some people when we get the deposit saved up." Connie looked around at the girls, then flopped back on her pillow and laughed loud. "Which is going too slow on account of too much partying and shopping!"

"But you see the L-whore every day." Michelle spoke out of her cloud of smoke.

"Who?"

"Lara! You're sure slow on the uptake. L-whore-a!"

"Well, not every day, but we try. We got it figured out when she comes and goes and eats and pees. All the basics. I still need stuff from you guys, though, for the newsletter people, so don't stop giving it up."

"Speaking of, here's what we're doing," Michelle said as she looked around for an ashtray, then let her ashes drop onto the coffee table.

"Dirk's in town, so we know he'll be all over L-whore's ass. She'll get moving around 10 or so. Holy shit, what time is it?"

So Dirk Durmont was in town. Lara knew to expect trouble.

She stood at her closet door and examined her clothes. The analytical mind that earned her computer programming jobs went to work, trying to understand the Granville situation. These rudies in town went after the actor like piranhas after a puppy. Or maybe they were more like fleas, pesky fleas; the stalkers were causing a lot of trouble, but they were mostly just annoying.

Except, that is, the unbalanced ones. They were dangerous.

And they were following Lara. What did they want? Did they expect her to pull him out of her purse, like some blow-up doll?

"I'm going to buy a big Dirk cardboard cutout and take it around shopping with me. That'd give these people something to look at," Lara murmured as she pulled out possible outfits, each one conservative and tasteful. Her hair was now washed and blown dry around her shoulders. It gleamed with highlights in a specific ash blond. Ash, not gold, ash. She had found a colorist who understood the difference and a stylist who was cutting trendy layers into her hair. Her face was done in neutral colors.

Tan twill pants, raspberry cardigan, tan slides. Lara dressed and looked in the mirror with a solemn expression. She nodded in approval but didn't smile.

Nicole would be Lara's first overnight guest in her new town. She wished she knew more about the popular restaurants, but they had talked about antique shopping and Lara knew every store and flea market in the city. And in several surrounding cities. Shopping was one of her favorite escapes.

Nicole was flying in from Peoria Friday and leaving Sunday, burning up extra airline bonus miles. Extra miles! Ah, the places Lara would go! Paris. She needed to make it to Paris before she died.

But first, errands in Granville. Paris another time.

"I've got a crush on you ..." Annoyed, Lara hit another button on her car radio. *"Evil love, now I kill for you ..."* She hit it again. *"I don't wanna lover from my mother's friends ..."* She grit her teeth, trying to contain her anger, and pressed her CD player. In spite of her intentions, her thoughts

turned hateful. Granville's own Suck Radio! Call letters S.U.C.K. Always the same songs. How could that be? The same negative songs, over and over. Irritating!

She took a deep breath. She would buy another CD. And another and another. There were always more CDs.

Saturday traffic was heavy. Lara stuck to side streets until she reached a strip mall that was home to several outlet stores. She parked and entered the largest, then browsed through women's sweaters, strolled along a rack of suits, pulled some high-heeled slides off the rack and strutted up and down, and finally arrived in the home decor section.

The walls were lined with shelves that bulged with folded comforters which gave way to rugs bent over and stacked. Lara walked slowly along the wall, draping her hand out to touch what came within reach. The rugs were hard and stiff, but her fingers sunk into the towels that came after. She had enough towels, leftovers from too many moves to places with yet another color of bathroom tile to coordinate with. Pillowcases were plentiful in her linen closet, too; with the wedding she'd acquired several sets and with the divorce she'd kept them.

Pillows were another matter. Men had a way of becoming attached to them and keeping them, so she owned only a few. She reached the pillows, which puffed out in spite of their little prisons of see-through plastic. She chose one with down feathers and a cover of blue-striped ticking and tested it by holding it up to her shoulder and dropping her head onto it.

A woman laughed.

Lara caught her breath and paused.

Tense now, she lifted her head and brought the pillow down to her chest. Forcing herself to breathe steadily, she dropped it into the basket and wheeled forward slowly, controlling each movement. She reached the end of the aisle, then turned and looked around her.

Three women were now in the home section, spaced far apart. The one with short brown hair styled curly on top was closest to Lara and was likely the one who laughed. To the left, in the middle of vases and pottery, a man with a long ponytail stood with his back to the store.

Lara shopped along, and was soon distracted from the puzzling laughter by the pretty things set out in front of her. She moved up an aisle of dishes and came back down through an assortment of notepads and stationery. Ahead of her now was the man with the ponytail.

Odd—he hadn't moved. In the ten minutes she'd spent examining white plates and patterned plates and plates in "California colors", he had stayed in the same spot. He and his ponytail and the broad shoulders Lara had noticed.

Nice. She felt some relief at the interest her body took in his. It had been a long time since Lara had even tried to meet a man. Actually, in the past, men had come to *her*. They'd come around, she'd date, she'd fall in love, she'd marry—and she had never learned how to meet a man. She knew her age would make it harder now. Fewer would come around; she might have to go out and find them herself.

The man stood still and she looked away, but Lara couldn't shake the sense of his presence, his maleness. But it was all too new, too difficult right now, too soon after the divorce.

And she had things to do, a project in front of her. Company was coming.

She sighed at the struggle inside her head, then turned and pushed her cart across the store to the checkout lane.

As she stood in line, however, she was distracted when the woman in front of her stretched up to see over the clothing racks. She seemed to be straining to look into the home décor area. Lara followed her eyes, puzzled. Was she looking for that man? Were they together? Suddenly, the woman turned and stared full at her. Lara quickly averted her eyes.

There he was, walking in that quick furtive way he used with some of his disguises. Alice exhaled smoke out the top of her car window and relaxed back into her seat. She loved to watch him walk.

Where to now, lover?

"That must be another one of his girlfriends."

Alice ignored the voice and eyed the woman who followed behind him. Her clothes and makeup were plain, her short dark hair curly on top. Alice had seen her before. This one showed up a lot, too, where Lara was. Dirk sometimes turned up around the same time.

"Not a girlfriend." Alice said as she sat alone. "Not his type. Hired. Like a bodyguard or an assistant." She watched the black SUV's doors close, then started her car. As she slowly rolled toward the street, she saw a small blue car speed into the lot. Again! Those girls! First the bodyguards showed up, then Lara, or Lara then the bodyguards, then that curly-headed woman, then Dirk, then all these women started pouring in. They were getting in Alice's way, but she did like seeing the grief they caused Lara.

What day was it? Saturday. They usually all showed up on weekends. So if Alice wanted to catch Lara unguarded, it'd have to be midweek.

"Those teenies are more his type, anyway. More than you, you know."

Alice put a hand over her left ear and followed the growing parade led by the unsuspecting woman in the red Monte Carlo. As she drove, a smooth wood handle slid out from under the passenger seat. Alice shoved the knife back into its hiding place.

A rabbit used to do that in the front yard, hold still as if it could make itself invisible. Until Michelle threw a rock at it.

"Let's see what toothpaste she gets."

The four Dirk Dolls gathered behind Lara at the end of an aisle in Discount City. Michelle stared at the back of her head and Stacy and Connie giggled while Delta tried to hold her breath. Lara stood silent, seemingly gazing at the rows of silver and blue boxes.

After a minute, Michelle snarled, "All she's going to do is stand there!" They moved on down the aisle.

"Let's find Dirk. He's bound to be here somewhere," Michelle said to Connie and Stacy, while Delta walked on to join Brittany, who emerged from the makeup section.

Stacy spotted a security camera, and lifted one arm while she performed an exaggerated runway walk toward it. "Do you suppose he's watching us? Is that where he went, in the back to look through the cameras?"

A familiar song, "Super Star Hero," sounded over the musak system and the girls squealed.

"It's the superman song!" Connie said. "You know he's in here someplace!" She waved at the camera mounted high on the wall. "Dirk! Hi, Dirk!"

Stacy joined her, hopping up and down and waving. "We love you! Come out and meet us! We are so much fun!" She turned her head to the side and winked big.

Michelle watched them, then eyed the camera. "I wonder where that's feeding into?"

She turned suddenly. "Brittany, you come with me." She gestured toward the three girls who were now twisting their necks back and forth to try to watch the camera and Michelle at the same time. "You others walk this store until you find Dirk!"

And she'd be looking for him in the back rooms. If she asked real nice, someone would let her see the security monitors. She paced away with Brittany following.

Lara hunched down near the floor to get at the tubs of small samples. Hand lotions, toothpastes, body gels—a treasure chest of guest room basket-fillers. She dropped a small soap into her cart and it fell next to two Tweetie Bird toothbrushes. Seeing the brushes reminded her to guard against the women who had been following her. Where'd they go?

"That's her!"

It was a woman's voice. As was becoming her habit, Lara froze in place.

"I don't see him anyplace!" A man replied.

Lara slowly turned her head and looked toward the end of the aisle. A middle-aged man and woman had stopped with their cart and were now watching her. She met the man's eyes and he stared long, then pushed his cart away while the woman followed.

Lara pulled herself up, feeling heavy. A realization sent a chill through her body. These people knew her face. She stood a long time, staring at a bin of tiny shampoos.

That man and woman—those strangers—knew her face.

They recognized her. Too many people seemed to recognize her. Had they seen a picture? How? Where? The most likely place these celebrity-obsessed types would have seen a photograph would be in one of those gossip magazines. Good grief, how disgusting. Lara felt her lip curl, but she forced her expression back into one of reserved composure.

But where were they taking pictures of her?

She stood alone in the aisle and tried to remember. There had been incidences. Sure. That time at the grocery store—an old truck was parked out solitary in the parking lot with a scruffy man behind the wheel. When she had glanced at him he'd jerked something down out of sight. She thought about the cars slowing in front of her house, and the odd behavior of the people while she shopped. Her face grew hot with shame.

Cameras? How vile! What gave anyone the right to take her picture?

Feeling like a slowing down wind-up doll, she walked her cart to the checkout, paid for her things, and went to her car, keeping her head down and letting her hair shield her. Home now. No more shopping. She'd had all she could take for the day.

Alice spied Lara slumping toward her car. Her slick blond hair fell forward, and she seemed unaware of anything around her. Alice's red sports car was soon creeping behind her as she walked along the parking lot aisle. Closer. Closer. Alice slowed beside her. Lara did not change her listless pace.

Dirk wanted Alice to do this. It's what he most needed from her, everyone knew that.

She slid her transmission to "P." The car jerked and she reached down under her passenger seat. If she moved fast enough …

Suddenly, a car loomed up behind her. Alice's concentration snapped. She turned her head around and scowled. Two men leaned forward in a white car and stared at her. Their passenger door swung open.

"Damn!" She yanked her car into drive and pulled away.

"You worthless shit. What are you going to tell Dirk?"

—∿∿—

How embarrassing. Lara had just hugged Nicole.

The visit had passed quickly and now ended as planned at the airport on Sunday.

And Lara had just hugged her. They weren't hugging friends and she felt she'd broken some rule. But worse—now Lara stood with tears in her eyes. Behind Nicole, Lara could see the plane attached to the gate with its slinky-like tunnel.

Nicole seemed okay with the hug. She didn't notice that Lara was clinging to her. "Come on up and visit. You're always welcome."

"I will! It's where all my friends are!" Immediately, Lara wished she could stick a sock in her own mouth. How pathetic did she look? But it was so hard to see her friend leave. This connection to the normal world, a world that didn't obsess about celebrities, was getting away. She was so alone in this weird place, this Granville.

But leave she did, and Lara stood at the window watching the plane until it lifted up from the runway. She stood a minute longer, mourning a loss she couldn't yet identify. Then she took a deep breath, straightened her shoulders, and resolutely turned around. She was a strong-willed woman. She had weathered many setbacks in her life and she would not let some group of gossips get to her. Lara strode to the escalator and glided down. The musak system blared out a rock song and her step picked up the beat as she walked through the bright corridors of the airport.

The weekend had gone well, as far as the visit was concerned. Good meals, good shopping, good conversation. But Lara's life was beginning to divide into two categories. There was the actual life she was living: her house, her work, her friends, her plans. But spinning around that was this strange world which was increasingly threatening to her. She and Nicole had toured the antique malls. And a woman in a red truck appeared everywhere they went. The woman had parked in sight of them, but never left the truck or took off her white visor cap. When they stopped at a trendy gift mall, Lara turned and saw the truck again; this time, the driver ducked down in the front seat but she was too slow to avoid Lara's eyes.

There was another follower, but this one she would have invited along if she'd had the chance. A good-looking blond man in a little car appeared several places they went. Twice when Lara glanced in his direction, he grabbed a newspaper and held it up in front of his face. He wasn't Dirk, but he was sure easy to look at.

Lara did the courteous thing and focused on her guest.

Now as she hurried through the airport, she thought about the woman in the red truck.

She had seen her before.

Lara first noticed her while hunting for a gift for Em. The wom-an had stood near her everywhere Lara went in the store. When she'd backtracked through to pick up something, so had the stranger. An internal hunch of Lara's connected her to Dirk Durmont, although the woman's clothes were conservative and her makeup in natural colors. She didn't have the painted-up "tart" look Lara was seeing on women around town, these dozens of Marilyn Monroe parodies who copied the makeup and hair but lacked Norma Jean's vulnerability and restraint.

And again, when Lara was at Home Store deciding on drill bits. She had glanced to the side to see the same woman crouching on the floor looking up at her. Studying her face, not the tools. Several times she'd seen her cruising High Street in the red truck. Lara's explanation for her being in the neighborhood was that, since Dirk seemed to own one of the large houses near her, this thin woman must be his personal assistant, fetching coffee and such.

Lara now reached the doors that led out to the airport parking lot. She didn't break pace as she shot a glance at the young man leaning against the wall watching her, but she mentally filed away the image of his face. She wanted to be aware if he showed up again.

CHAPTER NINE

Good-bye, Crazytown! Free at last! Lara sped along the highway feeling like she'd just jumped the prison wall wearing an orange jumpsuit. The exit suddenly appeared and she veered onto it, then skidded on the curve. Correcting the car quickly, she turned toward Sara's small town.

Soon she slowed, confused.

"Where are the houses? This isn't right!" She pulled into the gravel drive of a white clapboard farmhouse. In the distance was the cluster of buildings that made up Railton. She'd driven right through it! She headed back, paused at the only stop sign, and turned left. She drove until she was again surrounded by browning farm fields bordered with fire-colored trees.

"I hate this." Everything felt backwards. But she was in a place where she'd often been—lost.

She turned around again, but this time pulled through the intersection and drove straight until she finally recognized her friend's tole-painted mailbox. She parked near the garage, walked to the side door, and knocked. Silence. She knocked again.

The door swung open and a slender woman slightly taller than Lara stood laughing. Her words came in a breathless rush.

"Girl, did you ring the doorbell? We do have them out in the sticks, you know." She hugged Lara. "You look gorgeous! Come in, let me take your bag. How was your trip?" Her face was flushed with excitement.

"Sara! You look great! What are you putting on your hair? Neat waves." The two women exchanged girlfriend talk as they went upstairs to settle Lara in the guest room.

Back down in the kitchen, Sara waved her hand over trays of types of food that could be dangled from a stick and roasted over a fire. "You came just in time to help. Here, take these hot dogs out to that table near the fire. Where the fire *will* be, that is, once we get it started."

They carried food out, and as they walked, Sara talked on. "It's about a seven-hour drive, isn't it? We used to take family trips to the lakes down there. You'll know most of these people coming. They all work at United Insurance. Remember Darcy, and Heather, and Suzanne? The only one you don't know is Patty, and she'll talk your ear off if you let her!"

An hour later, a caravan of cars drove up and parked along the driveway. Doors opened and women exited, balancing dishes as they marched to where a baby fire was peeking out from a pile of wood and paper.

"Lara! How *are* you!" Hugs were passed around, and chatter, and eventually the roasting sticks. Each woman settled onto a hay-bale seat. They traded stories of what had happened since Lara moved—shifts in the company structure, Suzanne's hospital episode, Heather's wedding.

Then, inevitably, the question for Lara.

"So how's life in Granville?"

Lara inhaled deep and paused. Life in Granville. Up to now, when asked that question Lara had been able to push out a "fine" and take it no further. How could she explain her life—the increasingly bizarre incidents, the whispers, the stares, the strangers who were following her around? She wanted to talk about her problem, to get past the embarrassment, but how could she?

And worse. What if her talking about it created more rumors? So far, everything that happened was provoked by something out of her control. She had done nothing to cause any gossip.

As she sat and considered her answer, she looked absently out at the street, then noticed a black SUV had stopped in the road. A black SUV? Surely not the same one! She sat up straighter and peered at it. It accelerated and sped away. She looked around at the women glowing with firelight while they watched her, waiting.

"Fine," she answered and set a smile across her face. "Fine."

"Sara says you have a cute house."

"Oh, yes! Great house. It's a yellow Craftsman bungalow in this pretty neighborhood. Buckley and I take some great walks." She fell silent, thinking about the black SUV that often cruised the neighborhood when she took those walks.

"I go house-shopping tomorrow." Patty picked up the conversation and Lara was happy to let her. "The real estate lady is meeting me at nine and we're going the whole day. I don't know what I want, but a bungalow sounds nice. It's my first house, so I'm scared, but it's the smartest thing to do. I can't keep paying rent like this. Do you know how much rent is in town? For a decent place ..." and she talked on while the women ate their hotdogs and loaded plates from the side table.

The red sports car swerved, pilotless. As it hit the grass, Alice sat up in the driver's seat and corrected it back onto the road.

"They saw me. Damn!"

"You know you got too close. One hundred feet."

"That doesn't count when I'm in my car. And hell, *they've* been following *me!* What are they, some kinda nuts? And that's only Dirk's car back there. I don't know if he's in it."

Alice sped along the dark country roads until she no longer saw headlights behind her. They were heading back to the city they'd passed earlier; she'd find a place to sleep there. She would get up early and get back out to ... Railton, right? She'd watch when Lara left. Lara wouldn't be up too early. She never got out of the house until after 9. Then Alice could hook onto her car or one of the bodyguard's.

"One hundred feet, 100 feet, 100 feet."

Alice pressed her head with one hand, then pounded her skull. "Shut the hell up! Now—where is she heading tomorrow?"

"She'll shop, for sure."

She glanced behind her into the empty back seat.

"Dirk wants me to scare her off. It's up to me. She never should have moved to our city!"

She raced toward a motel sign, pressing her head.

"And if she's shopping she won't even see me coming."

Blood was smeared across the hood of the car and the hook from the killer hung from the door handle. Or the window. The women around Sara's fire had several versions of the scary classic, but they all agreed that the young couple parked at Lover's Lookout disappeared forever.

At 10 p.m., Darcy killed the fire with a lethal combination of sprinkled water and energetic stirring. Soon, not a red gleam showed in the dusty spot they surrounded and the women left, tired after much eating, storytelling, and laughing.

"What a great party! Success, girlfriend!" Lara helped Sara clean up and soon the two women walked up the stairs to their beds.

"We want an early start tomorrow, don't we?" Sara asked. "If I set an alarm for 7, is that okay?"

The next day, the weather was clear and highway construction minimal, both good things when driving toward Chicago. The two friends never ran out of things to talk about; it seemed a quick trip to the shopping center.

Granville and its strange population of Dirk-obsessed people seeped away from Lara's mind as they wandered through stores. It'd been a long time since she'd felt relaxed out in public and she breathed deeply in relief. But her tension rushed back when a camera flashed near her. She jerked her head up and spied a sales clerk hurrying away.

"Sara, did you see that? She took my *picture*!"

Sara was unconcerned as she walked on to the furniture section. "She must have been taking a picture of the display."

Lara looked around for a possible photo subject. The nearest walls held cabinet hardware—knobs.

"Knobs?" She was incredulous.

Sara had stopped in front of a wooden plate rack. "My father's making me one of these, in cherry. What do you think?" Lara moved on to join her. But as she passed two women at a candle display, she overheard one say "… then she moved down to Granville to be with him …" She stopped and stared. When they saw that she was looking, they hurried out of the store.

Lara, now thrown back into the surreal world she inhabited back "home", let Sara take the lead. They window-shopped their way to an upscale jeans store. As they walked, Lara scrutinized every group that passed; did these people know things about her? Or, more likely, had they heard some rumors that had no touch of truth?

"Women's is upstairs." Sara directed them and Lara followed her up the escalator as her eyes scanned the crowd.

The upper level was dense with racks and shelves. Lara again forgot her problems as she scoped out the sales. She found a "third-off" rack and began to examine each item. Suddenly, she sensed someone on her left. Too close. Lara moved away but the person moved with her. She looked up with a practiced "make nice" smile.

And froze.

Every muscle tense now, Lara steadied her breath, then forced her eyes down to the hanger in front of her, blind to the sweater it held. She released it and walked her hands and feet away from the person she'd seen. When she was on the other side of the rack, she looked up again.

The woman standing next to Lara had crept behind her as she walked. She had moved two paces but now stood fixed, staring up at what had stopped her. Her eyes peered into those of a tall creature in a brown wig and women's secondhand clothing. The man in drag seemed to be challenging her to move. Lara stared at the woman who was oozing a threat. She was slim, with bleached frizzy hair to her shoulders, and wore a black fake-fur jacket.

Lara's eyes slid over to the man. He wore an outdated butterscotch car coat, and his fake hair was styled in a bob with bangs hanging to his thick eyebrows.

Besides the people's strange appearance, something else was wrong. Lara felt as if she'd forgotten something, that her mind had misplaced an important piece to this puzzle. The spooky woman looked familiar. Hadn't she seen her someplace before? And there was something about her stance when she was standing next to Lara, but Lara's mind didn't let the thought form. It all made no sense.

Where was Sara? Lara spun around, suddenly needing to see her wholesome friend. Sara was across the room sorting through piles of sweaters. Lara hurried to her, picked up a bright blue pullover, and said, "I'm going to try this on."

"Cute!" Sara answered. "I'm about done. I'll wait outside the fitting room."

Lara rushed into the dressing room and shut the louvered door. Why did she feel this crazy need to run? She stood in the little space where women with less complicated lives had preened in pretty outfits. She turned to the mirror and faced a new worry. How could she undress in here? Would someone pop in and snap her picture? Were they watching her now? She glanced around the tiny room, then pulled the sweater on over what she was wearing. It fit lumpy over her clothes, so she pulled it off and left to join her friend.

The two characters at the sales rack were gone.

Lara and Sara finished their rounds of stores with Lara even more guarded as she watched the people around them. When they stopped at a bathroom on the way out, a short woman in a long brown wig and fake glasses followed them in. She stared at Lara while they waited for a stall. Lara shivered as she looked at her, then averted her eyes in distaste. Too many nasty characters; this was all too much.

They returned to the car and loaded their packages into the trunk.

Vigilant, Lara turned to look behind her. In the next row, a car had stopped in the middle of the aisle. She peered into it and met the eyes of a man watching her.

———w———

Midnight. Back in Granville the next night, Lara gave up trying to force sleep. She turned on the light. She had once read that if a person couldn't sleep, she should get up and do things until she was sleepy. There was something she could do.

A 9mm semi-automatic pistol rested in her nightstand drawer. It had been a Christmas gift. "Merry Christmas, peace on earth, and here's a handgun," she had joked with her friends. Now its presence gave her comfort.

She wrapped herself in a robe, then pulled the gun out and unloaded it. She found her purse, then carefully pushed the weapon into the main compartment. It was visible out the top of the bag. She would need to buy a larger handbag.

Lara turned and faced herself in a full-length mirror. She took a deep breath, then fast yanked the gun out but struggled as she pulled back the slide to cock it. She scowled and ran through the awkward motion again. It took much of her strength; this machine was not made for little hands with fingers that could gently tickle a cat's head or tap the top of a baking cake.

She quick-drawed her reflection once more, then stopped with the gun pointed toward her.

Lara stared, shocked at a sudden realization.

The woman in the jeans store—she remembered her! She was behind the wheel of that red car, the one that followed Dirk Durmont's truck so closely on High Street.

And that day in Chicago, she was standing with one hand clenched in her jacket pocket. Clutching something. Her eyes weren't on Lara's eyes. They were peering up and down her back.

Good grief. She was aiming!

Lara sank to her knees on the floor and huddled down with her head in her hands, trying to press her thoughts away.

Aiming!

She wouldn't sleep much this night.

CHAPTER TEN

Lara scanned the weight room. Maybe today she'd have a normal workout. Several days had passed since her trip to Chicago and she'd returned to Granville with even more stress to burn off. There were few people in the room and no one behind her, so she felt safe at the crossover rack.

A familiar rock oldie blared from the speaker above her head. She grabbed the hand grips, paused to catch a beat, then pulled them down and across her body. Moving to the song, she let the weights stretch her arms back up and out above her shoulders. She focused on the muscles of her upper chest and pulled down again with the music, as if she was performing a stationary dance. She leaned forward into the repetitions and as her hands came together at the bottom of the exercise, she pumped one-two-three as she criss-crossed the grips to intensify the movement.

"She'd be doing okay with *his* money."

Lara opened her eyes wide and stared into the mirror in front of her. It reflected her flushed checks and now immobile body as she held her breath. She also saw the trainers Jim and Joe behind her, sitting across the room with their heads together. They hadn't noticed her reaction to the words.

"Whose money?" Jim asked.

Joe muttered something and nodded toward Lara.

She forced air into her lungs and let the weights jerk her arms up without her usual practiced resistance.

"They must have known each other in California."

"Not that I don't think she's attractive…" Their voices grew inaudible as they continued.

Lara carefully released the handle in her right hand, then let the left weight pull her over to the side. She gave in to the sudden weakness in her knees and let herself sink to the floor. To hide her reaction, she pretended to move the machine's weight setting. As the two men whispered, she worked her diaphragm, trying to overcome her anger with forced, even breathing. How could this be happening to her? All these stories!

And they thought *she* was after some man's money? Unconscionable!

So that couldn't be her they were talking about, not this time. Their words were too ridiculous.

Weak now from confusion and breathlessness, she picked up her gym bag and lifted herself up, holding on to the crossover rack. She stepped backward to a column nearby and leaned against it. A young man on a bench near her sat still, watching her in the mirror.

As the trainers continued murmuring, Lara took a deep breath and pushed herself off the column. She turned and walked toward the men, staring them down.

"Shhh ... she heard us."

And to Lara's horror, they quickly and furtively looked away. They'd seen her and reacted, signs that they had indeed been talking about *her*.

The heat of her rage burned away her thoughts. She couldn't think of what to do; she just wanted to get away. Her face muscles clenched, her jaw tightening and her lips pressing together. She strode past them as they sat looking at the floor in silence, then shoved the door to the back stairs. Out of the corner of her eye, she noticed a tall lean man with a long ponytail sitting suspended on the chest expansion rack with his arms open. He watched her silently as she rushed out to escape before she lost control.

Lara hurried down the steps and out the front door, struggling to control tears. How many people were telling these stories? How many stories *were* there? She fumbled her keys, then jumped into her car, tossing her gym bag next to her new large purse.

Lara opened the purse and checked its contents. A pistol nestled next to her billfold. She paused a moment, then stomped the gas pedal and pulled out into the street without looking.

Faster and faster she drove.

She careened around the first corner, her tires squealing as the car slid. The windows of a nearby coffeehouse loomed too close. Many afternoons, groups stood outside the building visiting after meetings held behind the darkened windows. Fortunately, no one was in her car's way today.

Buckley enjoyed the extra walks when Lara decided to avoid the gym until the gossip died down. Tonight, though, he was nervous and several blocks from home suddenly pulled her to a corner.

"Where are we heading now, puppy dog?"

He took over navigation and made an odd turn.

For several nights now, Lara and her dog had hiked the streets, enjoying the brisk air and the trees topped with spice-colored leaves. Usually she went along with Buckley, letting him lead. But lately he'd been acting strange. Yesterday he had stopped, sniffed the air, then pulled her catercorner across streets to head toward home. And now tonight, he was rushing to get back. She followed him, reaching into the small heavy bag hanging from her shoulder and adjusting its cold metal contents.

Halfway up High Street, she pulled Buckley to a stop and stared.

Four vehicles—cars and trucks, all strangers—were lined up in front of her house.

What were they doing there? She stepped out of the shadows into the road. Two trucks and one car pulled away, leaving only a silver sports car stopped near her driveway. Lara watched the others drive off, then boldly strode across the street. She threw a look of defiance toward the driver of the remaining car. In the darkness her stare had no aim, but whoever was lurking around could just try to harass her, an angry woman with a huge furry guard on a leash and a loaded lunch bag over her shoulder.

The car pulled away.

Lara let herself in the back door. She hurried to the living room and looked out the front windows. All clear. No cars. Leaving the lights dim, she began pacing as Alien blinked sporadically.

"Alien! I have to do something. This stuff is all too weird. And I'm losing it. That last time at the gym, I almost started crying right then and there. That can't happen!" She walked across the room and dropped onto the sofa. She couldn't let these people feed on her life. Or on Dirk's. These stories were untrue and it was wrong to let them continue. She had a responsibility to the other victim.

"What can I do? I can't just turn and confront these people, can I? No! Like, 'oh, excuse me. I was eavesdropping, did I hear you right?' And then what? These people make me so mad. Would I outright call them idiots and vulgar trash? Where would that get me? And what about Dirk? They think we're having this relationship, so how would that make him look? Like he's involved with some mouthy coarse woman, that's how. I need to be cool, at least in public, and keep my mouth shut."

She looked up at Alien and thought a minute.

"What matters most is how far the rumors have spread, how big the story is. If it only involves a small group of people, it'll surely ride its course and end. How can I find out who knows what?"

Suddenly she stood.

It was … Wednesday? That mid-week church meeting was on Wednesdays. Clusters, or Home Groups, or Something Ministry.

Lara was a Christian, but lately her spiritual lessons came only from the TV. Finding a church home was on her list of things to do, along with getting in shape and giving up coffee. When she'd first moved to town, she'd found a small church with casual services, movie clips, and a funny pastor. She liked it.

But, to her abhorrence, the low people had begun to invade this holy area. Three young women had started showing up, always positioning themselves near her and staring. And she had overheard a group of teen-aged boys pointing her out with "That's Lara." Not unusual if they were much older, but she was far past the age for being a hottie in the eyes of teens. Too strange. And too much like the very real Dirk mess at the health club and grocery stores.

"I know what I'll do, Alien. I'll go to the church with the problem. It'll be like sanctuary, like in the movies. Sanctuary! I'll be careful what I say, of course, not tell them too much, but I can find out if they know anything, if the rumors have really spread that far. I'll visit awhile, then say that I have a silly little prayer request." She would phrase it so carefully, so lightly. Something about some gossip going around the gym and her workplace that was "becoming a distraction", that she's living such a dull life that people are trying to spice it up for her by linking her with someone she had never met. And since it involved someone else, she couldn't ignore it.

If the pastor knew anything, she'd get answers. If he didn't, she'd get prayers.

Lara looked at the clock. There was still time tonight to find Pastor Rick's Home Group Cluster Something. She grabbed her keys and headed out the door.

—◦∿◦—

"Look! 'Hollywood Hunks Naked'." Delta laughed. What was below the man's Speedo tan line was left to the imagination; all that was visible were his muscular upper body and his handsome face.

Michelle read from the Web page. "'See Tom, Leo, Dirk, Matt—100s of Pics.' Let's bring this one up." She clicked and waited. Delta, Brittany, and Stacy pressed up close behind her, peering at the computer monitor.

Stacy hopped once in excitement. "Ew, this is so cool! I wonder what Dirk looks like naked?"

"He's posed for regular magazines that way, so don't get your butt out of whack." Brittany didn't sound out of whack. In fact, Delta thought she sounded bored with seeing Dirk naked, but that couldn't be.

They were in Michelle's bedroom researching Dirk. First they had pulled their hair back in ponytails, then painted their nails from Brittany's bottle of Raspberry Shock. Michelle's mother was downstairs watching TV. She never came into Michelle's part of the second story that Delta ever saw and seldom spoke to any of them. She could bump into Miz Hamlin in Discount City and not know her.

Michelle lit a fresh cigarette and tapped her fingers on the computer desk. The desk had been her brother's, then he moved out. Her sister had painted the walls Easter Egg Lavender and made the floral curtains and the comforter. Delta could barely make the bedspread out, rumpled like it was under a pile of clothes, many still with price tags dangling. Some had those dark blue and gold tags from Goldberg's in Granville. Ma always said she'd die a happy woman if she could just once go into that snotty Goldberg's store and buy something at full price.

"Hell. They want a membership fee to see him naked." Michelle exhaled smoke onto the screen.

Delta pulled a cigarette out of her purse and lit it.

"You can't smoke in here," Michelle snarled. "I'm the only one who can smoke in here."

Delta stopped and stared.

Brittany jumped in. "Don't listen to her, Delta."

Michelle laughed and sang out, "Dum de dum de dum dum."

Brittany reached for Delta's cigarette. "Let me have that a minute." She inhaled hard, puffing her cheeks out, then blew smoke onto the computer screen. Michelle leaned back and waved it away, then gave Brittany a fighting look.

"Should we join?" Stacy said. "That would be so cool, to see all those guys naked. What does it cost?"

"We'll see if any Dirk Dolls have joined it. Speaking of naked men. What's Mark up to lately?" She looked at Delta.

Naked? "He's mostly wearing clothes, but doing fine. But hey …
can guys be Dirk Dolls? I think he might want in," Delta said.

Michelle moved her mouse pointer down the screen. "Isn't he getting enough? What's he want with the Dolls?"

"It's just that he's always asking what we're doing and where Lara
goes, and when Dirk's in town."

Michelle laughed. "So he's following Lara now. Cool." She was silent a minute while she moved her mouse pointer down the page of
Internet hits for "Dirk Durmont." "Wouldn't it be great to see my name
come up on this? Maybe someday. Here! 'Nickie's Dirk Dirt'" A click
brought up a Web page with a large picture of the bare-chested blue-
jeaned actor. The four girls squealed.

"There he is!"

"He is so cute!" Stacy shouted. "Like who can stand looking at such
a hunk without getting so hot! Look! It says he has another girlfriend!"
She pressed her finger onto the screen. Michelle pushed it away and
used her own finger to rub at the smudge.

In front of them, the page read:

"Nickie's Naughty Dirk Dirt.
    We love our starry-eyed angel
    And every breath he takes
    He is always the most hottest
    and our love we never fake.
But watch out, girls,
    Our Own Dirk has been seen with a steady.
    He and TV's Carrie Jo Miller,
    who plays our own Trudy, celebrity host of TV's game show "Are
    We There Yet",
    have been together like birds of a feather.
Will it finally be wedding bells for Hunkie-Poo? Stay tuned."

Brittany gasped. "But the paper said they were just friends!"

"Didn't she come to town? Some weekend I was working?" Stacy
was serving fries at Burger World now, getting money for Mountain
College but messing up her weekends.

Michelle scowled. "The Granville Dolls screwed up. It happened real
fast. She flew in and no one picked up on it." She stared at the screen. "I
don't think it's true. Like he's still partying in Granville, isn't he?"

"What if he gets married?" Delta whined. "That would be awful."
Wouldn't it?

"What will we do? He's our everything!" Stacy looked worried, too.

"He isn't getting married!" Michelle laughed but looked mad at the
same time. "Anyway, it'd be only his first marriage."

"I wonder if Lara knows?" Brittany asked as Michelle clicked over
to her email.

"Oh! Listen up." She spun around in her chair, making them jump
back. "This is the best. The Dolls are sending around a list of songs for
us to call into the radio. Everyone has to request them over and over so
we're sure she hears them."

"Songs. Like what songs?" Brittany asked.

"Here, I'll print this list. Call them in all the time. Or email the sta-
tions. We have us Dirk Dolls all over the country, so she can't get away
from us anyplace." Her printer hummed as she talked. When it quieted,
she grabbed the copies and handed them around.

Brittany read from the paper in her hand. "'Grannie With A Hot
Car'. 'Evil Love'. 'Warlock Lover'. What's this one, 'Arms To Hold'? Isn't
that about having a baby or something?"

Michelle laughed. "That's the best one! We're figuring if she doesn't
have children, it's because she can't!" She looked around at them; Delta
couldn't understand why she looked so happy. "And we know Dirk
wants babies, so there's no way he'll ever want to marry her!" She
laughed again.

Stacy laughed too, and Delta joined her, figuring something must
be funny. But Brittany stared, silent.

———ᘛᘘ———

The woman's naked back looked familiar. She sat on her feet, her
long blond hair around her shoulders, her behind propped up on her
heels. She leaned forward toward the nude man, whose legs were pushed
open by her body. Her hands rested on his inner thighs. He was lying
on a weight bench, the back inclined so his face was visible.

The second picture was clearer. Lara recognized the man now. It
was Dirk Durmont. She glanced through the four poses. In the last
frame, the woman had turned her head in profile.

Good grief! The nude woman was Lara!

Lara awoke, sickened and shocked. A nightmare.
Another one.
Sometimes, lately, Lara dreaded going to bed.

11-11-99
Journal,

I had another nightmare. I saw sexual pictures, four in a panel stacked vertically, fuzzy, as if they were on the Internet.

I need <u>facts</u>. Please God, some facts.

Halloween came and went okay. I arranged for Steve to come over to be with me, for safety's sake. I didn't write in here about the Chicago trip with Sara, did I? I guess I'm writing about the strange stuff more freely now. The happenings are becoming so frequent and obvious I can't ignore them. Like last week, at Pet Place, the cashier whispered to the bagger, and the bagger exclaimed, "She's <u>here</u>?!" The cashier gestured toward me and they both stared and clammed up. She <u>knew</u> my <u>face</u>. On and on at work, at church, the gym. The same thin curly-haired woman showed up <u>both</u> at work and church. Coincidence?

The problems continue at Brandt's Gym, of course. The men have started this thing with whispering, then leaving the room after the trainer gestures toward me. Then they come back and stare. This big <u>story</u>, this fabrication!! Where is it coming from? Time after time I've left, barely under control, and come home to sob from the anger and frustration. I'm afraid my feelings are becoming obvious. I don't want these people to think they're getting to me.

I went to the gym tonight. This time, the topic among the men was "I bet she enjoys the attention." I had to stop and analyze what all this mess is, 'cause I surely don't consider it "attention." Attention is what you get from friends and lovers, when people talk <u>to</u> you and listen to you or love you. <u>This</u>, <u>this</u>, is just watching and whispering and isolation! Almost the opposite of attention. Yes, people are being aware of me—still for reasons I don't know—aware of me and turning their backs on me. Talking about me, but never <u>to</u> me. This doesn't even count as <u>fame</u>. "Fame" is when you've done something that people know you for. Is it notoriety? (For <u>what</u>??)

I'm back to feeling very isolated. How can all this be happening? And there's no normal release, no escape. No man to cuddle *against, no one to talk to, no sex, little freedom to shop or exercise. I must remember that it's all temporary, simply a phase. Things <u>will</u> improve.*

When I pray, I sense it's not over yet, that "something" is going to happen. Patience and prayer, that's what I need now.

I went to see "The Thomas Crown Affair" with Georgia. Interesting. I'm keeping busy, but my sadness is back full force. I worry that I'll be let down when this mess blows over, when this intense recognition ends. But all the occurrences are so surprising, it isn't as if I think about them before they happen. No thought beforehand, but quite a bit after.

My greatest fear isn't a physical attack. Frankly, that would be a relief, as then all this would be out in the open. These women are starting to openly criticize and jeer, besides the pointing, staring, and whispering. There is too much cruelty in the world and I've never found a way to combat it.

Okay. Maybe this all is why I'm so sad today.

I wish for a physical attack to distract me.

"Hit me."

"Hit me as hard as you can."

CHAPTER ELEVEN

The store doors opened and closed again in a rhythm as people made a procession in and out. Lara sat in her car watching, forcing herself to breathe. Somehow she had to talk herself into going through those doors. It was the day before Thanksgiving, she was hosting the family dinner, and she needed groceries. She had to shop on this, the busiest, day of the year.

She took another deep breath, pushed herself out of the relative safety of her car, and marched up to the store. Inside, she yanked a cart unstuck from a row of jammed metal. The list was short; it shouldn't take long. After winding up and down a few aisles, Lara turned her cart toward the baking section. Several women stood with their backs to her. They looked at her, then spun their carts around in her direction and rolled toward her.

Lara glanced at them, then looked away and considered the risk.

Lately, groups of young women wearing clubbing outfits ridiculous in the stores, had been walking up to Lara, contorting their faces into ugly expressions, and saying "Ew!" "Is that her? Ew!" So embarrassing. And were these Dirk's "friends"? Were they going back to him with the same comments about her? Or what if he was lurking around the store watching the cruel scenes? The humiliation was too much.

These women today looked too old for that group. But nevertheless, she pulled backwards out of the aisle, and stepped on the foot of a person standing directly behind her.

"Oh, I'm sorry!" She looked at the blond woman grinning too close into Lara's face. She was empty-handed and didn't move but stood staring at Lara's groceries and blocking the way. Lara veered her cart to the side, got around her, and looked for an escape. The canned foods aisle was empty except for three men walking in her direction. She pushed her cart into the aisle. The men came nearer, then suddenly one leaned into Lara's face, making her reel back in surprise.

"That's the woman," the man said.

"I don't know. I don't see it," the tallest one replied. They stopped at the end of the aisle and watched her.

Enough! She rushed to the checkout lanes, a sense of helplessness making her legs heavy. At the register, she waited in line.

As she stood, relieved that the ordeal was almost over, she glanced up at the busy cashier. As the young woman rang up her customer's groceries, her eyes were fixed on Lara's. Lara looked away, embarrassed. She reached for a magazine to avoid the stare, then glanced behind her. Someone stood close at her back. She had no cart. Was she even carrying anything?

Finally it was Lara's turn, and the cashier rang her up. She pulled out her checkbook. As she wrote, the woman behind her leaned in close to her shoulder.

Mark revved his motorcycle and popped a wheelie up the street. Delta watched him from his big blue Chrysler and laughed. She had parked in front of Gramma's house behind a black mid-sized four-door. She and Michelle climbed out of the car and Delta rushed over to Mark, who was rolling his bike into the yard.

"Mark, you use your company manners like Ma said!"

"If Ma had any manners, she'd be here too," he snarled back at her.

"You know she has that sick friend in Granville."

Mark stomped his boot against the kickstand. He made a face like he did when Ma told him Pa's check was lost in the mail again and he'd have to give more toward his lovely room and board. Now he said, "Delta, that friend story ... oh, never mind."

Delta was determined that today was going to be wonderful. It was Thanksgiving and Gramma was having them all over for dinner, just like a TV movie. All the family was going to be together, except Ma and Pa and Uncle Saul and his wife and kids. That left Uncle Seth and his new wife Tillie. Aunt Tillie. Pa had said he was spending the holiday with his friend Hiram Walker, and Ma had taken off to see that sick friend. But Mark was along, and Michelle had agreed to come to make the family easier on each other. Soon they'd all be smiling and telling jokes.

As Delta hurried them up the sidewalk, Mark leaned in to her ear.

"Gramma'll like that dress for sure! Are you trying for the inheritance?" He laughed and swiped at the long hem. She'd found it in the back of Ma's closet. It was old-lady style for sure, with its ankle length and pattern of tiny flowers; she did hope Gramma liked it.

And when Gramma opened the door, she was dressed to please Delta, wearing the hot pink sweater set and tan pants they'd found at Discount City.

"Well, hello kids! Happy Thanksgiving! Goodness, Michelle, aren't you cold?" She eyed Michelle's bare midriff, pale between her low-slung jeans and short tight top. They all stepped into the warm house, and everyone sniffed in the smells of food steaming from the table.

Delta handed her the whiskey bottle she'd taken from Pa's case. It was new, never been opened. Mark had fought her on giving it away, but everyone knew it was polite to bring something when you went someplace for dinner. Gramma smiled nice and set the bottle on the table near the door.

A man in black from head to toe, even up to his shoe-polish hair, came forward with his hand extended. "Hey, kids. How've you been? I hear Silas ain't coming by today. Too bad. We'll have to catch him later. This here is my new bride, Tillie." Uncle Seth reached behind him and pulled a pale but raisiny looking woman forward by the arm. She grinned big, exposing tan teeth. Her dress might have come from Gramma; it was long and bleached-looking and hung on her like a sheet with shoulders and two bosom darts in the front. If she had a body, it was tiny.

The new Aunt Tillie reached her handshake around to the group. "So good to meet you all. So good to meet my new family."

Then she turned and made for the table, while Michelle pointed to her hair and made a face at Delta. Tillie's hair color was not from Discount City or certainly not the expensive places Lara McKeon went. Her hair strung down long and straight, and the color was deciding to go gray; three inches of nickel-color was making its way down her otherwise brown head.

They all sat where Gramma pointed them. There were six chairs and six people—perfect. The table was holiday-special with its clean pressed tablecloth, plates painted with tiny roses, and tall candles lit up like for company. And the food! Real, made in Gramma's kitchen. In the center, a white platter was loaded with a big pile of turkey, including drumsticks for Mark and Uncle Seth. More of the rosey dishes held mashed potatoes, stuffing, canned-berry sauce, and green beans. And there was gravy, served in a special bowl with a fancy spoon.

Gramma sat smiling at everyone a minute, then bowed her head to say grace. She blessed the food and the weather and everyone there at the table, then everyone not. Then she blessed the church and the hungry people and even the old red McNought house. Mark started reaching for the turkey, but pulled back when she started on Nancy Richardson's granddaughter's baby, the ailing pastor, the neighbor's gout, and all the sinners. Then she prayed for the grace to not mention the sinners by name and for anyone who was taking devil money.

Delta was starting to think she'd got the TV remote stuck on some churchy channel when Gramma finally said "Amen, and amen." Everyone must have been holding their breath, 'cause there was a mighty inhale all around as they grabbed for the food. They loaded up but good and dug in.

"So. Mark. I see you got a new bike out there," Uncle Seth said.

They were making polite talk, like on TV. Delta grinned, delighted.

"Yeah." Mark talked around a mouthful of mashed potatoes and continued eating.

Uncle Seth suddenly sat up straighter and looked like he'd answered the winning question on TV. "'Wasp!' I remember! They called you 'Wasp' when you were a kid! They still call you that?"

Mark had stopped chewing to give him the eye, then swallowed big and drew his eyebrows together. "Only some people. Mostly business connections."

Gramma interrupted. "Michelle, I thought your mother might come."

"Oh. She has this sick friend in Granville," Michelle said, then laughed.

Delta knew something must be funny, so laughed along. Then she remembered something. "Uncle Seth, wasn't that your first wife Louise that Ma said was in the paper? Did she ever get out of jail? I see your face is looking okay, considering she smashed it with the skillet that time. That was Louise, wasn't it?"

Gramma jumped in. "I declare, we McNoughts get around! I hope and pray none of us sitting around this blessed table today ever gets in the paper."

"No! Not unless we're dating Dirk Durmont or something cool!" Delta said.

Aunt Tillie laughed brown again. "Oh, honey, don't we all wish." She stopped and batted her eyes at Seth. "Except of course those of us who've got their own man now." She leaned back in to the table. "But I work with a woman who takes her son to scout meetings, and it's the same troop Dirk Durmont's nephew is in! She says he looks like him, the same cute dimples! And she's seen his mother, too, at some of the programs. I'm going to go along sometime so's I can get a look at them myself."

Delta glanced at Michelle sitting next to her and saw she had slipped her hand onto Mark's thigh. Delta gave her a mean look, but Michelle ignored her. Couldn't she quit that stuff for a few hours here at Gramma's house? She decided to occupy her with polite talk. "Michelle, Stacy tells me Connie said you went down to Granville yesterday. Did you do anything fun?"

Michelle stared at her a minute, then said, "What the hell does Stacy know, that fat bitch!"

"Tillie!" Gramma's voice sounded urgent. "I believe this is the first you've met your niece and nephew. Please tell us all about yourself."

Well, tiny Aunt Tillie could pull a lot of words out of that wrinkly face. It was like Gramma had pushed a "start" button on her head someplace. She lit all up and started in. "Well, you're sure right, Ma McNought! This is the first I seen of these kids and I still need to make the acquaintance of their daddy. Silas, is it? I understand he manages the parts factory here in Rockton. My Seth here has a fine position at the boat factory north of Granville and we're settling into our new house out that way. Now you all come out and see us whenever you can. Why, I should have you all over for Christmas! Or maybe Thanksgiving would be better, the next one, of course." She paused to breathe and laugh a little, then kept right on talking while everybody ate. No wonder she was so skinny-looking, if she always talked instead of eating. She reminded Delta of Mark when he got going on too many white pills.

—⌇—

"When you go get a child and bring it home with you to live." Lara's brother-in-law Ross was looking up at the dining room chandelier as he read from the game card.

"Kidnap!" Meredith, Lara's niece, shouted out, and everyone around the table laughed.

"Uh, the correct answer would be 'adopt'!" Ross passed the box of game cards to the next person.

The holiday was a success so far. Lara hosted Thanksgiving dinner, and after everyone ate too much and then more, most of the family settled around the table to visit and play a game her sister Danielle had brought along.

Lara sat in the chair near the kitchen. The air held nostalgic smells of roasted turkey, gravy, stuffing, and mashed potatoes. The dresser that served as a sideboard was still crowded with the remains of carrot cake, chocolate cake, fudge in two colors, and pumpkin and pecan pies. A carton of whipped topping was set out for use on anything or nothing.

By habit, Lara mentally reviewed her calorie and carb intake. She had eaten turkey, which was low in carbs and calories, some green beans without the sauce, which were low in everything, and some plain mashed potatoes, which were high in carbs but a good mood food. Because it was a special day, she had some yams and dressing and a small piece of almost everything on the sideboard. Way high carbs and calories, bad mood food.

High Street was visible from where she sat. From time to time, a car passed. Her body tensed as she watched each vehicle. Was it slowing? Would it stop? Could people actually take pictures of her sitting in her house? She tried to remember what she'd read about a recent celebrity lawsuit. The famous woman had won when a judge ruled that some places carried an "expectation of privacy."

Today, there were 11 people at Lara's, all family. They chatted now, lazy after the big meal. Ross had gotten a promotion at work, and the nieces and nephew had been coaxed into sharing a little about their lives. Lynn talked about her book group's best picks and the others added their favorite titles. For a moment Lara was peaceful as she looked around at the crowd leaning on her Irish linen tablecloth, all lit by the glow of the chandelier. It was a warm picture, like a Norman Rockwell painting.

Suddenly, her fantasy was broken by another car cruising past.

She straightened and watched it warily as it slowly moved from her sight. She hated this, how her bizarre Granville experiences made her so often think of low, dark things. But she had to be wary; it was smart to be a little self-protective. Seeing the car brought back a nagging worry. If people were stalking her, how long before they went after her family? All the McKeons were intelligent, well-groomed, and polite. But they were a variety of sizes, not Hollywood-perfect.

And the rumors. Surely her own family would tell her if they'd heard anything. She'd assumed they would, so hadn't asked.

Or would they be too polite to mention her supposed affair?

———∾∾∾∾———

Subj: DirkLetter Update
Date: 12/03/1999 3:23:04 PM Central Daylight Time
From: HotGirl11@mail.com (Karen)
To: DirkDolls (group)

Dirk Dolls,
Road trip!
Our favorite squeeze's favorite shoppee is hitting the road this weekend. Expect to find her at the Columns Mall in St. Louis on the way to her annual birthday trip. She's getting older and we're not!

A hot new development on the Dirk Front (oh what a front! and back!). An actual Dirk employee that does his Granville business has contacted us. Her name is Shirl Manier. She met with us DirkLetter editors (!!!!) after work, here at our building in a parking lot conference in her truck. She is so cool. She is going to give us everything we want to know about Lara (like about her going to the Columns this week-end), and this woman has sources! But she says she needs our help.

She says:
   1. We can follow Lara around, but only in small groups.
   2. We can not talk to Lara ever. It is none of her business what we are doing. It is only Dirk's and Shirl's business.
   3. And most important. Nothing is to get back to Dirk about what happens here in Granville. It is Shirl's job to report to him and we are to go straight to her with everything and she will tell Dirk what he needs to know.

If it makes Dirk happy, I'm sure we can all do it.

His truly,
Editor Karen

See you in St. Louis!

———∾∾∾∾———

Michelle stood with Delta, Stacy, and Brittany as they watched Lara from behind the jeans display. She had stepped out of the dressing room, but stopped at the sight of the young men and women gathered in front of the rack of business suits. She hooked the hangers in her hand onto the nearest rod and walked out. A saleswoman watched her leave then shot an angry look at the group left staring after her.

"There she goes!" Brittany said. "She won't be trying on anything else today." She picked up a pair of jeans from the shelf in front of her.

Michelle rolled her eyes. "She just got here and those jerks already pissed her off. Don't they know she'll march out of here if she gets fed up enough? St. Louis or not, she'll go right back out to her car, leaving us with nothing." She watched the two men rush out, pulling the women by the hand. "Who are those people, anyway? They're following Lara, aren't they? Let's go!"

Michelle had driven with her three friends all the way up from Rockton and she wasn't leaving until something interesting happened. They needed to find out if Dirk was there. It was December; there was a good chance he'd be showing up soon for the holidays.

They stepped out into the mall and watched the two couples trailing Lara. The men suddenly stopped and turned.

"Quick, don't look!" They all turned around at Michelle's command. "Now I'll see, but none of you do it." She looked back, along with Brittany. Michelle glared at her. "I told you not to look!"

Brittany smiled. "I just want to find The Gap, don't worry about me!" She laughed and scanned the storefronts across from them.

"We're going to lose them. Come on!" Michelle said and rushed on. She soon noticed another group of women across the corridor pacing Lara's quick steps. One had a cell phone pressed to her ear.

Stacy gasped. "Those girls are following her too! What did the DirkLetter say about not all of us showing up at once?"

Michelle laughed. "Yeah, right! Wasn't that what Shirl said? Well, those so-called editors don't know that I knew Shirl way back and I'm still not sure who she's working for."

"It's so like you to keep a secret, Michelle." Brittany grinned.

"It is so like me to use what I find out for handy purposes. Dirt on Shirl could be Dirk in my hand." Michelle said. She was bound and determined to find out who that Shirl actually was. Did she work for the tabloids, or for Dirk? She peered ahead while they marched, then said, "I think those two guys are bodyguards. Are they new? Why don't we know them?"

"Maybe he got more of them." Stacy said. "Or new ones. Connie said someone was fired for blabbing Dirk's business all over town."

Delta suddenly grabbed Stacy's arm and pulled her into a shoe store. "Hide! They stopped again."

Michelle and Brittany tried to act nonchalant, looking in big circles around the mall. After a minute, Michelle motioned to Delta and Stacy to come out.

"There's Abercrombie! Let's go shopping." Brittany said. "We came all this way, skipped out school, so let's at least shop!"

"You know why we came, so shut up about it. L-whore will hang here only a couple of hours, then she'll head up to farmer-land and we'll shop then." Michelle was getting fed up with Brittany's mouth. "One thing for sure. If those guys are bodyguards and they can lead us to Dirk, then we want to know them! If they're showing those two whores around, we can get with them, too!"

They walked and watched, until the couples disappeared into a large department store.

"Hurry! We can't lose her." They ran to the wide store entrance and stopped.

They all noticed her at the same time. A chesty young woman with frizzy blond hair had stepped out from between two tall racks of marked-down shoes. She stood watching Lara go up an escalator.

"Don't we know her?" Brittany asked. "Yeah, she's from Granville. Small world."

Stacy waved and called out to her.

"Hey, Alice!"

—⁓—

Lara came home from her birthday shopping trip with a clue. A woman in a bathroom on the mall had peered at Lara then told her friends she "looked like him." Lara didn't have to strain to hear the words—people spoke up around her as if she didn't have ears. She was surprised by the comment, but it could be why people peered at her and discussed whether they "saw it" or not. Had her face become like one of those illusion pictures with hidden images, and people thought if they looked at her right, Dirk would appear? She thought about letting them swoop near her, then crossing her eyes and sticking out her tongue. But what if Dirk was doing the same thing? Then there'd be no end to the stories of how much they looked alike.

It was December, and Lara couldn't avoid shopping for Christmas. She'd gone out of town for some gifts, but dropped into local stores for stocking stuffers. One afternoon as Lara shopped, a tall lean man appeared in the store bringing with him a woman and a buzz of excitement for the shoppers and cashiers. Lara then endured loud gossip about "which one" was his girlfriend. Was he intentionally showing up where she was? Didn't he know how these people tormented her when he wasn't there to fill their empty lives?

She needed help. Lara called an old friend, someone living far from Granville. It was the first time she'd told anyone the truth about the trouble she was having because of Dirk Durmont. Tori from Kentucky followed tabloid gossip and knew someone who might have a Dirk scrapbook. It would take a fan to help her, or a tabloid library if such a thing existed. If Lara was mentioned in some story, she'd never find it without help. If a story appeared in town, she knew Dirk would have the papers pulled off the stands before many people could buy them. If the papers even made it as far as Granville; he didn't strike her as a man who'd risk a lawsuit.

But the month passed and Tori didn't call her back.

Everywhere Lara went, her tension and the aggression of the people around her worked to chase her back home. She struggled to stay calm and became more skilled at dodging people. Her personal circle was growing as she made new friends, learned to "contra" dance, and joined a book group of fascinating women. But when she was out alone, the strange people closed in on her. She could count on trouble at the gym, and often the grocery stores, but now shopping at the mall was becoming difficult. She never knew when some group would suddenly swoop to thrust their faces into hers, or she'd look up from a display to find people staring and discussing her. It was petty and ridiculous, but being "that woman" was wearing Lara down.

New Year's Eve arrived. But it was an extraordinary day this year. It was the edge of Y2K, a new century, the year 2000.

Around the world, people partied while thousands of sober computer professionals, including Lara, stayed ready for anything.

Nothing happened.

Lara sat in front of the television with her journal.

12-31-99

Journal,

New Year's Eve, the big Millennium countdown.

Y2K.

I have to work tomorrow, January 1, and the next two days 6 p.m. to 3 a.m., then the next week. So far tonight, the year has changed in much of the world and nothing significant has happened. There are scores of books out predicting power outages and computer crashes and the end of our financial system. So far, nothing, except for lots of great celebrations on TV with fireworks and grand structures built.

I hate to make my New Year's entry about the crazy stuff that's been happening, but it's impacting my life so much and so thoroughly. There's so much staring and commenting that I'm almost a prisoner in my house. I'm trying to stay away from the harassment, but I hate staying at home. I'm so restless!

These groups of women—they're like predators, aggressive and cruel. And why does everyone think it's okay now to express an opinion about my appearance? It's such a joke. And now my face is aging, so there's that to contend with. I have no confidence. I'm hiding my face, looking away when people look at me.

Last night at the gym (I insist on going to the gym. I can't let myself get out of shape), two men were so gross, staring and gawking, that I left early. So today I dressed in thick sweats and a huge long sweatshirt and went in to try again. The scrutiny, the comments, I can't stand it! Maybe I should quit going there for a while, too, but I want to appear "normal", like this stuff isn't bothering me.

I need groceries, but I worry about what humiliating experiences I'll have—in front of Dirk, even, if he's there. How awful that would be.

I can't stand it.

Today I took Buckley to hike on my land at the lake. It felt good to be out someplace with no noticeable stalkers. I'm so tired of all this.

I just looked through the past entries. What a year! Funny—I was working at giving my appearance less importance, and look!

The world wants it to be the 1ˢᵗ order. And I was working on getting over shyness, and the world is full of rudies jumping me emotionally.

Incredible.

I mentioned months ago that "all this" was a dangling in front of me of something I can't have. The dangle has me exhausted. Back then, I could keep it in its place, but now it so emphasizes my aloneness. It's made worse by the fact that I couldn't stand going out for New Year's. What if people stared, what if I ran into Dirk and his date?

It's all too much to deal with.

Last Year's:

Best Moment:

* Thank God I haven't been abandoned in all this "crazy stuff." It looks like Dirk has had a hand (and staff) in trying to protect me. So for an instant a couple of times I felt protected, safe, which was a first in my life. I had never known those feelings, and it's important to be able to feel that God gives us protection. God knew it would take a wealthy and powerful man to lend me that emotion for an instant.

Worst Moments:

* Worrying that the church betrayed me. I overheard some guys talking in the gym; their story makes me think the church created more rumors when I went to that prayer meeting instead of helping me.

* All the things going on around me and not knowing what it's all about and not being able to figure out how to get the truth.

* The loneliness, the isolation being dealt to me by a city full of people who are whispering and staring and talking behind me and around me but never to me. I am so alone in this town.

Next Year Goals

Get the facts, what has been printed about me. What damage control do I need?

Work out four times a week at the health club. Focus more on weight-lifting.

Do something with my counseling degree. Begin a private practice.

Maintain weight. Am at okay 132.

Wish for:
Love, a lover, a companion. All in the same man.

My Day-to-Day Life:
I didn't go to Wagon Wheel City (with my season's pass) for the Christmas display. I didn't want to chance running into Dirk and his family and disrupting their good time. I've seen him around town a lot since I've moved here, and he always seems uncomfortable, which makes me feel the same way. But it keeps happening nonetheless.

Every workday, at lunchtime I have anxiety and a stomachache. What will happen if I go to the deli in the building? There, I'll likely face scrutiny, stares, whispers. If I go home for lunch, what will happen? Will I be creating a big photo op for some nuts in the parking lot or at my house? And do I care anymore if I do?

When I go to the grocery stores, I have to find which register doesn't have a group of women gathered because I don't want to have them stop talking and all stare at me as I check out. Usually some woman has shadowed me all through the store, then gets in line behind me (with all the other lanes empty, she'll stand behind me). It's so frustrating!

And Tori hasn't called with her tabloid research. Why?

Saturday I did a little shopping, testing "the situation." I'm so restless!! At an antique shop, the guys working there put their heads together and one said, "It's the chance of a lifetime!" When I left, one was hunched down in his truck, acting odd, and I worry he took my picture. It feels like such a violation! But surely there isn't a market for my picture! It makes me sick, people willing to victimize me just to make a buck.

This is stripping my life down to the basics. I'm in a situation in which there is nothing I can do but trust God. I'm powerless and must pray and wait. It's so hard for me.

Trusting in God, truly too difficult.

A spot of deep red dripped onto the carpet and shone like a ruby.

"Get that shit off my rug!" Blair shouted, and ran into the kitchen for a paper towel. Michelle mocked her after she left the room and everyone laughed.

"Sorry!" Brittany dabbed a cotton ball on the polish, then took the proffered paper towel and wet it with polish remover.

"So that's what Lara bought at PharmStore?" Stacy asked. "I bought that Pointed Pink that Carrie Jo Miller wears. Here, do my toes, okay? I can't reach." She pushed her foot over to Brittany, who sat on the floor with spacers between her toes.

"Let me get this done first. I thought Redstone was better for formal dress." She finished her toenails and stretched them out to dry.

"Like who's going to a formal?" Swirls of smoke joined a cloud that hung over the chair where Michelle sat. She examined the fingers that held her cigarette. Her nails were painted Pointed Pink and she'd be damned if she was going to change them.

"Well, I'm wearing a long gown, slinky and black and cut down to here." Brittany drew an imaginary line across the middle of her chest. "You wear what you want!"

Michelle put on a cool face, pretending she didn't care about Brittany's gown. But where the hell did she get it if she wasn't wearing what they did? She had to know. "So Britt. Where'd you pick up your gown?"

"You people better not embarrass me!" Blair interjected and positioned herself in the middle of her living room. She looked around at the five girls who lounged in a range of outfits from sweats to t-shirts to underwear. "The limo from the club should be here at 9, so be ready. Rocko's New Year's parties are great! I told him you're all hot chicks. Michelle, do you need to borrow a gown? I have some stuff I dance in."

Michelle snorted. Was she kidding? She looked up and down Blair's large body, clad now in a black spandex bodysuit. "Wear one of yours? What, you wear about a 10?" She stopped when Blair glared at her. "Like you need a bigger size across the top than I wear, I'm sure." She stared a minute at Blair's chest. "Rocko bought you those, didn't he?"

Blair ran her palms across her breasts and grinned. "Yeah, and he might do the same for you if you come dance there, beings you could use bigger tits. He says it makes him more money anyway." She laughed horsey. "Of course, he says he gets to see what he bought anytime he wants!" She laughed again, then grew serious. "But, for real, you got a dress, right?"

"Yeah, sure. You kidding? Sassy Lady's got a whole wall of sequins, so me and Stacy and Delta each got one. Brittany—I don't know where she got hers." Had she managed to swipe one from some place in St. Louis or KC? Without telling them?

Connie spoke up from the floor. "Damn, what a great year!"

"No kidding!" Stacy sat up straight, smiling like she'd won the lottery. "We saw Dirk, like how many times? Or maybe saw him, but it's the same thing. And this whole Lara thing is such a hoot. Look, we got her polish colors and her hair stylists, so we can figure out what she's getting done, and we got her workout all figured out so we can do that shit. And she shops in St. Louis, so we can always go there and get stuff, except when she goes to Chicago, but it's kinda the same."

Michelle suddenly stood up from her chair. "Dirk Dolls!" Everyone turned to face her. "New Year's resolutions! Getting more of Dirk!" Everyone cheered.

"And getting rid of Lara!"

Everyone cheered.

Chapter Twelve

"Alien, it's coming-out day!"

Lara swung her raspberry muffler around her neck and looked in the mirror. Her jaw was set in determination; things would be better now. The evidence was in front of her, and in front of every celebrity-obsessed person in Granville—Dirk had been in town with some woman. All the stalking and the stories about her "affair" would soon fizzle out and she could get back to living her normal life.

But in the meantime ... she pulled a paper out of her purse. She had made a list. These strange people were catching her off guard, shocking her and hurting her. The grocery stores, the mall, the gym—they were invading everyplace she went. Lara was embarrassed by their public criticism of her looks, her age, everything about her, even though she didn't care whether a group of stupid-acting people thought she was attractive. She didn't consider herself a beauty, but she knew that many men liked her looks. She usually preferred the company of men, and when she was these women's ages she was with her first husband. She'd never understand these women who ran in groups. Her female friends were intelligent and independent. Were these "women's women"? If so, Lara didn't want to be one. It looked boring.

What disturbed her especially, however, was their hatred. She'd heard this—"I hate her!"—flung at her, and saw it in their expressions. They didn't know her, couldn't understand someone who was so different from them, yet they hated her. It would be unacceptable for Lara to react with anger, with cursing, or with tears. She had to stay in control, whatever was happening around her.

She read from the paper:

Rules for this episode:
1. Do nothing to hurt, embarrass, or victimize the other innocent person, the celebrity.
2. Be Classy. Be Cool. Be Dignified.
3. Fight evil only with good. You do not fight evil by joining in with it.
4. If confronted with offensive remarks, walk away.

5. Do not waste time or energy thinking about the cruelty. There is no *solution* for the cruelty. Just as there is no *reason* for it, there is no *solution*.

6. Watch your back for rudies. If you even suspect them, walk out.

7. Shopping—Move fast (but not obviously fast). Get in, get out, no dawdling. Know what you're getting when you go. Make a *short* list. Use *cash*.

8. Remember, this is a God thing. Stay out of the way. Love *is* the answer.

She folded the paper and slipped it back into her purse, then looked up at Alien.

"I've been hiding out like a cloistered ... person, for weeks now. Today is the day everyone will have found something else to do, and will leave me alone. I am shopping, shopping, shopping in Eureka Springs!"

The last time Lara had felt so sneaky and free was when she was a teenager climbing out her bedroom window for a late-night walk. She checked the road atlas. Lacking a sense of direction, she'd compensated by learning to follow a map. She'd hold it in front of her and imagine a little car driving along making left and right turns. Never east and west; directions and compasses were somehow wrong things. She was waiting for the day when she'd see the headline "Map Directions a Hoax", followed by "Today a group of scientists admitted the creation of North, South, East, and West map points was a practical joke that got out of hand." Then Lara could say "Ha! I told you so" to those annoying people who pretended to know which way was North. Meanwhile she became skilled with a map. Sometimes she was surprised when she got where she wanted to go, and often she took accidental detours, but today it looked like an easy enough route. She would go in the down direction on the map, take a left, then a right ramp onto the highway.

Lara sped away in her car, eager to burn off her cabin fever. The weather was a late Christmas gift—sunny and 50s. A good omen! The radio played a series of light love songs and Lara sang along. She was soon turning onto the blacktop toward Eureka Springs. As she drove, she checked her rearview mirror.

That car behind her—hadn't it been following her all the way from Granville?

How was a girl supposed to show off her boobs if she wore a coat?

Alice pulled a fitted leather jacket from under a pile of clothes and slipped it on over her low-cut red top. She found zebra-striped stretch pants and wiggled into them. Sniffing, she wrinkled her nose, then grabbed a perfume bottle from the dresser and sprayed herself. She could ditch the jacket if it wasn't too cold; Dirk would want her to show herself off. She hadn't seen him yet at Rocko's where she danced, so she knew he'd be looking for her.

Music was blaring from the living room and she bumped her hips to the beat. A voice called out, "One hundred feet. Three-ty hundred, five-ty hundred, one-ty hundred feet!"

"Shut up!" Alice turned and shouted into the dim and dirty hall.

She grabbed the edges of the dresser and spoke into the mirror. "Today I'll catch up with you, Dirk Lover." Catching the rhythm again, she swayed and pushed her chest out, then ran her hands over her breasts. "You've missed these babies, haven't you? I know you're looking for me. Well, I'm going to show you that I'm right here in Granville." She puckered her lips and wiggled her hips while she watched herself in the mirror.

She left her apartment and was dancing her way out of the building when she suddenly stopped. Two men sat outside on the top steps smoking and blocking her way.

A familiar voice spoke from behind her. "Don't you talk to those men. They'll be turning you in to the police."

"Hey, gorgeous, where you going?" The man who spoke wore a jacket that used to be quilted and used to be sage green. Now its diamond pattern of threads was torn and its color dingy and blotched with stains. He was unshaven and as dirty and worn as the jacket, but he grinned up at Alice with the confidence of a well-dressed man.

Alice stared over the men's heads out to the sidewalk. Both had twisted around to face her, but there was an open space on the steps to the right.

"Leave her alone, George. You know she don't like us." George's companion was as whiskered and dirty, but younger. His plaid flannel jacket matched his brown shaggy hair.

"And there ain't no reason why she can't like us! Come on gorgeous, bend over and give us a smile!" He laughed ugly. Alice stepped wide past him as he grabbed at her legs. "We know where you work, you know. Can't you give us a little show?"

She pressed against the stair rail to avoid him and began to chant. "Stay away from the men, they'll put you in jail, stay away from the men, they'll put you in jail."

"Hey, wait there! We won't put you in no jail! We'll put you in our safe warm bed!" George shouted as she ran down the street to her car.

As she unlocked the door, she heard the other one say, "Leave her alone. You know she's crazy." She flipped him the bird. He started to stand, then sank down and sucked on the last of his cigarette.

—⁓—

A yellow light flashed a warning.

Lara slowed as she approached the intersection. She glanced to the right, then stared, alarmed.

A white truck was stopped at a small ice-cream shop. Two women in identical outfits were climbing out of the front seat. They walked toward the order window. Lara tried to see into the back seat of the extended cab, but the windows were tinted. A wave of worry washed over her as she tried to place the two familiar women. Where had she seen them before, and where was that truck headed?

Stacy's scream was shrill. "It's him! It's him!"

Michelle slammed on the brakes, but had gone past the little building before she could stop. She turned onto a small road and angled her car back to turn around. The girls watched as two women carried three drinks from the order window to a white truck. They climbed in and it sped away.

The Rockton girls sat while a stream of cars moved by in a steady line. Many of the drivers were young, female, and blond. Michelle scowled as she waited to break into the traffic. "Did the whole population of two states come out here today? Damn that email network. By the time we learn something, every bitch around knows it. We need an internal line somehow. Where's that phone?"

Stacy pulled the phone out of her purse, dialed a number, and handed it to Michelle as she chattered. "I know, it's like when we know something everyone knows it, so we don't have nothing special unless we get it ourselves, or make it up ourselves like with those shopping lists, then if we put it out there on email, everyone knows it so it's not special anymore …"

"Are you sure that was his truck?" Brittany asked.

Michelle found an opening onto the road, tossed the phone back, and raced off, cursing.

"Didn't you recognize those two girls?" Stacy replied. "They're around all the time when Dirk's in town. Always dressed the same, those freaks!" She struggled out of her denim jacket. Underneath, she wore a blue stretch top that exposed her chubby middle. She glanced around at her friends, who all wore the same outfit.

Michelle looked over at her, then rolled her eyes. What was that saying about not trying to make a small purse out of a cow's rear? She snorted, then narrowed her eyes at the vehicle ahead. "What I want to know is what they're doing in Dirk's truck. What makes them girls so special?"

"Are they from around here?" Brittany asked.

"I think they're from Granville," Stacy said. "They hang out following Lara when Dirk's not around. They're like groupies or something. Isn't that what we're trying to figure out, how to be his peeps?"

Michelle watched in the rearview mirror as Brittany made a grossed-out face. Like she figured. Brittany was thinking she was too good for all this. Well, one day she'd see who was too good, once Michelle had Dirk.

She drove on, then reached her hand toward the back seat. "Get Connie on the phone. We need to report this. And to figure out who those whores are. The Dirk Dolls don't need outsiders messing up our plans."

—

Eureka Springs had expanded, leaking new businesses along the highway near the turnoff to the original village. Lara was distracted by a freshly-built antique mall and almost missed the road that led toward the streets of historic brick buildings. She stomped on her brake and swerved to head down a hill and around a curve to the picturesque city.

"Little Switzerland," a brochure named it now. Over a century earlier, healing springs attracted the people who built a large hotel on a hill, and the city grew down the slopes and up again. Now the streets were lined with old brick storefronts that housed jewelry stores, trendy gift shops, and restaurants. Lara had visited it many times, and years earlier had seen the brick facades begin to deteriorate. But today the little town had an optimistic polish to it. Construction and restoration were underway on many of the buildings and the stone sidewalks were crowded with shoppers carrying bags. An effort to make it a honeymoon spot was blooming, judging from the number of tiny romantic inns sprouting up among wildflower gardens off the main streets.

Lara crawled her car down a long hill and parked. Maybe she could forget Granville and the strange people for a few hours. Across the street, stone steps led up to a landing with shop entrances, then farther on to an upper street. She strode up the steps in her hiking shoes, determined to burn off her frustration.

At the landing, she paused and popped into a shop that was strung with tie-dyed garments and Indian scarves, a 70s retro. Lara tried on rings, then stepped back out and hiked up more steps to the street. She moved in and out of shops, enjoying a rush from the immersion into colorful dresses, intense paintings, and gleaming jewelry. Original art galleries stood shoulder-to-shoulder with cheap import bazaars. Lara felt she was inside a kaleidoscope, refreshing after a year in which her own world had narrowed into a black and white tunnel.

Intent on a peaceful day, she ignored the sales clerks who studied her face. When a man leaned out a car door and hurriedly aimed something the size of a camera at her, she turned her back and walked down to another level of street. She managed to dodge problems, but she suddenly realized that she never stopped moving. She would walk into a store, see people stare, hear whispers, then walk out again. She wasn't feeling anxious, but she never stopped to shop.

She rationalized that she was there to walk and to look at pretty things.

She told herself it didn't matter that she didn't actually shop.

—∿—

The white truck was pulled up along a curb, the engine idling.

"I know you're in there, Lover. Can you hear me?" Alice stopped her car in the street alongside the truck and rolled down her window.

"Dirk! I need to talk to you!"

Cars were forced to stop behind her. A horn blared.

She stuck her head out and looked behind her. "Shut up, you asshole!" She turned back to the truck. "Dirk!"

Several more cars honked, then Alice saw a patrolling policeman had stopped on the sidewalk to watch her.

"Dirk! I'm at Rocko's. Did you hear? Rocko's in Granville!" She jerked her car forward and drove away.

—ᴡᴡ—

There he was again. That scruffy man was showing up everywhere Lara went.

Lara was determined to lose this one. He was the down-and-out type that made her uneasy lately, the sort of person she might catch taking her picture. Someone seeking a way to make easy money. Money! So many low-lifes trying to use Granville's Hollywood connection for some easy cash. Greed, simple greed. The women who followed Dirk around—they weren't innocents. Plenty of them likely wanted to latch on to a rich man.

This man was disheveled, his clothes rumpled as if slept in. A black pack was strapped across his back. The sight of it worried Lara. What was in it? A camera? Or worse, a weapon?

When she noticed him following her again, she stepped through the nearest door. It opened into a women's clothing store. Perfect. If he was just shopping, he shouldn't stop here. Lara ducked behind a tall round rack and peered out. She saw the man stop and look in the window, then turn his back and wait. After several minutes, he moved away. She went to the window pretending interest in a jacket on a mannequin and peeked out.

He was standing at the next storefront.

Suddenly, he removed a cigarette from his breast pocket and turned his back to her to light it.

Lara saw her chance and slipped out the door. She darted into the next shop. Looking out from the press of Christmas decorations and people, Lara watched for the man. He rushed to the window of this shop and peered in. Had he seen her?

He moved toward the door, opened it and stepped in.

Lara's breath came short as her anxiety grew. Was he a threat? If not, why was he following her? He stood a minute holding the door open and looking forward into the crowd. Then, as the man stood with the door open behind him, Lara came from the side and slipped out. Incredibly, he didn't notice her.

Once in the next shop, she peeked out from behind a dress rack. The man appeared outside and stopped at the window. He looked in, then searched up and down the street, seemingly frustrated. He hurried away, and after a minute Lara stuck her head out the door. He was pacing away from her, stopping to peer through windows. When he was a block farther, she stepped out behind a group of women and headed in the opposite direction. Free!

Lara crossed the street and continued up the hill. She began to again enjoy the beautiful weather and the quaint shops. A machine was popping out rainbow-shaded bubbles and she followed them into a hat shop, then moved on to dart through a door to check out the pottery. Two blocks up, she glanced away from a window full of silver jewelry and toward the street, then did a double take as she caught the eyes of the man in a familiar white truck. As she focused on him, he looked away with a stressed expression.

Goodness, couldn't he get out and shop like normal people? But with the thought was the knowledge that, sadly, he could not.

CHAPTER THIRTEEN

Uh oh. Gramma had that churchy look on her face. Delta bent deeper into the math book on the table in front of her but she felt her standing there looking at her.

"Delta, what's this I hear about your friends stalking some woman?"

Delta scrunched up her face and stared at the page of numbers. Even math was better than lectures from Gramma. Besides, they had terrible luck on that Eureka Springs trip the other week. They never managed to get near Lara or Dirk so they might just as well have been shopping on their own.

She answered her grandmother. "We're not stalking her, we're only getting information."

Gramma put her hand over the page. Graduation was only a few months off and this was the hardest subject, but she seemed to think something else was more important today.

"What do you mean, information?"

"Just sh…stuff. What she wears, where she goes, what she buys. And one day we'll catch her being with Dirk, we know we will!"

"Delta, look at me." She pulled her granddaughter's chin toward her. Delta pulled it back away. She hated it when her Gramma treated her like some little kid.

"Delta, Baby, you are stalking her. Now why are you doing this to that poor woman?"

"It's not stalking, Gramma. We're even making her famous!" Her face brightened as she spoke and she looked up at her. "She should be happy about it. Michelle says some stars pay to get magazines to listen to them and here we are, we have all this stuff on Lara McKeen, putting it around on our emails. People everywhere know her!"

Delta grinned, excited, but her grandmother's face grew more serious. Delta continued. "We made her a celebrity! She'll be thanking us when she figures it out. We know all about her—what she does for fun, where she went to school, her marriages. Did you know …"

"Delta, stop!" Gramma's words came out from between gritted teeth. Delta hushed up fast and looked back down at her book.

Gramma continued. "This is wrong, what you're doing is wrong! You've stolen this woman's privacy, Baby. What if she doesn't want everyone to know her business?"

This was getting confusing. Delta focused her eyes away on the wallpaper. Her grandmother still stood up over her. She sure could be tall when she wanted to be.

"Delta, I know you haven't had much raising, out in those hills in that trailer. I've tried to do what I could, but I worry I haven't made any difference. But you listen to me once." Delta looked up at her, surprised by the anger in her voice. "You have got to understand that there are different ways to be in this world. There's people who hold their ways private and behave with dignity. Then there's the loose sort who never think of whether they're being decent or how what they're doing is going to hurt other people. They're *trash*."

Delta narrowed her eyes at the word she'd heard uppity sorts hurl at her and her friends.

Gramma stared a minute, then softened her tone. She pulled out a chair and sat down next to Delta. "You girls like Dirk Durmont, don't you. Isn't that what this is all about?" Delta grinned, happy again, and nodded at her. "Well, Lord knows I'm sick of the mess his Hollywood has made of this place, but let's say he really liked Lara, or some woman like her. She's a church-going lady, isn't she?"

"Not now. Used to be."

"Well, say he wanted to meet a nice churchy gal to marry him and raise his children, and to please his ma. Now, you girls with your chasing him all over the place and spying on people he knows, you make it so he can't see anyone but loose types. Don't you see? You're not even letting him make his own choices."

"Michelle says he don't like no holy types anyhow. It's just a show."

"Delta."

Delta looked down again; she could sense that more bad stuff was coming. Wasn't this math book bad enough?

Gramma spoke. "I have never asked anything of you, have I?"

Delta thought a minute and shook her head.

"Delta, Baby, would you please, to make your old granny happy, would you please stop running with that Michelle? She is worse than no good white trash. She's white trash with bad ambitions."

She had gone too far. Delta sucked in her breath, angry now. She slammed her book shut and jumped up. Gramma was trying to make her mad with this hateful talk about Michelle! She saw her grandmother tighten her lips like she was trying to button them, but Delta had had enough.

She shouted as she loaded her tote with books, grabbed her jacket, and headed toward the door. "Michelle is my *friend!* You don't get it. We have this cool thing going, making that old whore famous, and you don't get it. Dirk does. Michelle says he loves us and thinks we're cool!"

And she was gone.

Lara examined the General Insurance policy on the desk in front of her, aiming a red pen at the paper. She circled the date. In the top right hand corner, the month read "Janua."

Always something.

The urge to use the bathroom was building up. For this she needed a strategy. Last week, she'd entered a stall in an empty restroom, and had soon seen the shadow of someone creeping quietly into the neighboring stall. The other person made no sounds other than breathing, so Lara got out as fast as she could. Since then, she'd used a variety of bathrooms, and was sometimes met with women who entered and pointed her out to each other, then left. Was something sinister afoot? A photo sought? These people seemed obsessed with whether Lara was pregnant. Her silly round belly—unfashionable, but harmless—was being peered at by so many people these days! Could it be that they sought physical evidence that she wasn't pregnant? Sickening.

Across the aisle from her cubicle, the phone rang.

"General Insurance, Darla speaking."

Lara studied the next policy. The month showed as "January." Great. The error was inconsistent, so harder to track.

"Oh my goodness!" Darla's voice was frantic. "That's terrible!"

Lara suspended her pen in midair and listened without looking up.

"You heard that on the news?" Darla sounded shocked as she spoke into the receiver.

Lara's hand became heavy. She lowered it and let it press against the paper.

"When did the plane go down? ... Does his mother know?"

Lara's middle suddenly felt gripped by a threatening hand. It hurt to breathe.

"That is so awful, to die like that! I'd hate to be his parents. ... Thanks for calling." Darla hung up the phone.

Oh God, don't let it be him. Lara's thoughts raced. *Don't let him be dead, don't let this be happening.* She sat motionless while Darla rose and stepped over to their boss' Cheryl's desk.

"Cheryl. Nancy called with the most terrible news ..."

Please God make him safe.

Lara's eyes filled. What was she *doing*? What was the matter with her?

Darla continued. "She heard on the news that Jack Lindsay's plane went down. There aren't any survivors that they know of. Isn't that terrible? I'll bet his mother's just sick."

Lara gasped and let herself resume breathing. Jack Lindsay? As she listened, she learned he was a world-ranked tennis player who'd gotten his start in Granville.

How sad and tragic!

But thank God it wasn't Dirk Durmont. Relief washed over her, and she realized how panicked she'd been. Then she felt her heart ache with a new sorrow. All her caution, all her reasoning—how had she gotten in so deep? What emotional smash-up was she speeding toward now?

It would not end, this strange war.

After work, Lara had gone to a grocery store and been chased by a young woman who paced her everywhere, several women with carts, and three men she recognized from stalking episodes in other stores. There seemed to be something about her eyes lately; they wanted to get a close look at them. In spite of her efforts to dodge the men, she'd collided into a display and they cornered her there to exclaim that "Naw!" they didn't see it. So many people trying to see something.

Some of them seemed to expect her to be a perfect beauty. Well, where did *they* get off? And didn't Dirk have a girlfriend now? End of the Lara story, right? But still they targeted her. Why?

Her trips to the gym ended in failure time after time. Men now sat in a line of chairs, watching her and whispering. She considered complaining to management, but the gym had become one of the few places she picked up information. She'd heard them talk about the money being spent. She only hoped they realized Dirk was putting it into Granville's pockets. And that the Lara Project wasn't a joke. There definitely were threats to her safety—people who hated her, some of them apparently unbalanced. What if something did happen to her, an innocent victim of his fame? He'd have to think his fame was like a toxic cloud that damaged anything he got near. What would that do to him?

One night at the gym, she overheard that Dirk was downstairs working out, and they had nodded toward her. It was so confusing! Was she in his way? She couldn't figure it out, so when she was done, she left. This nightmare was out of her control. If this man wanted to meet her, her phone number was in the book. He could always call, even only to see how she was handling the horrific mess her life had become. Because of him.

Her isolation grew along with her frustration and anger. Whom could she talk to? Every time Dirk Durmont's name came up, people spoke in hushed tones, as if in reverence. How could she talk about her problem with people who believed that a celebrity was almost a god? And Lara was beginning to suspect how base and dirty his life in Granville was. She was naive but not stupid. She gathered from the comments she heard that some of these women knew Dirk and others thought he was within their reach. There must be a reason for their attitudes.

2-13-00
Journal,
This "crazy stuff" has invaded all the areas of my life. It's taking all my strength to face the world now. How did that happen? I've kept it in its place—a passing odd phase—for so long. Now I can't do anything without it impacting me.

A day in my life:
I wake up, sometimes crying. Stress, or sorrow, realizing that this is my life. Sometimes I'm okay. And Mick kitty is there and I tell him that good things happen to people and that miracles happen, that something good might happen today.

I go down for breakfast and worry about who can see me through the window. I feed the dog outside, keeping my head down so no one can see my face. Is anyone taking pictures, is anyone looking? I found that an outside chair was moved to directly under the kitchen window and was dirty with shoe prints, so I've moved the chairs.

While I eat, I keep the light off so no one can see in, just in case. Then I shower. I peek out the window of the bathroom to make sure no one is there. Am I over-reacting, or being realistic?

That someone else's fame could make everyone act so strange—it's incredible! He is incredible-looking, I'll give them that. Definitely catches the eye. Tall, broad shoulders. Things he can't disguise. That jaw line.

Now I'm lonely, thinking of that beautiful man. Ouch.

A revelation last night, that my greatest sin is despair. It's a lack of faith, and that is so wrong. How does the verse go "all things work together for good for those who love Christ" or something. And I do believe that. Given how bizarre all this is, maybe it will somehow lead to great joy, or at least to some "good."

But I have to leave it in the hands of Dirk Durmont and God. I have no choice. An opening will come. And, in the meantime, I'll retreat again. I need to stay away from the mall for a bit. There's so much trouble there now, so many people cornering me. They must know I can hear them, but they don't care. How cruel they are, criticizing what I'm wearing, expressing amazement that I'm "that woman". I'll keep shopping out of town. I have to go to the grocery stores, though, darn it.

The other day was one of those "feeling my feelings" days. Every time I tried to leave the house, I'd burst into tears. It's the frustration of requiring a battle plan, a careful choice of stores, a list, a contingency plan for any event. It's exhausting! I couldn't stop crying so I stayed home.

But ... was I saved from some bad thing? The same thing has happened before, that I ended up not being able to leave the house for some reason. Once I suddenly got a stomach virus and couldn't go to the gym. And one Sunday I woke up with huge swollen lips from a toothpaste allergy, so I couldn't leave the house 'til evening. Was I saved from something awful? But I'll never know what might have happened, will I?

Yesterday, I cut my workout short. The gym was crowded—men everywhere, eyes everywhere—and when I picked up one offensive comment, I left. I don't have to be an exhibit.

I need to start watching the people who are giving me a hard time. There's likely only a handful that are unbalanced. I can't imagine many people would go out of their ways to harass me. I'll pay closer attention. It is illegal to stalk me, although I can't get the police involved without making a mess of things. So I won't. But I want to know.

What am I going to do? I don't want to have to move. I want to stay here. I want a friendship with Dirk, and this mess to be resolved. He must have friends in town, and they don't get stalked, do they? I want to see what's been printed. No rumors, just the facts. I want my life back, to find love, sex. Companionship. A family of some sort.

Tomorrow is Valentine's Day. I can't stand it. I was going to send cards to my friends who aren't attached; turns out I'm the only one! How odd for me!

I keep praying. I must keep the faith. What has given me happiness in the past? I'm happy when I'm in love. When there's a man giving me love and attention. And sex, ideally. Well, I need to base my happiness on more than that! Do I have to have a man around? Something is wrong there.

———

Michelle sat with roses framing her jaw. She glanced around the school cafeteria and grinned. She was obviously the only hottie in the whole place; no one else had flowers.

"I didn't think we could get flowers delivered here," Brittany said.

Michelle laughed. "You have to know the right people!" She sighed big. "Too bad for everyone else. Ha!"

"Who are they from?" Delta asked.

Michelle noticed the people sitting at nearby tables were silent, waiting for her answer. She looked around and stated loudly, "They're from that guy Dan in Granville, that's all." She leaned in and whispered to her friends. "He thinks I'm pregnant!"

Stacy inhaled in a laugh. "Ohmigod, I can't believe it! Why does he think that? You're not, are you? You'd tell us first, wouldn't you?"

"Yeah, you'd tell us, wouldn't you, if that happened?" Delta repeated.

Brittany sat back and rolled her eyes. "Didn't you pull this stuff last year?"

"Yeah, and the asshole believes it again!" Michelle laughed. "He says he's going to leave his wife."

Brittany scowled. "So you're lying about being pregnant for the second time, and now he's going to leave his wife for you. What if he does it for real?"

Michelle grinned. "Well, that's his problem, isn't it? His problems are not my problem."

"You're not pregnant?" Delta asked. When Michelle rolled her eyes, she continued. "Then why are you telling him you are?"

"Because it's *fun!*" Michelle laughed again. "And look, he sent me Valentine's Day flowers. That's better than any of you got! Besides, people like him are put in the world for people like me to use."

Stacy spoke up fast. "Brittany's going out with Jake tonight, and I bet he gets her something great. He did last year, and they were barely dating!"

Michelle ignored her. "I wonder if Carrie Jo Miller is doing Dirk tonight."

Stacy sat up straighter, excited. "Did you see it on the Internet? It said they went out last night, and that Web page showed this red teddy with nipple cutaways and had a contest of what sexual favors we wanted them to do to each other. She is so cool!"

"Do you think they're really engaged?" Brittany asked.

"She says they are, but he doesn't." Delta said.

Stacy wouldn't shut up. "She keeps saying they're getting married, but he says they're just friends. Connie says that's 'cause he likes what he's getting in Granville!"

"So, did Lara get any flowers for VD Day?" Michelle asked. If she did, the Dirk Dolls would make sure she didn't have them long.

"Connie says they'll be checking her all day today."

No one came back to the programming area without a reason.

Lara picked up the phone and again saw the woman out of the corner of her eye. This one was a stranger to the computer area, but she had repeatedly wandered down the dead-end aisle that ran past Lara. Each time she'd passed, she'd craned her head in and looked around her desk. By now, Lara wanted to grab her by the hair and force her head around and say "See? No flowers, no card, no nothing! Are you satisfied?"

She dialed the number printed bold in the phone book in front of her.

It had been a terrible day, with Lara's loneliness magnifying her usual problems. She had had many valentines in her life—so many roses, cards, dinners out, gifts. Each year of her adult life, even when she wasn't married to an obligated husband, there seemed to be one or several men around on Valentine's Day. And now, complete isolation. Even if she'd wanted to meet a man, she couldn't figure out how to go about it while guarding against attacks from the strange people.

"Pearson's Travel." A woman's voice on the line called her attention back to the phone.

"Yes! What do you have for trips for long weekends?" Lara craved distance between her and Granville. She described her need for a trip for one single, please.

"Well, we have several places I can think of. Mexico is always nice."

"Ah, a different country! The same continent, but I can't have everything. That sounds good."

"Great! We'll want to book that around the spring breaks so you can avoid those crowds."

"When is the *soonest* you can get me on a trip?"

And within minutes, Lara and her credit card had booked a trip to Cancun, Mexico. It was scheduled to leave in three days.

CHAPTER FOURTEEN

Waves upon waves upon waves. Hypnotic.

Lara leaned back against the deck rail and looked out over the ocean. Or gulf. Whatever it was didn't matter. For a few minutes here, nothing mattered. Not even that group of men with the serious camera who had walked out on a jetty near her. Or the man who occasionally paced past in front of her. She was having a rare moment of peace and would not let anyone bother her. In fact, maybe she would stay standing here for the next two days. The air was warm and the sun brilliant; back in the Midwest February it'd take a soft blanket and a fire in the fireplace to feel as comforted. She stood still, as if afraid to disturb an imaginary butterfly that had landed on her. From time to time, she leaned up to brush the back of her fitted capris and to shift her backside, which was pressed against the hard wood slats.

An hour passed while Lara breathed deep and let her mind drift away from the nightmare her life had become.

Then the man who'd been passing in front of her stopped. He walked over and stood next to her.

Go away, she willed toward him.

"What's your name?" he asked.

What?! Lara considered lying. She glanced toward him, then looked back out to the ocean.

Never an easy liar, she answered, "Lara."

"Are you staying around here?"

"No," she answered out of her need to be polite. Then, her peace broken, she straightened, said goodbye, and walked away.

The day had gone well. Except for the episode on the plane when two young women stared and whispered until they concluded that it was "her cheeks." She was so happy to be leaving the country that it didn't upset her this time. It simply made her tired.

She had booked a room in a restored hacienda downtown, a bus ride away from the main beach area. She hoped she'd find some peace there, be left alone. The locals worked and shopped nearby, and she was enjoying the immersion into a different culture. She had picked up a few groceries and a journaling notebook at a store where few people spoke English, and had marveled at the food bar where bowls of meats sat out uncovered and unheated. Luckily, she'd met two young American men in the bread aisle. They showed her how to pick up a tray and tongs and choose among the unwrapped rolls and pastries. Interesting. Some of the food looked scary, but she could live on yogurt and hard rolls—and cake—for this short trip.

She now strolled along the wooden boardwalk. Ahead, a bar in a dark pavilion jutted out from the pool area of a large hotel. She looked out at the ocean, with its beach full of people in scant sunwear, then glanced at the sand behind her. Her eyes caught those of a young man in a visor cap and held them briefly as he watched her from the shade of a dock. With all these women in bikinis, he was watching a 43-year-old pale woman in black capris. A shadow? So were they here, too? And what had *that* cost Dirk Durmont?

"That's Lara." A soft voice came from the poolside chairs to her right.

She tensed, but didn't look toward the voice. She walked on to the next hotel. There she found a building with painted pictures indicating restrooms.

After she had used the building, she stepped out and paused at the pool, staring into the clear calm water. She loved to swim, loved the freedom of kicking her legs in water, but hadn't packed a swimsuit. With all the comments and criticism directed at her face and clothed body, there was no way she'd show people any more than she had to. There was a pool at her hotel, in the center courtyard surrounded by four stories of balconies. She had stood near it earlier, and looked up to admire the overhanging plants, then stopped at the sight of a man watching her. A tall man in a hat and sunglasses was leaning on the rail with arms wide, looking down at her. Something about him brought Dirk to her mind. Was it possible he was in Mexico, too? And at her hotel? All the more reason not to wear a swimsuit. Not in front of a man who'd probably been with countless beautiful women.

She now turned to walk back to the quiet spot she'd found near the jetty. She settled back into her position against the rail and sighed. However, within minutes the local man was back beside her.

"Where are you staying?" he asked.

This she would lie about. "Not near here. With friends." She was a practiced traveler and knew the rules: Never tell anyone where she was staying and never let on that she was alone. Lara forced a smile toward the man and turned to walk back up to the street where she could catch a bus.

She stopped in mid-step. At the top of the wooden path, a tall man in a hat had quickly turned away. He bent into the inhale of a cigarette. Dirk? The broad shoulders, that behavior. Tense, turning his head away and down to hide his face. Who would hide his face from her except Dirk Durmont, or one of his associates from Granville?

How long had he been standing there?

And why? If he wanted to meet her, it'd be so easy.

But she wasn't surprised. Why not Mexico? Maybe a trip to another country was like a run to the grocery store for a man with so much money. She now sensed the tension emanating from his shoulder and realized how awkward she had made the moment. She detoured on along the beach, looking for another way up the hill.

—∿∿—

Subj: Where'd They Go?
Date: 02/17/2000 10:14:34 AM Central Daylight Time
From: HotGirl11@mail.com (Karen)
To: DirkDolls (group)

Has anyone seen Lara?

She is not at work today and doesn't seem to be at home. Our Gen Ins spies are working on a location. Someone said Mexico. Say what?

Keep us posted!

Yours in a DirkDaze,
Editor

IM: SassyGirl
To: DirkDolls (group)

OMIGOD! We're hearing she's in Cancun, like for real. That's in Mexico. And so is Dirk! Someone saw her!

Subj: In Mexico fer sure
Date: 02/17/2000 03:23:19 PM Central Daylight Time
From: HotGirl11@mail.com (Karen)
To: DirkDolls (group)

So, we thought he'd ignored her for Valentine's Day! All except for that little trip to Cancun to be wined and dined and s------ senseless! He probably owns a hotel down there and they're in the whole top floor. Somebody tell me what Lara is doing to get all this! I'm changing my hair color right now!

We have a Mexico connection, a Doll who's vacationing with her college roommate. But they keep losing track of her. Like duh! She's in the room with The Man, Dolls! "Room Service, please!"

—w—

Alice looked up at the flight terminal, tears forming in her eyes. She walked up to a uniformed woman standing at the counter.

"When does Dirk's jet get in?"

The woman raised her eyebrows. "Excuse me?"

"You know, Dirk Durmont. His jet. He's coming in from Mexico today, isn't he?"

"I'm sorry, I don't know anything about that." She took in Alice's red strappy sandals and fake fur jacket, then glanced around like she was looking for someone. Outside, the sky was dimmed to gray, the dreariness typical of February. "Would you like to purchase a ticket? You can fly to Mexico from Granville, but we'll have to put you through St. Louis."

Alice widened her eyes and nodded her head. "Oh, I get it! You can't say anything about it! It's secret. Well, I know he's coming back here, and I'll find someone who'll tell me when. Is your boss in?"

"Ma'am, if you want to purchase a ticket I'd be happy to help you. Please ring this bell when you're ready." She pushed a round service bell to the edge of the counter and hurried away through a door behind her.

Alice's tears came back and this time she sobbed as they coursed down her cheeks. The confusion was sickening. Why had Dirk run off with Lara? He meant to take Alice, didn't he? How could he be getting it all mixed up?

She thought she'd seen him at Rocko's. He must have seen her. She waited that night. She'd stood by the back door until the cleaning man told her to get on home, and Dirk had never come. Alice couldn't understand it. There had been so many tips, so many men groping at her. Dirk could see how popular she was. Why had he run off to Mexico and left her here?

"Lady? You alright?" A man in a gray uniform was walking toward her.

Alice stared, startled, then spun on her spiked heel and rushed out into the brittle air.

—∿∿—

Delta jumped a little and cringed when Michelle shouted, "Ew! Skinny!"

The girls sitting around the TV joined in with "Ew!" They'd ended up at Connie's folks' house after driving around Granville reminiscing over places they'd seen Lara or Dirk. Delta knew she was supposed to like this TV show, but she couldn't shake the bad feeling it gave her.

The thin young man on stage grabbed hold of the microphone like Pa sometimes did his bottle. Scared, looking for rescuing. He stood with his shoulders back and chin thrust forward, but fear showed in his eyes as he faced the audience.

"Look at his hair! What's he use on it, bird shit?" Michelle continued. "He gets his clothes from some garbage can."

They all laughed. Delta, too. There must be something funny even if she didn't get it.

The guy on stage sang his piece in a voice skinny as his body. He had chosen a slow tune about losing someone special who's looking at the same moon.

Stacy spoke over him. "I can't believe Dirk and Lara are in Mexico. Probably screwing right now. I can't believe they got past us. But we knew they were doing the deed, we just couldn't catch them and now they snuck away. It'll be in the papers next week, that we know. And on the Internet. Who do they think they are, running off like that?"

The TV singer finished his song, bowed, and watched the faces of the four judges sitting in front of the audience. He'd put on a frozen fake grin that didn't cover that spooked look.

Two of the judges were audience members picked out to be on a blind date. The man hugged the woman next to him, and she rolled her eyes.

"I wonder if Carrie Jo knows." Connie said. "Like according to her, they're getting married."

"Well, she better tell *him* about her wedding plans!" Michelle was sounding pissed off. They'd been spending a lot of time trying to figure who he was actually with. "And we better make sure Carrie Jo knows about Mexico. Does anyone have an email address for her?"

"Maybe Shirl does. Except she's working for Dirk, so maybe that wouldn't work." Connie spoke around a mouthful of popcorn. Air-pop, like Lara's. "But we *are* getting all this Lara stuff from Shirl and I bet she knows Carrie Jo. She tells us everything, she's so much fun."

"Shit! If Carrie Jo was in Mexico, the tabloids would know all about what she wore and what Dirk did and everything Dirk said to her." Michelle said. "That f-ing Lara is a major bore. No news never."

On the television, the first judge was talking. She was a big woman who used to be on a TV show they all watched. Everyone spoke out when they saw her.

"There's that Marjorie Storm. ... She's always too easy on them singers. ... She thinks she has to be nice because she's fat!"

Marjorie glanced over at the man sitting next to her then looked up at the young man on stage. She spoke in a make-nice voice. *"Gerald ..."*

"Ewww... Gerald!"

"You have a fine career ahead of you. I like your choice of song. It reminds me of my new CD of classic numbers that's coming out next month. I give you a ..." She flipped a card over and revealed a letter. *"... B+! Thanks so much for entertaining us."*

"See! She's too f-ing soft." Michelle was mad now.

The camera moved to the dating couple, who looked to be chewing on each other's mouths.

Stacy shouted out "Look! They're really going at it! Do you think they'll end up together for real? How romantic!"

The camera moved to the second judge, a red-headed man with spiked hair.

"Let's see what Charlie says!"

"Yeah! Charlie, tell Ger-ald he sucks! He sucks big hairy weenies!" Stacy rolled to her side on the floor, laughing.

The girls all got quiet to better hear him. Charlie Simpson was the meanest judge on the show "Sing and Date for Fame" and its biggest star. He now waited until everyone was looking at him. Then he rolled his eyes around and back and made a face into the camera.

"Gerald."

"Let him have it, Charlie!"

"Ger ... ald. First of all, get a stage name. You came on this show, national TV, with a name like 'Gerald'?"

Gerald gritted his teeth while he grinned, which made his thin face look like something in a Halloween movie.

"See! I told you!" Michelle shouted out. "Ger-ald, Ger-ald, your feet stink and you're old!"

Delta thought it was totally cool she could do rhymes without hardly thinking about it.

"And while you're at it, get rid of that outfit. Did your mother dress you? I'd like to see how she dresses! Or maybe I wouldn't!" The television audience was laughing along with Charlie. His face took on a look like he'd just won the contest, like he was forgetting that the people on stage were the ones trying out for it. He held up a square white card, proud as peaches. Slowly he turned it around and showed a big black "D." The camera pulled back and showed Marjorie Storm looking away embarrassed and the two dating judges frowning down at their cards.

The girls roared. "You go, Charlie! We knew he sucked, and see, he really did!"

This wave was the largest yet. Lara lifted her arms and rose up on tiptoe to avoid it, but the surf rolled over her feet and wet the bottom of her tan slacks. She made a two-step scissor walk away from the water, then glanced toward the lights of the hotels planted between the beaches and the highway.

A group of men stood at a railing, watching her. One of the men laughed and pretended to start climbing over the rail toward her. Her heart pounded. Why were they watching her? Then she realized they were at the edge of a crowded hotel deck overhanging the beach.

Okay. They were drunk, playing around. They probably couldn't even see her face.

The night had been perfect and she didn't want any strange happenings. This resort area was lined with miles of boardwalks and beaches, so she had enjoyed ambling in near solitude for the past hour. It was a night for magic, especially for someone with a mystical streak. Such serendipity—a perfectly round moon beamed down at her as she walked. She could almost feel a lunar power surge course through her, clearing her mind of its confusion.

She wouldn't worry about yesterday's trip to the street vendors, when in the dusk she had cut through a parking lot and encountered the familiar tall figure in the hat. He had spun his back around to her, blocking her view of his face with his left shoulder as he bent over a cigarette. She was embarrassed at catching him there. He wouldn't have expected her to do that, to take an unsafe, unlit shortcut back to her hotel. She had soundlessly moved in a big circle around him and escaped out the opposite entrance.

Today had been full of distractions. She had taken the bus tour that traveled through fascinating villages to the ruins of Chichen Itza. She ignored the row of young women in the restroom who stood and stared at her as she applied lip-gloss. She wouldn't think about the older couple who aimed a camera at her as she shopped. There was much to enjoy on the tour: the Mayan tour guide so passionate about his culture, the kind woman with an absent husband who shared the day with Lara, the children who danced for them at lunch.

A good day. She could learn to ignore the bad.

As she walked now in the sand, she spotted a formation of large rocks jutting into the ocean. They were blessedly deserted. Soon she was standing on the largest one.

From this high spot the moon seemed a magnet, drawing her up. Lara dropped her tote bag to the stone surface and stood with her palms out, enjoying the energy shower. She struggled to imprint this feeling in her mind, in her body, in her soul. She must find a way to carry this with her. It was an explosion of purity, blasting away the hollow sad ache that was so often a thief of her peace. Right now, all her strange problems seemed petty and foolish.

When she had worked as a counselor, she helped people think up a "safe place", a mental oasis to run to when the stress of living was too much. But always, her own safe place eluded her. Where had she ever felt secure? She had no answer. But this, this buzz pouring down on her from Something almighty—it wasn't safety, it was power, and it could overcome anything. Lara stood motionless and let it breathe for her.

Then a small voice began a song, the words in Spanish.

The mood was shattered. Lara's spirit sank back down to earth and she slowly turned her head. Behind her, a man and woman had climbed up and now watched her. She set her jaw; they would not rush her from this spot. She stood a minute longer, taking in the entire vista. Far to her right, the land curved and showed hotel lights. To her left, a smaller set of rocks was twenty feet distant. And there, sitting and looking toward Lara—not at the moon or the ocean—was a tall lean man. On each side of him sat a woman.

End of moment. She looked out at the ocean one last time, then climbed down past the couple and hurried to a bus stop. At the brightly lit street full of shops and tourists, a group of young women spied her and crossed the wide boulevard. They stared as Lara kept her head turned away, miserable under their scrutiny. Soon the women went back to the other side of the street.

An hour later, Lara was back at the hotel. She pulled out her notebook.

2-19-00 Saturday
Cancun, Mexico
   Success.
   That "hunted bunny" expression is gone, along with the feeling that I'm a rabbit in a field of foxes, darting away from predators. In Granville, I couldn't get rid of this look of pain and stress and that stressed me all the more! I could not disguise my expression, couldn't put on an appearance! It took a few days, but now I have a genuine sense of peace—on my face, not only in my soul. It had frightened me that I'd lost control of so elementary a thing as my face.
   I need to not let my calm be disturbed again. How? But even as I think about it, the tension starts building. I don't want to look like some stressed-out crazed creature who can't handle the attention. I need to work on my internals. On the plane, I started feeling lonely, insecure, and afraid that it's all going to stop and I'll feel abandoned. I must remember that it is love that I'm lacking and the attention of a lover and friends. That is the real stuff and I can

147

get that. I can't control what's happening around me and will not of course try to make this stalking mess last artificially. I need for God to provide me with the real things.

More lessons:
1. God sees us individually, focusing on each one of us and making us safe. We don't need to feel alone.
2. I now have a "safe place" to visualize. A real one that exists.

I think there have been Dirk/shadow sightings. I might have been walking into a real circus if photo-creeps thought I'd be wandering around in a swimsuit. I guess shadows might have saved me from that. But do people bug hotel rooms? Now that scares me. Still.

Are the shadows there to keep people from taking pictures, and to guard my safety and my privacy? Or is there a fear that someone will speak to me? And tell me ... what? What by now is such a secret?

If Dirk did protect me from attacks this trip, he made the way for God to bless me with a little peace and that rare spiritual episode on the rock. The man is winning my heart. How not, his being such a gentleman and a hero? What woman would not be won over? But it annoys me; I've resisted so long. I must remember—love is never a bad thing. And it's something his money can't buy him. But I need to keep my perspective and not to get too hung up on a misty figure that won't even materialize to have a conversation with!

The next morning, Lara stood in front of her bulging suitcase. Her new notebook would fit into the side compartment. Before she slipped it in, Lara stopped and opened a loose paper that was tucked into it. She began to scan the familiar list: "Do nothing to hurt, embarrass, or victimize the other innocent person. Be classy, cool, dignified. Fight evil only with good ... Walk away ... Be predictable ... Watch your back for rudies. ... "

She abruptly threw the paper down, sat, and covered her face with a pillow. Her breath became labored and she knew without looking that the anguished expression had returned to her face.

How could it be that she was living like this? How could it be?

CHAPTER FIFTEEN

Michelle set her cigarette on a soda can next to the computer. She typed:

Subj: AntiLaura Shops
Date: 03/02/2000 3:28:07 PM Central Daylight Time
From: OnlyOne1@mail.com (Michelle)
To: DirkDolls (group)

Dolls,
I have another shopping trip scoop. At Merker's, Bitch picked up cottage cheese, chicken, NoCare pantiliners, and two boxes of anti-snot cold pills.

She doesn't have a cold.

At PharmStore, she bought two birthday cards, hair conditioner (purple), and three bottles of drain cleaner, and six packs of batteries.

Okay, let's face what the L-whore is up to.

Send. She watched for a reply as she looked up Dirk sites on the Internet.

Subj: Re: AntiLaura Shops
Date: 03/02/2000 3:37:15 PM Central Daylight Time
From: HotGirl11@mail.com (Karen)
To: DirkDolls (group)

Dirk Dolls,
As official DirkLetter editor, may I remind the Dolls of email rules. Some of us send this to our company emails and it will be kicked out if the language is bad. No B-word, or Wh-word, or any swear words for that matter.

Also. Nanc, the Doll who's been dating Ron, says that Ron says that his friend Justin says that the guard squad says they know we're not following Shirl's rules about not all following Lara around all at the

149

same time. Shirl is not happy about it. So we need to find a way to do better what we're doing.

What was that last shopping email about? Lara is up to what?

Sincerely, Editor

\---

Michelle scowled at the screen, then typed.

\---

Subj: Re: AntiLaura Shops
Date: 03/02/2000 3:48:31 PM Central Daylight Time
From: OnlyOne1@mail.com (Michelle)
To: DirkDolls (group)

Dirk Dolls and Editor (Karen at General Insurance),
FYI, when you buy cold capsules, drain cleaner, lighter fluid, batter-ies, and fertilizer (like from farms in Illinois), you mix it all together with other stuff and make ... a word I can't use on your emails, but you can snort it or inject it for a great high. Not that I know anything about that. I do know people make a lot of money selling it, and can travel and own nice houses.

Do we all get it yet? Or if you all want to get it for real, that's another story I can tell you how to do.

\---

\---

Subj: Re: AntiLaura Shops
Date: 03/02/2000 3:55:03 PM Central Daylight Time
From: HotGirl11@homemail.com (Karen)
To: OnlyOne1 (Michelle)

Lara's dealing? Holy sh**!

That's why she has so much money. Do you think she's got Dirk hooked on that stuff? Oh no, poor Dirk!

I have IMs coming from all over! Let us know what else you find out! You are so HOT!

\---

Michelle stared at the screen. She was fed up. If she just mentioned Lara's name, wake up world, everyone went nuts. And that old whore didn't appreciate none of it. Hell, she was so famous, everyone practically knew when she was on the rag.

Well, move over L-whore. It was time to share the spotlight.
She thought a minute longer, then typed.

Subj: Re: AntiLaura Shops
Date: 03/02/2000 4:07:32 PM Central Daylight Time
From: OnlyOne1@mail.com (Michelle)
To: DirkDolls

My being a detective is NOT the only way I'm hot! I happen to have
great sources and one is very hunky and famous. He says I'm the
best thing he's ever found around Granville, especially when it
comes to certain favors, and I don't mean running for coffee!

Ask Dirk! He says it's his favorite day when he met yours truly.

Michelle

She was getting ready to shut down, when an instant message
appeared.

From: ClassChik@mail.com (Brit)
To: OnlyOne1@mail.com (Michelle)

Guess who Connie says someone says they saw walking around
downtown Granville. Dirk! WITH an "older blond" woman. Call me!

—w—

"Alien!"

Lara sunk down on her sofa with the local newspaper open in her
hands. She read aloud, "'Dirk Durmont Imposter Hits Granville.'"

Her recent trip to Mexico—her short brush with peace—seemed
long ago. She'd stepped right back into the Granville mess. Now what?
A fake Dirk? That would explain the circus at the gym Tuesday night.
Groups of look-alike young women had shown up with their yellow
hair and spandex. They must have been expecting a movie star to appear.
But this time their star was a fraud, some guy pretending to be Dirk
Durmont. Lara was curious what he looked like. How many men could
pass as one of the most beautiful men in the world?

She put the paper down and leaned forward with her head in her hands.

"Okay. If this imposter joker knows about my problems here he'll try to get a picture of him and me together and cause some trouble with the tabloids. Maybe he knows I've never met Dirk Durmont and thinks I can be fooled."

She looked up again and wrinkled her nose. "Ew!"

"Strategy. I need to stay out of all this. Avoid all the usual places. I need some groceries, but other than that, I can stay home. Out of harm's way."

The phone rang and Lara spoke to her neighbor Georgia for a few minutes. After she hung up, she sat again and stared out at the street. "A movie invitation. Never pass up a movie opp. So. Groceries and a movie. Easy. It *should* be easy, that is."

Later, Lara drove across town to a grocery store she seldom visited. She parked, checked around for signs of trouble, then hurried in. She moved quickly, and was soon halfway through the store, in front of the freezer case. She leaned in to check the price of green beans, then stepped back and bumped into someone close behind her. She turned, uneasy. A young blond woman with a vacant half-smile moved a step back but stayed uncomfortably close as she studied Lara's face.

Exasperated, Lara grabbed her cart and whirled around.

"She's here 15 minutes and it all begins."

Lara glanced toward the voice. Two men in white aprons watched her from behind the meat counter. She was just a show to these people! Lara shook her head and rushed toward the registers. Enough already. As she got into the short line, a different woman stood behind her, her head moving with each item that Lara loaded on the belt. Soon she was checked out.

"I'd love to carry your groceries out, ma'am!" The man who bagged her groceries smiled and looked eager to help.

She didn't usually bother the employees to take her cart out; she was healthy, she could manage it herself. But a thought came to her. If the Dirk look-alike turned up here, wouldn't having a strange man with her stop him from bothering her?

"Well, yes, thank you!" She accepted his offer.

The man beamed as he pushed her cart to the car, then loaded her sacks into the trunk. Lara closed the trunk lid with a thud, and turned to thank him again.

He lingered, still smiling, then said, "I want to say that it's been an honor!"

"Why, thank you very much," and Lara got into her car, puzzled.

Once home again, she hurried to her computer.

She had to find out—how did these women always know where she was? Was there some bug on her car? She needed to learn more about tracking devices. The women could be stalking the shadows, or "dating" them, so to speak, for information. But they showed up everywhere! Most likely they had some type of electronic communication, maybe even a shared Web site.

She logged on the Internet and typed in the search "Dirk Durmont."

The computer brought up scores of Web sites offering pictures of Dirk nude. She *knew* she did not want to see naked photos of a man she might run into at the grocery store! How embarrassing! She resumed scrolling through the pages, hoping for anything helpful. One Web site promised the latest entertainment gossip. Lara paused. She didn't want to look at this garbage. She'd so hoped someone—such as Dirk—would simply tell her what was going on.

But no one cared about what was happening to her except her.

She clicked on the gossip page and skimmed an account of an actor who ordered his Caesar salad without chicken, and then a list of celebrities who were quitting smoking. Boring. She backed out, then noticed a site promising the "Personal Journal of ... Dirk Durmont ..." Lara double-clicked.

Personal Journal of Dirk Durmont
Where I keep track of my thoughts for the book of my life for future generations.
Monday
Man I like couldn't find my socks this morning. Must have left them with LarMic at the pad when we smoked those joints. Oh wait, I think I see them, this lump in my jeans leg. Yeah, there they are, hitching a ride in my pants. I hate when that happens.
Hafta to learn the script for this movie scene where I kiss this woman for about two minutes, then say "Ah." Or I say that first, I can't remember. Hope she tastes okay, like Marlboros or Corona or something. I think I have it. "Ah." Be the "ah", live the "ah." This acting shit is hard work, sure as hell is.

Lara cringed in disgust. How gross this was!

153

But she studied the screen. This story had a character named "LarMic."

Some halfwit, I mean "fan", broke into my house again last night. Gotta put a lock on that front door. Keeps happening, like I'm laying there catching some major tube or a rank movie or shit and this nude chick comes walking through the damn door! And she's like "Dirk, I love you, f* me" and I'm like "Can't you see I'm working here" and she's like "But f* me first, give me your baby" and I'm like "Well, alright, I can spare about a minute here, then get the hell away."

Gotta seriously put a lock on that door. Who knows what desease their carrying.

Wednesday

Still working on that script. "Ah", then kiss. Or bice bers ..., dice bursor, ... turned the other way around.

Lara sickened at the cruelty of the words and quickly X'd the screens away, then shut down the computer. She felt filthy, as if the machine had been leaking diarrhea on her fingers. There had to be a better way to find the information she needed!

An hour later, Lara picked up Georgia for their movie rendezvous. Academy Award nominations had been announced and they were trying to catch all the films up for best picture. Lara enjoyed the privacy of the dark theatre for the length of the film, then stepped back out to the parking lot where she scanned the aisles for problems. She remembered a character in the movie she'd just seen who'd said he felt people's hatred like bees stinging him. She shivered, then spied it.

There. At the back of the lot. Trouble.

A large white truck was parked along the back row. A blond man resembling Dirk Durmont leaned out of the driver's window and grinned toward her. Lara bit her lip to keep from laughing. This guy needed Dirk lessons. He was smiling at her! If he wanted to look like Dirk, he needed to duck his head down and turn his shoulder toward her.

She and her friend found her car. As they left the lot, she watched in her rearview mirror. The white truck was following them. She drove slowly, taking a roundabout route toward home. Soon a line of trucks and cars was behind them and when she switched lanes, they did the same. Suddenly, the white truck turned onto a side street and sped away; the others went after it. By the time Lara made it home, she had no stragglers.

—◊◊—

Michelle shoved Connie and Brittany aside, then pushed up to the tavern window and peered through it. A commotion broke out on the sidewalk behind her.

"He autographed my ass! Look! He signed my butt! He is so COOL!" A young woman with long platinum hair stood outside the bar with her jeans pulled down to expose the top of her behind. Several men stared and a set of excited women bent to examine the butt stuck out in their direction.

"Look! It's his autograph, isn't it? I can't see it!" The woman tried to see behind her, but couldn't make the stretch. Michelle, Connie, and Brittany rushed over to the group. They squealed along with the other women.

"Yeah, it's his f-ing autograph."

"He is so cool!"

"Look, it says 'Dirk Durmont'!"

"You are so *lucky*."

The woman with the favored backside turned to face them, her jeans still pulled low. The men shifted to stand behind her. "Yeah, but I'm never going to be able to wash again! Clarice!" She grabbed the arm of one of the girls near her. "We have to get a picture of this! Let's go get your camera."

"Not 'til he does me!" and Clarice pushed through the crowd to return to the bar. Michelle and her friends crammed through the door while the bouncer shook his head and shrugged.

Near a booth on the far side of the dark room, people were pressed together watching a blond man sitting with a woman with frizzy hair the same shade. He was talking to the group seated across from him.

"What's going on?" Michelle shoved at a man who blocked her view.

"It's Dirk Durmont! He's been here awhile, talking to acting students and signing autographs. He's signing chicks' butts!" The man laughed. "Is that his girlfriend Lara with him?"

Michelle sneered at him. "No, she's at the gym. I just saw her." She peered around him to see Dirk. "How can I get closer?"

"Here, I'm taller, you get in front of me." He moved to the side and she pushed around him, then got closer still until she stood one person away from Dirk's table. She had to meet him tonight, she had to, especially since she'd been letting on to the Dirk Dolls that she was in with him. This was her best chance so far. No Lara, no Shirl, no gym rats, no interference.

The crowd burst into laughter and she strained to look around the woman in front of her. Dirk had stood and reached over the table with a black marker. Next to his table, a young woman stood with her bared butt thrust toward him.

Michelle leaned in to see him, the actor whose photo was tacked to her bedroom walls, who looked out from magazines on her dresser and from pictures taped to her school locker, the face that made the Dirk Dolls squeal. She smiled and pressed in closer.

Then she stiffened, startled. What the hell! She looked around.

Near her stood a woman she recognized. Alice. Tonight she wore a scarlet tube top, a smear of bright red lipstick, and the same puzzled expression as Michelle's.

Alice stared, confused. There were no voices harassing her tonight, only the laughter of the crowd around her. She had rushed over when she heard Dirk was here.

But who was this man?

She knew Dirk Durmont's face. She had studied it in pictures, on the screen, and in person many more times than he realized. This face in front of her was wrong. What were all these people doing, then? Was this his brother and was he sitting in for Dirk? No, she knew what his brother looked like, along with his mother, father, all his family. Did Dirk have a double for his movies that could go around and sign autographs, too? Or had he done something to change his looks?

None of this made sense, even in Alice's world where many things resisted reason.

Chapter Sixteen

Was this the break Lara prayed for?

She looked once more at the note in her hand. A slogan in red letters ran along the top offering "Best Deals for Your Wheels" and the name of an autobody shop. She drew a line through the business name and studied her handwriting below it. A company name again, and a phone number. But this was Dirk's brother's business, the information copied from a newspaper article.

Every day Lara's existence grew worse. She'd had another failed shopping trip to St. Louis, where people peered at, stalked, and openly discussed her. In Granville, she now shopped for groceries using a handheld basket, or two if needed, so she could move quickly. The stomach pain and breathlessness as she drove from store to store were increasing; sometimes she gave up and went back home empty-handed. Everywhere, the women trailed in after her. She tried now to memorize their faces. She wanted to note the most aggressive ones; mentally ill people could be dangerous. If they'd put so much energy into stalking her, what next? Some of them had lost touch with normalcy, with boundaries. But many of the women looked similar, so she was having a hard time differentiating them. A lot of them were young, blond, average size, with nondescript features.

And there was so much whispering! Thank God Lara had never done anything illegal, or even intentionally unkind, for them to talk about. Was this how famous people lived? Did Dirk have trouble meeting people, talking to them, because of dread of what they'd read or heard? And this "fame." Did it mean attracting crowds of sickos and aberrants?

But the gossip and stalking weren't the reasons she was about to call Dylan Durmont. There was something extra sinister in the air now. And she'd had a dream. In it, an Hispanic man was masterminding a plot that endangered her. She'd seen him leaning against a light blue car and knew he was intelligent and dangerous.

And lately, the characters showing up at the gym looked increasingly menacing. She feared some crime when the shadows were dismissed, if they were still there to begin with. Scruffy men were staring and pointing her out to each other, leaving her with an eerie feeling beyond the usual repugnance. She was becoming desperate to know which people, if any, were on her side.

She looked down at the phone number. This would be the first time she'd spoken openly to anyone local about Dirk, so a script was called for. As she sat on the bed next to the phone, Lara studied her notes.

"Be warm, funny, honest.

If his answering machine picks up, say:

Hello, this is Lara McKeon. I'm seeking a few facts, because (points to make):

    I have no facts.

    Can you or your brother help me out?

    Let me know if we can meet somewhere.

    My number is 688-9999.

    Bye!

If a machine picks up and it's another person:

    I'm trying to reach Dylan Durmont. Can I get a message to him here?

    My name is Lara McKeon, my number is 688-9999.

    I'm trying to get a little information, that's all.

    Thank you! Bye!

If he answers:

    I'm Lara McKeon and I'm hoping you can help me out with some information.

    (make points:)

    I need some facts. I need to know what has been printed about me. I know that Dirk ultimately is the target, but have I become a target on my own?

    Has the church caused any trouble for Dirk? It's important for me to know.

    About security. I'm grateful for it, but I need to know if it's there and when it ends, because then I'll need to be more watchful for myself."

She laid her papers out in front of her, picked up the phone, and dialed.

Journal,

Oops.

I called Little Brother, script in hand. My voice was <u>quaking</u>! Why?! Those people don't make me star-struck or nervous! Even when I met Mother Teresa I wanted to chat with her (not an option). Anyway, I started in about how I wanted a little information ... he was clueless. I think he was, for real.

Then I said, "Well. I guess I'm on my own. I'm very sorry to bother you" and that was it.

I was <u>not</u> prepared for that. I had assumed that Little Brother worked for Dirk in some of these matters. But I can understand Dirk's need to separate his family from all this fame business. How shady and low it is around this town, people's reactions to his fame.

But that leaves me ... stranded.

Well. At least, if the ball was in my court, I've returned it. Dirk has an open door.

—•—

Mark said it was early for kittens, but Stripey the mother cat finally led Delta to the mewing litter. She found them in the "parlor" of the stone house and made them a nest of old t-shirts. Now, as her brother sat on the trailer's front stoop with a cigarette gripped between his fingers, she gently stroked each of the small soft shapes. Their new names were Winken, Blinken, and Nod.

Suddenly, wheels made popping noises over rocks on the road. Delta peeked out to see who was driving up. Sitting on the ground as she was, she could barely see over the edge of the empty window. A mid-sized white car pulled to a stop next to Mark's old blue Chrysler. Delta saw him eye the car then make a face and smash his cigarette under his work boot. He looked over toward her, but couldn't see her through the bushes that grew wild around the abandoned house.

Gramma's car door swung open with a creak. Car wash water dripped on the ground. She grabbed the doorframe and pulled herself out.

"Oh Lord, give me my 'oomph' back!" She walked across the dry patches of grass and dirt and stopped in front of Mark, where she stood a minute watching him. Delta knew she was looking for a sign of what his mood was. It was the women's habit in the McNought family to always be checking these men for their moods, figuring out how far back to stay from them.

She must of thought he was okay, because she spoke up. "The worst part of getting old is losing your oomph, Mark."

He looked over her gray plaid slacks and pink sweater and said nothing. Delta knew the kittens would make them both smile, so she began to carefully gather them up.

Gramma hadn't seen her yet so visited with Mark. "How are you by now?" Her smile was a little fake, not showing much for teeth, like she was mad at him but wasn't going to say so right off.

"Fine." He looked off past her.

"And your Pa? Ma?"

"Just great, Gramma." He watched two squirrels chasing each other around a tree at the edge of the clearing. "Do you want to go in and see Pa?" He scooted over to make room for her to get up the steps into the trailer, but she stood silent, looking down at him.

"No. I came to talk to you. About the stuff I'm hearing around town."

Mark looked out at the squirrels again. One of them suddenly raced up the tree.

"And what I'm hearing from Delta." She paused. "What's this business about you having her stalk that woman in Granville?"

He was silent.

Delta cringed. Maybe she shouldn't have told her anything about that, how he was asking for the Dirk Doll reports about Lara's habits. Gramma was mad and now Mark would be mad and everyone was going to be mad at her.

"Listen, Mark, I've about given up on you. And I gave up on your Pa years ago, God forgive me. But Delta—maybe she has a chance."

Mark glanced toward the stone house, and Delta could see worry showing across his eyebrows. Was Gramma going to send him off into some fit? She bit her lip and struggled to get the squirming kittens safely into the crook of her arm.

He looked back at Gramma with a hard face. "Chance! What f-ing chance do any of us have!"

"You watch your mouth around me, young man! I'll slap you for that, like your Ma should have years ago!"

Mark's eyes scanned the yard, like he was looking for those squirrels again.

160

Gramma went on. "You've had chances, and you're a bright boy, but you chose some lazy way to make money. Don't be thinking I don't know what you do. You might think me and my friends are a bunch of silly old women, but there's nothing silly about our ladies luncheons. Somebody has to watch over this God-forsaken place!"

He stood and was walking away when his grandmother slapped him across his chest to stop him. Delta gasped. Had Gramma gone crazy, hitting Mark? She watched him as his left hand formed into a fist and tightened.

Gramma talked on, like there was no chance he'd hit her. "You listen to me just a minute! I'm not one to turn on family, but *here's* a threat for you. If that little girl gets involved with your deal-making and gets in trouble with the law because of you, you'd best be looking over your shoulder for trouble yourself!"

Delta grabbed hold of the squirmy creatures and began to stand. She didn't know what the law had to do with anything, but she knew what trouble was and it was showing up on Mark's face. No telling what he'd do if Gramma kept pushing him.

Mark's voice came out like a hiss between his clenched teeth. "Delta can do what she wants! She has a mind of her own."

"Oh, *does* she!" She challenged him with a shove of her hand. "What do you really think of her mind? Do you think she does anything on her own, or is she just used by you and that tramp Michelle!"

"Gramma!" Delta stepped out from the stone ruins with the kittens wiggling in her arms.

Mark jerked his head around toward her and Gramma snapped her mouth shut.

He leaned toward his grandmother. "Good job, old lady." He spat it out like a mad cat.

Delta continued. "Look what I found in your little house!"

Gramma stared into Mark's face until he turned away and walked to his car. Then she smiled at Delta and held out her arms. "Delta! What little critters have you got there?"

Lara glanced from side to side as she hunched down to retie her shoe. Four men were transfixed by a television at the far end of the weight room, looking like dogs waiting for a steak. They were strangers, of course, just dropping by. Not many people came regularly to work out. A few bodybuilders sometimes appeared for a few minutes then went downstairs to the men's club, and some familiar faces showed up from time to time, but most of the traffic was transient.

These men seemed distracted, so it looked like a squats opportunity. Lara sighed, relieved. It'd been a long time since she'd gotten a complete workout. Walking the treadmill was easiest to maneuver; she could put on her headphones and ignore what was going on behind her. Upper body exercises were doable unless men crept up and stared at her chest. She worried mostly about her lower body. She couldn't do squats at home; she needed the rack. And tonight it looked as if she had it.

Moving fast now, she loaded the bar with weights, then tightened her workout gloves. She peeked toward the men; some sports show had them engrossed. The radio introduced a song with a heavy beat—perfect. Lara lifted the bar onto her shoulders and focused her eyes on a spot on the wall. As the music played she moved to its rhythm, lowering and raising her body, then ended the set with a four-count pulse of her clenched gluts. She paused, then lifted her shoulders to return the bar and catch her breath before she began again. She turned to the side to stretch, then abruptly stopped and straightened.

Her breath became shallow.

The four men had abandoned the television and moved across the long room to gather near a bench behind Lara. As she glanced at them, they looked quickly to the ground and the walls, feigning disinterest. There were no weights near them, no pretense of a workout.

End of routine. Lara leaned on the bar and closed her eyes to block tears of frustration. She sunk to the floor to retrieve her bag and glanced up, hoping they had gone away. They all sat without talking. Waiting? She picked up her bag and walked past them, keeping her head down to let her hair hide her face.

Downstairs, the dressing room was empty. Lara leaned against a wall of locker doors, miserable, trying to get a grip on her emotions before she walked out to the lobby.

Suddenly, she turned and smashed her fist into the locker.

She gasped, shocked at the pain. "Ow!" She lifted her gloved hand up in front of her face. An intense burn raced up her arm. Dismayed, she stared at her fingers, afraid to take off the glove to see what she'd done to her throbbing hand.

Days later, the pain that shot up Lara's arm mixed with her revulsion as she grabbed the top tabloid paper. She winced and switched to her left hand. In the best of health, it creeped her out to touch these "gossip rags." But the people around her were becoming bolder and more hateful, so she had to force herself to find out anything she could. What was the point of acting like she couldn't feel a pea under the mattress when her life was falling apart? She knew she wouldn't lay hands on any helpful stories by buying off the rack—not this late in the game—but some business addresses and phone numbers might be useful. And she'd like the assurance that there wasn't some ongoing story that got pulled from circulation before making it to Granville.

She had stopped on her way home from a trip to Em's farm to take care of this distasteful chore at this grocery store. She picked up apples and cereal and cocoa, trying to hide her real mission, then found the racks of papers near the register.

Lara glanced at the front page headlines. Reading them made her feel dirty. Self-conscious, she snuck a peek around the store and noticed that a man stood at the front, watching her. No groceries, no shopping, just looking at Lara. She was embarrassed but determined and quickly pulled out one of each paper and dropped them into her basket. Back in the car, she glanced at a story. "Siesta's Husband Killed Her" was followed by an article about how an illness hadn't killed the actress, her husband had. How cruel! Lara cringed and shoved the tabloids down deeper into the grocery sack.

She had told Em about some of her troubles, that she was being followed around by obsessed fans who imagined she was involved with Dirk Durmont. Em thought it was plausible, that Lara fit a certain physical type, and her name didn't help matters after Dirk's relationship with Laura Starbright.

She had noticed Lara's wracked-up hand and asked, "So. When are you going to move?"

Move? Leave town? But there had to be another way.

As she drove back to Granville, a trendy slogan came to her mind, one she'd seen stamped on bright bracelets around kids' wrists. WWJD? What would Jesus do?

He would go about his good works and not be of the world.

Lara was getting sucked into this negative mess! She needed good works, some direction, and to enjoy the positive things—the shadows and SS, the superstar/superman. And her God lessons. He was her protector and she was the center of His attention, just as everyone was. She was His favorite, and so was everyone else. Except maybe the rude people.

She had to resolve to be bigger and better than the petty stuff that was going on around her.

Once home, she hid the tabloids under her bed without looking at them.

—⁓—

"I wanna see the famous butt!"

"She'll be here in a minute. Comes past here after lunch every day." Alice gripped the steering wheel, her car parked so she looked out over the General Insurance lot. Gina sat in the passenger seat, chomping a wad of gum. She danced at Rocko's, too, stripping off a mix of stuck-together animal skins. And she was a Dirk fan. Alice didn't have many friends, but Gina was being good to her so she was trying real hard not to mess it up. She'd even shown her this trick with her butt muscles, making them pop up and down. The guys loved it.

"Everyone's saying that Carrie Jo is shopping around for wedding gowns. Can you believe it?" Gina spoke around her gum while Alice cringed at hearing about Carrie Jo. "What do you think? Dirk says it isn't happening."

Alice kept quiet. She didn't want to hear stories about a wedding. Lara was enough trouble to think about for now.

Gina went on. "Not that we want him married to anyone, but if he had to, I want someone fun in the money house, someone like us. That Lara doesn't talk to anyone, unless she saves it all for Dirk. Anyhow, if he has to marry someone, I hope it's Carrie Jo."

"Maybe it'll be someone no one is thinking of," Alice finally replied. These women didn't know everything.

She liked that she'd found a place where her knowledge about Dirk paid off, even though this latest about the wedding was becoming a nuisance. A lot of women around here followed all the Dirk news.

Whenever she started telling stories about him, a crowd gathered, and then they told her everything they knew. She'd never been so popular. But rumors about weddings aside, these local women thought they had a shot at being Mrs. Dirk. Well, if anyone expected to marry him, they'd have to get past her. Alice had helped him get away from Laura Starbright, saved him from that big mistake, and she was working hard on this new Lara. Maybe she needed a plan for Carrie Jo.

A red Monte Carlo sped into the parking lot, made its way fast down the side lane, then pulled into an empty spot five rows up from the entrance.

"The same parking spot. Every day, that same spot. What a bore." Alice grit her teeth as she spoke.

"But she's the one who's screwing Dirk."

Alice twisted around and peered into her back seat. Then she looked at Gina, who was staring ahead as if she hadn't said—or heard—anything. Okay.

They watched as Lara left her car and paced toward the building, putting her on a path past Alice. Alice grimaced. What the hell was wrong with Dirk if he liked this woman better than her? She leaned an elbow out her open window. Her face twisted with hatred as she looked her up and down.

"Look at her! She's fat!" Alice announced.

Gina stared in silence.

Lara appeared not to notice. She looked the other way and continued on toward the locked entrance of the building.

———ɯɯ———

4-20-00
Journal,

Yesterday, an <u>unbalanced</u> rudie—a psycho—was parked out-side work over lunch. She was in the front row and I walked right past her! She had someone with her. How are these mentally ill people finding people to hang with them? She looked at me with so much hatred, her face was distorted and freaky. She looked like the one in the jeans store. I wonder if it <u>was</u> her?

I didn't get her license plate number; I get so overwhelmed with anger when these things happen that my brain shuts down! So all afternoon at my desk, I ranged from sadness to fantasies of breaking her arm. I'm afraid I'll go ballistic one day.

My new chant:

Don't engage, walk away.

Don't engage, walk away.

All my months of careful behavior will be for nothing if I create a situation that involves police. What a mess! And if these people are seeking attention, they'll aim right for tabloid coverage.

Today is the anniversary of the shootings at Columbine High and the bombing of the Fed Building. Psycho Day. So I laid low (due to that one hanging around yesterday). I didn't use the downstairs bathroom (which has access to outside) (and where that woman peered at me through the crack in the door two days ago—AUGH!).

I'm not much concerned about the latest psycho. I don't care much if someone shoots me, which is too strange and I should seek therapy for that attitude. I fear insults and criticism, but not death. Strange.

What to do? I pray and pray. So, this is faith. Believing when there is no hope and no help, believing that God is sorting it out.

When I went to Peoria, I had an appointment with a cosmetic surgeon to have my face looked at, as it seems to be on everyone else's mind. What a downward spiral, to be sucked into this. I need to find something meaningful to put myself into.

Tonight I should go to the health club. I had to push myself to go Tuesday. There are too many bullies! If I was a man, they wouldn't dare. I could turn and smash my fist into their faces, not some locker. Those cowards! But I went and it was "okay", except for all the young guys with their gossip. How tough am I supposed to be?

I need help. I can't live like this. I daydream about quitting, selling everything, moving.

Friday at the grocery store, I mouthed the word "bitch" at a rudie. It was behind her back, but who else saw it? In the checkout line, a man let me in front of him and looked around behind him to a Dirk look-alike in a suit. Was he staff? Was the other man Dirk? I hid my face because I had forgotten to control my expression so I must have looked sick and hunted, and I had developed a twitch in one of my cheek muscles. How stricken and strange was I looking?

Where will it all end? This all stops me from finding an ob/gyn, getting a mammogram. I can't do those things <u>here</u>! What do "famous" people do?

This year I think I'll go to France and a few places and try to get my life moving in some positive directions. A higher focus. Write. Counsel.

A part of me is laying the challenge out to God (an amusing idea). He said He'd take care of things, He <u>said</u> He would. Should I just let Him? Duh!

5-2-00 Tuesday

I bought a book on Post-Traumatic Stress Disorder.

It talks about PTSD causing the victim to numb out feelings and choose isolation due to dissolution of trust in people. That numbing could explain my lack of fear of the psychos. And anyway, what are the chances of anyone shooting and actually <u>hitting</u> me? Or trying to stab me, a known bodybuilder (to them), and not worrying about how I'd hurt them back.

Unless of course they came up behind me. Definitely a possibility.

I'm having a porch party Saturday. It should be fun, but it's getting me out shopping more so it's more exposure to strange people.

What will happen tonight?

CHAPTER SEVENTEEN

5-4-00 Thursday
> *Fame ... is a bad bad thing.*
> *It attracts the lowest people.*

The worst had almost happened.

The young man nodded toward Lara as he spoke to his friend. At the other end of the weight room, she honed her ears toward his voice.

"We'll finish up here and meet you there," he said to the two men in street clothes who were leaning against the open door to the back stairs.

"Yeah, okay. We'll be down at Maynard's. No cover charge tonight."

Her workout so far had been free from intrusions. Two men arrived soon after she did and stationed themselves near the tall windows that overlooked the street. They occasionally picked up a weight, but were obviously not there to work out. The two others had just joined them. Lara saw the man repeat his gesture toward her.

Shadows, apparently. There were the usual indications—they weren't working out and they weren't regulars. Every few minutes, one went to the windows and looked out into the darkness, peering across into the black windows of a similar old brick building, then up and down the street below.

The building across the street got a lot of attention from people in this gym. Sometimes men nodded out at the windows or young women in spandex thrust their bodies into exaggerated poses while staring into the night. Lara concluded that there was someone across the street peeking into the weight room, or people thought there was. She didn't blame the man whose work required him to observe people. How else was he supposed to go about it? Lara's compassion for Dirk Durmont and his inability to live like a normal man grew as her own life suffered. How could he improve his craft if strangers met him with bizarre reactions to his fame? How could he develop his work, his characters? Or his own *character*? Impossible. She only hoped that if there were voyeurs across the street, they weren't leering at or videotaping anyone working out. Especially her.

She returned her focus to her quadriceps.

"It won't be too long. See you down there." The door closed.

One more exercise. Lara slid off the leg extension machine and started toward the crossover rack. The two men glanced toward her and laughed as they walked to the same rack. One grabbed a handle and pulled it down without setting any weights.

Lara stopped, her face growing hot. Okay. They knew how to finish early so they could go party. All they had to do was to crowd her off the equipment. The squat rack was across the room from them, but she couldn't do a routine with these guys watching. She looked at the clock. 9:10. It was early, but there was little chance of getting anything else done. She grimaced and walked toward the door.

A few minutes later, she was out on the dark sidewalk beside the building. She inhaled deep, pleased to smell the approaching summer in the May night.

But the air was eerily still, as if suspended.

Lara reached her car parked at the curb and looked up and down the street. She moved around to the driver's side.

Across from her, a large dark blue car was pulled up along the curb facing the opposite direction as hers. So many cars, but so few people. Must be a basketball night.

Lara opened her door and leaned in to heft her gym bag across to the passenger seat. She heard another car door, then looked toward the sound. The blue car wasn't empty; the door had cracked open and a man was climbing out.

She stood still, surprised.

Something was not right. The man was walking toward her. Not to the entrance of the gym, but straight toward her.

Remembering some self-defense tip, she straightened and turned to face him off. Never turn your back on a mad dog, that was it.

Lara blinked, confused. He wore a white hat. Didn't the shadows wear white hats?

What did he want?

A deep metallic thump sounded.

Dazed now, Lara realized she was sitting in her car. The noise of the door locking had startled her back to awareness. Her hand was on the lock button. How did she get there? She didn't remember moving.

She hadn't yet realized that her brain had slammed a door on several minutes of trauma.

"What was *that* about?!" Confused, Lara watched in her rear-view mirror as the man walked down the sidewalk, his arms raised above his back in a feigned stretch. As he lifted his arms above his head, he opened the fingers of his right hand to drop something from it.

A car had pulled onto the street; it passed and went on down the road. A police car.

Bewildered, Lara turned the ignition and drove away. She chattered excitedly to herself as her subconscious took her on autopilot to her house. "A man? What did he want? I'm used to crazy women all around, but a *man*? What did he want?"

Once home, she clung to Buckley as he met her at the garage. She rushed through the back door, grabbed her gun, and searched the house, leaving all the lights burning behind her. But Lara didn't know what she was looking for. There was some danger, she knew that, but she couldn't remember what it was. Her body led her through motions of self-protection, exploring each room and peeking out the windows. Several times, a car slowed in front of her house, then moved on. When she was convinced the house was safe enough, she went upstairs and began the familiar routine of getting ready for bed.

But then she couldn't quit moving, she couldn't outdistance the thing that was after her.

Slowly, her memory returned.

Fame … is a bad bad thing.

It attracts the lowest and most evil people.

Tonight, after half a workout, I went to my car. Some young man got out of his car across the street and walked toward me. Toward me, not the gym entrance. He walked toward me with this look, a look of focus and concentration, focused on me.

At that moment, a police car drove by and he changed direction and walked down the sidewalk toward the front of the gym. What was that about?! Was the presence of the police car an accident? Was this all tied in to the fact that a guy in the gym kept looking out the window?

What is happening?! When will someone tell me?

And I'm supposed to sleep tonight?

Later ...

I took a bath.

Now I'm afraid.

I had considered staying dressed so I'd be ready if something happened. I was afraid to go down to the basement to do a load of laundry. I was afraid of noises and kept checking to make sure it was Buckley I was hearing. I turned on lots of lights and cocked my gun.

The look on his face, where I've seen it before. It was the look a cat gets when it's cornered its prey and is about to pounce. Not evil, not deranged, not lascivious, only focused and <u>ready</u>.

Was he hired by someone? By Psycho? Or was he extorting money from Dirk and failed? (I hope Dirk is not giving in to such tricks, paying people.) (Naw...)

He had stepped quickly toward her, raising both arms.

Of course. That's how you stab someone. With two hands. You'd use one arm to give force to the attacking arm. He knew how to do it correctly. Practiced?

He had dashed in on her, suddenly. But at the final instant, when he had stood over Lara with his arms raised high over his head, one fist clenched around something, a spotlight suddenly appeared. It shone on them as if they were on a stage. A car! That's right! The car had pulled onto the street and its headlights lit the scene. The man had frozen, squinted toward the lights, then smoothly changed direction.

It came back to me.

It all happened so fast.

When the lights of the police car shone on him he had his arms raised, ready to strike.

So then, the lights. He flinched, squinted into the light, still thinking, not startled. Oh God. He adjusted his pace, and I slid into my car and locked the door. It was his intent to stab me. My face? My shoulder, to show Dirk he was serious but...

It's all so awful. How sickening that this is where my thoughts all go.

He wanted to kill me.

Now I'll take my gun <u>with</u> me. Walking the dog. At the gym.

Hired. The look on his face was that of someone doing a job. Payday. Well, next time I'll be ready. Did the guys in the window see it all? Did they get him? Or,

Or was it all staged.

But it can't have been. I'm the unpredictable one. They can't know what I'll do. They couldn't stage something when they never know my direction.

He was going to use two hands. His stance, he's done this before. Too cool, too poised. He knows how to attack people. And no fear that I was staring him down, that I could maybe fight him. No fear. A man at work. Do the job, get the paycheck.

The next morning, Lara stared dumbly at the computer terminal. "ITV error value +2928.32—input PAMT023 error 42." Error report.

A man's profile appeared in her mind, lit up. Lara's shoulders rose and tightened; she unconsciously leaned in and gripped the edge of her desk.

She couldn't do this today. That near-miss last night was too much to absorb. Next to a row of black technical manuals, her small clock showed 9:30 a.m. One hour had passed and she was only a quarter done with this routine audit in front of her. She couldn't block the picture—now seared into her brain by the bright headlights—from flashing onto the screen of her mind. A surreal sick sense that something terrible was happening still gripped her, and her psyche was slowly leaking more of the memories from the previous night. She dug into her desk drawer for the herbal anti-depressants she now kept with her instant coffee and rice cakes. She popped an extra pill into her mouth, then brought up email.

Subj: Vacation half-day
Date: 05/05/2000 9:34:34 AM Central Daylight Time
From: lmckeon@genins.com
To: clenstett@genins.com

Cheryl, may I take ½ a vacation day today?

Send. She returned to her report, confident that her boss would trust Lara to have her work covered, and would agree to the short-notice time off.

What terrible timing; Lara was having a party on Saturday! But it was good to have something else to focus on.

She left work and drove to a grocery store she seldom visited.

Wandering the aisles, she was still unable to shake a woozy feeling, a detachment from everything around her. She knew she needed party foods: a case of soda, tortilla chips, chocolates, mints, wine. There were few people in the store and she was grateful; she couldn't tolerate anyone near her.

Lara moved her body to the checkout area and pushed her cart into line. She looked absently toward the front of the store, then realized she recognized the man who was pacing with a phone to his ear. She'd seen him around town—in a theatre parking lot and when Nicole and she shopped downtown. He was the good-looking man in the small red car who pulled a newspaper up to cover his face every time Lara looked toward him. She'd guessed he was the head shadow. If he was, today he was having one heck of a fight with the boss. He wasn't shouting, but he gestured widely with his free arm, paced, and spoke urgently into the phone. He waved an arm toward Lara and suddenly looked up to see her watching him. He immediately marched outside.

Damn. What a mess. Something definitely went wrong last night. But she didn't want people to lose their jobs over her. Of course, they wouldn't *have* those jobs if she wasn't in this mess. But no one wanted this to be happening, for Dirk Durmont to be spending so much money to keep his crazy stalkers from hurting innocent people.

It was all too much to think about. So she wouldn't. Lara dug out her errand list and studied it.

She needed flowers for her porch planters. Red and white. What were those flowers she liked? Petunias or geraniums or peraniums or something. The garden staff should know.

She loaded her groceries and drove on to Discount City. In the outdoors section, Lara let herself drift, sniffing in the musty smells and enjoying blossoms the colors of kindergarten crayons. She found flowers that required only partial sun and little water. Perfect. But as she pulled at the plastic to tear a cup from its greenhouse family, it ripped, exposing the fragile roots of one vulnerable plant. Lara gasped. She rushed to piece together the broken cup and pat dirt back over the skinny raw roots. Then she gently put the plant in her cart and nestled it against the others. Safe again.

She took a deep breath and pulled backward into the main aisle.

A man stepped into the aisle ahead of her at the same time and stopped when he saw her. He was wearing a dress shirt and dark slacks.

Lara had learned to watch for these inconsistencies—he was not dressed for garden shopping. He had fixed his eyes on her chest, but when he saw her eyeing him he looked away with an embarrassed expression. Not a jerk. A shadow? If so, his was a new face. Dark-haired, with intense eyes. Could they have switched shadow companies so quickly? Or was he another killer? Or maybe a normal guy? How, how, how would she ever know the difference anymore?

She pushed her cart into the line at the cash register. Immediately, she felt a presence near her shoulder. Her breath became shallow and panic gripped her. She forced her motions to remain slow and controlled, and turned to look behind her. A man stood near her back. This one was also wearing business clothes. Fighting to appear calm, she pushed her cart out of line and walked toward the potted bushes. Her right hand flew to her shoulders, which were now hunched up with tension. She forced her hand down and gripped the handle of her cart.

Lara became aware of her heavy purse digging into her shoulder and tried to feel comfort that she could defend herself. But if someone came up behind her to stab her, she couldn't get a gun out in time to save herself! And anyplace she went, people could come up to her, come up to her and do who-knows-what.

A large man in a t-shirt walked toward her.

Lara yanked the cart to put it between them. He passed. Her inhale was a gasp, and she realized she had been holding her breath.

—⁓—

Subj: What the hell
Date: 05/05/2000 09:04:19 PM Central Daylight Time
From: Beauty1@mail.com
To: DirkDolls@mail.com

So here's what I know. Some guy tried to stab Lara and missed! Darn the luck. Do you think he could be convinced to finish the job?

Just kidding. Right.

We don't know who it was, but we'll find out. Some bodyguard watched the whole thing out the window, but they shut him up real quick.

Back to you soon. Let us know if you hear anything. Did any of us do it? Promotion to Queen for that one! Just kidding. Right.

\--

\--

Subj: What the HECK
Date: 05/05/2000 09:31:30 PM Central Daylight Time
From: SexIsMe@mail.com
To: DirkDolls@mail.com

It was some guy named Wasp. Guess he has a big stinger, LOL. Anyone know a Wasp?

\--

Brittany spun the chair around and faced Michelle.

"You put him up to this," she said, looking like a school principal, mad as hell. Where did *she* get off?

"You don't know that." Michelle knew she was covered, that Mark wouldn't be stupid enough to tell anyone what he did. Especially since he'd botched it like a fool.

"Where is he now?"

The two were in Michelle's bedroom. Brittany had stormed in like she owned the place, jumping on the computer, spitting mad. She said she'd had some guy over, some boyfriend, and the instant messages on her computer started pinging so steady she had to look. She read a few notes and headed straight to Michelle's house.

"Where is who?" Michelle didn't like Brittany's tone. She would really have to drop her now.

"You know who. Mark."

"How the hell should I know? I don't need him tonight for nothing, so I sure as hell don't care where he is." And she sure as hell did not need to defend herself to anybody. "Why should you care?"

"Do you ever care about anyone, Michelle?" Brittany looked at her straight on. "What did you think you'd gain from this?"

Michelle had had enough of her mouth. "This is boring. Everyone knows that Lara is a trouble-maker, always in the way, and Dirk wants her gone too, everyone knows that. She's nothing but a big pain in the ass! Besides, nothing happened."

"It's not only this attack thing. What are you going to gain from *all* this? Hell, Michelle, we graduate from high school next month. What are you going to do then?"

"The Dolls got jobs in Granville. They'll fix me up."

"Jobs? As strippers? Is that what you want?"

"Money's good." Michelle took a drag on her cigarette and glared at Brittany. "Listen, it's nothing to you, anyway. You're getting way boring. We don't want you in. And here's news for you, I am so in."

"According to *you*! You think I believe those stories you're telling about you and Dirk?"

Michelle narrowed her eyes. "Maybe you can take your boring Dirk-less ass home now."

"Yeah, I need to call Jake and apologize for taking off so fast."

"Jake?"

"Jake. The guy I've been dating for a year and a half. A real guy who loves me and takes me around places. We're going to California and finding a beauty school for me out there."

"Jake who?"

Brittany laughed. "It doesn't matter. You wouldn't remember anyway. Just know that I'm going on to do something with myself, and you're … what, being a prostitute?"

Michelle was way pissed off now, but she kept her voice cold. "We are not prostitutes."

"Oh, right. You don't get paid!" Brittany laughed again.

"Get out now."

"No problem, I'm going. But think, Michelle. What are you heading for? Being a professional groupie and a stripper? Or do you actually think you'll be the one Dirk marries?"

"It could happen."

"Don't fool yourself! You'll see the one he marries. It'll be Carrie Jo, the woman he's dating, really dating. He'll marry her and she'll help him with his career. He won't end up with some hill girl who puts out for anyone. Hollywood has enough of them, if it's anything like Granville."

Brittany turned back to the computer, then clicked on the screen a few times until it went black. "Oops!" She grinned, picked up her purse, and went to the door. She stopped and looked back.

"Michelle, when you get bored with waiting around here for something real to happen to you, look me up at my spa in California. I'm calling it 'Just Brit's'."

Michelle smirked a smile.

Brittany walked out, then stuck her head back in.

"One more thing," she said.

Michelle looked up.

"Don't do this to Delta. Keep her out of it."

"Delta can take care of herself!" Michelle snarled back.

"You don't believe that," Brittany said, and left.

———ᘞᘞᘞ———

Another set of headlights appeared, from a distance looking like cat's eyes in the night. Delta took a long drag on her cigarette and held it in until a black SUV crawled past the trailer. It made a loop to turn around, then went back down the road. That was the third black SUV she'd seen since she'd been waiting out here.

The dark became thick again, and the air more still. Nature seemed to be stopped and listening, sitting as quiet as Delta as she watched the road. Five cigarette butts surrounded her on the ground in front of the old floral sofa. Her floppy-eared dog slept at the far end of the couch, settling for the armrest after his mistress had pushed him away from her lap.

The front door creaked and a rectangle of light shone on the dirt. Her mother leaned out to see if Delta was where she'd left her, then propped herself against the doorframe.

"He'll be back soon." Ma sucked on a cigarette and blew smoke out of her mouth with a lippy noise. "But it ain't like him to not come home without telling us."

Delta wished she'd shut up that worry talk. It was like wishing bad on him.

"Where do you think he is, Ma?" Delta studied the red glow at the end of the white stick in her hand. Mark had been so funny lately, talking about how she should go stay with Gramma if he wasn't around and go on to beauty school to learn fingernails. And he'd sworn her to secrecy, calling out the blood vow they'd made when they were too young even for smoking. Then he'd shown her a metal box buried behind the old house; it held paper-clipped bundles of twenty-dollar bills zipped tight in plastic bags. He and she were like pirates with a hidden treasure.

But it didn't mean anything if he didn't come home.

Delta took a drag from her cigarette, then continued. "Some of his friends don't seem like nice people. Even the sheriff worries about him."

"The sheriff?"

"Yeah. He comes around asking about him sometimes."

"And what does he want?"

"Only to take a walk in the woods and around the hills, that's all."

Ma's voice turned hard. "You don't be telling nothing to anyone in uniform, you hear?"

Delta looked up to study her mother's face. Had she done something wrong? But Ma was staring out into the dark with spacey non-seeing eyes, so it didn't seem too bad.

They were silent for a few minutes. Then her mother spoke.

"Well, you don't be sitting out here too late. Tomorrow's a school day."

"Tomorrow's Sunday, Ma."

"Yeah, whatever. If he doesn't show up tomorrow, we'll start asking around, okay?" She closed the door but put some mighty force behind it. The loud bang it made was like a gun going off. Delta and the dog jumped.

CHAPTER EIGHTEEN

Lara's demons set up house in her head, but she knew how to handle that.

She stayed frenetically busy.

She set out to have her porch party on Saturday as planned. She planted flowers, baked cookies, cut up fresh vegetables, and filled bowls with candy. On Saturday, she vacuumed and swept and polished, then filled a copper bucket with ice and three bottles of wine.

Blessedly, her friends knew her routines and started drifting in at the official starting time. They brought food and chairs and found the drinks and utensils they needed to enjoy themselves. The party was a success in Lara's tired eyes. She enjoyed the company of all these nice people who were unlikely to attack anybody, especially the hostess. She stayed mostly inside, and when outside, positioned herself so a porch post guarded her from the vehicles that cruised past.

The next day, Lara packed her gym bag with a radio, weight-lifting gloves, a towel, and a pistol. She'd been distracted by the murder attempt, but her body craved exercise and these people would not steal her work-outs from her. They would not win!

And she would not disappear from the gym as if something had happened.

She drove to downtown Granville, parked behind Brandt's Gym, then pushed through the front doors of the old building, her jaw clenched. There were no crowds in the lobby, only a few men in sweats. She walked upstairs and easily found an empty treadmill. As she paced along to her headphone music, she watched out the window to the street below. Alert now, she noticed which vehicles passed by more than once and which paused in the street where Lara knew she could be seen in the upstairs window.

She was waiting for an old dark-blue car.

Suddenly, a large white truck pulled up and stopped still in the street. She stiffened. Lara glared at the driver hidden behind the darkened windshield and raised her chin a little higher. Did he think *she* would run away from any of this? She flung the sharp thought out through the window into the head of the driver of the truck. The vehicle paused a minute longer, then slowly moved away.

Half an hour later, Lara had worked her way to the crossover bars. She would do light weights today; it was all so exhausting, her life. But as she counted the reps, she heard two men at a bench near her.

"Yeah, it shocked me!"

The other murmured some reply.

"I knew him in high school. We called him 'Wasp'. I never figured him for someone who could do something like that!"

Lara looked into the mirror and scouted the room. They were the only people there. The young man who spoke looked familiar. Wasn't he one of the guys in the gym on Thursday, the night of the attack? So he had seen it all from that window, where he'd hovered that night. And he knew the attacker. Wasp. And now he would gossip about it and everyone would get excited about the story.

And no one would help her. Lara sunk down to pick up her heavy bag and walked out.

5-8-00 Monday

Talk about major PTSD <u>now</u>. I can hardly work, can't think, can't focus. Flashbacks, flashbacks.

I called Steve about setting up a will for me. I got his answering machine.

It was a miracle I was saved that night. I don't remember getting into my car. The lights, his face, his stance (he moved so quickly into attack mode, so fast) and the next thing I remembered, I was sitting in my car, locking my door. It was God's hand.

Description: Lean, skinny, not a bad face, even good-looking. Baseball cap (white?!), grungy greasy-looking big gray t-shirt with a "3" on the back. Dark eyes, dark curly hair, what I could see showing out of the cap. Tall-ish, 5'-11", 6'?

And no one will tell me what is going on.

I'm convinced that, for Dirk to attract so much evil, he must, in his heart of hearts, be a very good man. I pray that he be protected from evil—physically, mentally, morally.

I need a more convenient gun. My semi-automatic requires me to chamber it, taking muscle and focus and coordination. I went to Bass Pro Shop and a nice man shopping there told me I need a .38 Special (or .357), double-action (you can just press the trigger and it'll shoot) revolver. Now I need to find a place that sells them.

They found a dead body yesterday and I hoped it was the attacker. Then I saw the picture and it wasn't, and I was disappointed. God forgive me.

I want to find this Web site a radio DJ talked about. It lists people subscribers want killed. Am I on a list?

Some guy got severely beaten up by 15 men this weekend. I hope it's him. His name was in the paper, so I'll try to find his high school yearbook picture in the library. I called the hospital so I could go look at him, but he'd already checked out.

If it wasn't him, where is he? Now that I can ID him, where is he? Concerned about finishing the job? By sneaking up behind me. Which was the plan to begin with, to get me while I was getting into my car.

Stab me in the back.

Kill me, I guess.

—◊◊◊—

Delta saw him first. She ran toward him like a wild little animal seeking safety, but when he saw her coming he turned his back.

"Mark! Mark!" By the time she'd reached the edge of the school parking lot, he was slipping around the back of an abandoned bus garage. She followed, and saw him climb into his car. She ran to the passenger door, then stopped. He'd slid away from the driver's seat and sat hunched in the middle. She opened the door and leaned in as Michelle, Stacy, and Brittany gathered behind her.

"Delta, don't look too close, I ain't feeling too good right now." His head was down and he held one hand up along his face, guarding him from the girls now peering through the windows. "I'm glad you been making it to school. Ma taking you?"

Delta felt silly with relief. "Where've you been? Geez … me and Ma been worried sick. And when I sit outside waiting for you some big black funeral-looking thing comes crawling by, 'bout giving me the creeps. Do you know them folks? Tell them to stay away if they can't come up to the door like normal."

She stopped talking when he dropped his head back on the seat, inhaled deep, and rolled his eyes. He had a bruise along one jaw, but a few days beard growth was beginning to disguise it. But something else was different. Like after that time he spent in jail. He could shut out everyone and get real hateful, and Delta knew he was doing that now. She sniffed big; his clothes were dirty and he hadn't showered for a while. "Mark, let's get on home and ..."

"Delta, I need you to do some stuff. I need you to drive me home so I can get my bike. Is it still there?"

She nodded slowly. Where else would it be? "Yeah, sure, Mark. I wouldn't take your Harley."

"I know that, Delta, not you." He sighed. "You can drive this car home and you keep the keys. It's yours for awhile. You'll need it for that beauty school, anyway."

Delta's face grew sad. "Mark! What are you talking about?"

"You can drive this, and you will take it to beauty school and learn fingernails like we planned."

She nodded and he glanced at her. Delta saw his right eye was kinda torn and runny.

"But first." He breathed deep again. And again. He looked like he was in slow motion, like someone had dumped water on the fire that kept his engine going. Delta waited, but he didn't speak.

"Are you sick? Do you want me to call Ma?" she asked.

"No! I'll be okay. I'm taking a little vacation, is all. I'll be gone awhile." He sat up straighter. "Okay. Tell that bitch Michelle to come in here a minute. Tell her ... you listening?" Delta nodded slowly as he glanced toward her. "Tell her to come in here a minute and she is not to open her mouth. She is not to say one thing to me, not one thing, or I will kill her and she knows I can do *that*." He emphasized the last word, as if he was having a run of bad luck but he was happy to find something he could do so easy as snuffing her best friend. "Tell her she is nothing to certain people and that I got big bosses who don't care shit if some hillbilly tramp in Rockton lives or dies."

Delta stood straight and almost bumped heads with Michelle, who was close at her shoulder.

"I heard him," Michelle said sharply, then shoved past her and climbed into the car.

In a few minutes, she sent Stacy to fetch her car. After Mark climbed out of his car, she directed Delta and the other girls into it. When they saw his face, they all got spooked looks, but no one said anything. Then Brittany drove them in the Chrysler on a roundabout tour through the hills while Michelle took off with Mark hidden in the small back seat of her car.

———

If a man stood six feet tall, his heart would be—there! Lara drew a circle up and to the right of the bull's-eye. The green marker squeaked and she cringed at the noise. She faced the target, now mounted 20 feet out from the shooting booth. A 10-foot distance was more practical, but didn't it stand to reason that if she got good at hitting someone—not "someone", it was only a target, right?—at 20 feet, she'd be able to manage 10 feet?

She put her hand over her heart and eyed the circle. Perfect. She'd heard in a movie to aim for the center to have a better chance of hitting something. The torso was also home to several vulnerable spots. Hit one of those spots and the attack ended. It was the most logical place to aim. This green ink was her second choice of colors. At first she'd picked out a cherry-red marker from her box of Christmas crafts, then decided red was way too obvious for a heart target. Using green was much more civilized.

She walked back around to her station and waited for the go-ahead announcement on the intercom. She loaded two clips for the gun and jammed one into place.

Suddenly a loud boom sounded.

Lara's body jerked and her shoulders hunched up. Headphones covered her ears into which she'd jammed rubbery plugs, but there wasn't enough protection to escape the shock. She forced a deep breath, then sat and pressed the handle of her gun against the table to steady it. Another loud blast, but this time she was tensed in advance for it. A man with a black rifle was stationed in a nearby booth. She had noticed him as she walked by and had shuddered. He wasn't a hunter wearing jeans or cammies. This man with the polished rifle and telescopic lens looked well-groomed and sophisticated in his clean black shirt and trousers, his dark hair slicked back with a touch of gel.

What or whom was he intending to shoot?

His weapon blasted again, deep and cannon-like, and Lara's body jerked. She straightened, picked up her pistol in her right hand, and steadied it with her left.

Blam!

Her target showed a fresh hole, an inch below her green circle. Good. She shot again, then set the gun down and practiced picking it up and shooting two consecutive shots at the torso she pictured twenty feet in front of her. She once more raised the weapon to aim. A chill gripped her spine and she forgot everything except that she had an enemy.

Blam, blam! Two new holes appeared near the green circle. She grinned.

Several minutes later, a speaker crackled.

"Cease shooting. You may all cease shooting. Unload your weapons and leave them with the chambers open in your booths. When you are finished, step away from the booth."

Lara retrieved her paper target and set up a new one, drawing in another green circle. Back at her booth, she spread out the tattered page. She knew she'd fired off 55 bullets. She counted the holes. 54!

"Score! I do believe I have a knack for this stuff." She smiled at the target.

Soon the range resumed shooting. Lara practiced standing, then sitting, in different spots in her booth, quick-drawing the target. Finally her hand tired and she fired and missed the target completely. She cursed to herself.

The sound of men's voices nearby startled her. She peeked around and saw that the two men who had set up in the booth next to hers were now standing behind her, watching her. She rolled her eyes and shot toward the target.

"She isn't getting near the bull's-eye at all!" one said.

The other man defended her with, "She just took his f-ing head off!"

Ah, he'd noticed; she wasn't aiming for the bull's-eye. Lara was tempted to speak up out of pride in her marksmanship, but kept quiet.

"He drove her to it."

He *what*? She put her gun down and breathed deeply, exasperated. He drove her to it. Odd. Drove her to what? Owning a gun, or learning how to use it? And which "he" were they referring to? The famous guy or the knife guy? And must they aggravate her while she was holding a loaded gun? Fools! She resumed practicing, but watched the men's reflection in her eyeglass lens.

After a few minutes, she turned her head to the side, speaking to them without looking. "You're making me nervous, standing behind me like that." She gestured wide with her free arm. "Would you move away, please?" Here she was with this gun in her hand, and they were irritating her.

They moved back a few paces, and one of the men went back to their booth. The other, however, stubbornly kept his place nearby.

Lara stood still, controlling her breathing while her gun pointed down at her side. Her face grew hot as her anger rose.

Suddenly, another man's voice startled her and she gripped the gun tighter until his words registered. "Don't stand behind her like that. You're making her nervous," he said. Lara looked around and saw that an employee of the range had appeared.

Both men moved away, but the ranger stood a safe distance back, guarding the space behind her.

Lara pulled her gun up and fired. She slowly smiled as she noticed the small hole, fresh, in the center of the heart.

—◊◊◊—

Stacy reached over and grabbed Delta's hand. Delta jumped a little, then giggled.

"Can you believe this? I am so excited!" Stacy bounced in her metal fold-up seat and smiled wide while Delta watched, trying to figure out what she was supposed to do. She eyed the black hat with the big flat diamond top, amazed that this goofy thing was a sign they were finally smart enough. Delta hoped the billowy black robe looked better on her than it did on Stacy.

"This is real different, I'm sure of that!" She had promised Gramma she would do this graduation ceremony and had let her order the robe and strange hat. This whole high school mess would soon be over! They'd worked hard, her and Gramma.

And Mark. No one knew how much he'd pushed her to get done with school, to not be making the same mistakes he had. But now today he was nowhere in sight. He might not even know she was here dressed up like a choir member from TV church, being grinned at by grownups who were excited for some unknown reason that didn't involve drinking or sex.

The principal Mr. Sanders started calling out names and handing each student a thin black book, like they'd practiced last week. Delta imagined she could balance that thing on her flat hat, but she was too nervous to try. There were only three short rows of black robes on the Rockton High football field today. It was a small class to begin with, and had gotten smaller each year what with pregnancies and dropouts and jail. A handful of them who'd made it through hadn't bothered to come today. Michelle and Brittany skipped out on the ceremony, but they'd all celebrate tomorrow night at the big party at the lake.

"Lindsay Dalton." Mr. Sanders didn't use a microphone, the crowd was so small.

Delta watched as the cheerleader turned and waved at the audience, then walked up to the platform, swinging her long shiny hair as she moved. Delta knew she was going to the state university next fall and that she gave blow jobs to the football coach.

"Tommy Johnson."

A tall sandy-haired boy stood and said loudly, "It's 'Tom'!" then sat down again. The crowd began to applaud, but the clapping slowed and became a murmur of confusion. Mr. Sanders waited with a smile and a black book, then noticed Tommy wasn't leaving his seat. He stared, then repeated, "Tommy … uh… that's Tom Johnson." The boy stood and the crowd clapped with renewed energy as he walked to the front to receive his diploma.

Stacy and Delta were almost alphabet twins today—McNought and Morris. Almost. Buddy Minion had to move over one, and he did so without much fuss.

Mr. Sanders summoned Betsy Lamont.

Delta almost couldn't hear him over her own pounding heart when he announced "Delta McNought."

She stood, suddenly tearful. She heard clapping, but didn't trust herself to look at anyone. Why was she feeling so silly and sad and excited over this goofy black thing that might have been a painted old copy of Snow White for all she could tell? She focused on moving her feet as she walked. It seemed she'd gone a mile before she was standing next to Mr. Sanders. He handed her the diploma with one hand and shook her hand with the other.

"Congratulations, trooper!" he said warmly, looking her right in the eye, and Delta bit her lips to pain her some so her teary eyes wouldn't give her away.

Then, to make it all impossible, as she stepped off the platform she heard a piercing whistle. There beyond the far goal post, she saw sunlight gleam off a shiny motorcycle, and there was Mark waving one arm. It was all she could do to keep walking, blind as she was to her seat but finding it through her tears.

"I will sure as shit be glad when this is over," she said as she sat, but Stacy was gone to the front already and didn't hear.

"Note—Clothing optional."

Michelle crumpled up the flyer and threw it out her car window into the night. She'd read the party announcement to her friends but didn't let on about the nudity thing. Not that it would embarrass her to be naked on Rocko's party barge, but she knew Brittany's and Delta's bodies would get more attention than hers, and Stacy would refuse to take anything off and make them all look strange.

That's it, that's what she'd do. She'd pretend she didn't want Stacy to feel uncomfortable so she was keeping her clothes on out of goodness. She'd pull a Lara Church-lady on them.

They followed a red sports car as it wound toward the lake. When it pulled onto the grass and stopped, Michelle parked beside it. She saw a woman with big tits in a tiny bikini top climb out and look around. What was her name? Alice, that's right. She danced at Rocko's and Michelle was pretty sure they were going to let her, too. She hoped keeping her clothes on tonight wouldn't make them not want her. There were other things she could do to show them she wasn't shy.

As they stepped out of the car, Michelle shouted to Alice, who was rushing ahead toward the lights and music. "Hey!"

Alice looked all around her. She was a strange one alright. But she sure knew how to get the dope on Dirk. Handy that way, but way strange. Alice in loolooland.

"Back here!" Michelle called out. "Where else would we be?" She laughed, and Alice turned around to face them as they walked toward her. "Which one of the guys does the hiring? For dancing at Rocko's?"

Alice nodded, said nothing, then pointed to the barge. She turned and hurried away.

"Well that's real helpful!" Michelle snorted at her friends as they moved toward the lights.

A muscular man with a tan showing out of his white shirt helped them step from the dock onto the boat. An engine hummed and party lights shone an array of colors onto the many made-up, and fewer whiskered, faces. The smells of cigarettes and belched beer dominated the odor of stale fishy lake water. Heavy beat music boomed out and a sloppily drunk woman wiggled her fleshy butt in time to the song. Several middle-aged men stood around her, smoking and laughing as they leered.

"Clothing optional, ladies," the shirted man said.

"Don't hold your breath," Brittany snapped at him.

"What if we want to get naked, Brit!" Michelle pretended outrage.

"Suit yourself, then, but I know you won't show your stuff to *no* one unless you're getting something out of it."

Michelle laughed, then led them to the beer keg where she spied Connie waiting in line with a plastic cup. She wanted to get along with Brittany tonight. She and that boyfriend were leaving for California soon and who knows how long it'd be before she got back. Or before Michelle got out there with her. And with Dirk. There was definitely a Plan B to decide on. What if she didn't hook The Dirkman in Granville? He did have that house in Los Angeles and that's right where she'd head.

Several beers later, they were leaning against the rail, high and laughing at a chunky young girl who was rubbing the crotch of the man who stood guard over the entry gangplank. He grinned down at her but kept his head moving in a side-to-side refusal, even as he reached up and grabbed her breast.

"So. Are you going to try to get a job at Rocko's now that school's over?" Connie asked Michelle.

Michelle smiled big. Connie wasn't an idiot, or else Blair had filled her in on how to get ahead in this town. "Yeah. I will soon be an official dancer at Rocko's Club for Men. They pay great, and I'll get lots of tips. I'm gonna find an apartment like Blair's. Maybe I'll look in her building. Lots of the dancers live there."

"What about you, Delta?"

"I might dance," Delta said. No one paid attention to Michelle's scowl. "But Gramma wants me to go to beauty school and do fingernails. Brittany, too." Delta held out her multi-colored fingertips and wiggled them. "She wants me to learn fingernails and go out and work for her when she opens her place. She's calling it 'Just Brit's'. Cool name, huh?"

Michelle narrowed her eyes. Her head hurt; too much conversation. So Delta was thinking she wasn't going to strip? Michelle would be relieved if she stayed away from her business—especially with all the attention that booby dumb blonde stuff got her—but she hadn't decided if she needed her around or not.

She squinted from the throb behind her eyes. "Does anyone have a joint?"

The girls around her shook their heads.

"Just when I could use a dealer!" Michelle laughed. "Speaking of which. I wonder what old Lara's up to lately? Like hiding under the bed waiting for the next attack?"

"Not hardly." Connie looked over and stared at Michelle as she spoke. "I heard she's going around like nothing happened. Like maybe it's only another story someone made up."

"Oh, it happened. At least, the part where someone tried to kill her. But maybe she's used to it, in her line of work."

"I did hear she bought a gun. And is a good shot, from what Tony's friend Sam says. They say she practices out at the range in Argent, and does okay."

Michelle forced out a loud laugh. "So she's surrounding herself with weapons and bombs! We got her running now!"

"What do you mean 'we'?" Connie was really no dummy.

"Well, Dirk Dolls, listen up," Michelle said. "We are not all just talkers around here. Some of us are taking action about getting this L-whore bitch out of our picture and out of our man's pants."

Stacy squealed. "What did you do! Ohmigod, are you about the murder attempt? Say it *is* so! It's like that cops show. Who done it? Our own Michelle!" Then she looked serious at her. "But who did it, for real?"

Brittany turned her back to them and looked out over the water.

Michelle leaned against the rail and grinned. "I do have friends, and lots of them are men."

"It's that married guy who sent you flowers!" Stacy was excited. "Who always thinks you're pregnant!"

Michelle shook her head and grinned.

"That Bob guy at the liquor store!" Stacy said.

"Hell, no. He won't even let me swipe a six-pack!"

191

Connie interrupted. "You are kidding, aren't you? You read that DirkLetter, didn't you? Karen said that Shirl said to leave Lara alone, like for real. You never know when she's going to pull out a gun and blast someone's head off!"

Michelle laughed again. "Well, I don't know how they're going to get the message out to everyone who's stalking her now. Every time we see her, there's a whole gang of hags and homos dogging her."

"Let's talk about something fun," Stacy said. "Let's decide who Dirk's going to marry."

Suddenly someone yanked Michelle's arm and she lurched to the side.

"Relax! For being so drunk, you're sure uptight!" A muscular man dressed only in skimpy swim trunks and tanned to a coffee brown pulled her a few feet away from Connie. "Rocko is getting a private party together on his boat, and wants you along." Blair was standing a few feet behind the man. Beside her was Alice, who was staring at everyone who walked by like they'd just stolen something from her.

Blair nodded at Michelle. This was her chance to get in with Rocko, the owner of the classiest dance club in Granville. A similar man—tall, muscled, tanned—was talking to Brittany, who rolled her eyes and walked away. That bitch! Was she going to ruin it for all of them? Not for Michelle, that was for sure.

She leaned into his chest, bit at his nipple, then looked up into his face.

"Sounds like fun."

She followed him toward the dock. Connie's voice drifted toward her, with "Where are they going?", then Brittany's, "Let's go on to your house, Connie. This party's over."

What bores. She knew Stacy wouldn't be invited to Rocko's boat, which left only one of her little army unaccounted for.

"Michelle! We get to go on that big yacht over there!"

Michelle turned to see Delta's excited face, now beside her. Damn.

—∿—

Suddenly Lara's brain was working again. She hadn't realized how foggy and distracted the attack had left her until one day there were a few hours without flashbacks and the sense that she was floating above her life. Then an entire day went by without dissociations. She went into the summer ready to fit the existence of this real killer into her activities. Buy gas, watch for killer, shop for groceries, watch for killer, use mall coupons, watch for killer.

Every strange man was now possibly one with a knife. None could stand behind her—it would be stupid to allow such vulnerability. At the gym, she requested that a trainer walk her to her car. She bought a kit to make out a will. When she left for work or errands, she was aware of how her house and underwear looked in case she ended up in a hospital or morgue. She carried a gun wherever she could without getting caught by a metal detector or risking harm to any children.

The crowd at the gym became increasingly strange and sinister; even the trainer commented on "the psychos." Her workouts turned as bizarre as the characters around her as she determined to keep exercising in spite of the danger. Time after time, men crept up to her back as she attempted squats or pull-downs. They would creep and Lara would turn to face them, and they would step back to their original positions, over and over, like a macabre dance. They would appear at the gym for a few days, watching and creeping, and then disappear.

She surmised that for so many men to want to hurt her, there must be a lot of cash involved. The reward couldn't be just sexual favors from some whorish women. Someone had a bounty on her, someone with money. Money! What else mattered to these people? But what did they intend to do? Did they think they could stab her and that would be the end of it? Lara knew it would take a great deal of injury to keep her from coming up swinging. These men would attack and run like the cowards they were, but Lara would chase them and fight them until she was unconscious.

And the person who hired them—or hired the one who hired them—what was her or his purpose? Did someone think they could run her out of town? Or scare her? Ha! It would take more than the threat of death to scare her, or to run her off. They had underestimated Lara's strength and tenacity.

She considered calling the police about the knife incident. But what would that accomplish, besides creating a report that the tabloid reporters could see? She didn't want to do that to Dirk. And she knew that when it came to her safety, she was better off relying on him than on the police. She worried about when he would pull his protection and the thought made her panic. But that was the goal; this had to end somehow. He couldn't keep pouring money into this; it was all wrong. How could Lara end the extortion and craziness? She didn't have any answers. If it was extortion, Dirk could not give them money! Where would it all end? After her, who? His family? Some little child somewhere? It couldn't be fed into or it would never stop.

Shadows still seemed to be around, but they were different somehow. There were now some burly types. But of course, now Lara had to consider that *they* might be out to kill her. They hadn't yet, so maybe they wouldn't, unless they just hadn't found the right time.

Which led her to a thought that haunted and sickened her.

She was in the middle of an incredible mess. She'd somehow embarrassed Dirk Durmont. She'd had a look at his lifestyle in Granville, was often face-to-face with women who'd apparently had some type of relationship with him. And now she was a witness to a murder attempt that hadn't succeeded. Her very existence was a problem for a man with so much money and power that it seemed people would do whatever he wanted.

What if he was the one who wanted her dead?

It was all so ugly.

But all Lara could do was pray and keep moving forward, to do the task in front of her. So she shopped and researched firearms and ordered a more convenient gun, a .357 three-inch barrel J-frame double-action revolver. She would not be a sitting duck again, so vulnerable to attack. She would be someone these people feared, just on her own, shadows or no shadows.

Dirk was working on a big project so she had been trying to be stable and not a distraction. This murder attempt was such bad timing!

Or was the timing intentional?

—◦◦◦—

The big blue car was following the Monte Carlo, and tailing it was a red truck. After that came a beige SUV with two guys with white hats.

Behind them all, Alice peered out from behind the wheel of her car. That guy in the blue car—what was he up to? The skinny one with dark hair. She was seeing him around a lot lately. She glanced out her rearview mirror and saw Levi's rusty red compact. No surprise. He must have a whole drawer full of photos of Dirk and Lara. That didn't bother

her any, as long as he didn't take pictures of Alice. Not while she was near Dirk, anyway.

That skinny guy was connected somehow to that shapeless blonde from hillbilly land; she'd seen them talking after work one night. That girl needed to buy herself some boobs. Rocko would take care of that; Alice heard he did that for the girls. Hillbilly girl hung out with the thin blonde with the real tits. Big, for being real. She wasn't so bad, and was being nice to her. Alice had taught her some dance moves at that party. Delta, that was the nice one's name.

But too many young chicks were racing around Granville trying to get Dirk.

And somehow this older one, Lara, had his attention. What was she doing to get him to follow her around like he did? Him and his little army. And all this time Lara was marching around with her nose up in the air like she was looking past them. But she saw what was going on, or she wouldn't be shooting so much at the range. That night when she almost got stabbed was a work night for Alice so she'd missed the whole thing. Damn the luck. Alice could have snuck in after that guy missed and gotten Lara herself when her guard was down. Damn.

Lately Dirk was giving her something to watch, though. All the girls were talking about his getting married and it looked like it was that TV show woman, that Carrie something. Alice didn't believe it for a minute. For being almost married to a woman in California, he was sure hanging around town an awful lot.

She knew what he wanted. He wanted to come right up to Alice after one of her best shows and give her a big kiss and ask her to marry him. Too shy, just too shy.

And too distracted by other women.

Well, that was something Alice could fix.

CHAPTER NINETEEN

Lara watched in the dark as Buckley panted, then sat. Summer's furnace was warming up and soon it would be too hot for him to walk with her. That would put her alone on these brutal streets of Granville.

Was the danger increasing? But what was worse than people wanting to kill her? Sinister characters popped up around her like spiders coming out of hiding holes. Just a few days earlier, Lara had let her stress over a family medical emergency distract her. When she'd left the hospital, two steps out into the night a small fierce man rushed toward her and thrust his face into hers. But at that instant, something behind Lara grabbed his attention. He glanced over her shoulder, then leered back at her and rasped out "Hi!" She lurched away, shocked, and the vicious man dashed off.

Now Lara let the dog rest a moment, then gently tugged at his leash.

"Come on, puppy. Are you going to make it?"

He stood and they moved farther down the sidewalk. Suddenly, Buckley turned and paced up a brick walk toward a two-story white house.

"That's not our house, doofus!" Lara pulled him back. He paused, then came back to her and walked on with her in tow.

Two houses farther along, he again veered toward a strange porch.

"Buckley, what are you doing?" Lara stopped, amazed. He knew this wasn't their house. Maybe he was tired, maybe his eyesight was worsening, but his nose and intuition never failed him.

A picture flashed across her mind, a lit-up image. *Watch for killer.*

She whirled around to look behind her.

There! A man was following them! He stopped as she stared. So Buckley had been leading her up to these houses, to safety. Was this man only some guy out walking? No. Buckley never reacted to harmless people, except to beg for a petting.

She tugged the leash and they hurried across the street. Once on the other side, Lara turned again. The man hadn't moved. She eyed him as she reached into her black bag and gripped the handle of her gun. Easy to grab, if she needed to.

They hurried home, watchful for trouble.

———~~~———

With the wavy blond hair, short dress, and barely-there makeup, Delta looked like a kid. She sat and giggled at her reflection. Rocko had said something about her being old enough to do it, but as young as they could get away with. And now she looked even younger! He'd like that.

The closet doors hung open and she walked over to stroke a big pink boa. Its feathery fingers fluttered with her movements. Once she and Michelle had come in here to play dress-up. This was her favorite piece, this fluffy thing. She'd worn it with a pink shiny gown and high spiky shoes with glitter straps. Those were sure funner shoes than these flat black things she was now wearing with cotton socks. That day, Alice had come in and shown them some dance moves. She was nice, Alice was. She said she was going to marry Dirk, but Michelle later told Delta she was nuts. Of course, everyone knew that Michelle planned to marry Dirk, or at least have his baby. That would be fun.

Life was fun now. Dancing and hanging out with her new friends sure beat going to high school and hanging out in Rockton. She still hadn't mustered the nerve to tell Gramma that she wasn't in beauty school. And Brittany was gone to California, so she didn't have to tell her nothing about not learning fingernails.

Michelle was letting her live in the apartment she'd found in Blair's building. She took Delta's paycheck and some of her tips and took out the rent, then put the rest in a bank account for her. And she had Delta following Lara around some, because the DirkLetter said Shirl didn't want to hear about them messing with Lara or "the deal was off." So they were being real careful about how many people were seen near her.

Mark still wanted her to follow Lara, too, to tell him where all she went and on what days. And Gramma liked Lara, so it made everyone happy that Delta followed her. She should learn how to copy her ways. Already this "natural" makeup was way what Lara would wear.

The work was easy—she stripped to music out there on the stage, then went out and partied with Rocko's friends after. And there was so much money, she couldn't believe it!

Gramma's face suddenly came into her head. She turned her back on the mirror. She couldn't tell her about beauty school and spending all the tuition money she'd sent her on shopping with Michelle. Maybe she shouldn't see her until she could tell her truthful things.

—⁓—

Michelle took off her bikini top and tossed it to one side, feeling like a movie star.

"We're not supposed to be topless out here, are we?" Stacy quickly sat upright on the poolside lounge chair and looked around.

Michelle laughed, then eyed the two young men who'd entered the pool area and were now steering toward her. They walked by the row of women and leered at Michelle's naked breasts. "Let the f-ing pool police come run me out if they don't like it. I live here now and I need a tan all over in my profession."

"What'd your mom say about your new job?" Stacy asked.

"Ha! You mean my op-por-tun-ity at the phone company? She's happy I'm settling down and getting retirement benefits!" Michelle snorted. She was so happy to be rid of Rockton. Forever.

Delta rolled over on her stomach and untied the thin strings of her pink bikini top. "Rocko wants me to stay pale, so I gotta cover up in a minute."

Stacy spoke up. "Lara uses a bunch of sunscreens to keep herself pale like Laura Starbright, but Carrie Jo gets a tan."

Connie spoke from where she lay next to Stacy. "Yeah, sunscreens. Lara gets this SPF 45 at Discount City." She sat up and looked across the pool. "There's Blair!" She turned to a slim dark-haired woman lying next to her, a new friend and Dirk Doll from TeleSales. "Nadine, look, there's the Blair I was talking about. She gets us into those parties." She waved big. "Blair! Hey!"

Blair had unfurled her towel onto the cement across the pool from them and next to a large muscular man. She looked up at the girls with a tight smile and wiggled her fingers in a stingy wave.

"Well. Why isn't she coming over here?" Stacy asked. "Like who the hell does she think she is?"

Michelle lifted her sunglasses and looked over at her. "That guy next to her drives a Lexus. She's been trying to get his attention all summer. I guess we're too much competition for her! I can see why she thinks that. Look at her thighs! Each one is two of ours." She laughed.

"I hear she's partying with Dirk Durmont," Connie said.

"Her and my pet hamster! That bitch is just so much talk," Michelle said, angry now. "He never mentions her to *me*, in any case."

Stacy's eyes got big. "Michelle! You said you were never supposed to talk about Dirk and you! It's his rule! And what about all that stuff going around about him getting married?"

Nadine sat up fast. "Michelle's doing Dirk? No way!"

Michelle grinned from where she lay. "I can't say a word. I am sworn to secrecy about what he and I do together."

Nadine squealed. "Just like Lara, keeping their love a secret!"

Michelle grit her teeth at the sound of the L-name. She looked over and saw that Blair was now lying on her back with her big tits bared. Copycat. The man next to her was raised up on an elbow checking her out.

Stacy swigged her diet soda and spoke. "I got an email from Brittany yesterday. She got into that beauty school, and Jake has a job. So right now she's probably on some real beach, like at the ocean."

Delta sat up, holding her bikini top over her breasts. "Did she ask about me? Michelle has our email on her computer. She says Britt emailed me once, but then forgot all about me."

Michelle watched as Stacy looked over at Delta. "Yeah, sure. She sounded like she'd just emailed you. Did you tell her you were dancing, 'cause she said you didn't sound right. And she had a funny message. She wanted me to ask you if you knew what some word meant. Let me think ... embezz ..."

Michelle interrupted. "Here come those two guys back again, looking us over. Stacy, talk them up and see if it's worth me giving them my number."

Stacy's usual motor mouth stalled. Michelle peered over at her, then noticed what had caught Stacy's attention. A white cargo van had pulled up to the pool fence and two men climbed out. Their skin shone with greasiness and sweat spots darkened the armpits of their open shirts. The muscular black man wore denim shorts and sandals, but the big white guy with stringy long brown hair had torn his dress slacks to make shorts. In spite of the summer heat, he wore heavy work boots with grayed white socks rolled down.

Nadine was watching them, too. "Class group you attract here. Look at that one guy's clothes! What a hunk!" She laughed.

"They give me the creeps. Do you guys know them?" Stacy asked.

"Are you Michelle?" The women were startled back to poolside by a man's voice. The two younger men who had walked by were now back. One of them was looking down at Stacy.

Michelle spoke. "You're definitely not seeing Michelle if you're looking at her." She grinned. "And it's Mikala, my name is now Mikala. Can I help you with something?"

He glanced at the women, then around the pool enclosure. "I heard you might fix us up with party supplies, so to speak."

Michelle opened her mouth to speak, then let it hang open. Everyone turned at the sound of heavy boots on cement. The two men from the van were marching toward them. She looked back up at the men seeking drugs. They looked squeaky-clean and scrawny next to the men walking up. "Hafta to get back to you with that one, boys."

But she needn't have said anything. When they saw the rough guys, the men hurried away.

Michelle lay back a minute as the two greasy characters stopped and leered at the women. Delta grabbed her cover-up and wrapped it tight around her shoulders. Michelle fought the urge to cover herself to avoid their stares. She sure as hell was used to men looking at her. What was it about these guys that gave her the creeps?

"You're blocking my sun, guys," she said.

The black man spoke while the booted man leered at them and chuckled to himself. "We heard you ladies might know a Mark McNought."

Michelle heard Delta gasp. She looked over at her with the meanest face she could muster, signaling that she should stay shut up. It must have worked, because she glanced at Michelle and pressed her lips tight.

But the men had seen the exchange. The one spoke again. "Don't go thinking you're hiding anything. We seen you around. Which one of you's his sister?"

The women sat silent. Michelle could smell their sweat and unwashed clothes. She had to think fast. Mark was still her best hope for getting rid of Lara and getting herself a millionaire boyfriend. He was worth keeping around.

Stacy started to speak. "What do you guys want with Del ..."

"You guys don't have any business with us," Michelle said in a rush, "so why don't you move on. Maybe we know Mr. McNought but we are not his keeper."

"Oh but you do have business with us," the thug-looking one with the raggedy clothes said. He moved to stand directly in front of them and laughed.

The black one spoke. He seemed to be the brains of the pair. "We have a message for McNought. We seem to have the same interests, but it is all ours now and we do not want to see him anywhere near it."

He paced along the row of women, staring down at them. They sat silent, breathing shallow through their fear. He stopped in front of Michelle. "Same with you ladies. You're running around where you're not wanted. You need to stay home and tend to your knitting. Understand?"

The women sat silent.

As if at a signal, both men grinned, then the grimy-haired one next to Delta lifted his heavy boot and kicked her pale thigh with it. Delta let out a short scream. She pulled her legs up and wrapped her arms around them.

He laughed. The few men in the pool enclosure turned at the sound of her screech, but they all stayed rooted where they were, looking tensed-up and bug-eyed like cats who'd just spotted a rottweiler.

He spoke again through gritted teeth, angry now. "You ladies get it?"

Michelle answered fast. "Yeah. Right. I suppose we can take up knitting." She grabbed a towel to cover herself.

"So we understand each other." Suddenly, the black guy looked around the parking lot and slapped the thug's arm. They turned and rushed away.

The girls sat speechless until they drove off. Then Stacy's words came running out so fast they almost tripped on each other. "What the hell was that about? Son of a bitch! Are you okay, Delta? What a couple of craz-ola creeps! Michelle, what were they talking about?" She went on, ranting about gangs and criminals and a murder last week in some other state.

Connie and Nadine surrounded Delta and checked out her leg. Everyone else around the pool stayed frozen in place.

Michelle forced herself to take a deep breath. She wouldn't let herself speak until her voice was steady. After a minute, she said, "I don't know what they were talking about. I don't know."

But she had an idea. The "business" they had with them. Who it was they were all running after.

Why did everything have to be about Lara? Why did she get all the attention?

———《》———

Alice bent over her notebook computer, steadying it as it wobbled on the motel bed.

Her hand shook as she tried to locate another celebrity gossip site. For an instant, she considered taking one of her old pills; so much wasn't making sense and now this latest was just crazy.

> "His publicist denies reports that Dirk Durmont is getting married. ... Friends say they'll be in Los Angeles for the 'fictitious' event. ... Family members are reportedly making travel arrangements. ... Three wedding planners claim involvement in a huge ceremony occurring ..."

"Ha! He's done with you now! And they're going to find you and arrest you."

Alice stood up and looked around the room. What was that shit about arresting her? She wasn't getting too close to him, anyone could see that. For all they knew, she was doing like they said—100 feet.

"Hell, no one's trying to arrest me. I need to call Mom and find out."

She walked to the phone and paused, looking down at it.

"Don't use that phone! They'll find you for sure, you fool."

She didn't need them to find her, especially if they were looking. But that part wasn't actually happening, right? The reality was that there was some type of wedding going on. But that couldn't be. It was just stories, gossip gone wild. And who cared where she was, anyway? She'd told the dance manager Reeza she was taking a couple of weeks off, so Rocko wouldn't be looking for her. Who knew or cared if she left Granville for a little while?

All the rumors—they made her head hurt and she had to find out for herself. Dirk couldn't be marrying that woman from the TV show when Alice was right there in Granville waiting for him. And she was close to getting rid of Lara, if the dark-haired skinny guy didn't do it first. Somehow things kept going wrong when either of them got close enough, past all those bodyguards. By now she knew which bodyguards were serious and which ones were there to pick up on women. It'd been so easy to distract them; she simply made sure the little "fans" knew where Lara was and all those slutty girls showed up to make out with the supposed security guys. Funny!

Several times Alice had gotten close to her. Then that woman had turned and looked right at her, or made a quick dodge to another direction, like she knew Alice was standing there.

But what were these stories about Carrie Jo Miller? She'd thought if she got rid of Lara, Dirk would be free to be with her.

She took a deep breath and looked in the mirror. He couldn't be marrying Carrie Jo. She was driving out to Los Angeles to make sure.

She'd fix that one, she would. Easy.

—⁓—

7-19-00 Wednesday
Journal,
On and on it goes.
I went to Merker's and got stalked by a particularly mouthy rudie. She had this hideous look on her face, like stalking me is cool, while I'm mostly repulsed and disgusted by all this. She told her friend she couldn't believe what I'm driving when I look like I do, when she has an old beater. I take it she was implying that all she got out of her fling or whatever was … a fling or whatever and I got a car. That this young woman should even think that that's how women get cars!

I'm so discouraged about Granville. I know I'm seeing its worst sides—these low-functioning, backwards people. But during a prayer session I got the directive "stay where you are." So I won't consider moving yet.

It's a circus at the gym. Exhausting. Always a new set of faces. One of the ironies is that I'm living in a town where the men who are looking at me are paid to do so or want to kill me! Sometimes

I have to remind myself that maybe some men are simply looking at me. Men do that!

But last week, this street person showed up. He was standing in front of the TV swinging weights around. He had long stringy brown hair, heavy work boots, shabby shorts; he might as well have had a "thug" sign on his back. That night, I had had it with people everywhere staring, staring—criminals and thugs. I went down and played racquetball awhile. Then I went up and could work out; the strange-o's had all gone.

Tonight Thug was there again. He made a point of coming over while I was doing chest expansions and checked out my face, ID-ing me. He wouldn't want to stab the wrong woman now, would he? I couldn't look him in the eye, darn it. Now I hardly know what he looks like. I didn't linger and went down to the racquetball courts. That Thug makes me nervous.

When I came back up to the weight room, he was gone.

Joe the trainer is quitting Brandt's Gym. Rats! I'll miss that he knows so much of the history of this "stuff." He knows about knife guy and he's commented about the weirdo rotation in the weight room. And he's a muscle guy, the type these cowards would fear. I had told him that the last time I used a locker someone had tried to break into it, that the door was all bent up. So the last time I mentioned going down to the locker room, he said, "You don't want to go down there, not now!" And we both knew what he meant, given all the problems I've had at the gym.

I'm head-tired from all the confusion. I must be looking very stupid, which is hard for me to take, although much of my ignorance is by choice. When I pray for guidance, which is often, I always get that I should live my life "normally." Now I see the wisdom in that. If I had let this change me, where would I be, now and when it all dies out? Thank God I have a spiritual base and a counseling degree; likely this won't make me crazy. I need to hang on to what is real—my life, my plans, my God. I'm planning a trip to France. It's something I've always wanted to do before I die. I checked out some French language tapes from the library.

I need more plans.

I'm going to New York City with Nicole in October. That should be neat.

My prayers today:
That Dirk doesn't get bored and exasperated with all this and do or say something that humiliates me.
That the rudies and killers will soften their hearts toward me. "Love is the answer." Let <u>them</u> love <u>me</u>.

———

Like a little girl, Lara dreamt up a pretend family. There were five children—three natural and two foster—and they were all kind and loving. They would revive this old orchard she was walking through and put a horse in the barn over there. The big stone house ahead of her had history, beauty, acreage, and was open for pre-auction tours this weekend.

Apparently, much of Granville was going to bid on it, or, like Lara, sought a free peek at a great house; the traffic on the remote farm road had been dense. The estate was easy to find—she simply followed the line of cars.

She now walked up wide steps to the stone porch that spanned the building. The house stood two stories high, with an attic Lara imagined loaded with trunks of vintage outfits in perfect condition except for a touch of dust for authenticity. She stepped into the foyer and swept her eyes up the grand staircase that curved to the second floor hall. What a great place, like a doll house grown up! People strung through the rooms, and Lara ignored them as she enjoyed her tour. But when she stood in a line slowly moving up the stairs, a light flashed. She turned and met the eyes of a woman holding a camera. Lara turned her back to her.

A man in the line was telling stories of being raised in the house, and she listened as he relived childhood games of hide-n-seek. The building didn't disappoint her; it was definitely fantasy material.

Later, outside again, Lara walked wide around the yard and headed toward the barn.

She stopped abruptly.

Dirk? Here? The tall lean man had suddenly turned his shoulder to her and bent over a cigarette in a familiar motion. He stood still, but was in her path to the barn.

Why did this keep happening?

Lara looked back at the house and pretended interest in an old window. Original glass, a crack in the lower right corner.

What should she do? He'd turned away so quickly, as if he was unhappy to see her, embarrassed. All these nutty women were causing her problems because of him; he probably *was* embarrassed. She must have surprised him, taken him off-guard. He was touring the house, and here she was, in *his* way, blocking him from getting in.

Unintentional, but how rude of her.

She changed direction and walked across the orchard to her car.

7-23-00 Sunday
Journal,

I'm so confused about Dirk Durmont. I have to assume that he wants me to stay away. Well, he's the one to decide that; it isn't as if his number is in the book. Mine is.

The house tour—that's the type of thing that bothers me. Can't he do tours without people harassing him? Duh! Haven't I learned by now how people limit him? But can't he go around okay in disguise? So couldn't he go <u>with</u> me, not around me? Here I am, so alone, and if he wants to hang out, can't we? But he would have to risk the gossip. Well, the gossip is all out there, what does it matter now? I don't think they could come up with much more, not that I know what they've come up with. Well, romance of course. That must be ticking the girlfriend off.

There seems to be a lot of activity lately. My "story": One of his officially deranged fans has been in town hiring people to stab me, but now there's a warrant out for her. People figure she's following me, so they're following me to catch her. And if she's that blonde I saw in the parking lot, she's mouthy, so she's telling everyone how she's going to kill me.

I'll do a bunny run at the south side Merker's tomorrow.

She wouldn't have a <u>gun</u>, would she?

———

"Tonight's the big night."

Lara tried to ignore the whispers. She knew Dirk was in town, carrying confusion with him as always. Now her workout was going okay, but there was an odd silence in the room. Until she overheard Joe's words.

"He's going to talk to her tonight. I can't wait," he continued.

The man next to him whispered something and the trainer replied, "He's downstairs right now."

Well, downstairs didn't put "him" any closer than he'd been already. Lara looked at the clock. Time to go home. He knew where to find her if he finally wanted to talk to her and help straighten this mess out.

Her number was in the book. And his wasn't.

CHAPTER TWENTY

The DJ's words, this announcement—Lara couldn't believe it! Her heart pounded. What were they saying?

Rain hit heavy and loud against her car roof; she turned up the volume. What awful thing was happening now? She stepped out of her car, forgetting to shield herself, letting her pant legs soak in the downpour as she walked into work.

How would she get through the day?

8-04-00 Friday

Dirk Durmont is getting married tomorrow.

Oh God, I hurt so bad and I don't even know why. I cry and cry, it won't stop.

If they had only announced their engagement, how different this would have been for me! Fewer psychos and rudies (none?), no murder attempt, no criminals. I've been so hurt and abused these months, and they could have prevented it! There have been all these criminals stalking me, but has anyone but me cared?

I hurt so bad. I need to keep the faith that God will fix this.

And I tried so hard to stay detached, to keep my heart out of all this—but it wore me down.

There is nothing to do but hurt tonight.

What now? What tomorrow?

How cruel, how callous, these people are, to let all these things happen to me and not tell me anything. Unless all the "talk" I've heard around me has been a way people have been trying to tell me things. Who was that woman talking about when she said, "It's sad. She's digging up all this stuff about her and showing it to him. Just out of jealousy." (It was said along with the body language. I don't think everything is about me. There is always body language.) Who is the one who is ruining me, the one ruining my life? Who could "dig up things about me"?

———⟋⟍⟋———

How dare she! She was holding back, Michelle knew she was. Trying to get him all for herself. Now look!

The door shook as she pounded harder.

The peephole darkened, then a chain rattled and Blair looked out the door. She stepped out and glanced up and down the hall, wearing only a push-up bra and thong panties.

"What, no sidekicks?" She was the tallest of the dancers, and big, leaning toward a fat fleshiness.

Today Michelle was especially happy that Delta was taking over as the most popular dancer at Rocko's, that Blair was losing her spot as queen stripper bee.

"You knew about this!" Michelle shouted, too angry to bother with her usual oiliness.

Blair opened the door wider and Michelle stepped in. The living room was still bare, like a model apartment for the complex. No pictures on the walls, no knickknacks setting out. The only decorative piece in the room was an ashtray on the coffee table. Next to it, a pack of Long Lady cigarettes spilt open. The room smelled of perfume sprayed over ashes.

She didn't need an explanation for Michelle's temper. "You heard as well as I did that he was telling everyone he wasn't getting married," she retorted.

"I thought you had an insider line!"

"Yeah, I thought so, too. But she's everyone's inside line, isn't she? That chick who works for him, that Shirl. Guess she's been lying to all of us."

"Shirl! With the short curly hair?" Michelle's anger was becoming fierce. "Yeah, I *guess* she lies. I know her. Whore! And that damned email letter said Carrie Jo was marrying him, but we believed Shirl."

"Shirl did not know, for real. I really believe her—she is so pissed. And she says she's so on our side, especially now."

"On our side, like how?"

"Like she wants Lara out. Everyone was watching *her* ass while they're planning weddings and shit we don't even know about. The Internet was right all along, and we're watching Dirk and Lara like it's some damned movie! But—we *were* watching Dirk, which is what we want no matter what Shirl wants."

"So where does all that leave us?" Michelle fumed.

Blair ignored her anger and spoke evenly. "Exactly where we always were. Why do you think he didn't tell us he was getting married?" She walked to the table, pulled out a cigarette and lit it.

Michelle glared at her. What the hell was she getting at?

"Because maybe it doesn't matter," Blair said. "He was here in town all summer! Obviously he still wants us around."

"But not for wife-shopping anymore!"

Blair narrowed her eyes at her, then looked away. "Okay, maybe we were all hoping. Maybe even Shirl!" She rolled her eyes. "But we need to face it—he married the one with the biggest PR, the big Hollywood story. But it's only his first marriage. There's time."

Michelle inhaled deep. "So you think he'll still be around?"

"Hell, maybe so. They'd been engaged all this time, but how much were they actually together?" Blair exhaled smoke at Michelle. "So ..."

Michelle stood still, waiting. After a minute, Blair spoke. "Much as we hate her, Lara seems to draw him here. Shit! When that guy tried to kill her, everyone came running in on white horses like they were filming a movie." She stopped and looked at Michelle, who stared back.

"And what?" Michelle shouted. "What the hell's your point?" So he might like this Lara whore. Big deal.

Blair stared at her, then spoke slowly like she was stupid. "So more of the same will get us more of the same. Maybe it isn't Lara bringing him here so much as what keeps happening to her." She bent over the ashtray and tapped out some ashes. "Shirl may want Lara run out of town, but as long as we have her here, we have a ticket to the Dirk show. But. We have to be real careful. Mess with her, but not go too far. We can't let Shirl know what we're doing—as far as she's concerned, we want Lara gone too. And if Dirk figures us out, that will only make him mad. We did get him coming around when we told him how cute he was with that crush thing." She raised her voice to a whine. "Oh, Dirk, you are so romantic!"

Michelle narrowed her eyes, suspicious. "You're saying you did that, you and your friends?"

"Yep. And Shirl's been working it, too, getting him to listen to her reports about 'the Granville situation'. That is, her stories about the amazing Shirl and how she's expertly handling the situation! Worked him but good." Blair walked to the door, opened it, and leaned against it. "Well, it's been fun, but I'm dancing tonight. Need to shower."

Michelle turned to leave.

"But remember," Blair said.

Michelle stopped and faced her again.

Blair continued. "This thing with messing with Lara, keeping on her all the time. The stories, the threats, the chasing around. It'll be fun to keep Dirk in town, but no one can know we're behind it, ever. Or if they find us out, it was all for fun, we are just fun-loving little innocents!" She laughed ugly.

Michelle faked a giggle and left.

———————

8-05-00 Saturday a.m. 6:45
Journal,

What did I want? I don't know.

I've kept hold of reality. He's a man who hasn't cared enough to even talk to me, or call me. Sex is so complicated, and much as I like it, some casual fling wouldn't cut it for me. I wanted to know him, to meet him, be friends. So, the things I want can still be had.

But, it … crying more. I hurt so bad.

If only they had announced their engagement. So they— what? Preserved their privacy? And I've been through all this. I'm so damaged, my life is so damaged.

Have I been used? Was I a tool to distract attention from their wedding plans? At the expense of my life? How callous are these people? But I can't believe that of Dirk. I really believe he's been more confused than anything. I've prayed and prayed for God to direct this and I must keep faith that He has.

Dirk was committed to the girlfriend all this time.

I've structured my life around this stuff. I had to, it took over! Now what? My heart is screaming. I have to remember that I will feel better again! This isn't forever. I have to try to gather my "lessons" —God alone can make me feel less abandoned.

I'm making no sense. How am I going to cope? I hurt! I can't stand the pain. I won't stop crying. Something in my soul is screaming "No!" I don't understand. What is wrong with me? "No" to what? The wedding? Why should I care? "No" to another change in my life? Definitely. "No" to losing his attention? Of course. "No" to the past months, the not knowing what has happened to my life, how much privacy I have lost, whether I was used as a tool so they could plan their wedding. Yes, without a doubt. "No" to the possibility that someone ruined my life in a plot to get what she wanted, and she won.

God must help me. I hurt so much.

8-07-00 Monday evening

I feel better. Caffeine and St. John's Wort in bigger doses. Prayers. Tears—are they all cried out?

How can I fix this.

I took Buckley walking around Granville Lake. In the daylight. With no gun. I don't care if someone kills me; life is too hard. I've had it. And just the luck—now, no one wants to kill me, just when I've lost interest in protecting myself.

Maybe there are shadows. I don't know what to think. I want them to be there, I don't want everything to change overnight.

Like they did.

It is God I must depend on. Dirk is plenty powerful—his money and fame make him almost a superman—but God is the main protector here. I need to trust that I'll be saved in some way. Given how bizarre this situation has been, maybe I can expect some incredible event to come out of it. Please no more pain.

I need help. I worry the gossips will start stories that I'm a jilted lover now, taken advantage of and used and then dumped. They'll delight in my rumored humiliation. I worked only a half-day today. I couldn't cope and my eyes are awful! Too many tears, too little sleep. My pain is finally showing on my face. I'm so afraid people will misunderstand and think I've had this affair or obsession or whatever with Dirk. And maybe I <u>do</u> have a dependence on him—not good. But am I not allowed to depend on <u>anyone</u>? Except God? Maybe not.

I think part of my emotional reaction has been terror. What will these people do to me now? What's going to happen to me? How much humiliation? I've been blind-sided every step of the way in this mess. If I had only known what was going on! All I've gotten has been a series of unexplainable attacks.

I must trust God, that He will protect me and make this come out good for me, whether He's using Dirk Durmont or not.

```
---------------------------------------------
```
Subj: DirkLetter
Date: 08/07/2000 3:15:03 PM Central Daylight Time
From: HotGirl11@mail.com (Karen)
To: DirkDolls (group)

Dirk Dolls, are we calmed down yet?

My computer is burning up, along with my keyboard. But were we right, or were we right. Carrie Jo Miller was the winner.

Have we all found the pictures on the Web? They showed up yesterday with a list of everything she wore. Carriejoanddirk. They're making a gown like hers, so we can get a copy, and the same flowers, which someone says were an assortment of daisies to symbolize country love, and orchids to symbolize rare something.

It's so romantic! About five wedding planners are saying they did it, so it's hard to see which one actually did, unless they all did. One of them did Mindy and Luke's wedding and remember all that cool stuff they had like greyhounds running around the guests legs to symbolize freedom, and someone released wolves back to the wild (over in a valley someplace) to symbolize nature conservation. They had an opera singer who sang with Dead Fever to symbolize we're all getting along, then a plane flew overhead with a banner that said something like "death do us part", or "don't never do part". And it cost a fortune! Cool!

We Dolls in Granville should know people who went to it, right? FIND OUT the real news! Who went to the wedding and who went home with who afterward?

Married or not, we love our Dirkman forever.

His always,
Editor
```
---------------------------------------------
```

—⁓—

So many people were crowded together on the street below. Alice peered down and saw more running up. What were they shouting?

"Jump! Jump! Jump!"

Alice had hoped it'd be higher, this old water tower. She'd hoped to be high as the sky; from here she could still see the vicious expressions on the people's faces. There'd been a dog like that near her house growing up. A thick chain held it back, but still it lunged at her when she walked by on the way to school. Always showing its yellow teeth, slobber coming out its mouth. Mean, wanting to hurt her.

She'd tried to get up on the roof of the department store, but some man had stopped her. Usually men let her do stuff, winking and letting her by, then grabbing at her while she walked past. But that old guy in the gray coveralls had blocked her from the stairs going up to the roof.

Alice suddenly lifted her arms high and spun. There was music playing someplace. She knew this one.

"Anyway I see it, I need you here ..." She'd put on Dirk's favorite dress, the silver shimmery sheath that slid off when she dropped the straps. Her feet were bare. She liked to dance with her feet free.

She swayed with her eyes closed, her mind in a different place now. There was no crowd, no water tower, no shifting boards underneath her as she moved. Only the music in her head. She was so tired. This should be Granville; the signs had said so. After the wedding she'd driven and driven until she saw those signs.

She'd tried to stop them from getting married. It was all a mistake. But the police were everywhere! And the crowds. She couldn't make Dirk hear her from where she stood.

"Jump! Jump, you crazy bitch! Jump!" Ah, she knew that voice. Always those voices. Had they been right all along, that Dirk didn't want her? How could that be true when she was so sure they belonged together?

A siren was sounding and coming closer.

"Now you have my heart ..." She shuffled forward as she danced.

Then suddenly the splintered wood under her bare feet was gone.

—◦◦◦—

Delta thought it was awful news. "So she isn't going to dance here anymore?"

Reeza's face was always serious so Delta couldn't tell if she was sad tonight. Gramma would call her "hard", with her heavy black eyeliner and long frizzy coal-black hair. Shoe-polish hair, Michelle called it. Blair had told them she used to dance, but she was too old now and hadn't kept out of the sun so her skin was crinkled like tree bark.

Delta snuck a look at the women crammed too close into the dressing room, checking whether they thought her comment was stupid. Unsure, she turned to the mirror and picked up a lipstick to fiddle with.

Reeza continued. "There were things we didn't know about Alice. Like the police looking for her. We need you all to tell us outright if you have the law after you, okay?" She paused and looked around at the women. No one said anything. "It would serve you good to keep the police out of here, okay? We have enough problems."

She opened a blue notebook with a sparkly cover. It looked like the one Delta had had for English class. "We don't want to increase staff right now," Reeza said. "So you dancers present here can pick up more hours. Delta, Rocko wants you to have first choice. Come up and show me what extra nights you want."

Delta spun around away from the mirror, surprised she'd been picked first. Was it alphabet "D"? As she stood to go look over Reeza's shoulder, she heard Michelle whisper to Blair. "Shit, she won't be able to figure out that schedule. But I was right about Alice, wasn't I. Loolooland."

8-15-00
Journal,

I seem to be having an emotional breakdown. Today I have a better grip on things. I slept without a sleeping pill for the first time in days. At work, I struggle all day to stay level, then I have to pass people in the hall with my face all wretched and desolate. I'm setting myself up for all sorts of rumors with this emotional reaction. And I still don't understand why I feel so bad. Even now, I was feeling okay but when I sit and think about it, there is so much pain. I have been so frustrated for so long; it has gotten to me more than I realized.

I don't want to let my feelings for Dirk to diminish. I haven't mentioned "the Crush" thing much; it seemed so egotistical. And I just wanted it left alone. Maybe it's the counselor in me. If people don't let him leave that star thing behind sometimes and be a normal guy, how can he keep growing and developing as a person? I was determined to just let him be. But this has gone on so long and so much has happened. Keeping my composure has worn me out.

And it has just been God's will that I haven't met some guy to go out with along the way. I'm alone all the time. I could have fallen for a man if God supplied the right one. It isn't as if I've been "waiting by the phone" for something to happen with all this mess. I've been living. Accommodating this "stuff" constantly, but living.

I need to trust God that this will work out positive for me. I need to remember I can rely on God and He wants me to rely on only Him. I've been depending on Dirk Durmont—sort of. I must remember it's all in God's hands, it always has been and He will fix it for me. I know God can't leave me alone with a beautiful man who has my heart. I'm sure, if given any encouragement, I couldn't have left Dirk alone physically. And it's not God's plan for me to casually mess around with men. Oh, how I wish I'd been blessed with a decent husband along the way. What a curse. I can not marry to get sex again. That has never worked; marriage has been so bad, so destructive for me. I pray for a lover, but does God want that for me? Why not?

I wrote a poem that sums up a lot of my reaction. It's about how I started out wise and ignored the stories around me. This part of the poem haunts me:

> But my soul, oh my soul—unattended—
> danced with the hero ...

So much of this has been out of my control, including me.

Another day, and it was time for work again. Lara sat in her car, listlessly looking at the General Insurance building. She wished she had a job that didn't require thinking; it was hell trying to focus on computer projects.

Last week, a woman had jumped off an old water tower. She didn't die—she "only" crushed her leg. How tragic, that she was so sad she wanted to die and now she was still so sad and possibly handicapped. Sickening.

Lara's first impulse was to go see her in the hospital and try to help her. This town was so callous, they were probably gossiping about her and leaving her alone with her demons. But what if her kind act became another source of pain? What if the woman was a manipulator, or as low and bad as these others? Still, Lara resolved to be bigger than her fear of being hurt. She'd find the newspaper article with her name and hospital and go see her.

Then she'd come up with a plan for staying alive and for salvaging some dignity. There seemed to be shadows, so she hadn't been completely abandoned. Not yet, but it stood to reason that she soon would be. Why would Dirk care to protect some woman in Granville when his life was going so well? But how could she think up solutions to this problem when she could barely get through each day? One step, one step, one step—that was all she could manage. Not one day at a time—she was down to living five minutes at a time. She couldn't think up a way to defend herself from the people who were stalking her. Lara was destroyed and the bad people had won.

No! It was not over yet. God would win! Maybe she'd lost some battles, but the war was not over. She could make a life for herself here. She still had her house. She could—yes she could—have a home.

She lifted her body out of her car. It took all her strength, but she pushed herself forward.

CHAPTER TWENTY-ONE

"What the hell am I doing out here?"

Michelle stood in the night, dragging on her cigarette as she peered up and down the abandoned street. She could not believe she was doing this. When she'd gotten the phone call, the voice on the other end insisted on the place they'd meet. And here she was, waiting in this dark alley in downtown Granville.

Buildings loomed over the sidewalks making the street a tunnel. A block away, a shadow shifted and she peered through the night. Was something there? She shivered and watched, then realized that walls of red brick buildings capped off both ends of the street on which she stood. She was in a brick box! Roads crossed at each end, but she wasn't visible unless someone was spying down from a window. At the thought, she eyed each window nervously, then looked again toward where she'd imagined movement.

Why had this woman chosen some hidden alley for their meeting? What was Shirl Manier's big secret? This was far different from their first meeting at the gym. That wasn't so long ago, but it seemed like ages. Michelle was dancing at Rocko's now, and Dirk had married that TV star. And Lara was still around causing trouble for everyone.

She jumped when headlights came from around a corner and eased toward her. A red truck swerved to the curb in front of Michelle's car and stopped.

The woman behind the wheel was slim and wore plain makeup, if any at all. But her face was almost hidden under a big visor cap pulled down low. She slumped down in the driver's seat.

"Michelle?" She looked out from under the brim.

"Shirl Manier?" Michelle peered at her face. This was supposedly the woman she'd met at the gym. That day, she'd handed her a business card. Michelle inhaled sharply, remembering. That business card! What was the number on it? She was sure she still had it, probably stuck in some purse. She watched her face as she spoke. "So. Shirl. What's up?"

"I heard you might have a phone number I need."

"Yeah?"

"There's a guy. Mark McNought. Friend of yours."

"Mark? Yeah, sure." Funny that Shirl hadn't called Delta. And how everyone was looking for Mark lately. There must be more to this than she figured.

"I need his phone number. I want to ask him a little favor. I'd pay him, of course. I heard he might … well, do me a favor."

Something wasn't right. Michelle understood the Delta thing, why Shirl hadn't called her. Delta could be real slow, but she was starting to catch on to things. She wouldn't let anyone pull any shit on her brother, anything that might get him into trouble or send him back to jail.

But this Shirl. Even the voice, the manner. Where was that uppity business-like stuff? The "Dirk Camp" crap?

"I could get his number," Michelle said. "If he wants you to have it. But I sure ain't standing out in some abandoned alley with it. What's wrong with the gym?" Smoke-out time.

"The gym?"

"The lounge in the gym."

Shirl's eyes were darting down and around. Nervous? "Which gym?"

Gotcha! Michelle smirked. This "Shirl" was so busted!

Shirl's voice came out rushed, breathless. She was way nervous now, no doubt about it. "Listen, this is … I can't go parading around public with this stuff. I thought Mark was a discrete guy."

"Oh he can keep secrets alright; that's required in his business, if you know what I mean. But what do I get for my efforts, for the phone number?" Did these California types think people were stupid here in the Midwest?

Shirl laughed and looked over at her, calm again, direct. "And what exactly are you getting here in Granville?"

What she was talking about? Michelle sneered to mask her confusion.

Shirl continued. "You girls around here! You all think you're going to become Dirk Durmont groupies and he will buy you everything you want." Her voice turned mocking. "Or *your* Dirk will pick you out as his one true love and want to *marry* you!" She rolled her eyes, snorted, then paused. After a minute, she looked Michelle up and down. "If you're looking for a sugar daddy, a girl like you has a much better chance in L.A." Then she sang out in a hillbilly accent, "California is the place you oughta be."

Michelle grit her teeth, but didn't show her anger. She'd learned there was nothing to be gained by showing reactions to nastiness. Where had she heard that? Lara's face came to her mind and she scowled. Damn!

Shirl was staring at her.

Michelle asked, "So what the hell's your point?"

"You help us get this woman Lara out of Granville. You get me this Mark's number and do me some favors. And when she's gone, we can all get back to our real lives in the real world, in L.A., far away from Hootersville. And you can come with us. I'll introduce you around, help you find work and a place to crash. You'd like it out there. Lot of opportunities."

Los Angeles. Where the real money was and where hundreds of Dirk Durmonts wandered the streets. Including the real one. Michelle knew she couldn't trust this woman, but she knew something else. This wasn't Shirl Manier and the real Shirl and maybe the real Dirk would be mighty interested in what this woman in the big hat was up to. And Hat Woman wouldn't want them to know, that was for sure. Useful information. Handy.

"Shirl, you got a deal." Michelle promised to get Mark's number to her.

But as she started to drive off, Michelle called out, "Hey, Shirl!"

She looked bothered, but stopped.

"Shirl, who *do* you work for?" Michelle asked.

The woman stared at her with hard eyes.

After a minute, she said, "For myself, Michelle. Like everyone around here, I work for myself." She drove away.

——◈——

Lara did a double-take when she saw the man near the free weights.

Cute. And he had looked at Lara like he was interested in her, not with the bold personal stare she usually got in Granville. Was it possible that she could attract some nice decent man? Now that Dirk was married, the rumors should be vaporizing. She should finally be able to get a life going for herself, to get back on track after this derailment.

She managed a set of squats, glancing at Cute Guy in the mirror at rep number five. He was pumping his biceps, really working them, not leering at her! Maybe there was a normal man in Granville, and maybe she could still be interested in one.

He must have just arrived. Lara had started her routine with leg lifts on the crossover rack, but stopped when she spied a familiar blond woman standing nearby staring at her. The woman had left when Lara caught her eye and glared. This was her second week at this new gym and the problems had apparently switched health clubs with her. One fresh twist became evident—a trainer had stepped into the middle of a group of gossiping men and said, "Break it up. We don't do that here." Was someone on Lara's side? But that one employee wasn't there to block the men who stood and leered, or to question the women who loitered in larger numbers.

"I don't think she's so cute." The comment came from beside her.

No! Not now! Lara hefted the weight back in place, pressed her forehead against the bar, and glanced to her right.

Four men had gathered at the crossover rack next to her. Three stood as one straddled a weight bench. Tight white t-shirts were stretched across their bulging stomachs and too-small gym shorts rode up their pale flabby legs. They were obviously not gym regulars.

"So you saw the pictures?" They continued talking.

"Yeah, I saw those last December."

"Were they cute?"

"No!"

Pictures! What pictures? Were there actually fake photos somewhere on the Internet, as she had dreamt? But surely by now these people would have blurted out some remark about them if there was.

Blurted something out. Like they just had.

This man had seen something, definitely. She couldn't face the group—her shame was too great. If those pictures existed, how could she face any decent man? Had Cute Guy seen them? As she picked up her bag, she glanced toward the trainer's desk and saw a man sitting there leering at her as if he was watching a porn movie.

The men continued. "She heard us!"

"Shhh!"

And now there was no doubt they were talking about her.

She noticed the normal guy look toward her, then toward the four men. A man near him whispered something to him, and he nodded and continued to stare at the group at the crossover rack. Lara crept out, keeping her head down to hide her humiliation. She wouldn't come back to this place, not at night.

The bad people had found her there, and they were brutal.

Delta sat up straighter. "There's Lara, leaving already!"

Michelle had been watching a beige SUV parked in the last row. She whipped her head around. "Hell. Did you make her mad?"

"Don't blame me! I got out as soon as she gave me the evil eye. It must have been someone else."

The two women watched as Lara slumped out to her car. As she was climbing behind the wheel, Lara noticed Michelle's car and paused. She stared a moment, then drove off.

Michelle lurched her car around to follow her. The beige SUV and a beat-up little red car were in front of them. "Where the hell is she going? I am not in the mood to chase her butt all over town."

It didn't make much difference to Delta where they went. Lately, Michelle had been letting her off wherever Lara was and telling her to go in alone while she stayed out and scoped out the parking lot. That Levi with the red car sometimes showed up and kept Michelle company, hatching plans and whatnot. It was much easier getting near Lara without a crowd, anyway. The cashiers were even getting to know Delta. They'd say, "Well, here we go again", or "There they are, showing up like clockwork." Friendly. They didn't seem to mind her a bit. But sometimes Lara would march right out, like shopping or exercising made her mad. The gym was the worst—like today. Lara hadn't been there long and there she was, sliding right back out like she fell off the merry-go-around after only three turns. Lara was no way interested in anybody looking her over while she did those machines.

With only Delta going in places, Shirl was happy because there was only one of Delta. And Michelle was happy because she said they were keeping things stirred up so the shadows would stick around and get Dirk to come back. And Mark was happy when he dropped by the apartment and they talked about things. He called Lara his Unfinished Business or Unfished Bitchness, depending on how much he'd drunk.

Delta had told Mark about the bad men with the boots and white van. He laughed and said he had almost as many enemies as Lara, and wasn't that a hoot. He'd taken his car back. Good enough, it was so gross anyway. And when she'd parked it at the grocery store, Lara was onto her in a heartbeat. No elephant of surprise at all.

Now Michelle was driving through the dark streets like they were in a stock car race.

"I know what we'll do!" she said.

Delta cringed. Michelle's plans usually meant bad news. Soon they were rolling past Lara's house in time to see her garage door moving down. The rear lights of two cars were visible turning the corner a couple of blocks ahead.

"Let's go see what she does!" Michelle pulled to a stop at the curb.

She jumped out and Delta followed, and they both ran in a crouch through the dark, looking like people in a TV cop show. They stopped beside Lara's backyard fence. Delta peered through the wood slats, looking for the dog. Buckley seemed like he was a nice dog, but the times they'd sneaked around the house he never had taken a liking to them. He wasn't out tonight. Lara seemed to be keeping him locked up inside lately.

And there she was. The two watched as Lara came out of her garage and paced toward her back door. Her gym bag hung open and her right hand was buried in it. She reached the back door and craned her head around to look into the darkness behind her.

"I'll bet she has her gun. There!" Michelle whispered.

Lara froze in place and stared right toward them, looking like the Terminator. It was like her eyes bored through the fence and she could reach her hands through the wood and snap their necks in two, then shoot them full of holes. Delta took off running. She didn't care if Michelle followed her or not, but they reached the car at the same time. Soon they were racing around the blocks, Michelle laughing like she was crazy and Delta wishing they were back at the apartment.

Then Michelle pulled over in front of a big stone house loaded with fancy windows, and stopped. She sighed big, like she was happy, and pulled out a cigarette. "It's illegal running around trying to shoot people. Yeah, we can say she was trying to shoot us. I'll get a picture of her with a gun, that's what I'll do, and sell it. 'Dirk Durmont's Girlfriend, Gangster'."

She smoked a while and looked over at the house. "Some house, huh? Wouldn't it be great to live in a place like that?" She glanced over at Delta, then went on. "There are loads of great places in L.A. And loads of money. Wouldn't it be great to live somewhere with loads of money and mansions?"

Delta liked the house, but didn't answer because Michelle kept going on like she was talking to herself, all worked up over that shooting incident. Of course, there wasn't really a shooting incident.

"I'm going to live in a great place. Better than L-whore's. A girl like me, I can find men who'll give me stuff. Maybe this Dirk thing is going all to hell, but I can do it easy in L.A."

Michelle blew smoke out her window. It was looking like they were going to be there a while, so Delta got a Long Lady out for herself.

"Funny thing, Delta." Michelle laughed in that witchy way she had. "I can sit here and talk to you and you probably don't get half of what I'm talking about."

Delta took a drag off her cigarette and kept looking out her window. On her side of the street, this other house looked even nicer, with a trimmed lawn greener than a crayon and loads of flowers in boxes at the windows. Brittany came to mind. She had told her some good things to know. She would even say, "Delta, this is good to know" and that helped her remember. What came to mind now was the time Brit had told her that if you just keep your mouth shut, people will talk and talk. They might think you're slow—and she said that happened to her, too, 'cause she's blond and don't speak out much—but don't pay any mind to that. Sit and gather facts. More times than not, there was stuff to learn.

Delta thought this was a time for that "good to know."

Michelle talked on, just like Brittany said. "I got me a new idea. This Shirl, she's the most crooked one of the whole bunch. She's not even really Shirl! Who knows, maybe there isn't a real one. But whoever she is, she's no fool and I know if I help her, I'm getting a ticket to good times in California. She knows all sorts of people and she's setting me up with someone who'll put me in a house just like this."

Michelle took another long inhale, then blew smoke out in a thin line. Delta sat silent. A little rabbit hopped out of the bushes next to the house, then saw them and froze in position. The only thing on it that moved was its soft brown fur ruffling in the breeze.

She continued. "All Shirl needs is for us to run L-whore out of town."

Whoa! This was different! Didn't they like Lara being here, to please Dirk? Delta took a drag of her cigarette and exhaled hard. Maybe she'd need help figuring these facts out.

"And Lara is so running, isn't she? Look how fast she ran out of that gym tonight! You know it was only some jerk trying to scope out her damn butt, or someone razzing her about Dirk. But you hafta hand it to her, she don't give up easy. What with Mar ..., er, somebody already almost killing her and here she still is, right where no one wants her."

Delta turned and looked at her. It was getting hard to sit quiet while Michelle was making no sense. But she'd gather facts, then maybe someone could help her with them.

"But we're wearing her down. She can't make a move without our knowing it, or without Levi taking a picture of it, and how long can a person go on like that? She already leaves town to shop and get laid. Well, she can go away and stay away. Somehow or other, we are going to make her get her ass out of Granville."

Delta made her mouth stay shut, but she knew she was frowning. Get Lara out of Granville? Was that what this was about? She looked at the rabbit. It hadn't budged. Gramma never said "good to know," but there her face was, looking at Delta in her head like she was standing right in front of her. What Gramma said was that sometimes there's something a person is meant to do. And if you didn't do it, no one else would.

Michelle and some people were trying to run Lara out of town. She was sitting there admitting it. Delta knew that wasn't right. That wasn't being a good Dirk Doll.

She had to do something.

Lara seemed to be getting used to Delta. She'd see her and look like she knew her, and she didn't always rush away, not if Delta was alone.

It was up to Delta to warn Lara.

But how?

8-20-00 Sunday
Journal,

Nothing has changed, nothing has happened to fix things. I need a miracle now.

I didn't call that woman in the hospital, the one who jumped off the water tower. I'm ashamed of myself. It's only cowardice.

Later

Okay, I went and called the hospital and no one answered in the room they connected me to. I'll try tomorrow. I must have courage. Cowardice annoys me so much; I won't tolerate it in myself.

I try to keep getting out, being "normal." I don't mind people staring so much, but I have to avoid their cruelty somehow. I go for drives a lot and flip the station when any sad song comes on.

I joined Shape It Fitness Center, but even in a new gym people quickly close in around me. And they gossip loudly, and of course they stare. So I leave. I'm being too sensitive, but I need to indulge myself for a while. I won't go back there in the evening—that crowd is ruthless. I need to do what I can to protect my psyche for a while. I'm being a wimp, I realize, but only for a while. Maybe I'll try going back to Brandt's Gym Tuesday. I haven't been emotionally ready yet. There are too many memories and sorrow, with Dirk hanging around there so much, and so many people talking about it.

Please God, fix this, it can't be this way.

I can't stand any strangers near me. I'm this raw gaping emotional wound and am so afraid of people sticking pins in me. In the bathroom at work, strange women keep showing up and reacting to my face. So I turn and walk out. I imagine they think I'm acting odd, but I don't care.

I'm reading "Experiencing God". One point startled me: Do I love God? If not, everything is a mess. Thoughts on love: Why do we make love so complicated? It is the purest power we have. Yet it becomes painful? Does it demand expression? Or does it feel so good being with someone/something you love that the absence becomes painful. It's not the love that hurts, but the loss of that great feeling of peace (love) you have with the beloved that causes sorrow.

That feeling should be there with or without the person there.

8-25

I went to Illinois, to Sara's wedding. It was so moving and beautiful!

Then I went over to Em and Paul's. It was fun, of course. We made a fire. A trash fire, but we got silly and did Native American dances around it like the scene in "Dances With Wolves."

I'm trying to focus on my trip to France; a change of continent will do me good. I leave Friday. I bought a voltage adapter so can now curl my hair anyplace in the world.

Time must pass. That's the only thing that can help me heal. And prayer. I haven't been able to pray for weeks now; my thoughts are so sad and intense I can't stand closing my eyes. I do simple prayers, like "help me God". He knows what I need, right?

I worry now that I'm coming across as negative to people. I need to not assume everyone is going to attack or hurt me. It's been a hard few days. At the health club there was a lot more gossip and stares. Then Friday, I went to Discount City and Circus Shoes. Some girl with long blond hair seemed to attach herself to me as I was leaving Discount City. She kept turning her back to me when I looked at her. Then she turned up at the shoe store with other women, all watching everything I was doing. I wish I knew what they wanted. I don't mind if they copy me, but this following me and staring makes me so nervous. What do they want?

Then, when I was in line at Circus Shoes, this woman with huge eyes stared at me in shock while her husband whispered in her ear. But her eyes were so big, she looked like some kind of insect! If these people knew how they look to me—their expressions make them look like creatures. Vile.

I went back to Circus Shoes on Sunday. I could get half off on a second pair, but Friday I was too tense to find the second one. I need a low-heeled boot for Paris. There were stares, whatever. Then, when I was in line, I got another hate-filled stare from some woman, like on Friday. It worries me. Is there still something going on? More rumors? I'm so confused.

Then Tuesday after my workout at Brandt's . . .

Lara had found a parking spot across the street in front of the building, a good thing in spite of the need to parallel park. As she left the gym, she let the heavy doors close behind her. Farther down the sidewalk, a man was walking away, his back to her.

As the door closed with a bang, the man turned, met her eyes, and changed direction.

He came toward her.

Lara registered his abrupt turn-around and rushed to her car, her keys in one hand and pepper spray in the other. He stepped out into the street and was only two cars distant when she slid behind the wheel and locked the door. The man paused, then continued pacing along the center line past her car door. He came to the next street and angled across to the far corner.

I'm an idiot! Why didn't I go back into the building? It was luck that I made it into my car before he reached me.

Why won't God send someone to help me?

CHAPTER TWENTY-TWO

The men called out again as Lara passed.

Three times now, she had walked by and these men had shouted at her! In French, no less. She was in Paris now, excited to be far from Granville, hopefully in a safe place where someone wouldn't try sneaking up to kill her. But now what? She had rushed past these people the first time on her way out of baggage claims into the terminal. There, a lady with a clipboard had told her the tour company didn't have a telekinetic luggage-handling system, so she'd rushed back into the claims area, slipping through an exit door as it closed. She'd found the carousels and her gray tweed suitcases, which looked hayseed bumping along amid the sleek black duffels and attachés.

This was not the U.S., where airport terminals were fresh and huge with halls wide as four-lane highways. This old building was dim, as if the years had leached out its light. And it was smaller than the airport where Lara had begun her trip, but no less busy. People were crowded together more tightly, not seeming to mind the constant jostling of other too-close human bodies muttering a dozen different languages.

And now, these men. She needed to get back to the clipboard tour people, to let them whisk her away to someplace nice. Were they so desperate to carry her bags? She looked back at them with a grimace meant to be a smile and said, "Je ne comprends pas," that she didn't understand.

They answered, "Customs!"

Lara froze. Oh! Goodness. She slowly turned toward them with her suitcases and an embarrassed grin. She saw now that "they" were two men and a woman standing behind a fold-up table.

"Customs?" She walked over to them, suspicious. They were dressed casually in blue jeans; they could be criminals. "Ou est votre ... uniforms?" She gestured to their outfits.

They each pulled out black ID cases, and as she studied one man's badge he lifted the edge of his jacket to expose a gun in a holster. Lara widened her eyes and nodded.

"Okay. Pardon moi. Dans Etats-Unis, il y a beaucoup des criminals." She realized she had pronounced the English "criminal" with a heavy

French accent, as if that made the word French. *Dans Etats-Unis, aussi, je suis une idiote. In the United States, also, I am an idiot.*

09-02-00 France. Paris.
Journal,
    I'm so tired I'm senseless.
    My flight—Granville to St. Louis to Paris—was overnight and I didn't sleep much on the plane. It's 6:30 p.m. here and I'm so tired.
    Paris hasn't magically healed my soul the way it was supposed to. Traveling alone can be lonely. Well, this trip doesn't have to heal me; it can be <u>educational</u>. I can learn about France.
    I don't know if there are shadows. When people stare at me or react to me, I startle. I don't know if people are good or bad. I trust no one, even with the smallest things.

Later
    2 a.m. Can't sleep. A movie is on TV, in English, thank goodness. The translating/speaking French is exhausting!
    There's a scene in this movie where some guy realizes his buddy is depressed, so he calls and calls, then goes over and tries to drag him out. I want to be more like that. We can make a difference in each others' lives. It takes courage.
    I tried again to call the woman who jumped off the water tower—well, I called the hospital she was in. She wasn't there anymore. I blew it. She's not in the phone book. I hope she's okay. Is anyone helping her?
    The men here in France are beautiful and sexual looking, exuding testosterone! They're not crude, but there's something hungry in their faces. It's exhausting, looking at them!
    I need to try to be nicer. I have to assume some people are okay, that not everyone has bad intentions. I need to have more sympathy for the guys at the gym. This movie reminded me that men are vulnerable, too. They have needs. And those needs drive them to act, well, like pigs, in the case of some of those at the health club. Many have been cruel, but some are simply trying to connect. I must try to understand how they're thinking and cut them some slack. I'm lonely, they're lonely.

If she hurried, Lara could make it to the church on time.

Daily, the tour bus transported the group to interesting places then turned everyone loose for a few hours. Lara's mission this trip—besides finding the cure for her sorrows and some authentic French fashions—was to light a candle in every grand cathedral she came across. There seemed to be one in every town.

One by one, Lara went into the church and tiptoed over to the racks of candles glowing before a statue of Jesus, Mary, or a saint. She then slid a large coin into the cash box and lit two candles, one for her and one for Dirk. After that, she prayed fervently for both of them—both—to end up in some positive place from all this. Lighting holy candles appealed to the Catholic schoolgirl in her, the 7-year-old who drew pictures of Jesus and expected miracles and visits from guardian angels. One never knew; maybe candles made God listen harder.

Today, the bus brought them to a little town with a film school and rows of shops where she found a wooden doll with painted yellow hair and a bright red dress. She shopped for clothes, but was quickly discouraged by the clerk who followed her too closely, almost touching her body. She gave up and hurried back to the quiet church she'd visited as her first stop.

As she stepped back into the hushed interior, several members of the tour turned and waved in her direction. She smiled and waved back, then moved over to a niche with a candle rack. She fished a coin out of her pocket and winced at the loud clunk it made as it fell into the metal money box. Two more candles. And maybe an extra one for good measure. She lit them, stared into the flames and prayed, then stepped back outside onto the stone plaza.

"Deux." Two.

Lara stared toward the voice and saw a man turn away from her gaze. Two? She'd made two trips to light candles. Had he noticed, was he counting? Surely not. She dismissed the idea, then spied the bus at the corner and rushed toward it.

"Well, this bites my butt!" Michelle spit the words out, then sucked hard on her cigarette. Her chair was surrounded by the haze of drifting smoke swirls. News about L-whore was always bad news.

"What did you expect Dirk to do, with her acting all suicidal and shit?" Stacy sat cross-legged on the floor in front of a raggedy baby blue easy chair. Delta had hauled the chair home from a flea market, along with a coffee table and a set of china plates.

Connie looked around at the women sitting in Michelle's and Delta's living room. She spoke up. "We all know Lara wasn't the one who jumped off the water tower! Everyone has that story screwed up."

Connie was sticking up for Lara? Michelle thought that was bullshit.

"She may as well had," Stacy said. "Hell, I'll jump off something if Dirk would fly me to Paris to cheer me up." She took another swig of her beer.

"Do you think he would if we did?" Delta asked with that clueless face of hers. "Is that where Alice went, too? Paris?"

Connie scowled. "Do you think that's what happened, that Dirk 'flew her to Paris'? Didn't you get that email from that girl at the travel agency that said Lara came in and bought a ticket herself? She put it on her charge card. Maybe people can just buy tickets."

Michelle glared at her. "Whose side are you on, anyway?" Her apartment was their new hangout, and she expected her company to side with her. She could count on Stacy, who would agree with anyone if it got her away from Mountain College and her nursing classes. But Connie was unpredictable with way too many opinions. Still, she worked at TeleSales, which gave her the inside track to Lara from working in the same building and all. Michelle would dump her, but not yet.

Connie backed down. Michelle knew she'd seen her give her the eye and felt smug. She was getting real good at digging up dirt on people and spreading it around if they crossed her. Now no one wanted to get on her bad side. Maybe Connie hadn't done anything worth talking about, but Michelle could always make something up.

Connie's voice turned make-nice. "It's just that maybe when we've worked awhile, got promotions ... or look at you guys already, making so much money in one night and all. We can save up and go on trips ourselves. No one has to 'send us' anywhere."

Michelle felt her face grow hot. "Shit, you know as well as I do that he's there and they're screwing in some Paris hotel even as we speak."

How was it that Lara was getting so much? And Michelle wasn't?

Stacy put on that same brainless look Delta had had when she was talking about jumping off buildings. "Or I bet he has a castle there in the French countryside, with servants. And they bring Lara breakfast to eat with Dirk, in front of the big stone fireplace. There are fancy dogs and sheep running over the grounds, and a horse stable so they can take rides together across the fields."

Connie stood. "You're forgetting he's *married*."

Michelle snorted and rolled her eyes.

"Anyway, I have to go," Connie continued. "Some guy I met at Jesters is going to call tonight." She picked up her jacket from the back of a chair. "You know, Taylor says he and the guys around here are real sick of Dirk Durmont messing around with women their age, and they won't touch a woman who's doing 'Hollywood'."

Michelle snorted. "I'm sure, like they're really avoiding us. I don't have any trouble finding a prick when I want one. And they know any chick in this town would dump them flat if they had a chance at Dirk. Hell, that's why half of us moved here!"

"Well, anyway," Connie said, "I'd appreciate it if you didn't tell any guys we know about our chasing Dirk around. Or his girlfriend." No one said anything as she let herself out.

Michelle, Stacy, and Delta sat silent, drinking their beers. Michelle knew she'd have to dump Connie now, and that she'd get Lara if it was the last thing she did.

But it seemed that everything they did to hurt her got her more of Dirk's attention.

Now France. Damn!

"I wonder what she did with that dog," Michelle said.

Delta and Stacy looked at her, waiting for her explanation.

After a minute, Delta said, "You mean Buckley? Lara's dog?"

"Yeah, that big hairy one. If she's in France, where's the dog?" Michelle asked.

Stacy had the story. "Connie says that Lara's sister Diane goes over to the house to take care of him, so he stays at the house in the yard. Why?"

"In the yard. Does anyone know Levi's number?" When Stacy and Delta just stared, Michelle continued. "You know, the guy with the little red car, always taking all those pictures." She grinned and swigged her beer.

Then she looked at them both, back and forth. "Remember when that guy showed up pretending to be Dirk? The paper called him The Imposter. Well I got me a plan."

Two days later, Michelle was sweet-talking a massive—and angry—dog. A low growl rumbled out from his throat and Michelle pushed the gate back shut.

"I don't think this is such a good idea, Michelle." Levi stood close behind her, a heavy camera hanging from his neck.

"I need this dog, damn it!" She grinned maliciously at Buckley through a crack in the fence. "Good dog, good Buckley!" Buckley stood still, his ears lifted. She tried the gate again. He growled.

"Son of a bitch!"

"Michelle, we can't use this dog. Maybe you can just be walking along the sidewalk. Here, put that hat and sunglasses back on."

Michelle set the wide-brimmed hat on her head and slid on the large sunglasses. She snorted. "Do I look like her? Without the dog? If these pictures look convincing, we could make a fortune selling them!"

"Yeah, you look great. Come on, let's get out of here. Someone's bound to tell Lara if people are hanging around her house."

They hurried out to Levi's car parked on the street. He stood a minute by the passenger door and directed Michelle. "You walk a ways in that getup. I'll drive by and take some shots."

Michelle began an exaggerated stroll down High Street. Soon she heard a car and turned with a big smile, but froze at what she saw. A large white cargo van had slowed in the street; two greasy men stared out the windshield at her. The longhaired man in the passenger seat shook his head at her before they accelerated and disappeared around the next corner.

Michelle stared at the van until it was out of sight.

"Act natural! Like you're taking a walk."

Michelle gasped, then saw that Levi's car was crawling past. He was whispering loud out his window. "You're not changing your mind, are you? This was your idea, you know."

She faked a toothy smile and stopped so he could get the shot.

"Be taking a walk!" Levi said.

"I don't know how to look like I'm taking a walk!" Michelle grit her teeth. Was her voice quivering? She squinted down the street, angry. Those van bastards were ruining her photo shoot. She spoke extra loud to show she wasn't afraid of those jerks. "Who the hell besides L-whore takes walks?"

"Keep it down! You wanna get us arrested? Now look natural." Levi smirked. "What it takes for a professional to get a few good shots!" He drove on, then turned around in a driveway and came back past Michelle. After a few passes, he pulled to the curb beside her.

"Good job, gorgeous! I'm sure we got some good ones," he called out to her.

She climbed into the car, relieved to be behind a locked door again. "So you're going to split it with me if you sell them, right?"

"Yeah, sure. Like we said."

"And I have a few more ideas. I have this idea for the gym."

"You know, this might work. Does anyone really know what she looks like? She's so damned jumpy, dodging away from the cameras. A big tease, is all. No one knows what she looks like up close," Levi said.

"Or naked!" Michelle laughed.

—*w*—

The word for car was "voiture." Maybe. Lara tried it and the women seemed to understand. They did own cars, possibly like these tiny boxy models she saw crammed into all the available curb space. Lara guessed that the three women were walking rather than driving because 1) it was easier than getting one's voiture popped back out of the parking spot, or 2) it was not too far to the theater. However, they had walked with her for six blocks already and the cinema didn't seem to be in sight.

These kind Parisiennes had invited her to go along with them when she asked directions to the Opera House. She didn't understand how she got lost, and was relieved when she saw the women walking. They tried to tell her what streets to follow but when she got confused they decided to take her there themselves. She was very grateful, merci beaucoup.

As they walked, the women explained that they were going to a movie starring an actor they were sure she knew. Lara tensed, then relaxed when they repeated the name a few times. She couldn't under-stand them, but she was sure it wasn't "Dirk Durmont." Their efforts at conversation were starting to fall flat when the women stopped and pointed across the street. They explained that she needed to cross over and go to the front of the huge stone building. When Lara asked about a side entrance she saw, they slowly and loudly repeated their instructions, apparently fearful that she'd get lost crossing the street.

"Oui, je comprends! Merci beaucoup!" Lara nodded her understanding and smiled as she waved and left them.

As she walked away, she passed a man standing on the corner. He quickly bent over a cigarette.

She toured the Opera House and Montmartre with its Sacre Coeur Basilica. Several miles and hours later Lara decided to head back to the hotel. She pulled the Metro map from her tote and made her way to a station. All this Midwestern girl knew about subways was that tourists in New York City got attacked on them and Chicago's downtown system was home to a cheeseburger shop. There weren't many in her part of the world. But this subway station in Paris wasn't the dirty underground alley she expected. It more resembled a tunnel connecting hospital wings; subterranean, but surfaced in clean white tiles and brightly lit.

A subway ride back to her hotel—such an adventure! Lara sunk onto a bench to wait for a train.

A few minutes later, two young women strolled in and sat nearby. One looked Lara over, then began speaking to her friend in animated French. Lara wasn't one to eavesdrop, especially in a foreign language, but when the girl's voice rose and became shrill she caught her words.

"...quand s'il est marie, elle folle ah ah ah ..." and with the last syllables, she circled her hand near her head in a universal gesture, singing the words out like a siren.

When he got married, she went nuts?! No! Lara's eyes went wide and she stared at the woman, struggling to hide her alarm.

Then worst. The woman saw the look of comprehension on Lara's face, murmured something to her friend, and abruptly stopped talking. It *was* Lara? No! How could this be happening?

Lara stood and walked toward the platform. She heard one of the women gasp. Oh, for crying out loud! What were they thinking she was going to do now? Soon the train arrived, and she stepped in through the nearest door.

Once inside, she found a seat and forced herself to breathe steadily. She knew she'd been recognized on this trip. But she wasn't sure who people thought she was. A group of Americans at a sidewalk café had seen her struggling with a map and a man had said, "See? It *is* her. You never know who you'll see around here!" But this woman at the station seemed to know the Dirk gossip.

Another young woman entered the subway car and took a seat facing Lara. And she stared. They were surrounded by empty seats and this woman sat across from Lara, and now stared.

Go away, go away, go away. Maybe it was some cultural difference, the staring. Like in Granville. Or could it be that the Dirk-obsessed "fans" were here, too? Lara tried to distract herself by studying the map on the wall. She knew her hotel was in the suburb at the last stop.

A half-hour later, the train reached the dot at the end of the map and she stepped out into another white-tiled corridor. She walked up steps and emerged in a grassy park near a terminal of busses and taxis. The sky was still light, but the blue was deepening in the dusk. Beyond the park, tall buildings lined the streets. None of them looked like her hotel; it must be a couple of blocks away. Holding a map, she peered up at a street sign. She studied the map. She looked up at the sign, then at the map, for a long time. Where was this street? It had to be on here someplace. It was a small town, this little suburb outside Paris. Not so many streets that it should be hard to find this one.

Near the bus terminal, a man in uniform sat in a booth, reading. Lara walked over to him and in her faulty French asked him where she could find the street with her hotel. He looked at her with raised eyebrows, not understanding. She showed him the map. He nodded, and gave her another confused look. Then he spoke really really fast, and in French, and Lara didn't understand a thing he said. She smiled and nodded and walked away.

Well. Maybe if she walked around, she'd recognize the neighborhood. She'd been out yesterday buying coffee and washcloths. She'd know the shops.

She headed across the park and walked over to a boulevard lined with tall apartment buildings. A large formal sign greeted her with "Porte de Vincennes." Porte de Vincennes. That didn't mean "Welcome." It took a few seconds for her internal translator to re-read it in English, then a few more for the awful comprehension. Lara whipped out her subway map.

"Oh, f*ck!"

She slapped her hand over her mouth and looked around, mortified. Did people around here know that word? But no one was within earshot except those in a car that had pulled up to the corner.

She studied the map. There, there was La Defense, the town with her hotel, and there, at the other end of Paris, there was Vincennes. She had taken the subway the wrong direction and gotten off at the opposite end of the line! Idiot!

She turned and backtracked, biting her lips to keep from laughing out loud. Exhausted, but recharged by adrenaline and some relief after her confusion, she reached the subway entrance. Near the stairs, a man watched her walk up, studying her face. When he saw she was fighting back a grin, he began to laugh, then ducked his head down over a cigarette to hide his face.

Lara didn't have time to wonder about how much he looked like the man she'd seen near the Opera House. It was getting dark and she had a distance to travel yet.

—⁓—

The seatbelt light turned off and Lara reached for her tote. The seat next to her was empty, so she'd spread out her carry-ons. Extra space on this long flight home was a luxury and she felt blessed.

The week had been too short, but any time away from Granville was too short. It'd been a good trip. Someone had told her that France was fun but to expect to be very tired and to have bad hair. Lara had to agree. The adapter she'd brought for her curling iron turned out to be good only for larger appliances. So, besides learning that some Louis king had portraits done of his legs, she'd developed hair-styling tricks using mousse and her fingers. What a trooper. And she'd finally adjusted her sleep schedule, but now she had to undo the seven-hour difference.

She thought about the past week. She'd lit candles at majestic cathedrals all over France; would they work? She'd prayed over them with the usual requests: for God to guide her to be doing the right things in the Granville mess, and that those right things didn't cause her sorrow; that someone would tell her what was going on and what was printed; that this terrible problem be resolved positively for her and Dirk; for their mutual protection from evil; that she would feel God's love, and not this hollow sad feeling that even now on the plane was beginning to nag her.

She gripped the angel pin perched on her lapel. She had to remember it was God's love she needed, His protection and peace. For all she knew, He was all she had to save her from these people who wanted to hurt her. Dirk had never spoken to her and she didn't even know if he was helping her. She pushed back against the seat and pulled a thin blanket around her shoulders.

She felt so alone. But there seemed to be shadows on this trip, and quite a bit of recognition, unless people thought she was someone else. How silly it all was. In a shop at Mont St. Michel, a man and woman had moved in close to her, then the man whispered, "it's not her." Not her?! Lara became defensive; she wanted to confront him with the news that it certainly was her! But did they think she was someone else, then saw she wasn't? Who did they think she was? Her?

She'd bought a French newspaper and now pulled it from her bag. But as she turned to get it, she noticed a woman across the aisle and one row back watching her. Lara shook the paper to open it and glanced back. The woman was writing in a notebook. Lara read a moment, then dug into her tote for the arts section. Again, the woman watched her movements, then wrote.

Was that woman aware of her, observing her and writing something? Or was she simply glancing in Lara's direction? There was always wariness now, always a peppering of the strange over events. Would life —would perceptions—ever be "normal" again?

CHAPTER TWENTY-THREE

Lara peered along the steel barrel and into the tiny V-shaped scene of the gun's sight.

Blam!

Shocked, her hand flew back, rammed by the recall. She lowered the gun and blew on her stinging palm. Rats! The kick on this .357 Magnum was hard on a hand sensitive enough to pick up a ladybug without injuring it. She'd named the new pistol "Snubbie", but snub-nosed or not, it blasted like a small cannon.

"Cease shooting," a husky voice blared through an intercom. "You may all cease shooting. Unload your weapons, leave them open, and move your sign to white."

Lara got ready to tack up a new target. She wiped her hand along the front of her dark t-shirt and studied the fine black dust that colored her fingers. Shooting was dirty work, like really dirty. She picked up the stapler, packed her guns into a bag to guard them with her, and walked past a crowd of men and women sitting on benches behind the booths. She seemed to be the only woman there with a weapon. Strange. Didn't they know they should learn how to handle a gun, that it was that kind of world? Instantly, an image of the lit profile of a dark-haired man entered her mind, and she shook her head to erase it. Not that she intended to shoot anybody.

But Halloween was coming up. Didn't these women worry about that? Maybe they should. Lara had come out today to polish her skills before the holiday. It was on her list: buy candy, find biker gloves for her costume, practice shooting.

Out beyond her booth, she attached a target to the board, but held off drawing her usual green circle. Too many people were watching her with that bold stare; someone might figure out what the extra mark was for and think her low.

Back at her booth, she sat and waited for the ranger to clear them for shooting.

It was that kind of world. Didn't everyone know that? Lara thought about her recent trip to New York City with Nicole.

She'd returned from France late September and had barely got her sleeping back to her time-zone before she was packing for her trip to NYC. She and Nicole had met up at the airport and spent a long week-end shopping and catching a show. The trip went well and things were "normal", except for the large serious cameras aimed at them and the stares and the comments.

And except for that incident at the Dallas Airport.

She had been on her way back to Granville, on a layover in Dallas. After a hike through the terminal, she'd found her gate and settled into a plastic chair, one of a row mounted to the floor. The view out the dark window had her attention until suddenly she noticed the reflection of a young man in jeans rushing toward her back. Beyond the glass, airplanes taxied and hummed, while inside, the man closed in on her. But as she watched, he swept past her and circled back to his starting point.

After a few minutes, he glanced around and again crept toward her. Two rows behind her, another man lounged in a chair, his khaki-clad legs stretched out in front of him. He seemed to doze, but Lara saw his eyes were only half-closed. The terminal was empty. Only Lara and the two men were visible along the wide hall. As the younger man swooped in, Lara quickly contrived a plan. If he raised his arm to stab her, she would drop forward onto her knees and he'd be blocked by the row of plastic seats.

But the faux-dozer—whose side was he on? What would he do?

Lara tensed as the man paced toward her. When he was behind her, he paused a step, looked at the other man, then rushed past her.

The attacker paused on the other side of the terminal, scanned the area, and prepared for a third swoop. He moved in faster this time. Lara tensed, ready to act. He charged toward her, but again eyed the other man and passed her.

Enough! Lara jumped up and turned to look at him.

The young man abruptly stopped and met her eyes. He hurried away.

"Resume shooting!" The intercom jolted her awareness back to the range. Lara picked up a gun. It was that kind of world, a place where a woman should know how to defend herself. It looked as if the bad guys were winning.

The crowds milling around were making her nervous; it would be a short session. She used up two loaded clips for the semi-automatic and slipped .38 Special bullets—weaker and easier on her hand—into the revolver. Snubbie was her new friend and source of security. Rocket the Gun Dealer had told her it needed 200 rounds to be broken in. That amounted to four boxes of fifty, and she was on box number three today.

Later that night, Lara tried to think of ways to distract herself from her lonely ache. Shopping was too stressful in Granville. Eating, too fattening. Hanging out with a man—there weren't any. Drinking, maybe later. Traveling—she'd been on two trips in two months, enough already.

Diversions. She felt she'd been wasting her time, her life. And all that effort she'd put into her relationships with men when they'd failed anyway. All her mistakes, her bad choices, all that time, all those years, wasted. "Forrest Gump" had been on TV earlier. The movie's main character went through life without planning, letting life happen without trying to control it.

Sometimes you have no control.

Lara walked downstairs to her office. She flipped on the powerstrip to her computer.

When she'd moved to Granville, she'd had a plan. She would start a counseling practice. She would work as a computer programmer and be a therapist on Saturdays to build up a clientele.

A good plan. Until, of course, Dirk Durmont.

Now, some people wanted her dead and others wanted to hurt her. It would be foolhardy to face strangers alone in a counseling office. These stalkers were vicious, and dangerous. She didn't fear them, but she knew she wasn't safe around them. Her dream of a private practice was being crushed along with the rest of her plans, destroyed by ruthless people. What did they want from her? Whatever it was, Lara wasn't going to let them just take it! She had to find out what was going on. She'd have to just dig until she uncovered something. But the Hollywood stories were such filth! Her disdain for sleazy celebrity gossip stopped her from taking her research very far.

Well. She had to toughen up. Her contempt for low-acting people was getting her nowhere.

She sat in front of the computer, typed "Dirk Durmont", and hit enter. She clicked past the first few pages of sites with nude pictures and reports from adoring fans. At the fourth page, she stopped. She randomly chose GossipLand.

Hollywood Musings by Sam Snedley
Thank you to my many fans and friends for the super dooper tips and write-ins about your fav Hollywood Hunks and Honeys.
Steve Wilton, legendary funny guy, went into Rhonda's Veggie Teahouse and Bosco says he sat right behind him and watched him eat. Steve left only a $2 tip. Maybe he needs to make a new flick if he's getting so tight, and we don't mean his a—.
Ohmigod, I can't believe who's sitting right outside on the plaza smoking a cigarette. None other than Carrie Jo Miller, now not known as Mrs. Carrie Jo Miller Dirk Durmont. Friends say that the neighbor's dog has been barking so much that the newlyweds hafta yell out the window. Not getting enough beauty sleep, celebrity lovebirds? Everyone is watching for the expected bambino which friends say is on the production schedule, and I'm sure we'll all be the first to know.

Boring. Was some guy actually getting paid to write this stuff? Lara clicked the site shut. She paged down more until she saw PersJournal. Ah—she'd seen this one before. This guy seemed to know something about Dirk and the Granville stories.

Personal Journal of Dirk Durmont
Where I keep track of my thoughts for future generations.
Sunday,
Like here we are, married and shit. So far so f-ing good. Day Two, if you count yesterday when we were getting hitched, but we didn't like wake up married or anything. Thank gawd, 'cause when that other chick found out I was heading for my wedding after we got it on, she was pissed! Women, who knows.
We're here at Abner Land, it's a real hoot. These characters do hillbilly shit and shit. CarrieJo—oh, that's who I got married to, what the hell. Anyway, when we got here and I took her up to the room in Hillsa Heaven, she kept saying like "Not really" and I'd say "yeah really", and she'd say "not really" and I'd say "yeah really," then she took my charge card and said

she'd meet me back in California at her place. Like what's that about? Women, who cares. It was an okay start, though, with me doing the housekeeper and she getting it on with the pool boy and dice mersa ... the other ways, anyway. Then me getting that blowjob from that older woman I'm taking along with us, back behind the building.

Lara had braced herself, leaning away from the obscene text. But she moved closer now. Older woman?

I'm getting real tired of LarMic whining so much. If she doesn't quit laying there all bandaged up and whining about getting stabbed, I'm going to take a knife and finish the job. Shut her up for good ...

Tears formed and streamed down Lara's face. A joke! This was a joke to these people! Someone trying to kill her was funny to them. A sob escaped, and she stomped the power strip to kill the screen. She stumbled up the stairs and pushed back into a corner where she knew no one could see her through any window, then cried uncontrollably, desperately. What would stop these awful people? Did they all know what she was going through and only laughing at her? There was no answer, there was no help! And Dirk. Could that be true, that he was going to "finish the job"?

Or hire someone to do it. Like the first guy was hired.

By whom?

—————

The weight room was crowded, and the faces unfamiliar. Lara sighed, annoyed. She was acting on an urge to work out early tonight and here she was, probably the only actual gym member, crowded out by people who were just dropping by. One treadmill was open, in front of a blond woman who sat pumping the pedals of a stationary bike. Lara felt uneasy about the exposure, but set her jaw and stepped onto it.

The woman cackled.

Lara didn't change her expression as she started the treadmill. Her radio headphones were in place on her head, but she kept the music turned off.

There was a maxim used in the counseling profession. "If you always do what you've always done, you'll always get what you've always gotten." It was time for Lara to do something different. She wouldn't ignore the woman; she would watch what she did next, after that crazy laughter. Lara fiddled with her radio, pretending to flip it on. In front of her, a big bare window blackened by the night acted as a mirror. She walked along on the treadmill, watching the reflection of the room behind her.

The woman on the bike thought she had a blind target in Lara. She forced more ugly laughter and leaned toward the woman on the bike next to her. "I'm sorry, I can't help it!" She said, and laughed. "Look at her socks! Hahaha!"

She looked up, and suddenly stopped. Lara's eyes, the green like granite now, stared steady out at her from the reflection in the window.

A sick expression passed over the woman's face. She quickly looked away, silent now.

Fear?

Lara stepped off the treadmill and turned around to face her directly. The woman glanced around, not able to meet her eyes. Lara sneered. Fear! This woman was afraid of her! What did she think, that she was going to shoot her? Well, let them be afraid, all of them! Cowards. They could snipe at her behind her back, but they couldn't face her. Disgusted, Lara headed toward the free weights. The rudie hefted herself off the bike and moved toward a treadmill.

Behind the treadmill, a stair-stepper stood empty. Lara stopped and eyed the machine.

Well. What the hey. She'd take a look at *her* socks. Who were these people? Here was Lara's chance to get a good look at one. She had already seen she was over 30 and overweight by about 25 pounds, and her face was round, the skin spotty. Her hair was an overprocessed yellow with a wide brown stripe at the part.

Lara climbed onto the stair-stepper. She glanced at the woman's reflection in the window, not directly staring, not being rude. The woman still had a sick look on her face. Lara knew the expression wasn't guilt for being cruel; these people had no consciences!

It was fear Lara was seeing.

Her socks—they were dingy and rolled down at the ends of short chunky legs. Had Lara seen her before? Maybe she looked familiar, but so many of them looked alike to her by now.

Two minutes later, the woman stepped off the treadmill.

Lara smirked. Couldn't she take it, her victim standing behind her? She heard her ask someone where the bathroom was. So it was her first visit; she didn't even know her way around. As she walked out, Lara stopped the stair-stepper and looked around.

Crowded still. Men stood near the weights, watching her. Then, through the glass door across the room, Lara saw a dreaded sight. Skinny Bitch. This one was always trouble, she and her boyfriend. They showed up in the gym from time to time, bringing different sets of friends and playing at exercising while working at gossiping about Lara and Dirk. They made cruel comments and sexual remarks. She had never stopped her workouts, never showed emotion, but now she couldn't see either of them without wishing she knew how to spit.

But tonight, if trouble had a scent, the air in the gym was a toxic gas. These people acted so strange, like they were criminals or crazy or both. There was no telling what they'd do next. Lara heeded her instincts and left by the back stairs. She passed the blond rudie, who still could not meet her eyes. In the lobby, Lara paused when she saw another unfamiliar woman walk in. The woman saw Lara and immediately turned toward a phone mounted on the wall.

Something was too wrong. Lara turned her back on it all and hurried toward the racquetball courts.

Michelle huddled with Delta at the corner of the building, both shivering in short leather jackets.

"What are you guys going to do to her?" Delta's voice was whiney, uncool. "It's cold out! Colder than a witch's toes."

Michelle lit another cigarette. "Don't make it your business what we're doing."

"Maybe I *want* to make it my business! You aren't going to kill her, are you?"

"Hell! Much as we may want to, killing her wouldn't get us nowhere! We just wanna mess with her, just for fun.'"

They stood eyeing the people in gym clothes as they went up the wide stone steps and through the double front doors. Several women had passed—some they recognized—but not the one they were looking for.

"Where the hell is she? Week after week, f-ing month after month, she's been dragging her boring ass into this place at 8:15 every Thursday night. So where is she?" Michelle's phone rang. She flipped it open. "Leaving? She hasn't gotten here yet! … She hasn't been out this way. … Yeah, we're watching. … Front … Okay, yeah … right."

Michelle snapped her phone shut and walked down the side of the building with Delta hurrying behind her. They stopped at the edge of the parking lot.

"Well, shit!" Michelle said. "There's her car! When did she get here?"

"You're not going to jump her at her car, are you?"

"No! Hell, she walks around out here with one hand gripping a six-shooter like she's in a cowboy movie. She'd blow our heads off! We have to catch her unaware, away from that gym bag." Michelle turned and shot a hard look at Delta. "Now we're sure she's here, you have your part to do. Get with it."

Delta gave her a funny look, then turned quick and left.

Michelle watched her climb into the little blue car. It was Delta's car now—that is, it would be if Michelle ever got the title work done. She'd sold it to her, made her a deal when she'd bought a newer white one. All Michelle had to do was take payments out of the money Delta trusted her with every week. She figured she could keep doing that for a long time before Delta even thought to ask about it being paid off. She hadn't ever asked about the bank account Michelle said she was keeping for her. Good thing! Michelle laughed.

Delta drove away. Great. This would fix Lara but good. If they didn't do what they planned here at the gym, Delta was making sure what Lara found when she got home would make up for it. There's no way L-whore would be staying around Granville after tonight.

Delta had her part to do, alright. And she knew what she was going to do about it.

She found Lara's house and pulled to the curb in front of it. In the seat beside her was a plastic bag, cold and squishy with a hamburger mixture.

Delta knew that Michelle had fixed the meat up the way she wanted it.

Headlights from a passing car surprised her and she drove down a block farther and stopped. Better to park away from the actual scene of the crime. She grabbed the bag and crept in the dark to the yellow house. At the end of the driveway she came to a short stone wall. She knew it was like a trick wall, though. It was low on this side, but dropped down the other side far enough to keep a dog big as a bear from getting out.

Delta sat on the wall and swung her legs over. Peering down into the yard, she prayed to the fairies that the big dog Buckley wasn't nearby. Because she had two things to do tonight. She had to get into the yard, and she had to get rid of this bag of poison hamburger, and she had to bring the dog's collar back to Michelle. That was three things. She had three things to do tonight.

She'd asked if there wasn't a way around all this, an easier way.

But no.

When she'd asked Reeza for advice, Reeza had looked at her out those gypsy eyes and said Delta's a lousy liar and she had to do these things or people would know she hadn't done anything.

So Delta knew she had to follow Michelle's orders.

Michelle had told Delta to poison Lara's dog Buckley. That would be the thing that would get Lara good for standing in the way of everyone's plans to marry Dirk.

But it was a wrong thing to do. It took less than the time of a flea-jump for Delta to figure that out. What she couldn't figure out was how to get out of it herself and at the same time make sure no one hurt that poor floppy-eared dog. When Michelle had told her the plan, she had to zip her lip and walk away to think about the problem. Luckily, Michelle thought Delta always went along with everything. That's because she always did. So she never said more about it. Delta was going to poison that dog and that was all there was to it.

She was afraid to say no. If Delta didn't agree, then Michelle would ask Stacy and she would do it, thinking it'd make everyone like her more. The only way to save the dog was to poison him herself.

But how was she going to manage that? She needed help.

Reeza's eyes about bugged out when Delta told her about her problem.

"Who is telling you to poison some woman's dog!" she'd shouted.

Delta said nothing, keeping her lips zipped tight.

Reeza gave up easy, though, and said, "I see. Well never mind, I'll deal with that one later. Seems we need a way around this."

And here Delta was, lowering her body over the wall into Lara McKeen's back yard.

And there came Buckley! He trotted around the side of the garage, ears raised and tail high. He rushed at her, growling deep. Delta lost all her breath and pushed her body back against the stone. She almost dropped the little bag, so she stuffed it down her bra to keep it safe. She tried to hold still, not even blinking, like the TV said to do around a rattlesnake. Her breath came out in scared gasps. The only thing moving on the dog was his quivering upper lip, which was lifted a little to show his teeth. The low growl continued.

"Nice dog." Delta's voice came out in a squeak.

He growled louder, then moved his eyes as he watched her hand creep up the wall. She immediately flattened her palm against the stone. Delta's heart pounded in her ears. He couldn't be a bad dog; she'd seen him trotting along beside Lara, grinning all the while. He was just so super-sized.

Suddenly his eyes turned more curious than deadly. His nose started quivering and he snorted once toward the middle of Delta's chest.

He'd smelled the hamburger!

He sniffed again and leaned in closer.

She couldn't let him get the poison meat. "No dog!" she commanded, but the words came out weak as a church-whisper.

He was getting closer and closer to Delta's body. She slowly lifted her foot toward him, hoping he'd take the offer of chewing on her rather than on something that would kill him. And there she was, balancing on one leg, trying to ward off that huge tooth-lined doggy-mouth, when the vines around her lit up. Headlights! A car was coming up the driveway.

Delta crouched down lower. Buckley lifted his head and pointed his nose toward the loud metallic sound of the garage door rising. He forgot about Delta and any smelly old meat. With one motion, his entire huge body was turned around and he was running around the garage to meet his mistress. This was Delta's chance for a getaway. She watched as the car disappeared into the garage and the door lowered, then hooked her elbows onto the wall and pulled herself up and over. She crept down the driveway, then ran along the sidewalk toward her car, one hand pressed against her chest to keep the bad meat from flying out and hurting some unlucky little creature.

"Delta!"

She flung herself behind a tree. Michelle's car had come out of no-where, and sat idling in the street with the window down.

"Did you do it?"

Delta didn't want to see Michelle right now. She peeked around the tree and whispered loud, "What are you doing here? Aren't you at the gym?"

"We lost her!" Michelle said. "Nobody could figure where she was hiding, then all of a sudden she was out at her car. The whole thing fell apart. Where's the collar?"

The collar.

Michelle said she had to bring back the collar. Reeza had said that sounded like something the Wicked Witch would demand, then said that was the easiest part. Delta needed a dog collar, and Reeza had one, old and dirty and around her own dog's neck. She'd picked up a fresh one for Misty and handed the old one over. Delta would be happy to get that stinky collar out of her purse and give it to Michelle.

But it was in her purse, in her car.

She stayed behind the tree and looked down at her hands. They held nothing. How was she going to fake a collar until she got back to her car? She looked around at the ground, and picked up a stick. Not hardly.

Car lights came around the corner and a beige SUV stopped behind Michelle's car. Michelle flung her arm out to wave it around, but it stayed stopped and tapped its horn. Michelle drove on and Delta bolted toward her car.

She'd had three things to do. She'd gone into the yard, and she'd be giving that collar up soon. Two down, one to go. She still had to get rid of the hamburger. Easy, Reeza had said. It didn't matter what happened to it, it just had to be where it couldn't hurt any creatures. So she would flush it down the toilet, bag and all, and she could honestly say she saw it get swallowed up.

———

The employees of Rocko's Club for Men had little trouble putting together Halloween costumes. This was one night they could go out in their work clothes and fit in.

Michelle led a colorful group onto High Street. She and Delta strutted along in stiletto heels, fuzzy bright boas, and sequined gowns. They had helped Stacy and Connie into leather corsets, mini-skirts, and masks of leather strips with eyeholes. They each carried a whip which they dangled as they stumbled along the sidewalk in the steep-heeled boots. The whips were Michelle's idea and totally brilliant, if she did say so herself. If used right, they could slice gashes into flesh. Perfect for tonight's activities.

The two sheepherders—Gretchen and Vera—were from Lakeland near Rockton and were hanging out with Michelle because they knew she was totally cool and would introduce them to Dirk one day. Lots of the girls from the hills wanted to be stars, either working at Wagon Wheel City doing a "Singing to America" act or meeting Dirk and becoming really famous. Michelle thought they were much more fun than Connie and her bunch, who were dating boring guys and taking classes at the college. Boring.

The streets and sidewalks weren't visible under the swarms of children and their escorting adults who crunched through gold leaves shaken down from the oak trees. Vehicles rolled along the street like a funeral procession, some stopping occasionally to gape open a door and spill out monsters, angels, and cartoon characters. Many of the over-30 set had trick-or-treated this old neighborhood when they were children and were now passing down tradition to the younger ones. They remembered that brick house where someone always hung spiders from the trees, and there, the owner still dressed as Santa and shouted "Ho Ho Ho!" when she opened the door. And, sure enough, a monster still jumped out of the pile of leaves in front of that two-story white frame. Hadn't he passed? Maybe so, but it looked as if someone had inherited the Frankenstein costume.

Michelle and the others reached a point across the street from a yellow bungalow and stopped.

Gretchen grinned at the people strolling by and asked, "Can we meet Dirk tonight?"

"You know one of these is him," Stacy hissed. "How can we tell? Can we see any shoes out here in the dark? He'd be wearing some good ones. Let's see—he's tall, so we can rule out the short guys unless he's hunching down to fool everyone. Do you think he'd do that?"

"I don't think he could hunch all night," Delta said, "so if we see someone looking hunched, watch him to see if he straightens when no one's looking. Mark's out here someplace, too. He was over at the apartment earlier wondering where we'd be."

"Why is Mark out here?" Connie looked worried.

"I dunno." Delta answered. "He always wants to know where Lara is, so when I told him that she'd be sitting out like usual on Halloween, he said he'd be around in costume. Don't use his name if you see him. He likes to go around secret."

Michelle peered across the street at Lara sitting on her porch in a heavy leather jacket. "Look at L-whore-a! A biker! What a dyke," she hissed. She bent forward and shook her breasts, which were wired up high enough to hurt. "Look at real women, you dyke!"

"So that's the woman!" Gretchen laughed as she and Vera leaned in to stare across the street. "I can't believe it! This is so cool! Did you hear how when that man tried to kill her, that Dirk cancelled his movie and ran up here to defend her, and then—and then—the murderer mysteriously disappeared."

Vera grinned as she stared at Lara. "I can't believe we're really seeing her."

Gretchen continued. "They say Dirk moved her to Granville after Laura Starbright broke his heart. And when he married Carrie Jo Miller, Lara jumped off a building to kill herself! But she didn't die, so then he flew her to his castle in France to show he loved her, that it was his agent made him marry Carrie Jo."

"Let's get closer." Vera stepped into the street.

"No!" Michelle shouted, then lowered her voice. "We have to be totally cool. Like, Dirk doesn't want a fuss made, so don't say anything to her. Okay?"

"Yeah, sure," Vera replied. "You know what I heard? I heard that she's into witchcraft and put a spell on Dirk and they're trying to find someone to break the spell, like a virgin or something, but her powers are too powerful!" She stopped to gasp. "And that's her right there!"

Michelle had had enough of this excitement over L-whore. "Well, ladies, sorry to disappoint you, but I heard—and from a good source— that she's his drug dealer, and that's why he goes over to her house." Suddenly, she leaned forward and stared. "What the hell! Isn't that her dog?"

Buckley was sitting behind the storm door with his big tongue lolling out. She whipped around to face Delta.

Delta looked like she almost grinned, but then got real serious. She spoke fast. "Oh my goodness, that big dog must take a lot to get him down. Last time I saw him, he was sicker than a dog. Now there he is, big as life."

Michelle screwed up her eyebrows. What the hell! That didn't even sound like Delta, saying so much in one breath.

"Where do you suppose she hid her gun?" Delta kept talking. "I know Mark knows she's got guns. He knows more than any of us."

Stacy, breathless from the cinched-up corset, gulped some air and looked long at Lara. "That jacket's big enough to hide a bunch of guns. Who's that guy?" They watched as a good-looking dark-haired man came out the door and sat next to her. He opened a bag of candy and poured it into a black plastic kettle.

Connie stared, then spoke. "Oh. Yeah. He's her lawyer. Every celebrity needs one, you know. He works downtown." She shifted her corset up.

Michelle scowled. "Damn. Dirk will never show up if she has a lawyer with her."

"What's she so afraid of? She can't sue us, can she?" Stacy asked.

"You know that stalking is illegal," Connie spoke loudly, putting on that college snot attitude she was getting. Several small groups stopped and looked at her.

"I don't want no one suing me!" Delta whined out. "I'm still thinking how I'm going to pay Gramma all her money back."

Michelle rolled her eyes. "No one is suing us. Hell, if L-whore wanted to sue someone, it'd be Dirk Durmont. But you see how slippery he is! We can't even see him, much less catch him."

Suddenly, a white cargo van stopped in front of them. A greasy-looking man with long brown hair glared at them from the passenger seat. He lifted one hammy middle finger and shook it at them.

Stacy gasped. "Isn't that the guy from the pool? The one who kicked Delta?"

Delta's eyes grew big. "What are those guys doing here?"

Michelle looked hard at him. Around his neck, shaped around his stringy hair, stood the collar of a black cape. Was he in some kind of costume? She quickly moved down the sidewalk and waved the women along with her. "Keep moving. Let's find Dirk and get out of here. He's around here someplace." Suddenly she pointed. "There's a tall one!"

The women hurried to stand behind a man in a Grim Reaper costume. He stood on the sidewalk until three children ran up and pulled him to the next house. The women groaned.

They walked a few more steps, then Michelle grabbed Stacy's arm and said, "Gimme that whip a minute. I'm going to show you girls how it's done." Michelle pointed to a shiny gold paper on the ground. "Watch me get that!" Taking the wooden handle in one hand, she raised the leather lash above her head, then brought it down fast. It cracked against the paper, sending it shredded in two directions.

She smiled big and turned.

And screamed in pain when a hand darted out and gripped her wrist.

"Ow!" She dropped the whip.

A man in a vampire costume—a mask hiding his face and a black cape hanging from his shoulders—held her arm while she struggled. The other women gasped, then stepped back to run away, but bumped against men wearing the same disguise.

The vampire who'd grabbed Michelle flung her wrist down.

"You bastard!" she shouted. "That hur ...", but she stopped as he stepped closer.

He turned to take in the group of women, but they couldn't see his eyes to know where he was looking. Then he faced Michelle and spoke. "You listen to me!" He sounded real mad and looked around at the women again. "Listen up, *Dolls!*" He spat out the last word. "I don't know what you're doing out here on High Street, but you go find someplace else to trick-or-treat. There is no way any of you are getting near that yellow house across the street."

Michelle started up with, "You can't tell us where ..."

But he was gone. So were the others. The women looked around, confused. The vampires surrounding them had all faded back into the crowd. One was pacing fast across the street where he spoke to another and pointed back at them. They then stepped toward Lara's house.

Michelle looked over at Delta. Her voice quaked as she said, "Do you know what Mark is dressed like?"

"Yeah, he changed at our place. He's a vampire."

The women peered around at the crowds. Vampires were everywhere. There might have been a dozen tall figures in black tuxes and capes, their faces hidden behind masks.

"Hell," Michelle whispered.

A vampire cat. It must be a character from a children's TV show.

"Really, I saw one!" The tiny blonde in the caped cat costume was confident.

Lara smiled at her and said, "On TV. You saw a vampire cat on TV." She dropped more candy into the proffered bag. Her knowledge of kids' shows and their heroes came mostly from Halloween night. A Chinese girl warrior was popular this year, along with a group of blue people with special powers. She now looked over at Steve, who shrugged and shook his head.

Halloween on High Street had become Lara's all time favorite holiday and she was determined to keep the crazies from stealing it. But so many people hated her, it would be stupid for her to open her door to strangers in masks. At the last minute, she'd tried to hire a bodyguard but the security companies were all booked for the evening. When her friend Steve agreed to join her tonight her great relief surprised her. She'd been more worried than she realized.

The little girl shouted now, excited. "No, I saw one here! There's a vampire cat around here!"

Beyond her on the sidewalk, her mother rolled her eyes.

"Around here? How do you know it's a vampire?" Lara asked.

"Because it has a cape!"

"A cape! Well, I'll have to look for it." Lara turned to glance around at the porch behind her.

"Oh, it's *invisible* now."

The mother lost patience and called for the child, who ran off to the next house.

After she left, there was a lull in the crowds. They sat a minute, enjoying the warm air that prompted them to sit out on the steps to hand out candy.

Steve stood. "I'm running in for a minute. Do you want anything, besides more candy?"

Lara smiled up at her friend. He had no idea what a help he was being. One day she'd tell him. "No, nothing for me, thanks."

After Steve went inside, Lara shifted her jacket and grew uneasy. She had considered dressing as a Sitting Duck, as a joke, but this biker costume was a more practical choice. The thick leather jacket offered some defense, the sunglasses hid her eyes so she could watch for attacks, and a motorcycle chain draped across her body was like armor over her heart, good protection from a knife.

But now she felt vulnerable sitting out with masked monsters—many of them adult-size—wandering the sidewalks. She knew she couldn't carry Snubbie with children around, so she'd left the gun in the house, hidden in the living room. Her plan: if she had trouble with the crazies she'd let Steve delay them while she ran inside. If an assailant followed her in, he would then be in her house and intending her bodily harm. And he'd be close range, so she wouldn't hit any innocent parties.

But right now, a good plan would be to get Buckley to sit beside her until Steve came back. The dog had been standing watch at the storm door, making tongue marks on the glass while the children waved at him and laughed. Lara stood and opened the door, guiding him to sit on the porch behind her.

"Good puppy," she sat, turned back around, then jerked in surprise.

Where had *he* come from?!

A tall man stood in front of her. Lara leaned back to take in his costume—a tux and a cape, with a full mask hiding his face. She glanced at his visible hand; it carried no weapon. One hand, however, was tucked out of sight.

Buckley leaned in near her shoulder. His usual pant had ceased and she could sense his tension.

Then Lara saw the mini-vampire on the sidewalk next to him. The toddler walked up to her and hefted a bag higher than his head. Instantly, she forgot her danger.

"Well, hello! Aren't you too cute!" She laughed, lowered herself down a step, and leaned out to drop some candy into his bag. He accepted it silently, then turned and waddled away. The man turned with him, as silent as the child and as the grave.

"Happy Halloween!" Lara called after him. Her voice held a touch of sarcasm.

Chapter Twenty-Four

Subj: DirkLetter
Date: 11/15/2000 8:35:07 AM Central Daylight Time
From: HotGirl11@mail.com (Karen)
To: DirkDolls (group)

Dirk Dolls,

We're still waiting for that first baby with Dirk's smile and fortune, but there's no news yet.

We have some business to pass on. Shirl Manier, loyal Granville Dirk assistant, told us that she will give us stuff on Lara M as long as we keep to our agreement. Which was to never tell anyone outside Granville anything we know or see, and that includes the tabloids and bodyguards. Everything is to go through Shirl first and only.

She also says that whoever said that someone wants to "make it look like suicide" isn't funny. And that Lara has a "sensitive nature", so you who are making faces at her in the stores should do so only when absolutely necessary. I know some of you think she is into witchcraft and has put a spell on our Dirk, but you must not attack her unless she makes you.

Also, there is a lot of radio requesting for certain songs about witches and evil women. Shirl wants us to stop it and to put only the songs on from the list she gave us. Let me know if you need another copy.

Finally, we can follow Lara around but we are never to talk to her and we follow her at our own risk. There are reportedly some dangerous types hanging around.

Yours in Dirkville,
Editor Karen

Lara lay huddled into a corner of her sofa with a notebook across her knees and a pen in her hand. The successful Halloween and upcoming holidays had her feeling cheerful, almost happy.

"Alien!" She waved high and the light blinked. "I've decided since I have no life here, it's the perfect time to write a book." She grinned. "It's a regular writer's life. I'm alone all the time, I can't go anywhere without trouble so I don't go, I don't know how I'm ever going to meet a man much less trust one. So, my book begins."

She wrote a few minutes, then peered out her front door to see if any cars or people had stopped. She looked back up at the corner of the room.

"The book will be about a woman who moves to a town to begin a new life. But the town is enchanted, and the people are kind, and she finds a man to love, and good things happen to her. And she lives happily ever after to the ends of her days." She wrote more, then spoke. "You've made a good point, Alien. Of course there has to be a villain. She'll be a vulgar woman who reads tabloids and has dried-out bleached yellow hair. Everybody hates her."

Lara laughed, then wrote quietly for the next hour. Then, ready for a break, she leaned back on her sofa and looked out the front door for cars crawling past. She eyed Alien. She could not escape the sense that she was being watched, all the time now. She worried she was a show for more than the people staring at her and gossiping about her and Dirk. In her own home, how safe was she? If this man had endless money—and he did, by most people's standards—and if he could find people who'd do anything for money, would he bug her house?

Of course he would. He would monitor everything she did, every phone call she made. So the better question was: where were the bugs? Lara had searched under her furniture, in her vents, and behind mirrors. She didn't know exactly what she was looking for, but there had to be some physical device, a camera or recorder. How tiny were those things these days?

Now she sat and eyed Alien, her confidant in this matter she couldn't discuss with anyone "real." Talking to him comforted her. And, as a counselor, she knew that giving voice to her problems sometimes led her to understanding them.

But what was the little light on the wall, really?

Technically, Alien was left over from a security system a former owner had installed. A label on her front door warned the world that this house was protected by A&M Security. She wasn't being charged for an unordered service, so she'd accepted her fanciful Alien as some forgotten motion detector, disconnected from the main system. Besides, she'd had enough on her mind with working and decorating and being stalked to worry about why it was blinking at her.

But her life was worsening and she needed to know if it was another menace. By now, she had tracked the rest of the security system. A box near the back door held a numeric keypad and a small display window. In the basement, a gray metal case that mimicked her fuse box was loaded with wires that led into little receiving holes labeled with room names. The entire box was connected to a plug that looked like a telephone hookup.

The box near the back door probably controlled the system. Now Lara went to stand in front of it and, with the confidence of a computer professional, keyed in a random number.

"Invalid Entry" appeared in the viewing window.

She punched in other combinations—her birthday, the current date, seven 7's. It answered with "Invalid Entry, Invalid Entry, Invalid Entry."

On impulse, she pressed the numbers for Dirk Durmont's date of birth. The window displayed "Do you wish to access?"

The box had responded.

Interesting.

Lara pressed "Y."

The box answered with "Do you wish to end access?" Did she wish to stop punching things in? Yes, for now, until she figured out what she was doing. She pressed "Y."

And all hell broke lose.

A horn sounded throughout the house, blaring from some un-known place. Lara jumped back, covered her ears, and reached out to push more keys. "N", "N", "N"! The horrid noise continued.

She ran out her front door and stood on her porch. Was it coming from under the porch? Surely the neighbors could hear! What were they thinking?

Back inside, she struggled with the phone book. Her hands shook as the nerve-wracking blare continued. She called the police. Had they received a signal? The operator was confused, but not ready to send squad cars to her house. Next she called A&M Security.

"Ma'am, you don't have an account with us."

"But how do I turn this off? Can't you hear it? It's terrible, this awful noise!"

"I'm sorry, ma'am, I can't help you. We can't do anything from here."

Lara hung up, and slapped her hands over her ears. She ran into the basement, opened the small gray box of wired connections, and began pulling the lines out. She tried to remember where they all went so she could put them right later, but her panic at the blasting overwhelmed her. And still the deafening noise continued.

She ran upstairs and found a wire that led to a spot above the kitchen pantry. She climbed up on a chair and eyed a small box, then yanked hard at the spliced wires, oblivious to danger from the live current. The earsplitting sounds had to stop!

Then, as abruptly as it started, the alarm went dead.

Lara remained balanced on the chair and breathed in deep, her nerves shot. She climbed down and waited for neighbors to knock on her door to see if she was okay. No one came.

Suddenly, a sick dread gripped her middle.

She'd disconnected wires, killing the power for the security system. But what else had she destroyed?

She moved toward the living room at a funeral pace. She was only trying to stop the noise. She didn't mean to hurt anything.

Then she looked up at the corner near the front door and saw her worst fear realized. The little box was dark. She waved her arms, paced to the back of the room and up the steps, positioned herself in every spot of the room and still it didn't respond.

Dead? No! Now with fresh panic, she rushed down to the basement and shoved wires back into little holes. Back and forth up the stairs she ran, looking for life in the corner of the living room. But finally, after an hour of desperate effort, she had to admit what she had done.

She had killed Alien.

She had destroyed her only friend in this nightmare. Shock hit her. In her isolation in Granville, she had befriended a little light on the wall. How pathetic! But now she had destroyed even that. She sunk to the floor and sobbed.

"I'm sorry, Alien! I'm so sorry."

Later, Lara sat staring bleakly at the cold corner of the living room. She couldn't leave the house today now; her face was a mess from her tears.

She had to face it. It was time to move away. Her life in Granville was ridiculous, so isolated and lonely. Her world was becoming smaller and smaller as she limited what she did and with whom. She'd given up on finding a church home and she couldn't think of a way to meet normal men in such a crazy place. Shopping required a trip out of town. She clung to the few new friends she'd made and filled her time with work, house projects, and struggles to work out at a gym.

How long had it been now that she'd been victimized by this faux fame, that she had been reciting her list of celebrity rules and living like a prisoner? Two years. But what was God directing her to do? Last winter, before the murder attempt, she'd felt that moving would be running away. She wasn't someone to run away from anything! She could fight them; she wouldn't give up!

But she needed a life. And she needed to trust God to take care of her future if she took some risks. Funny—she might have appeared brave through this terrible year, but it wasn't too difficult for her to walk into situations where she might be stabbed or shot or photographed. It took some courage, but not so much.

But when faced with her life, she was frozen by her fears—her fear of aloneness and her fear of poverty. She needed courage about the real things, courage to take risks with her life.

Death didn't scare her. Life did.

She had to remember the lesson: trust *God. He* is the one.

But moving meant losing her house. Throughout this nightmare, she'd found comfort in knowing she had something they couldn't take away—her beautiful house. Well, they would have taken it. The thought of the loss filled Lara's eyes with tears once more.

She had to get away to think this out. She'd take a trip, that's what she'd do. She'd go to the ocean. Where was that brochure about that island, the one in South Carolina with the old houses? Pawley's Island, that was it. She'd plan a trip. She wouldn't think about this awful business until she was distanced from it.

CHAPTER TWENTY-FIVE

Freedom!

Lara ran, letting her legs carry her blind through the fog toward the thunderous "om" of the ocean surf. She turned and the waves chased her back up the shore. Here near the water the sand was springy, giving an extra bounce to her steps. No one could see her; salt-scented mist draped curtains around her movements. She ran zigzag farther up the beach.

Then she stopped so fast her feet dug a little hollow in the sand.

Suddenly anxious, she searched the heavy air around her. The world had become a small room with damp gray clouds for walls. Where were the weathered beach houses that stood shoulder-to-shoulder in a huddle beyond the sand dunes? Lara faced the noise of the waves to orient herself. The houses should be at her back. She turned around to face civilization, but the mist still hid all signs of the living. The heavy cloud that had dropped onto the island was becoming menacing.

She rested her hand on Snubbie's bag, which was strapped across her body. Good to have, although she'd be better off with a compass right now. Or a chunk of garlic to ward off ghosts. While reading up for her trip, she was dismayed to learn that the area around Pawley's Island was home to more ghosts per capita than any other place in the nation. Scary. Her first day here, she had skimmed the local history books in a corner of a gift shop. She was relieved to read that the ghosts haunted places nearby, but there were none on the island itself.

Except one. The Grey Ghost. But he was unstable, showing up only once in a while to warn people of disaster. Lara peered through the fog. Lordy! How would she even know if she was seeing a ghost in all this? She shivered, then paced toward where she imagined the houses.

As she'd left her little rented cottage this evening, the fog felt like a blessing. Construction workers were renovating the house across the street and each time Lara stepped out, they looked over at her and murmured to each other, making her uneasy and shy. When she'd gone out into a cover of fog today, she was relieved.

Now, however, she clutched Snubbie as she walked.

The sound of movement nearby startled her. She stopped and

peered toward the noise. Had it come from the ocean? But the water was behind her. Wasn't it?

Scared now, she rushed straight ahead. Suddenly, a dim glow leaked through the mist. A streetlight! Lara exhaled the breath she'd been holding and ran to it.

Home, safe again. Lara looked up from her journal and admired the cozy beach cottage. It was cute, with wood furniture pieces painted the same bright white and a scheme of coral and plum running through the pillows and silk flower arrangements. Pretty. The first night here, she'd heard the sound of footsteps creeping up the long stairs to her porch. Now the porch door was locked, the front door was bolted, and blankets were draped over the shaded windows. Lara had created a snug little cave.

She looked down at the notebook in front of her and flipped back several pages.

Another New Year's Day had gone by quietly. She'd tried to begin the year with a new attitude, to pick herself up out of the months of frustration and pain. She had grown, but nothing around her had changed. The ruthless people who stalked and tormented her simply didn't care what they were doing to her. It hurt, but at least she wasn't letting them control what she did. She was proud that she'd kept to her list of rules and had never lost her cool. Not publicly, that is.

But she factored danger into most things she did now. For this trip, she'd chosen to drive 21 hours so she could have her guns with her. How long would it be before someone succeeded … in what? In killing her? But why? She'd given up trying to figure it out. It was as if understanding the world of fame required her to expect low behavior—even stupidity— from strangers. There was no reason for it, that's just the way it was.

But how could these people still get to her? Their attacks were so petty and ridiculous. Was her exhaustion making her more vulnerable? Was it PTSD?

What*ever*.

It wasn't her war! They didn't know *her* at all. Their problem was with "their" movie star, whom they either dogged after to pilfer money and attention from or hated because of their own shortcomings. If they thought that by running her out of town, they had won something— a chance at Hollywood, an affront to Dirk—okay, they could have Granville and she'd take the rest of the world.

Ultimately God would win.

In the meantime, what were her options? She picked up her pen.

02-13-01 Tuesday

Pawley's Island. Does Granville exist? Is all that mess really happening?

I need a life. Whether they're harassing me or not, I need a life. I'm here to clear my head and hear from God what I'm supposed to do next.

Options:

1. Stay in Granville.

Problems with staying: If I don't resolve this with Dirk, it's too humiliating to stay in town. Also, so many people hate me and the mentally ill ones will always stalk me. My life is in danger. And my reputation and privacy are shot; I don't want to see a doctor or go to a dentist with the chance of rudies victimizing there.

So: It's not an option. "Feels" all wrong.

2. Sell my house, leave. Look for a job anyplace.

Problem: Go where?

3. Go away for a while, distance myself so I can heal a little, then decide. All I need is the next <u>step</u>; I can never know the future.

Problem: Then what? Decide later. Go away and write, finish the book I'm working on. That way I can put off the trauma of losing my house or I can decide to keep it.

What does God want me to do?

What do <u>I</u> want to do?

She couldn't do it. She couldn't give up her house, her plans! What was she going to *do*? Surely there was a way out of this mess!

"Happy Valentine's Day," Lara said to herself. She lazily viewed the ocean from her seat on a wooden staircase that led up a sand dune. She was working on her gratitude list for the day, counting up five blessings. One, she was at a fairly warm beach in winter. Two, she wasn't in Granville with people peering at her while she arranged to flee the country, like last year.

A couple of dogs ran past, teasing each other with a piece of driftwood, mouths open as if they were laughing. Buckley would like it here, unless he'd spend his time bullying the other dogs. Still, he'd enjoy scaring the smaller dogs. Three. Her third blessing was seeing happy dogs run by.

Four—some TV station was running a monster movie marathon. It was perfect for this Valentine's Day. So far, she'd seen the Fly and a werewolf movie. They made her think of past relationships. She muttered her version of a werewolf poem, "Even a man who looks okay, and takes you out at night, can become a monster when the right mood hits, and the moon is full and bright." That was the trouble with marriage—one never knew what they'd turn into once married.

Suddenly, a large dark shape caught her attention. She froze and stared toward the surf. Something was in the water, just off the shore. There it was again! She'd recently read about some shark attacks. Had they happened near here? She fished in her pocket for her glasses, worn only to drive, watch movies, and identify monsters.

Emboldened by the fact that a shark attack on land was unheard of—so far—she stood and walked toward the waves. Then, directly in front of her, a group of four rounded bodies broke their fins through the water. Dolphins! Lara was seeing dolphins! She didn't know that such a special creature lived here. She stood, mystified. They seemed to be putting on a show for her, dipping and coursing back and forth. Then, just as suddenly as they had arrived, they disappeared. Lara searched the water for several minutes, but they were gone.

Five. Blessing number five. She'd seen dolphins. Happy Valentine's Day.

02-16-01 Friday
Pawley's Island
Journal,

I had the best dream! Dirk was in it and finally showing his face. In fact, he kept making comic faces at me, funny faces like Charlie Chaplin and the Stooges—old movie comedians. I laughed and called him a Professional Face Maker. Then he kissed me, and that got me so worked up that my heavy breathing woke me up. Rats! I want more dreams like that!

It's my last night here, and there are no answers for me. I thought that if I emptied my head, or at least moved a few thoughts out, God would say, "Well, finally! That's what I was waiting for, a little room." And then He'd drop in a new idea, the right one. Not so.

My life—what do I want? If I could have the perfect life, what would it be? There is no five-year plan that God gives to anyone. Like that plaque I brought with me: "I don't have to know where I'm going, but at least I'm on my way." I only understand that I need to step out in faith, that there are no guarantees.

What do I want? Not the status quo, that much I know.

I had thought I got a revelation, to change my work schedule but stay in Granville. It felt good, like an answer.

It felt good, for about 20 minutes. There is so much that's painful about Granville, so many problems. And humiliation, confusion, danger. I don't want to go back there.

I'm worried that when I'm alone and barricaded in my house, I soothe myself with daydreams that things will be okay. Is that called "optimism", or "escaping into fantasy"? And then I face reality and it's too sad. I am alone and I can't see a way to fix this on my own. Okay, faith in God should give me dreams— call them "prayers"? But will they be answered? What is going to become of me? I did get dolphins on Valentine's Day. That's a God thing. But really, what is going to happen to me? I don't want to go back, back to all that mess.

But she had to go back. Tonight she'd packed her bags and cleaned out the refrigerator and tomorrow she'd begin the long drive to a very cold town.

—⁓—

Karma.

That's what Rocko called his plan.

He liked his dancers to sign up for the Rocko Karma Plan which encompassed health insurance, disability, and a savings deduction. He said if he kept his girls' money safe, they'd make him rich. Karma.

Alice had told him the fall from the water tower was an accident. It was an accident, as far as she knew. But it was all so hazy. She'd been dancing for the guys that night. It seemed something terrible had just happened. Right—Dirk had married some other woman. It was too confusing. So she'd driven home, that's all. She knew he'd get back to Granville eventually. He'd come home, sometime.

Then she was dancing and they were shouting to her. *Dance! Dance! Dance!* Wasn't that it? She couldn't remember.

Then she was in a hospital.

Her leg was hurt bad, broken in several places. Not her face though; it was okay. It took a couple of surgeries to get her leg right, but it would be fine. The nurses called her lucky.

The voices called her stupid.

As she lay in the mechanical bed, she had watched the door warily. She learned that if someone didn't come in through it, she was alone. One nurse—Denise—searched the room when Alice asked her to. Then Denise talked about her "meds" and calling some family members, but when Alice wouldn't tell her anything she gave up. A social worker came by, but she gave up, too. So the voices went on, but if Alice ignored them, no one could hurt her because of them.

It was an accident, so she was insured and a good part of the hospital bill was taken care of. The remainder of the bills was covered by the savings deduction account. After two weeks, Rocko's muscle men came to carry her and her big cast back to her apartment. When they'd seen the photos of Dirk all over the place, they joked with her about her movie star boyfriend, but she kept her mouth shut so they couldn't arrest her.

She'd get better and then she'd straighten this mistake out with Dirk.

The guys had left her there on her sofa and went out to a grocery store with the plan to fill her refrigerator.

They didn't come back.

Alice woke up from a pain-pill doze when the door opened again. The two men creeping in and peeking at her were not at all the pair of muscular men who'd left. Shuffling in with two bags of groceries were George and Dave, the bums she'd seen so often out on the front steps of the building. They told her later that Rocko had told his guys to slip them some cash to look out for her awhile. But they took her into their care and kept her there long after it was worth money to them.

The scruffy characters showed Alice kindness. They fetched her prescriptions and kept her in food, then ran her to sessions with doctors and physical therapists. George walked with a deep limp, so he promised her he wouldn't let her get into some gimpy condition. When she was ready to try walking, they held her arms while she tottered up and down the halls, then outside and around the block. George even drove her around some while she watched Lara, making sure she wasn't getting with Dirk. Alice explained to him that this woman had ruined her life and that she was going to fix her somehow.

The two men became her friends.

Then she was ready to dance. At first she was slow and unsteady, but all she needed in her line of work was to sway and take off her clothes, and that she could manage. But Rocko wouldn't take her back. She'd lied to him and Reeza about her police record and he wouldn't tolerate that.

There were other places to dance, though. Tonight, she was starting at Lively Lady. She studied her naked reflection in the mirror, and practiced a short routine. Not bad, for sitting on her butt so long. It'd sure be nice to have some money coming in again. And to connect with Dirk. She'd get word to him that she was dancing there so he could come see her. The Lady wasn't as upscale as Rocko's, but she could make a decent living while she worked things out in Granville.

She had something to finish in this town.

If it wasn't for Lara McKeon, she'd be with Dirk Durmont and maybe even married to him, right now.

—◦◦◦—

Ah, a DirkLetter. Michelle balanced her cigarette on the edge of the table, letting the ashes sprinkle the carpet. She swigged her beer and clicked open the email.

```
---------------------------------------------
Subj:  Fat for a reason
Date:  02/24/2001  4:55:03 PM Central Daylight Time
From:  HotGirl11@mail.com (Karen)
To:    DirkDolls (group)


Dolls!

Did you hear the news? It's all over the Internet and the newspaper!
He said so himself—Lara's pregnant! We've been right all this time.
---------------------------------------------
```

Damn. How was she getting away with all this? She must have seen Dirk and told him when she was on that trip to the coast. Then Michelle laughed and belched out some beer. At least this was something the L-whore couldn't hide for long! She typed:

```
----------------------------------------------
Subj:   Re: Fat for a reason
Date:   02/24/2001  5:19:03 PM Central Daylight Time
From:   OnlyOne1@mail.com (Michelle)
To:     DirkDolls (group)


This time we're going to catch her. There is no way out. If she sneaks
out of town to get rid of it, we'll be right there.
----------------------------------------------
```

More emails quickly arrived.

```
----------------------------------------------
Subj:   Re: Fat for a reason
Date:   02/24/2001  5:24:53 PM Central Daylight Time
From:   NancyJonn@mail.com
To:     DirkDolls (group)


What do you think they'll name it?
----------------------------------------------


----------------------------------------------
Subj:   Re: Fat for a reason
Date:   02/24/2001  5:33:09 PM Central Daylight Time
From:   HotGirl111@mail.com (Karen)
To:     DirkDolls (group)


Dolls,

Okay, let's hear from you. What will we name the baby?
Editor K
----------------------------------------------
```

Lara exhaled, exasperated, and dropped her head into her hands. On the table in front of her, the newspaper lay open.

"Dirk Durmont's Wife Not Pregnant

In a retraction of yesterday's news story ... a baby on the way ... Dirk Durmont has denied that his wife, Carrie Jo Miller of the television game show 'Are We There Yet,' is pregnant."

So if people thought there was a "baby on the way", and his wife wasn't expecting, who would they think was carrying it? She'd come back from Pawley's Island and stepped right back into chaos. She knew the rudies would be staring at her abdomen. They did that typically, but for the next couple of months they'd be more blatant. What would protect her from them? Dressing for work, she finally chose a navy blue suit with a long jacket. As she hurried into the General Insurance building, she wasn't surprised to see three young women sitting outside on the planter eyeing her as she walked. Inside, several others in the halls examined her body as she went for coffee.

Saturday arrived. Lara had grown bored with the whole pregnancy issue and her jackets by Thursday, but out of laziness finished out the workweek in suits. Today she'd do a reverse. She thanked God for a thin day and pulled on figure-flattering jeans and a tight black t-shirt. For a jacket, she wore a short fitted blazer that showed her lower body.

Now she had errands to run, and she hoped everyone who'd been spying on her would look like royal fools when she showed up un-pregnant.

A favorite shopping center was holding a big sidewalk sale, and Lara made it her first stop. Soon she was sliding hangers along the racks set outside the stores. A "Sale Inside" sign baited her into a shop, and she headed to a wall rack labeled "30% off." Too soon, her shopping was interrupted.

"There she is," someone behind her whispered.

Lara steeled herself, but didn't show a reaction.

"It's her, all right," the voice continued. "She has some nerve, showing her face around here."

Lara pulled out the skirt of a long dress, then turned to the side to glance behind her. A dark-haired woman, 40-ish, stood with a younger woman near a round rack. As Lara turned and peeked at her, the woman quickly looked away.

Lara tried to detach, tried not to react to the woman's hatred. What did it matter what these people thought of her? She lifted the dress down and moved past the clothes and shoppers to find the dressing rooms at the back of the store. She entered one of the little rooms and slid an old heavy curtain across the doorway. Without undressing, she held the garment up in front of her and peered into a tall mirror. Was the color too orange? She never wore orange, but liked a certain shade of red. Undecided, she hung the hanger on a hook and reached up to find the care tag. The color was iffy, but the price was low and if it was machine washable, maybe she'd buy it anyway.

Suddenly the curtain whipped open!

Lara whirled around, shocked.

There, with one hand gripping the curtain, stood the woman who'd been gossiping in the store. She moved her eyes up and down Lara's body, then said with sarcasm, "Oh. Excuse me!" She smirked into Lara's face.

Lara stared back at her, not trying to mask her hatred and disgust. The woman gave her body one more leer, then let the curtain drop closed.

Bitch! Only in Granville! In a lifetime of shopping, Lara had never had some woman charge in on her and leer at her body. Thank God she was fully dressed.

She stood a moment composing herself, then returned the dress to the rack and marched out of the store.

CHAPTER TWENTY-SIX

Trips to pick up kitty litter had been annoying, but fairly safe. Until tonight.

The scarf tightened around Lara's neck and choked her. She gasped, then quickly unwound her muffler and draped it again more loosely.

Then she stepped out of Pet Place into the cold night.

Through the door, she had seen the white cargo van pull up to the curb. A familiar chill rushed up her spine as she studied it. She'd dreamt this. And it wasn't good, it was a bad thing. Increasing her dread was the fact that a similar vehicle was mentioned in the paper recently. The newspaper reported that someone had seen some men jump out of a cargo van and kidnap a woman off the streets. Days later, an updated story suggested it was bogus, that the "kidnapping" was fake.

A practice run?

She stood, waiting for someone to climb out of the vehicle. No one moved. The driver wasn't visible in the dark interior. Lara cased the parking lot. Behind the van and facing it, was an SUV with its engine running and lights on. As she watched, a black SUV pulled into the lot and stopped out away from her car. Another car joined it.

She waited. No one climbed out of any of the vehicles.

Quick and determined, she pushed her cart out into the parking lot. She needed to get to Snubbie. She passed behind the van. There were no people anyplace except those sitting in the stopped vehicles. She paced across the lot, trying to shake off the thought that cold weather was perfect for a kidnapping. If robbed of a coat and shoes, anyone would be an easy captive.

When she reached her car, she swung the heavy cart around to face the van and lifted the trunk lid. She opened the passenger door and created a fort with the car, the door, and the cart rack she'd parked beside. Pulling out Snubbie's bag, she slung it across her body and slid off her right glove to give her a better grip. Then she stepped behind her car and hefted the heavy litter into the trunk, watching the van as she worked. All the vehicles remained motionless. Their idling engines were the only sounds in the night.

Finished, Lara slammed the trunk lid down, jerked the cart into the rack, and sped away. Minutes later, she was back barricaded in her house.

Home again.

The nightmares would not end, those when she was sleeping and those when she left the house. She couldn't escape the low people. When had the world grown so ugly? She had lived years now in Granville trying to clutch on to her life while piece by piece it was stolen from her. She analyzed and itemized, and it came down to one choice. She could postpone it as long as her psyche and body could hold up, and as long as some deranged beast didn't kill her, but the fact remained.

She had to leave town. She had to lose her home.

Lara analyzed, and she prayed. And the still small voice echoing in her mind's ear began to tell her to leave Granville. The war was not lost—God would win—but the war was not hers and surviving meant leaving.

She had to let lose her grip on this house, the first home no one could take from her.

Well, God could.

But this God, this God she was supposed to trust—He had watched her suffer so many times in her life. He had heard her prayers, her begging. And still He allowed for one horrific event after another. Wasn't He as hard-hearted as all the rest? How could Lara trust such a Being? And when she trusted, she hoped. When she hoped, she ended up hurting.

She didn't want to hope any more. She couldn't stand the pain.

However, while looking out from the darkness in her mind, she missed seeing two things:

1. Although she hurt, she never feared.
2. As each of her plans was blocked, a fresh idea replaced it.

Problem: She missed seeing the hand of God.

He was slouched against the far wall, staring Delta down as she peered through the peephole. His foot tapped fast and he fidgeted with his cigarette, jittery, like he'd taken some of those white pills. Those always put him in a good mood.

She giggled and swung the door open.

"Mark! Where do you keep yourself these days? Sometimes we see you all the time, then weeks go by."

He automatically grinned at his little sister as he paced fast past her. But once inside, his face turned serious. He circled around an easy chair and dropped down into it.

"I needed to tell you I don't think I can stick around here much longer." He propped his foot up on his knee and jerked it to some internal beat, then drummed on the arm of the chair with one hand.

"I don't mind if you stay here, and you know Michelle will let you. She'll probably even let you sleep in her bed!" Delta rolled her eyes and smirked. She sat on the arm of the sofa and let herself fall backwards onto the seat.

Mark stood up and looked down at her, then sat again. His right foot resumed the rhythm.

After a minute, he spoke. "You know what Gramma's up to lately?" Hearing her name made Delta so sad she feared she might cry. He looked at her face, then didn't wait for an answer. "She knows you didn't enroll in that beauty school. That you been taking her money for shopping. Or for your 'friends'." He snorted.

"She don't send it no more. Anyway, I can pay her back. I'll tell Michelle I need to save some money for that."

"Delta … that Michelle. You keep your money away from her."

Delta frowned and started making shapes with her hands. Here's the church, here's the steeple. She hated this money talk, especially when it had to do with Michelle, who was not an honest person. Even she could see that giving her cash was like setting a match to it. "I heard Rocko handles some of the girls' money, so they'll have some to keep them when they're old," she said.

"Smart man." He took a pull on his cigarette, then tapped some ashes out into an open beer can on the coffee table. "Gramma blames me for you dumping school. And Brittany—she says you're not sounding right."

"Brittany!" Delta brightened and she looked over at him. "You talked to Brittany?"

"And you haven't? She wrote me this letter out to the trailer and says you email her and you're sounding like some cold-ass criminal, and that I turned you into that …" he stopped.

Delta was staring at him, not understanding. Neither spoke while

Mark's foot counted out a minute. He suddenly dropped his cigarette into the can.

"Delta, when did you get a computer?"

She shook her head. "I don't have a computer! I don't like them. I use Michelle's when I want to read email. Mostly she reads it for me. I got an email from Brit only once, then none others."

Mark snorted. "So. And Michelle uses your computer name, doesn't she." He shook his head. "Okay. Delta, I want you to call Brittany, on the phone, yourself, and you tell her what you're doing. And here ..." He took a crumpled envelope out of his jacket pocket. "Read this. She wants you to go out to California and learn fingernails, like you and her were talking about."

Delta sat up and took the letter.

"Like Gramma was talking about." He sunk back into the cushions of the chair. "That Gramma is scary. You know what she's got them doing in Rockton? You know that big old house?" He raised his eyebrows.

"The red house? The family 'state?" Delta smiled. "I know she grows a garden behind it."

"Yeah, that's the house, the one they had way back. It was going up for auction, so she convinced that damn church to buy it for an old folks home! She and her old lady friends are fixing it up and she got them to hire her to run the place."

"So Gramma's going to be the boss of her old house! Cool."

"And she's going to move in there, probably picking herself the best apartment. That's gonna leave her house empty. She wants me to talk you into going down and living in it, and getting back to some God-fearing shit like she always talks about." He stopped and shook his head. "She's something."

He fixed his eyes on the closed curtains as if he was looking out and beyond. After a minute, he looked back at her. "But she scares me, Delta. I don't mind telling you that. She has this shitload of stuff on me. And I think she might use it and get me put away, sent to prison, unless I get away from here. All this crap about that Lara McWhatever. Somehow she knows all this shit. Those damn old lady church groups—they got their noses into everything! She always warned me. She said they were praying up a storm for me, but they knew what I was up to."

He stood up fast. Delta startled and sat up. She watched him warily. Anger was taking over his face like in those old werewolf movies when the nice sad man looked at the moon then sprouted hair and pointy teeth. He paced back and forth across the room as he talked.

"It's that Lara bitch's fault! Yeah, I screwed up, missing her … missing the chance to take care of it. As long as she's prancing her ass around this town, I'm f-ing shit on a flea. I gotta get this mess done with, then I might disappear awhile. Head up to KC. Or not. Don't tell anyone I said that. But I wanted to tell you, so's I'd not just disappear or something."

With his final words, he paced back to the door. Delta stood and followed. He put his hand on the doorknob and continued, "I know you're doing real good for yourself, but Gramma would hate this stripping you're doing, you know that."

"Dancing! It's dancing."

"Yeah, whatever. But you give Brittany a call, and Gramma, too. Maybe that'll get them off my back." He stepped into the hall. "You'll see me when you see me. And one more thing. You tell that Michelle to keep her ass out of my life! I got big problems and she's, she's shit on a flea compared to those other guys!"

He gave Delta a long look, than paced down the hall and was gone.

Delta closed the door without emotion. He'd come back; he always did. He was in some crazy mood tonight. Probably too many of those little pills. Or some whites with a big black one. She used to watch while he mixed up the little bags, and he'd explain what they did when put together. He was so smart! But it'd be tomorrow at least before he made sense again.

She leaned back against the door and opened the letter he'd handed her.

Dear Mark,

I hope you get this somehow. I have this old Rockton address for Delta in my address book.

What is she doing? I email her and I can't get a straight answer from her about coming to California. Jake and I have a nice apartment two blocks from the beach. It's small, but has a sofa, so she can stay here and look for jobs. I'm getting done with my studies at Design Couture for the hair part and will start the esthetician part this summer. So I'll be working very soon. Jake got a job apprenticing at a Chevy dealership. He'll be ranked as full time mechanic next fall, so will be making the big bucks then.

I'm enclosing a little piece of paper with my address and phone on it. Give it to Delta direct. NOT Michelle. Please do not tell Michelle I wrote. She does not look after Delta right. Michelle looks after Michelle.

I hope this correspondence finds you and yours well.

Sincerely,

Brittany Bannister
enc.

Delta grinned, happy with thoughts of her friend. She'd call her on the phone, that was for sure, but first she needed to talk to someone.

She needed to talk to Reeza. See what she thought of her doing fingernails in California.

—⁄⁄⁄—

Lara knew she had to leave town. The facts were in.

But the facts must be wrong. God wouldn't make her lose her house. And sure, it was "His war." Okay, whatever, but there had to be another way out of this.

She began to pray for solid signs that she'd heard right, that she really should move away.

Soon after, a sign walked by as she was standing in line at a grocery store. She knew him—the height, the hair, the build, the lanky movements. Knife Guy. Lara watched his back as he left the store with no groceries. He wasn't dead as she had hoped, Godforgiveher. And he was more muscular, as if he'd been working out. Why would he need more muscle? And more important, why was he able to work out at a gym while she couldn't? Her face flushed with her anger.

The next week, she set out again for groceries, trying to ignore her shortness of breath and stomach pain. Her counseling diagnosis: anxiety disorder, with possible panic attacks. She ran down a mental list of stores. She'd been to all of them in town and had multiple bad experiences in each.

Then she had an idea.

Knife Guy was showing up again, so shouldn't she try to force him out and be done with it? As she drove, Lara glanced down at the black bag on the floor. She'd last seen him at Merker's on Meadows Road. Was he watching for her there? Was that going to be the site of his next attack?

And here she was, with Snubbie.

She turned toward Meadows Road. Maybe, just maybe, he'd show up there. And she'd be ready.

The radio suddenly intruded on her thoughts.

"...we're all homeless boys and girls. It's such a lonely, lonely world...". One of her favorite songs was playing, Todd Rundgren's "Love Is the Answer."

"... Light of the world, shine on me, love is the answer. Shine on us all, set us free, love is the answer."

Oh, for crying out loud!

Tears of shame filled Lara's eyes. What was she doing? She was trying to bait a criminal to attack her so she could defend herself— what was she *doing*?

She was becoming one of them.

Lara sniffed big, ashamed, and turned to travel across town to the supermarket in her neighborhood. She prayed for God's forgiveness and pulled into the parking lot of the store. She drove toward the farthest row, then suddenly slammed her foot hard on the brake.

There, parked out away from the other vehicles, was a large blue car. And hunched down behind the wheel was a thin man with dark hair, wavy where it showed from beneath a white cap. Knife Guy.

"I'll be damned," Lara whispered, her prayers forgotten. "Well, I'll be damned!"

She parked in her usual spot, and sauntered into the store, hoping he'd seen her. She walked gracefully in spite of the drag of the heavy bag on her shoulder. Within minutes, however, the strange detachment she felt toward the things that were destroying her life took over, and she was soon focused only on her list. By the third aisle, all she had on her mind was frozen green beans.

Lara angled her cart toward the freezer cases. Green beans, green beans. Then the cart abruptly stopped. She shoved it. Beside her, a tall metal rack loaded with children's kick balls shook. She pushed the cart again, then realized it was attached to the rack. Stuck on some kiddy display! Glumly smirking at the colorful balls, she moved to the front of her cart, turned, and bent down to free it. She glanced up ...

And she saw him.

There, in the aisle she'd just left, was Knife Guy. White cap and baggy shirt, untucked—to hide a weapon in his waistband, of course. He grabbed a can from a shelf and pretended to read the label.

Lara paused only a few seconds.

She jerked her cart free and pushed it on toward the frozen vegetables. She found them nearby and saw that the glass of the case reflected like a murky mirror. Perfect. She pulled her cart up behind her to block the attack, then waited while she watched in the freezer case door. Soon the skinny figure would appear, and this time she was ready.

At her left, the air stirred. Something was approaching. She glanced up and saw a man coming toward her. Not the killer, but a familiar face. Dirk's driver? She met his eyes and he walked on behind and past her.

So they were here? Or not. What difference did it make? What good did it do her, if they only hid?

Lara stood a moment longer, impatient now. What was taking Knife Guy so long? She had groceries to find, and she refused to go through the store looking over her shoulder for some criminal. She grabbed her cart, spun it around, and walked toward the front of the store. Where'd he go? She saw nothing unusual. Clerks were running the registers, a few people were checking out, groceries were being bagged. The scene was strangely normal. She went back to the aisle where she'd seen him. At the far end, a young woman crouched near a low shelf. No one else was there.

Where was he?

Lara's jaw tightened in anger. He would not stalk her like this! She would end this now! But where'd he go? She marched up the aisle, determined now. The woman at the end looked up at her and Lara forced a grim smile. She passed the end cap and looked around the meat and dairy cases at the back of the store.

Nowhere. Had he run off?

So again, a close call. But the thought came to Lara that she wasn't the only one being rescued by the odd events, the miracles, that stopped Knife Guy. *He* was being prevented from committing this crime. Did God consider him something worth saving? Lara was in no mood to think about it. She had things to buy. Coffee, cocoa, cottage cheese. And green beans.

Delta lifted her dress to the crowd.

She swayed to the music and teased the men now hooting at her. They liked her so much! She turned around, lifted her dress from behind, and wiggled her butt. Always move to the music, like Alice had said. Where was Alice, anyway?

The song was about being bad but wanting to be good. Delta kept up to the beat, counting every movement, 1-2-3-4. She swayed frontward, then turned again and hopped a few times. Hop, hop, hop! The men shouted; they liked it when she made her butt jump up and down. She swayed around forward again and let her dress slide all the way off her and down to the floor. Act surprised, Rocko said. She opened her eyes wide in pretend surprise and scanned the room. She smiled as she squinted through the bright stage lights, meeting the eyes of the audience. At the back near the door, several men stood in a row, then ...

Delta gasped and froze. She was looking into a familiar face.

She grabbed to cover her breasts and crotch, but she didn't seem to have enough hands. She backed up until she ran into the curtains, then raced off stage and down the hall, running naked and blind into furniture, walls, doors, people. Frantic and sobbing, she turned doorknobs and beat on every door she could see through her tears, using one hand while trying to hide her nakedness with the other.

Several people stood in the hall, staring and speechless, too confused to help her.

"Let me in! Let me in!" she choked out. Then a door opened and she fell into it. It was the dancers' dressing room.

She dove into the closet and huddled with her face smashed into a corner, still heaving sobs. The night's performers pushed in around her, trying to learn what had happened. One of them threw a robe around her naked body. The only sound they could get from her was a series of choking wet gasps. The women drew out tissue after tissue from a box on the dresser, trying to keep up with her tears.

Reeza pushed through. She stood over her and shouted at the women. "Break it up, Ladies! Delta! What are you doing?"

Michelle walked up to the edge of the crowd in the dressing room. "Is it her period or something? Hell, what a bitch! See what happens when you let someone like her get extra dances?"

Reeza stood up from where she'd been crouching down to pat Delta's shoulder, then turned and glared at Michelle. For an instant, Michelle worried whether she was carrying a switchblade. Reeza pushed toward her, grabbed her shoulders, and shook her. Michelle tried to pull away but the grip was hard and tight.

Reeza got her face too close and hissed, "I don't want any of your fat lip. I want one thing from you, and that's to go out and shut those men up!" She pushed her away. "Go! You can have your extra dance tonight, Mik-a-la!" She exaggerated the syllables of Michelle's stage name.

Michelle backed away, smoothing her hair. Okay. An extra dance—that would be good. More money. And listen to those men hollering! They were so ready for her! She turned and rushed to the stage, then swept out with her arms wide.

She shouted over the noise. "Now, calm down, boys! Mikala's here to make you happy!"

"Delta! Baby Girl Delta! We want our little naked girl back."

Michelle let her anger show for only a second, then bared her teeth in a big fake smile. What the hell did Delta have that these men liked so much? Well, they'd like *her* tonight. If she had to do lap dances on each and every one of these hillbillies, they'd like her tonight.

"Well, boys, you got a grown-up woman now!" And she suddenly jumped her legs apart and pulled off her short sequined costume. She had hoped for a special program to introduce the new tits Rocko bought her, but tonight would have to be the night. She grabbed her ballooned breasts and propped them up. She had their attention now.

"How do you looove ... these babies?" She shook them toward a man in the front row, and the men roared. Laughing, she looked around the room.

Then she stopped, her eyes narrowing.

At the back, near the door, stood a woman with gray hair and a sweater set from Discount City. Marianne McNought stared back at her with undisguised hatred.

Well, that old lady was going to get a show!

Michelle twirled around and looked over her shoulder as she moved her hips in a practiced grind. She shook her butt, then swayed until she faced forward again.

Gramma was gone.

Through the funny glass of the peephole, Reeza's nose looked even bigger and her hair sloped off to either side, making her head look pointy. But Delta was too worried to find it funny. What kind of trouble was she in for missing work this past week? She opened the door a crack, and Reeza pushed into the apartment. As she moved, the fabric of her purple gown flowed around her legs and hips. She swayed as she walked, like she was using the dance steps she taught the girls.

"You've been giving your dances to Michelle?" Reeza's voice was kindly. Something Gramma used to say came into Delta's mind, something about catching bees with honey. At the thought of her grandmother, her eyes filled with tears.

Reeza walked into the living room. "I'm going to sit myself down here and you busy yourself with getting me a soda, Baby Doll."

She dropped into an armchair and looked around. "You girls ever decorate these places? You're most of you in this apartment complex, aren't you? When I started out, I decked my place out with those bright scarves from India, like at Imports Place. And like this dress here. The men liked that, I'm telling you! I used to dance, you know." She took the beer Delta offered her, then looked at the can and laughed. "All you got is alcohol around here? Figures! Now you sit over there on that sofa and let's have a little visit."

She pulled the tab off and took a big swig, then continued. "Yeah, I danced like you do. Was real popular. Got me some good friends back then, and now I'm doing okay being Rocko's Vice President of Operations and all."

Delta blinked and wondered what a vice president of operations was. Must have something to do with keeping the dance notebook.

"Got me a house and a good job and some cash, like I was saying."

Delta sat and watched Reeza. Was she doing her manners right, using etiquette? Usually someone was around to tell her how to act. When it was men, it was easy, 'cause they just grabbed at her and did what they wanted and they liked that fine. If it was girls or someone else, Michelle was there.

"Michelle lives here, too, doesn't she?"

Delta nodded slowly. Lately, when Michelle's name came up, trouble was on its way.

"It's good to have roommates, but not if they're not looking after your own good." Reeza leaned forward in the chair. "Do you understand?"

Delta looked away. If she nodded, it wouldn't be the truth and she might ask something harder. If she shook her head, Reeza would think she was stupid. Delta hadn't called Brittany yet, like Mark said to do. Something told her that once she did, she'd know a whole lot more about Michelle than she wanted to. She was putting that off.

A pack of cigarettes laid between them on the coffee table. Delta picked it up and held it out. "Would you like a cigarette?"

Reeza shook her head and leaned back again. "Why haven't you been coming in to the club this past week?"

Delta kept her eyes on the cigarettes in her hand.

Reeza went on. "I've been asking the girls what's going on and getting an earful. They say Michelle told them your grandmother came in and scared you real bad."

Tears suddenly flooded up in Delta's eyes.

Reeza was watching her, and made her voice softer. "I know what that's like, when family judges you but then they're not there to help you when you need it. I know what that's like. You're doing real good for yourself, Delta, and one day they'll be proud. I guarantee that."

Delta looked up, feeling a smidgen of hope. Could that be true?

"Tell you what." Reeza continued, scooting up again in her chair. "Rocko and I got a real good idea on how to make them proud, even your grandma. If you drove back to your town one day in a shiny new red car and wearing real nice clothes, and if you bought your mama and her a good house to live in, would that make them proud?"

Her Ma in a real house? Not one that shook when she walked and sounded like a rock-fall when it rained? Delta looked straight on at Reeza and nodded.

"Ah, I thought so. Well, Baby Doll, all you need is enough money. I hear from the girls that you give your money to Michelle and she just takes it."

Delta spoke up, defending herself. "Then she pays the bills and buys food with it, and we shop together for clothes. She does the hard stuff, like adding up the bank notices."

Reeza nodded slowly. "Like I thought. Do you know how much you make a week, Delta?"

Delta shook her head.

"You make a lot. You make more than Michelle, and I think she's taking advantage of you."

That didn't sound very nice, so Delta narrowed her eyes at her.

Reeza looked serious and went on. "Do you trust Rocko and me?"

Delta nodded.

"Good, because we like you plenty. You got this 'fresh' thing going that we don't see too often. Honey, I think you're going to look like a sweet little thing for 20 more years! And the men—they can't get enough of you. What we want to do is get you into Rocko's national group."

Delta frowned. Now what was she talking about?

"You don't know about all the businesses Rocko has. Well, he has a set of special girls he takes around to special men. Like famous men, and men with a lot of money. Some out west, so you might even meet Dirk Durmont!"

Delta brightened. "Dirk? You can get me in to meet Dirk?" Michelle would be wild happy when she heard about this!

Reeza smiled big when she saw Delta's grin. "Maybe so. I see you're interested. Rocko wants to help with your bank accounts, too, like Michelle's doing. We'll do right by you, though, and even teach you how to watch your money yourself. And don't worry about Michelle. Our people will talk to her and she'll be fine with it."

She stood and put the half-empty can on the table. "I'll be leaving now. Rocko will talk to you about when you can travel. You come on in and dance tonight. We miss you!"

Delta watched as she closed the door behind her, then sat awhile grinning to herself. She might be getting with Dirk, like Michelle and Mark wanted her to do! Maybe she'd get in with his friend Lara, too.

Reeza was right. She'd make Gramma proud.

———

Lara remained a prisoner of her plan for a simple life in Granville, for a role in a Norman Rockwell painting. She prayed again for a sign that she should move. It immediately arrived at Brandt's Gym on what became her last day there.

When she went in that day, one man was in the weight room, in a far corner pumping dumbbells. She began to set up the squat rack and he quickly left his weights and moved to a bench behind her. Lara grit her teeth, then headed to the treadmills. The man remained in place at the bench. One treadmill mile later, she stopped and moved to the crossover rack. She had set the weights and grabbed a handle when the door swung open and three people sauntered in. Strangers, of course. Two men and a woman. They gathered around a bench behind Lara. And stared.

"Don't look at her!" the woman suddenly blurted out. Was she trying to help Lara, or causing trouble?

The woman's words got one of the men fired up. Lara tried to ignore him, but in the mirror she could see the man leering at her. He was trouble, the usual type. Unattractive, probably didn't "date" much, might hate a beautiful man like Dirk who attracts lots of women. So, this being Granville, he might hate Lara, too.

"You know she despises...", the woman continued, then murmured more.

Lara's jaw stiffened. How dare they think they knew anything about her! They didn't know what she liked, or what she "despises"!

At the woman's remarks, the man turned more mean, like a mad dog urged into a fight. He moved to stand behind Lara, showing his teeth in a macabre snarl.

And then, incredibly, he began hopping up and down!

A monkey dance! Like the two women Lara nicknamed the Vulgar Twins, the women who mocked her workouts. What was *wrong* with these twisted people? Lara cringed in disgust, slowly released her hold on the machine handles, and walked away, careful to show no reaction to this maniacal man now staring her down. She headed to the leg extension machine at the far end of the room, then sat and began counting reps.

The man's voice sounded from across the room. "See? She's fat!"

Lara grit her teeth. *Ignore him! Ignore him!*

"Can you imagine having sex with that? Oh, Lara! ..." He groaned out sexual sounds, moaning "Lara ..." while the woman with him insisted, "Stop it! Stop it!"

Lara froze in place, too repulsed to move.

He'd said her *name*. This vile low-functioning piece of trash had said her name! A sickening feeling of violation washed over her. That this pig had actually used her name—disgusting! And sex?! With that? Hatred overwhelmed her, flooding her mind with a hot darkness.

Why hadn't she left when they'd come in? She didn't want to become paranoid, but she had to be! These awful people were everywhere.

Fighting to control her anger, Lara slowly pushed her body off the machine, picked up her bag, and walked carefully to the door. Once in the stairwell, she tried to think around her hatred and forced herself to stop to listen, wondering how far the man would go. After all, these were people who knew about the rumors; maybe she could learn something. But as she stood, she saw through the open door that the man who'd been in the gym lifting weights was watching her. He had witnessed her humiliation.

Sick and devastated, she left.

03-20-01

I can't think. Humiliation. Hatred. I can't stand what these abusive attacks turn me into. I hate these people! Their cowardice, the evil.

I fantasize about retaliation, but there is no answer. If I confront these maniacs, they will only get worse. Yes, I can humiliate them with words. It'd be easy. (My hatred! It's constant!) But then it would be me they hate. Right now, they have this crazy problem with Dirk Durmont. They are major losers and they believe their moronic stories about me, whatever they are. Anyway, their attacks are based on their own nuttiness. If I confront them, they'll go "Duh, oh we hate her" and there will be no end. (My hatred, uncontrollable.)

I don't want to go back to Brandt's Gym. It's where these nuts go to brutalize me. They can call it a "power" they have, that I want to avoid them. But it's the same power someone with strong body odor has—people are repulsed. These people—they are gross so I will stay away from them.

How has my life gotten so screwed up? How have I gotten into such a mess?

I am stunned by all this.

Lara's activities narrowed still more. With no health club membership, she tried to walk more often, but the memories and bleak thoughts that dogged her along the dark streets hurt too much. And walking had become another source of tension as she endured malicious slurs thrown out from car windows and the remarks of people sitting on their porches, the ubiquitous "that's the woman, isn't that the woman." She had to stop or risk PDG—public display of her grief. The ugliness around her grew like a mold. Strange danger-tinged characters continued to stalk her, and the vicious comments became louder. Lara could barely leash her hatred toward these monsters. She searched for a solution, a way to fix the impossible mess, some understanding.

She finally began to reach out to local people for answers although it strained her to form the words, to face the embarrassment of admitting her bizarre problem, and to risk adding to the gossip. As the harassment at her workplace grew, she asked her boss if she'd heard any of the rumors. She casually mentioned her problems with the gym to her book group, then members of her family. No one had heard anything. In fact, one woman told her that people made it a point not to mention Dirk Durmont so they wouldn't be accused of name-dropping.

The only helpful comment came from a long-time resident who exclaimed, "Oh, those are the white trash people!"

As simple as that. The "white trash" people. That was why Lara's associates hadn't heard anything. This obsession with celebrity gossip and the mindless stalking were part of the "white trash" world and her friends had no connections to it.

And still Lara wouldn't give up. She could not let them win. She called a lawyer in Chicago, not someone local who might be awestruck over, or afraid of, a celebrity. He never returned her calls. She tried cruising the grocery store parking lots to record license plate numbers. The women raced off, but then showed up in the stores by the time Lara hit the coffee aisle.

Surely there was a piece of information that could act as a key to open a door back to her real life, some safety, and her future. She assumed the rudies communicated over the Internet; she'd heard a "DirkLetter" mentioned. But she knew that if it was distributed via an email address list, she'd never find it. She had hunted for a helpful Web site, but found nothing. She contacted libraries and learned they didn't carry copies of tabloids. Past issues seemed to be only in the hands of obsessed fans or the papers themselves. So she called a tabloid. She used a different name—not fake, but now unused—and rented a post office box in another state, just over the line in Kansas. She told the lady on the phone she needed Dirk Durmont articles for a scrapbook for a friend. Not untrue; she wanted the scrapbook for herself and she was her own good friend. She made the drive to Kansas over and over to pick up piles of new junk mail until it became obvious that the tabloids were ignoring her.

Shopping as a hobby was lost long ago. It had once been a peaceful escape for Lara, a chance to fill her head with pretty images of coordinated outfits and decorated rooms. Now she never relaxed. Everywhere she went, she assessed the people around her or searched for ways to avoid them. They advanced, she ducked away. She was constantly aware of the movement of air around her. Who was approaching and from what direction? When she couldn't slip away, she'd freeze in a position that hid her face, tuning up her ears to listen to the whispers that gave away people's interest in her. Sometimes she studied the faces that looked familiar. Were they stalkers?

Lara needed a powerful friend. And one day, she overheard the name of the perfect person. Lakeesha, the rich and famous actress, was known for her kindness and philanthropy. Lara had been a fan for years.

She bought a card:

> "Do you ever feel
> that your guardian angel
> went out for a smoke?"

Perfect. Inside, she copied over a carefully composed message:

Dear Lakeesha and Associates,

I'm involved in a bizarre situation with a very famous man, and I need powerful help. I'm not a celebrity myself and am mostly concerned about tabloid stories that will haunt me the rest of my life. I need to know what's been printed but don't read tabloids and have discovered that they don't keep libraries that are open to the public.

If you are willing to help, please contact me. If you can't help, if you know anyone who is trustworthy and can research this for me, please let me know.

She tucked a check into the envelope along with the card. If she sent a donation to Lakeesha's Project Heaven, they'd have to answer

her if only to send a receipt. She said a quick prayer, then sealed the
envelope and mailed it.

04-23-01
Journal,

> *"You gain strength, courage, and confidence*
> *by every experience*
> *in which you really stop to look fear in the face—*
> *You must do the thing*
> *which you think you cannot do."*
> *- Eleanor Roosevelt*

*I'm putting together a little "courage book" with sayings and
articles that will motivate and inspire me.*

*I'm going to ask Cheryl if I can work part-time, three days a
week. That would give me more time to work on my life. I can't see
quitting and drifting, so I need to work on a plan.*

*I had an odd dream: I was at Discount City and women start-
ed showing up dressed in their underwear! One of the Vulgar Twins
wandered in wearing some raggedy old cotton briefs and a t-shirt.
Another woman wore long johns, cut out around her shoulders
and legs, showing garters. I was appalled and asked the one in long
johns, "What are you people <u>doing?</u>" (I was wearing my black suit
from the boutique in SoHo). And the woman explained, all excited,
"Dirk Durmont is in the building!" I answered "Well? So where are
your clothes?" The dream ended.*

Is Dirk exposed only to lewdness, never anything nice and normal?

*The women who've been milling around all these years—what
do they want with him? And now he's married. Do they just want
to meet him? Have sex with him? Or is he really trying to make
people into stars?*

*I'm going to Em's for Easter to avoid being in town when Mr.
and Mrs. Dirk are here. This is so painful for me here in Granville
and I don't want to live around it.*

*It was a bad day yesterday. I went to the drug store and some
girl pointed me out to her mother using that "eewww!" sound,
making an ugly face. Crude, coarse, horsey girl. <u>That</u> helped my
mood! Then I went to Magnolia Canyon to hike. An hour drive*

for a workout.

I struggle with whether I'm handling the hate attacks, the Nut Crowd, correctly. Am I supposed to love them? Naw! And evil can't be destroyed, it will always be there. It seems all you can do is stay on your path, ignore it, walk past it and let it fester into itself. That is the victory—not engaging with it, but walking on and letting it turn on itself.

Some of the shadows seem to be working for the other side now. At the Nature Center I recognized a shadow sitting on a bench with some woman who was leering at me. I had to walk past them and up a hill while this woman leered at my body. It makes me sick, the violation. Then, I went out of town and on the way back I went grocery shopping. In Merker's, about four groups of people stalked me around the store. There's only one way that so many could have known I was there on the way back from a trip—shadows are selling out.

My anger toward Dirk is hard to control. I worry of the ways I may be being victimized, the things this man may be doing, and how far he'll go. People believe anything these lowlifes make up— they'll believe Dirk's stories, whatever he tells them. Perceptions, always perceptions. Theirs, mine, his even. The destruction of my life is a game to them.

I have to get out of here. But I can't get a picture of a future, no dreams.

I don't have a minute of peace, ever, anymore. I have a running nightmare going through my head—these homely crude people ridiculing me, victimizing me, Dirk's back turned toward me. Images of cruelty, victimization, gossip. I walk across the parking lot and worry about the people in the cars. Are they telling stories, taking pictures? Will one get out with a knife when I have no weapon with me? Is someone aiming a gun at me? Are there shadows today or did Dirk call the whole thing off? Am I abandoned? Was I always?

I must admit, though, that even though people are ridiculing me and trying to destroy me, I'm liking myself more and more through this. I'm surrounded by evil, cowardice, and avarice, and in this mess I have been good, I have courage, I am steadfast.

I'm very very sad, but I'm the good guy here.

293

Worries:

* I worry that this city is ruined for me <u>and</u> for Dirk Durmont, which is what I wanted to avoid. But these nuts and hateful creeps have been here all along. They just focused their aim on me when I came to town. Unless this stuff happens all the time here, innocent people being destroyed by celebrity-obsessed brutes.

* I worry that the nuts will have a vacuum when I leave. They'll need to fill it with something, or someone, else.

I can't think anymore. I have to stop.

———

A letter from The Lakeesha Organization! Lara rushed into the house to read it.

Dear Ms. McKeon,

Thank you for writing us. Lakeesha receives an overwhelming number of requests similar to yours …

Lara laughed bitterly. Oh really! So many women were having bizarre problems involving celebrities!

…and although she is unable to accommodate them all, please know that she wishes you the best.

What did this mean?

Of course Lakeesha wouldn't have seen the original letter, but did it fall into the hands of anyone who would even tell her about it? At least Lara hadn't told them the "famous man's" name, but they knew her city and they could possibly find out her story. What if someone corrupt had gotten her letter? Or what if they were all ruthless, callous people?

CHAPTER TWENTY-SEVEN

Next stop, Chicago? It could happen, if she moved. Lara dug through the pile of Sunday Tribunes until she found a fresh one, its pages tightly packed. Sunday mornings, it was becoming her habit to visit this large chain bookstore and buy a newspaper and a real cup of coffee. She would take the paper home and spread it out on the kitchen table, then work the puzzles and scan the optimistic job section and the depressing real estate ads.

She had forgotten that habits in Granville were a bad thing.

Paper in hand, she straightened, turned, and policed the bookstore. Only one customer was checking out, talking to the man running the register. Another clerk stood flipping through pages in front of her. She moved toward the registers. As she walked, a woman stepped in front of her and went up to the one available clerk. Lara took her place next in line, frustrated now. Minutes passed and she grew anxious.

Suddenly someone shoved her!

Her body jerked forward and she stiffened to catch herself. Her mental radar clicked on. Was that push accidental?

She had noticed someone, a large heavyset man, moving toward the line behind her. He had walked in a few minutes earlier with another man. She had seen him before in a grocery store, so he was possibly a shadow. That day at Merker's he had moved in too close to her and had crowded her as she tried to shop. But she had sensed a harmless attitude from him, as if he wasn't a bad person, he was just bad at his job. He might have just now clumsily bumped into her.

She stepped forward to give him more space. A rope was set up to organize the lines, and now Lara was beyond the opening, with the rope behind her. Her jaw tightened in annoyance; she didn't want to look obtrusive, stepping outside the rope divider.

He shoved her again, harder.

Lara inhaled sharply. What was he *doing*? Her face grew hot, her anger now kindled. She stepped up again, this time well beyond the rope opening. Her mind raced. What should she do? She was next in line; what was holding things up? The same two women stood at the counter, tying the cashiers up in rambling discussions.

The man shoved Lara again, this time hitting directly against her purse. An awareness suddenly struck her. Snubbie! Was he checking to see if she had a weapon?

"What are you doing?" A male voice whispered, objecting. Probably the thinner man she'd seen with the big one. "You know she hates that."

So it *was* intentional! This man was shoving her, assaulting her, for real. Why? Was he trying to get her to react?

She edged up to escape the creep behind her, and now was almost past the clerks' windows. She would not play their game! She would give them *nothing*! She was there to buy her paper and that's what she would do. Lara couldn't think clearly through the blaze of her anger. She forced herself to breathe steadily, and her rehearsed lines came to her. *Do not engage, walk away. Do not engage, walk away.*

A clerk was finally free. She paid for her paper and hurried away, eager to escape. She passed a young woman standing near the door and staring at the man behind Lara.

Once safe in her car, Lara reached for the bag that held Snubbie. She hated to carry it into places where innocent people shopped, but now she slipped it into her purse. Something strange—more so than usual—was going on today. She needed protection.

And she needed to show these people that she was unpredictable. It was best if they feared her. She didn't have a weapon when the man shoved against her purse, but she did now.

Michelle had pulled into the bookstore parking lot with Stacy and Nadine. Her phone rang.

"You're kidding! Ha!" She shrieked, and the other girls joined her. "We'll take it from here, see where she goes. So that fat guy is staying behind, looks like. Later!" She tossed the phone down and looked around at her friends. "You will not believe this! That bodyguard Larry who's dating Joannie was in there shoving Lara around! But damn the luck, she didn't shoot him. Now we're going to watch her go running to her Dirk Darling to tell him how bad those bodyguards are!" She laughed and sped along, keeping Lara's car a half block ahead.

Several minutes later, Michelle's car careened through the downtown streets. She lost sight of Lara and slowed to get her bearings.

Suddenly Nadine shrieked.

"What!" Michelle hit the brake and the three lurched forward. She looked back and saw Nadine staring out the window, her eyes bugged out like she'd seen a ghost.

Nadine pointed. Michelle followed her finger. Up the street they'd just passed, a white van waited along a curb. Two men sat in the front seat, watching them.

"Oh shit." Michelle didn't want to run into those guys again.

"That's the same van, isn't it?" Nadine whined.

Stacy looked at the vehicle and popped her eyes open big. "That van is the one from the pool! Ohmigod! And those bastards are looking right at us."

"Hell!" Michelle stomped on the gas pedal and they sped away. A block up, she stopped in the middle of the street.

Nadine and Stacy both screamed. Michelle turned and saw that the van had followed and now blocked the intersection behind them. She accelerated, then stomped on her brake and cursed. Ahead of her, a large light-blue car had pulled across the next intersection.

Nadine began to sniffle. "Damn you, Michelle, you bitch. What the hell have you got us into? They're going to kill us!"

Michelle lurched her car in reverse, then spied an alley. She turned sharp and sped away, bumping the car over broken cement behind old buildings. As they entered the next street, a silver car followed by a small fleet passed them. The caravan turned at the corner and sped away.

The bodyguards. They must be chasing those other guys, the ones in the white van. Was someone actually trying to get L-whore today? They were getting rid of Lara! Killed or kidnapped, it didn't matter. Michelle laughed, triumphant. Finally, L.A. here she came!

Lara had one more errand yet this morning. Downtown, an old bank had been converted into a small used bookstore. She drove to it and was relieved to find easy parking across from the store and few customers in it. She located her book group's choice for that month and soon was back out in the street. The bag with her book bumped her leg as she moved toward her car and her purse weighed heavy on her shoulder. She stopped to unlock her car door.

Suddenly she sensed something behind her. She rushed to slide into the driver's seat and punched the lock button.

Snap!

The sound was unmistakable—someone had snapped his fingers!

Agitated now, Lara peered out through each of her car mirrors. She watched as three heavyset men moved along her back fender and walked behind her car to the sidewalk.

They had been following her that closely when she jumped into her car.

Where had they come from? The few businesses besides the bookstore located in this lonely part of downtown Granville were closed today. Where was their car? No place that she could see. She hadn't seen them in the bookstore; their size would have made them obvious in the small space. She watched them now. All three stood in front of a store window with their backs to her. The building was dark and the display dusty. If they spoke to each other, they didn't move their heads.

Lara stared at them for a couple of minutes. None moved. Finally she drove toward home, drained.

One of the men had snapped his fingers. She shuddered. A missed opportunity? For what?

———

This was getting as hard as catching a wild cat!

And Delta should know. A cat used to come by the trailer, leaping down the hill when Delta went out with extra chicken nuggets for the critters. She'd called it Snowball because of its long white hair, but it looked more like snowplow leavings what with all the dirt on its coat. Snowball would grab a piece of chicken in its mouth and growl with its ears pressed flat, looking so fierce that no one got near until it backed away a safe distance. Delta knew if she'd reached out her hand to pet it, the hand would likely come back shredded, so she let Snowball have plenty of space.

Lara could be just like that cat sometimes, like tonight. Delta had followed her to this grocery store—after trailing her through that other store and then following her car to the park and back—and now couldn't get Lara to stand in one spot. She seemed ready for a fight, like she was hanging on to something someone was trying to take away. Delta didn't know what she was guarding so fierce. There were stories going around about almost every part of Lara's life, but she hadn't heard about any thieving.

In any case, Delta had to try to warn her about the dirty dealings around town. Helping Lara was one thing she knew would make Gramma proud and help ease over all the mess she'd made of their plans for beauty school. Still, every time she got close, Lara took off. Even if she wasn't looking at Delta, she'd catch wind of her and go off in another direction. Delta went to the next aisle and looked down it. Lara was peering at the spices; she saw Delta and hurried away.

Maybe it was just as well. If that woman got mad enough, she might pull out a gun and shoot her. No one ever knew what Lara was going to do. There were stories now about her sharpshooting with a gang from Kansas City. And Delta didn't know what she would say if she could walk up and have a visit. Well, she could warn her about the white van creeps, and the bodyguards going bad, and even tell her the stories about some crazy person stalking Dirk. This whole mess was turning worser and worser and it was right that Lara knew it, if only to keep that dog safe.

Delta saw her come out two rows down. She beelined toward her, but Lara got herself quick to a register. She paid for her stuff and hurried out while Delta pretended to play with the rack of tabloid papers. Delta followed her toward the door.

Suddenly, two men appeared out of nowhere and blocked her way. They both wore white caps.

"Where do you think you're going?" the fat one asked. The other guy stood quiet, staring around him nervous, like he was looking for trouble to come jumping out from the bread aisle.

She knew the big guy. He was a bodyguard, and was dating that Dirk Doll Joannie. But Delta had heard from Stacy that he'd lost his job. He'd gone to the bookstore and hit Lara or something and broke all the rules.

What was he doing here?

Delta looked up at him and answered his challenge. "Where am I going? Where I'm going is out the door." She looked beyond him through the windows and saw Lara escaping into her car.

"We saw what you're doing," he replied.

"Doing? Like shopping? I don't think you saw nothing, 'cause nothing happened."

He reached up and shoved her shoulder. Well, that sure made her mad! She backed up a step. She'd be telling Mark about this one.

He went on, snarling. "You stay away from Lara McKeon, do you hear? If we catch you talking to her, you are in big trouble."

He went to shove her again, but Delta ducked away.

She glared at him, ready to fight if she had to. And if she couldn't run fast enough first. She hissed out, "I know about you. You're not here guarding Lara. They fired you."

He laughed. Delta made a mean face to scare him, then ducked around him and darted out the door. She ran to her car as fast as her legs would carry her.

Lara was far gone. But seeing that man's ugly snarl had put an idea into Delta's head. There was something else she could do to please her Gramma, something bigger than being Lara's friend. Something only she could do.

You can get used to hell if you live there long enough.

Lara's grandmother used to say that. Or someone told her she'd said it; Lara had barely known her grandmother and she'd been dead for many years.

Now she faced off the stalker of the evening. His crazed eyes peered out from a wrinkled dirty face above disheveled clothes. As he followed her, his movements were made more strange by a deep limp. Lara rolled her grocery cart fast to get away, then slowed to shop in the baking section. He appeared again at the end of the aisle, near the front of the store. She turned her back to him and pushed her cart away. She headed down the next aisle, but stopped when she saw him at the end, watching her.

Back and forth they went, his stalking, her dodging.

It was common now for Lara to be harassed by bizarre-looking people. Men, women, young, old, all sizes, some dirty, some familiar like the young blond woman she'd seen again last week. The month had been especially stressful; a string of new predators had shown up. One night two police cars rushed through her neighborhood shining searchlights. Georgia next door told her they were searching for an escapee. Lara called the police to see if they'd caught him, but they knew nothing about it. A few days later she'd gone for a walk, and a police car went by and flashed a searchlight behind her.

Tonight she quickly decided to stop wasting her time and to go home. She pushed her cart with force to the front and found a checkout line one person long. Several male clerks stood near the registers while the intercom called for another. Had they noticed the man and were actually going to help her? Or had they gathered to watch her struggle?

She glanced back and saw the rough man standing behind her. She immediately stepped out of the line and wheeled back into an aisle. He followed. She turned with the cart to face him off and he went to another aisle. She got back into line, and he moved in behind her, this time holding a roll of paper towels. She again sped away. This time he didn't follow.

She paid for her few groceries.

Then she prepared to leave the store, to go outside where the man probably waited. Her absence of fear gave her thoughts clarity; she simply prepped for the next step, as usual. She slipped her weighted purse onto her right shoulder, so she could easily access her weapon. Hooking her single bag of groceries onto her left hand, Lara turned toward the entrance.

She paused. On a bench near the doors, the scruffy man sat looking at her. She exited while watching his reflection in the dark window, then hurried to her car.

Alice pressed her hands against both ears and watched George and Lara from her car. She couldn't talk him into carrying a knife. George said he would scare her by creeping up and talking dirty. But from what Alice could see, it wasn't working. Lara wasn't spooked; she looked ready for a fight.

Alice knew where she got her confidence. It was from Dirk. No one had caught them together yet, but she knew Lara ran to him with her complaints. Then people who crossed her disappeared off the streets. Just like that, gone. Well, one day Alice would have Dirk and she knew the first thing she'd want from him. She'd tell him to get rid of Lara, that's what she'd do.

She started and jerked her hands down when George opened the car door. He climbed in behind the wheel. He was driving tonight—it'd been a long week and her leg ached.

"I saw you both in the store," Alice said.

George sounded mad. "She is slippery, like you said."

"And did you see all those guys ganging up near the front? There weren't any bodyguards this time, though. Maybe they're all back in

California by now." She looked out the window as George pulled the car out toward the road. "I wish she'd go away! But here she is, still in Granville bothering Dirk."

George breathed deep and drove on without talking. Sometimes Alice wasn't sure he believed her about Dirk. But he was helping her with Lara, so that's all that mattered.

A few minutes later Alice said, "You know she carries a gun."

He laughed. "I don't believe it! She's bluffing you scaredy cats. No woman is going to touch a gun with a ten foot pole unless she has to."

Alice didn't bring up what those guys said about Lara when she hit that target at the shooting range. They said she laughed.

—⁓—

The situation was getting worse, if that was possible. Scary-looking men were aggressively stalking her now. After the incident with the limping man, Lara had tried grocery shopping several nights later. Again, another scraggly man had stared her down then followed her out to the parking lot.

She'd leave Granville ... when she was good and ready! Until then, she would not be moved, or killed, by some low-life. She really wanted to make all this trouble go away so she could keep her house and live happily ever after. There had to be a way. She sat in front of her computer, looking for ideas. If she knew her enemy better, maybe she could better protect herself.

She fed the usual celebrity name into an Internet search, then automatically clicked past the first few pages. She stopped and opened a site.

Late-breaking Hollywood News by Freda

I told you first about the breakup of Shasta Purple and her hot rocker hubby Wheels Rapcity. The BIG NEW scoop is that the Mrs. Wheels Purple Rapcity is expecting a little set of tires, and who do you think is the father. Only Shasta knows for sure.

Friends of Carrie Jo and Dirk say they're waiting for baby news. They also tattle that the celeb couple didn't do it, make it, get it, or dirty-deed-it until they'd dated six months. Maybe if their friends stayed away from their bedroom window they'd get more baby-making done.

Boring. Lara clicked the site shut. She paged down and stopped when she saw PersJournal. So far it'd been the only site that acknowledged her—an "older woman" and someone who'd been stabbed.

Personal Journal of Dirk Durmont, or,
Former Personal Journal of Dirk Durmont
    Well, fans and friends, I'm getting real tired of Dirk Durmont's lawyer's breathing down my neck, so:
            I now officially cease and desist
            the Personal Journal of Dirk Durmont.
                    I hereby apologize
            to all his family, friends, and associates
                who I may have offended.
    Please enjoy my newest column, Stories from the Hall.

Gone! This was the only site she'd found that hinted of the Granville mess, and it was gone! Lara continued reading, curious about the new column.

Stories From the Hall
    Like I was eating this sandwich, and Tony the Bone ;-)
came in and said "Did you go on the fire drill?" And I said "No man, I hid in the john!" He laughed his ass off! Funny! Then Jack-O Jack-Wad came by and wanted to shoot some weed, and I told him you can't shoot weed, man, like make up your mind what or whom you're shooting. He cracked up!

She stared, incredulous, then tossed her head from side to side in a Valley Girl imitation. "Ohmigod, dude, how lame! Like, if you can't totally dis somebody's rep, you don't have nothin' to say? Like, what's that about?"

Lara smirked, then slowly closed down the site. She'd lost a potential source of information, but this time it didn't bother her.

———

Michelle shoved the apartment door open, then stepped into the dark living room. She was surprised to see Delta watching her from the old easy chair.

303

"What the hell! Did we forget the light bill?" She flipped the switch and the overhead light glowed pink. The color was Big Blair's idea—a pink light bulb made them look hot. Delta's eyes looked strange, almost serious.

Michelle dropped her purse onto the dinette table and walked around to the refrigerator. "What's going on? Did the cat die?" She walked into the living room with a beer and sat on the sofa. "Oh, yeah, we don't have a cat."

Delta stared at her like she was that bully back at Rockton High, the one the football team finally beat up.

Michelle continued. "Why the f are you sitting here in the dark? Are you pondering the condition of the world?" She snorted a laugh, held her beer up as a toast, then swallowed.

"You're such a liar," Delta said evenly.

Michelle stopped and stared her down. Which thing was this about? Her grandmother's money? The checking account, the car, the stuff she'd told Rocko? A practiced liar, she knew to keep quiet, to not admit to anything and let Delta bring it up. Act dumb. She shifted in her seat until she was sitting like Delta, then grinned like a fool.

"You're a big fat liar," Delta repeated.

"Well, Delta, Baby Girl," she whined out the nickname, "sticks and stones may break my bones ..."

"I talked to Brittany. On the phone." Delta's face was strangely steady. The usual blank look in her eyes was gone, replaced by some awareness. When had that happened? Had she been getting smarter for real?

Shit. "Well, hey! What'd Brit have to say?"

"She said you pretended to be me and sent lying emails around to people. And you said I was stealing from Rocko. That's a dirty, rotten lie."

Michelle was undecided whether to keep grinning. She switched to a sincere look and drew her eyebrows together. "I'm sure she has it mixed up. You know how silly she can get."

"Michelle, I am not an idiot."

Michelle laughed, then stopped herself abruptly.

Delta continued. "I know I'm not smart. I know you and Brittany love those old computers and are real good at working them and I'll never give a rat's tail what the Innernet says. But at least I *know* what I am, and that makes me smarter than you."

Michelle blinked. What?

"I talked to Rocko, too. See, I know who's smart and I'm learning how to figure out whose side they're on. Rocko loves his money, I know that, but that means he'll make me earn money. For him and for me. And Reeza—she's showing me about bank books. Funny thing is, she's the most honest person I know besides Brittany and Gramma, and I'm smart enough to figure that out."

Michelle was dumbfounded. When did all this start?

Delta continued. "I've made a decision."

Michelle stuttered, then laughed. "You? You've ..."

"You're moving out. We will no longer be roommates. I don't want your type around me. You're mean and you lie, and I am finding a better sort to hang with."

"Now, Delta, let's all calm down." Michelle was wearing herself out with this sincerity act. But it used to always work with Delta.

"Rocko told me he'd send someone to help you move. He thinks I don't know what that means. He thinks I'm dumb, and maybe that's okay. But I do know what he means. He's saying you'd better get your things out, or you'll have trouble with him. He keeps an extra place downstairs you can use until you find something else."

Michelle laughed, outraged. "I'm sure! You bitch! You think you can do this to me? After all I've done for you! You will be so sorry." She swigged some beer to calm her voice. "Well, when Dirk hears about this, you will never get in with him, never!"

Delta sat quiet and stared. The expression on her face confused Michelle.

After a minute, Delta spoke. "Do you think I believe all that about you and Dirk Durmont, me who lives here with you? Really, Michelle, how stupid do you think I am?"

06-05-01

> *"I haven't failed.*
> *I've found 10,000 ways that didn't work."*
> *—Thomas Edison*

I must conquer this.
My problems are extraordinary, I have days of debilitating

depression, my life is a mess, my head is so screwed up.

Whatever.

I must be stronger and more focused. Years have passed with these Granville problems and I've not gotten things done. This must change.

I saw Sara (pregnant with twins!) when I went to Illinois. She is so spiritually wise, and gives me such dead-on wisdom. She told me that God is a lamp onto our feet. No farther than that, just to our feet. We can know only the next step.

I told her that I felt God wanted me to ignore the tabloid stuff and for me to stay with higher-minded things. When I told her that I had to know anyway, that it would come back to cause me trouble later, she said "And you don't trust God to protect you from it harming you later?" I have to admit that I don't. God hasn't protected me so far—look at my life, such a mess! Trust is a huge problem.

I caught a TV program about Post Traumatic Stress Disorder. They said that a trigger can occur and put you back emotionally to the time of the trauma. My triggers are anything that brings the wrong thought up. A song on the radio—even now, writing about songs on the radio starts it for me. I shudder, I tear up, feel so much sorrow. Another trigger is seeing Dirk on TV or in photos doing Movie Guy stuff, being the star.

Damn. I am so wounded and angry.

Sara lent me a book about why God lets bad things happen. It was depressing, but rang true.

Book notes:

> *God ...*
>> *has not forgotten you.*
>> *did not cause this problem in your life.*
>
> *Your problem ...*
>> *is no surprise to God.*
>> *will be used by God for your ultimate good.*
>> *shall pass.*
>
> *You ...*
>> *are loved by God.*
>> *will recover, with God's help.*
>
> *Why did it happen?*

to learn to live by faith, not sight. (2 Cor 5:7)
to be pruned to bear more fruit.
to learn more about God and His character.
because evil exists and sometimes good people
are its victims.

Because evil exists and sometimes good people are its victims.

Chapter Twenty-Eight

It was a hot day for a hike. Lara hesitated, but her body won. It craved a workout, if only to burn off some of the stress of living with constant scrutiny, danger, and worry about her future.

She headed for the wooded trails in a park near the edge of town. In spite of the heat, she'd tossed an oversized linen shirt over her shoulders, hoping that its long length would protect her body from stares.

Once on the trails, Lara strode along at a fast pace. It felt so good to move! Even the weight of the heavy black bag slung across her body didn't slow her down. Half a mile later, she was deep into the park, past the clusters of people who crowded the paths. She breathed deep, enjoying the fresh air and solitude.

Suddenly, a light flashed on the trail ahead.

She stopped short, aghast at what was in her path.

The man with the camera noticed her abrupt stop. Lara recognized him; he hung around the gym, gossiping about her and Dirk. He stared toward her, then the man he was photographing—Dirk Durmont—turned to follow his eyes and caught hers. A rush of horrible emotions made her dizzy. He immediately directed the woman with him to look at some scene ahead of them.

Lara felt sick. She strained to think. Where could she go? How could she escape?

She would not go forward to overtake them, no way. If she turned around and they hiked behind her, they would be following her. What if they caught up? Should she turn around and run? But she was a lousy runner; if she ran, they might still overtake her. Frantic, she glanced around and noticed a small ravine nearby. In two steps she had paced to the edge and jumped down into it. She squatted next to the creek that ran at its bottom and pretended to hunt for rocks, barely breathing as she listened for the group to pass behind her.

No sounds.

Minutes later, she heard someone running from the direction she had come. Lara glanced up and saw a trim dark-haired man run by, watching her as he went. She turned to look back up the trail.

Dirk and his people were gone. She scrambled out of the ravine and retraced her path, now frantic for the quickest route out of the park.

How dare he invade her space! With his money, he had complete freedom. It was Lara who was now a prisoner, because of Dirk Durmont. He could always find out where she was. Those times he'd shown up in the same places as Lara—they couldn't have all been coincidences. And with him came the women surrounding him and creeping up like spiders in a horror movie.

She hit a section of the trail where no one was in sight and began to run, trying to remember the quickest way back to her car. She reached a trail below the nature center building and looked up. A man was watching her; she recognized him. The driver—or was he also a bodyguard? Was he watching for her, showing her where Dirk was now so she could leave without running into the celebrity's group?

Or, did they fear her?

Did they think she was a threat because of the weapon she now felt compelled to carry? Because of Dirk Durmont.

How dare they! Monsters!

She was not the nut here!

Later, Lara lay on her sofa and eyed the large mirror above the sideboard. Hanging it was one of her first projects when she'd moved in. After she painted the porch, she found the elegant mirror and placed it to reflect the fireplace across the room. Above the fireplace, two huge pictures were propped on the mantel, visually balanced by bottles in carefully chosen graduated sizes. The room wasn't perfect yet; nothing in the house was. But she had ideas, pictures torn from magazines, and gallons of paint purchased. The house was her home. When she'd moved in, she had joked to her friends that she wouldn't leave until carried out in a coffin.

How could this be happening to her? In the past, before Granville, she'd made mistakes that caused her losses and pain. She'd made some bad decisions and put her trust in the wrong people, the wrong things. But not this time. She'd done nothing wrong in Granville, nothing to deserve this. But in spite of her innocence, something ruthless and cruel stood in her path everywhere she went and that was the way it would always be for her here.

06-16-01
Journal,

 I fear running into Dirk Durmont. When I saw him at the nature center, I felt such sickness and rage.

 And these obsessed nuts will always be here in Granville to be near Dirk. There is nothing to do but leave! It all makes me sick. This crap isn't about me; they don't even know me. But I don't have to stay in a town where something so insidious is even possible. Everywhere I go, I look over my shoulder, I look around, ready to take off if anyone gets near me. And they do. Now that same blond woman keeps showing up everywhere I go.

 Friday while I was leaving a restaurant, this waitress watched me walk out and said sarcastically, "Well <u>that</u> makes my night; I've seen the famous butt!" When I'm in a better mood I can smirk at the fact that these people have their minds on my ass and that's damned pathetic. My mind is usually full of such interesting stuff, and they're obsessed with my "butt".

 The reality of losing my house makes me nuts. But I can't stand the pain and the stalking and the abuse of Granville. And that I'm being ruined and victimized by a man whom God has so blessed, and by his deranged followers and all the people he has bought. I'm sick from it all. I want to think well of Dirk, to love him, but I'm fearing the worst. I fear he is a bad man, completely self-serving. I read about another trivial lawsuit he has filed. He sues people while he has ruined me and avoids taking responsibility.

 My review time at work is coming up. I will tell Cheryl that I unfortunately don't see a future in this town and will ultimately leave. I'll tell her that I don't know where to go but I can't stay here.

 I'll keep "packing my bags" and writing and this is my life for now.

09-23-01
 "We must be willing to get rid of the life we've planned,
  so as to have the life that is waiting for us."
   —Joseph Campbell, author

 A catch-up.

 It's been intense lately. September 11 is one of those days that will go down in infamy. Terrorist planes attacked the US—the

World Trade Center and the Pentagon. Thousands are dead, so much shock, tragedy, grieving. It's sickening. And constant media coverage. I'm trying to avoid the TV and the newspaper stories. It's too much, too sad. Horrible violent dreams.

I've rented a house on Pawley's Island again, this time for the entire month of January. This cements my plans to quit my job and leave Granville. The rental is pricey, but if I spend a few dollars to fix myself, so be it. I need some good experiences. In my most debilitating depressions I think of my savings account and realize its lack of worth. I don't want to spend another winter here while Dirk comes to town for the holidays, showing the world and city how happy his life is and I am so ruined because of him.

I had a dream about a demon—a skinny dirty little man— that was crawling, clutching and clawing, toward me, but being dragged back by a heavy chain. Twice it tried to drown itself in a dark well, but I—cold, but morally obligated—pulled it out. It wanted to destroy itself, but I, its victim, was too "good" to let it. A bad day for a monster.

I feel set upon by demons. At work now, some woman has been sitting outside on the planter ridiculing me as I come back in from lunch. She looks me up and down, pointing at me while drawing in the people around her with her comments.

09-27-01 Friday
I worked four extra hours today, trying to make money while I can. Unemployment will be frightening.

The men remain a great problem. Some make cruel comments. The only place I go now is the grocery store and they leer at me there; some are bizarre-looking and most are vulgar. Last week, I had a dream, typical, about some man who was going to shoot me. When I woke up, I was so depressed I couldn't move. My body quit. In the dream—whatever. I can't even stand to write about it.

Em and my Illinois friends remain supportive. Paul and Em are creating this little fantasy farm with chickens and a pet goat and kittens everywhere. It gives me something uplifting to think about.

I went to a movie last week with Tom Mitchell, a guy from the folk dancing crowd in town. He's attractive and nice, but I told him I'm leaving the area. He still wants to run around as friends, which is nice. If my life was normal at all, I could get involved with him if he was interested in me.

But—when Tom and I were on the way back to my house, I saw a condom tucked in under the windshield wiper of his car! I pointed it out and made a joke about it (having had a beer earlier helped the joking part), thinking that was better than his driving around and seeing it later and being embarrassed. He stayed non-committal about what it was, so I told him that maybe it was a breath mint. It was, of course, a condom. And it <u>was</u> funny, unless it humiliated Tom. And unless it was because of me. Because, when we were walking to his car, we passed a group of four yellow-haired women, laughing in that horsey open-mouthed way. So, it might have been the usual lewd behavior of some Granville skanks, sticking a condom on my date's car. Harassing me on a date.

I told Cheryl that I would be leaving Granville. The weirdness, stares, comments at work continue. More and more from the smokers outside when I come back from lunch.

I can not let myself talk or think about all this, my mind and psyche can't handle it. God help me. Why won't He help me?

12-01-01

> *"There is the risk you cannot afford to take,*
> *and there is the risk you cannot afford <u>not</u> to take."*
> *—Peter Drucker, author*

I just wrote my resignation letter.

My leaving is necessary; I usually block any thoughts about it and keep my emotions under control. Being unemployed is terrifying, but I have to believe that God has something better for me. I've read that when the devil steals from you, God gives you back something much better.

A revelation, though. I hope in my life I someday find a man to be with, but if I don't, I can still make someone of myself. With God, I can go out and achieve something, whatever it is He's trying to do in this mess of my life.

When I think about Dirk and this nightmare I'm living, the sorrow is too much. I can't take it on. Later, another day, another place.

313

Darn. The terrible rage and misery starts again when I get near these topics. Too much pain. Just to go away, that's all I can do right now. And to not hope. I need to give up hope.

12-04-01
Happy birthday to me.

To Lara on her birthday
from God

Today, for your birthday, I give you:
- *good friends.*
- *the radio game, the right song at the right moment.*
- *health, a strong body.*
- *intelligence. (So use it.)*
- *protection from physical harm through miracles, people acting as angels, and angels.*
- *protection from evil for you. And for Dirk, since you pray for him.*
- *a life that has been so full of strange events and traumas, you are the envy of bored people with "ordinary" lives.*

Happy Birthday!
Love,
God

To Lara on her birthday
from Lara

For my birthday, I want to make up daydreams and stories of things that would be nice to have happen. I don't have to deal with reality; that will always be there. I want and need dreams this year. So—
* Wouldn't it be great if I wrote a novel, and sold it? And I sold movie rights and it touched many people's minds, hearts, and lives. And it made me enough money that I never had to worry about money again.
* Wouldn't it be great if Dirk and I met and became friends, loving and enjoying each other and praying for and helping each other

for the rest of our lives? They don't stalk his friends, do they?

* Wouldn't it be great if I could keep this house and have a beach house and a condo in Chicago?

* Wouldn't it be great if I met a man who loved me, whom I loved and felt safe around and who liked sex and would be my companion? Who would stay with me, and travel and see movies with me. And who liked to iron. ;-)

* Wouldn't it be great if, day by day, I worked happily at work God wanted me to do and that I loved doing?

*"And we know that all things work together for good to them that love God,
to them who are called according to His purpose."*
—Romans 8:28

CHAPTER TWENTY-NINE

"She went to the ocean to finish her novel."

Lara repeated the line as she paused at the bottom of the long weathered staircase. It was a romantic notion, so writer-like. She climbed the grayed wooden steps with her load of suitcases and shopping bags, then stopped at her new temporary back door.

Buckley had already refused to make the climb. Later tonight she would double his pain medication and try again. It'd been expensive to add him to her house rental and she wanted him to enjoy the trip, a vacation in this—perhaps his last—year of living. Right now he seemed happy curling into a sleep pose in the sand under the house.

Lara unlocked the door. She dropped her bags inside and immediately paced across the wooden floor toward expansive glass doors. This one large room served as a kitchen, living room, and dining room and as she moved through it she thought about how she'd rearrange the furniture. She reached the doors and slid them open, then stepped outside.

The deck overlooked the beach and ocean. There was no one in sight here on Pawley's Island in January, and few lights visible in the now familiar row of weathered old beach cottages mixed with brighter new houses. Lara breathed deeply and intentionally, enjoying the fresh ocean air and solitude for a minute before she turned back to finish unloading her car. After that, there was a bed to make and groceries to buy.

January 1, 2002
"A 'journey of faith' is a different sort of journey . . . . Abraham set out, not knowing where he was to go (Hebrew 11:8). Moses wanted to stay put in Midian, but God said 'Go, and I will be with you' (Exodus 3:12). The Israelites in the desert . . . (did not) reach their destination for 40 years. Apparently the journey itself was a goal, a necessary means of forming them into a people."
—Fr. Mark Stengel, The Abbey Message, Vol LX No 2,
Subiaco Abbey, Subiaco AR.

A New Year.

And I've lost everything. It's been in the most painful way, at the hands of a man so famous that my face is regularly rubbed into news of his activities.

I spent last night, New Year's Eve, in a motel room in Charlotte NC, sobbing into a towel while some couple had loud sex in the next room. I tried to shop but the mall had closed early. I thought of finding a church, but I got so lost when trying to find the mall that I couldn't take on the search for a church. I made it to Pawley's this afternoon.

But, on the "faith" side: This is supposedly where God wants us, with no plans. I'm in so much mental and emotional pain that I can't imagine God had a hand in this, but my life is His to create for me now.

Something evil stole my life from me, and He promises to restore it.

For 2002, my resolutions, hopes, and plans are:

1.

2.

3.

open.

What a year. I don't even want to look back at my past year's resolutions for 2001. Best and worst things—did I even record them last year? It doesn't matter. Things are changing, __will__ change, regardless of the past.

Now:

* Worst of last year: That Dirk Durmont did not clear up this mess for me, when it would have been so easy for him. I will not recover from the anguish and grief this one fact has caused me.

* Best of last year: The realization that my "sensitivity" may be an aptitude I need to attend to and develop.

01-02-02

I'm now a writer full-time. I'm not afraid; this has been so long coming and I've worked so hard on my courage, that right now I'm okay.

I gave my letter of resignation to Cheryl, but when she came to *my cubicle to ask about announcing it, I started to cry! I cried! At work! I don't <u>do</u> that. So embarrassing.*

We agreed to not announce my leaving, to just let word get around, and she would tell anyone she needed to. It was a rough few weeks. So many triggers. Ned wanted to get me a cake and have a going-away lunch and I sent him an email about my rage at my victimization and that this was far from a normal situation.

So I got through it. Most people were sympathetic and kind. Adrienne Taylor gave me a journal! How nice. She told me about her art adventure in Greece and Italy, and having to wing it in Greece. I asked her if the sheer survival part, the searching for rooms and such, was so much work it ruined her fun. She replied that her trip was about developing her art, so she took those problems and put them into her painting. An inspiration, as always.

Buckley is unhappy here at the ocean. The strange smells, the sounds. The surf is very loud and won't stop. The refrigerator makes noises, and something creaks. I worry about ghosts.

But here I am and I will work. I must. I hauled my old computer with me and will set it up tomorrow.

I expect a lot from this spooky beach house. I have no choices. I can't stay in Granville, I can not stand the pain. I've quit my job, it's winter there, I am stalked and harassed when I leave the house, I can not stand the pain. I fear running into Dirk Durmont, I can not stand the pain. So here I am, like it or not. I'll push myself to finish my book, <u>use</u> this time and place.

I brought the pain with me, of course, but maybe the distance will help me detach from Granville and my house and maybe, maybe, God will provide me with a solution and a place to be, and maybe I'll finish my book and sell it.

01-06-02

Buckley has adjusted a bit. We're walking every day. This is a healing environment, and beautiful. Today it was sunny and 50s, so I took a couple of good walks. I saw dolphins, popping up exactly where I imagined they would, as if they read my mind over some distance and came to please me. I saw pelicans flying along in a train, almost beak to tail, inches above the water. This evening, I walked Buckley along the creek and watched the sunset. Such colors—dusky corals, plums, some mauve, and the sky a medium gray blue.

But for hours every day, the depression rips into me. Whatever. I won't let myself off the hook of writing my book. As far as I see it, this emotional pain and rage will be a part of my life until Dirk Durmont helps me. And after all these years of his ducking responsibility for what he did to me, I have to face that that is all he is going to do. I am okay only when I can distract myself.

Today God gave me a beautiful day and dolphins. I'm in a beach house with the ocean outside my door and the movie channel on TV.

Lara heaved the computer monitor onto the table, then collapsed into the molded plastic chair. Soon she could start typing her hand-written manuscript. She crawled through the tangle of wires and cords, sorting them and finding homes for all the connectors. Then, with a prayer, she pushed the main plug into an outlet. The green light on the CPU blinked—it worked! After a week bumping along in her car, the outdated machine now hummed while familiar logos appeared on its screen.

Lara set out to clean up the memory. She'd sweep out the old files to make room for this fresh new project, her novel. She double-clicked on the uninstall program. It moved through the system and at times flashed Lara a question, to which she usually answered "yes." The software would know what to keep. After a few minutes, she closed the program. She clicked on the word processor, expecting to start page one, sentence one, of her novel. But a cold gray box with a cryptic error message appeared on the screen.

Say what? She couldn't access *what*? She clicked the box away, then tried again to open the word processor. The same error message popped up.

She thought a minute, then rebooted and went to the word processor via another path. Error.

Lara grit her teeth. "No way. Don't even think it," she scolded the computer.

She brought up the DOS window. Why, oh why, had she never learned DOS? On the blank screen she typed in "Run", then hit enter. The command sat steady; nothing happened. She tried typing "Windows", enter.

This time the computer came back with "Invalid command."

Lara's breath came quicker as she grew anxious. She spoke sternly into the monitor. "You will not do this to me. You will not do this."

There had to be a solution. Lara clenched her jaw and sat back to think. She would type her book here in this little beach house, just as she planned. It was what she had in front of her to do. She would type her book.

Anything else was unacceptable.

The next day, she sat with a list of DOS commands recited by the techie who answered the computer help line. He'd also given her bad news. According to the error message, she'd blown away some important file. The fix involved reconfiguring the whole system. That was possible if her brother-in-law could find and mail the packet of computer CDs and diskettes.

For now, she sat and entered one DOS command after another, her tension mounting. Over and over, the screen returned "Invalid command."

Frustrated and angry, she stopped, folded her arms, and stared a dare into the screen.

"Who do you think you are? Do you think you can stop me?" The blank screen stared back. She suddenly slapped the side of the monitor, making her palm smart. "Well, think again, you worthless piece of plastic!"

A local newspaper had listed a used computer for $100. "You can be replaced, you know!"

Lara called the number. Nobody was home.

01-10-02 Friday
>*"I pack my trunk, embrace my friends, embark on the sea,*
>*and at last wake up in Naples,*
>*and there beside me*
>*is the Stern Fact, the Sad Self, unrelenting, identical,*
>*that I fled from."*
>>*—Ralph Waldo Emerson.*

I have to trick myself into working on my book, trick the depression away. I can't let myself think about my life.

*My rituals: I get up at sunrise and drink some coffee while lis-
tening to a Catholic chaplet on EWTN, some cable station. Then I
do the yogic "salutation to the sun" with the early sun making a path
over the water and lighting me up in orange. It's a neat experience.*

*I then feed Buckley and take a short walk with him along the
beach. I return to the house and have a writing session of four pages.
I shower etc., and run around town a little. Once back, I take a
good long walk, then write another four pages. A good schedule.*

Part of Lara's daily ritual had become sitting in front of her computer trying to force the technical problem away. She *would* type her
book. Somehow she would do this. She called the library and learned
she could use their computer, but only for limited times and with
people creeping around as she typed. Unacceptable.

She now stared at the familiar error message on the monitor. She
could almost recite it, she'd read it out to so many people over the
phone. Annoyed, she grabbed the mouse and roughly clicked on other
programs. The same sour message appeared on the screen. This had
gone on too long. She had a plan out here on Pawley's Island and she
would carry it out. Her anger grew.

She leaned her face into the computer.

"I don't know who you think you are! I don't *care* who you think
you are! You will not beat me, do you understand?"

She jumped up from her chair and slapped the side of the monitor.
It shook from the impact. She shouted into the screen at her invisible
enemy.

"Do you understand? You will not win! You will not do this to me!"

She leaned in closer to the glass, her years of frustration making her
lose control. "Who the hell do you think you're dealing with?! You will
not stop me!"

Lara paced now, senseless with anger and shouting.

"Did you think this would stop me? There's a way around *you*!
There's always another way. Did you think you'd win? Well, think
again, you friggin monster! I do not care ...," She beat her fists on top
of the monitor. "I do not care what you do, you will not beat me! Yeah,
you're a goddamned error message, or some vacuum-eyed white trash,
or a nut with a knife. *Or* some soulless celebrity! I don't care, I do not
care who you are!"

She sat with a thud and leaned into the computer, fierce with rage. "You will not beat me! You will not win!"

Gripping the edge of the table, she forced her breath to steady. She moved deliberately to calm her actions and clicked her way along a shortcut to a letter she'd typed long ago. Maybe she'd write a note to that god-forsaken monster. She brought up a document, glanced through it, then searched for another. She'd use one of these as a base, then write a letter to that son of Satan.

Then she stopped, staring. Suddenly she saw it.

She was in the word processor! She'd found a back door in.

She would type her manuscript.

Her month reprieve was thieved away in pieces, as if stolen by one of the ghosts Lara feared. January ended and Lara made the long drive back to Granville, where the world was wintry cold and the people strange. She had told her neighbors that she might move away and now some people wanted to see her house. The inevitable was looming.

Not long after her return, Lara stood waiting to check out at a grocery store and noticed a tabloid cover featuring a photo of a woman with a large hat, huge sunglasses, and long blond hair. Other people in line eyed the paper, then her. She ignored them; she was too numb to care anymore.

What she had in front of her to do was to get her house ready to sell. The neighbor's friends might buy it. They'd waited weeks for Lara to finish her painting and reorganizing projects, and she needed to call them soon.

Today she had to fill her porch planters, that's all she knew. The house had to be perfect. She drove to Home Store, parked, and strode toward the gardening area. It was early in the season for flowers, but behind a chain-linked fence rows of colorful blooms dotted the dark shelves like confetti. Lara didn't see the sign until she was close enough to read "Garden Center Opened Weekends Only Until April 1." There was no arguing with the large chain wrapped around the closed entrance.

She spun around and paced back to the car. When she reached it, she turned as she opened the door.

Then she straightened and stared, surprised.

A tall thin man wearing a cap and a large shirt—untucked—was moving away from the garden center and down a nearby row with few cars. To be where he was walking now, almost even with her in another row, he must have followed her toward the fence.

Lara felt no fear, only a reminder of a chore on her list, something to take care of before leaving town. She was two years late, but she would do it now.

The spare blue room looked familiar and Lara tried to remember if she'd ever been to a police station. Not likely. Why would anyone like her be involved with the police?

The lobby wasn't like what she'd seen in movies. It was empty except for a bench and a window that offered a darkened view to the outside. A policeman behind a service window looked up at her from the paperwork in front of him. Along the back wall, a door led probably into the area where TV shows pictured investigators at desks and detectives in small rooms questioning witnesses and perps.

She glanced around and ducked her head down. Had anyone seen her come here? What would Dirk think? Did it matter now? She walked up to the window and spoke to the man in uniform, who wrote on a pad as she talked. Describing her problem was harder than she imagined. She hadn't discussed this with enough people to be practiced at finding the right words.

"So you want to report a man stalking you," the officer said.

That wasn't it. "He isn't exactly stalking me, that one isn't. I've only seen him four times."

"Ma'am, why do you think he's stalking you?"

"I didn't say he was stalking me. I want to report an attempted assault. Or an assault." When he'd come at her with a knife, she'd told a few friends. She had to explain why she'd become so guarded and jumpy. And why she kept a weapon at hand. But these were all new friends; they didn't know that she had changed, that a friendly kind woman had turned into a major spook. Only her friends back in Illinois were really aware of her problems and how they affected her. But one thing her friends in Granville had impressed on her was that, even if he hadn't stabbed her, the event was an assault and she needed to go to the police so he couldn't go around attacking anyone else. Maybe it had taken awhile, but here she was, being a responsible citizen.

"Can you describe what happened?"

Lara glanced around the station. A man had come in and stood nearby, looking out the window. "May I just speak to someone?"

The policeman picked up the phone and directed Lara to wait.

She sat for the time it took to read two sections of a newspaper left on the bench. She counted three deep breaths to calm herself and reviewed her story in her head. Finally, a man in uniform opened the door in the back wall.

"Lara McKeon?"

She cringed. Did he have to say her name so loud? She got up and followed him to a small room furnished with a metal table and several chairs. This she recognized from the movies. This looked like that scene in that movie where some character destroyed a woman's life by stealing all she had and making her desperate. The woman had become a criminal herself.

Thought stop, thought stop. Lara tried to clear her mind.

She chose a chair that put her back to the wall. Two police officers had come into the room with her. One held an open notebook and pen. He spoke.

"I see that you are being stalked."

"No. It's an assault case. I've seen him several times, but they say up front that that isn't enough to call it stalking. *He* isn't stalking me, anyway. He just tried to kill me, and he keeps showing up, so I wanted to report it. I'm leaving town because of all this, so I wanted to report it before I left."

Was she making any sense? The officer wrote something, so maybe he understood her.

"And when did this happened?"

"May 4, 2000."

"Two years ago?"

"Yes. But I didn't want ... I didn't want it in the newspapers then, but I see he's still following me around."

"What happened on ... ," he looked down at his notebook, "on May 4, 2000."

"I had been working out at the health club, Brandt's Gym, the downtown branch, and went out to my car, when he came at me with a knife."

"What street was that on?"

Darn. Street names. Details. "I'm not sure. It's beside the gym. I think the front is on Jackson Street, but I don't know the side street."

"What time was it?"

"Around 9 at night. I always left around that time, so I think he was waiting for me."

"What's his name and where do you know him from?"

"Oh, I don't know him, but I heard that his nickname is 'Wasp'." This is when the movie detective picks up the fact that the victim knows more than she's saying. Now he'll ask clever questions to get the truth.

But this wasn't a movie.

The officer wrote a few notes. "And he came toward you with a knife? What happened then?"

"A car pulled into the street at the same instant and caught him in its headlights, so he stopped and changed direction. Actually, it was a police car that saw him." Okay, so he missed the fact that Lara knew the perp's nickname. Now he'd wonder why a policeman saw the whole thing and didn't do anything about it.

But he gave her a blank look and said, "We didn't have any reports of any assaults that night."

Lara stared. How did he know what was reported two years ago? Surely these people weren't all bought by the movie star. But the policeman didn't look like he was hiding anything. Maybe Granville was still a peaceful enough town that knifings were unusual.

He wrote more in his book, then copied some numbers onto a small slip of paper. He handed the paper to Lara. "We're making a police record of this. Next time he shows up, you call the police and use this number, and we'll know there's a previous report on him."

Lara took the paper. A thought slowly formed in her head.

There was now a police report.

With an official report, if she ever did have to use Snubbie, it was clearly a case of self-defense. Clearly. She was incredulous. Why hadn't she done this long ago?

They didn't buy her house. Not those people, but maybe the next ones would. Or maybe no one would and this whole nightmare would disappear. But just in case, Lara needed to find a place to go so she wouldn't be homeless.

She had returned from the coast with her typed manuscript, as planned, but it needed length and polishing. So now she had two things in front of her to do: 1) finish the rewrite of her novel and, 2) find a place to live.

Lara traveled. Raleigh NC was reported to be a fine place of growth and opportunity, trendy in the 90s. She headed toward it, but got lost on the roads time and time again. At one point she went around a loop highway four times before she realized she was going in circles. She didn't need to see any more "Wrong Way" signs to know she hadn't found her new city.

On the way there, emergency vehicles passed her along a winding mountain road, making her panic. What if the shadows were there and something had happened to them? Because of her! The thought made her sick. It was a familiar feeling by now. Just last winter, she'd chanced going out on icy roads, then on the way back from her mother's house, had passed an overturned jeep. Her sorrow and sense of guilt were overwhelming! Would she ever know if the driver was okay and if he had been driving on the ice because of her?

And now this wreck in the hills.

But then she realized that if anyone wondered about Dirk's shadows, they should try to imagine that terrible sense of responsibility, what it felt like to cause some innocent person to be hurt. Because maybe that was a little bit how Dirk felt about the Lara Project.

After North Carolina, she headed toward Chicago. The cost of housing quickly ran her out.

She came home from one of her trips to find Buckley sick. His 14th birthday was two weeks away and Lara had increased his pain medicine to keep his huge body mobile. She dreaded the trip to the vet's she'd have to make the next day.

That night, she had a dream. She saw Buckley running up the stairs into her bedroom, more animated and vigorous than he'd been in years. He ran toward her, his ears lifted, curious at his renewed strength. Two steps into the room, however, he dropped his nose to the ground and sniffed his way toward a corner, where it seemed someone called to him. He trotted a couple of steps, then disappeared.

The next morning, Lara stood a long time in the kitchen before stepping out to check on Buckley. She wasn't surprised to find him lifeless, his huge body diminished and dead. Such a good dog to the very end, he had run to her in her dream, full of the new life that death had given him.

Within the month, Lara finished polishing her novel and turned it over to two friends to preview.

That same day, she visited a real estate agent. But she held on to the thought that if her house didn't sell, she'd know God didn't really want her to move, that it was all a mistake and a miracle would fix her life.

A week later, she sat in front of her computer, trying to control her trembling fingers. She was grateful for the physical barrier of the machine; no one would know her distress when they saw only her typed words.

Subj: House Sold
Date: 04/17/2002 2:15:03 PM Central Daylight Time
From: LaraMc777@mail.com
To: SauderFarms@mail.com;JCMusic2@network.com;TinaGirl @goodmail.com; SaraKyle @mail.com

Hello friends,

My house sold. It went so fast. In five days I let a dozen people in to see it and the sixth day someone came back to buy it. I don't know where I'm going to go now.

Please spare a prayer for me. I am sick about all this, and about losing my house because of this mess in Granville. This is the worst thing that has ever happened to me, and you all know some of the things I've been through, so that's saying a lot.

Thanks,
Love, Lara

She hit "send", then slipped back to the floor where she'd lain sobbing much of the day. Her face hurt from the days of salt tears, but she could not stop. She only hoped the neighbors couldn't hear her anguish.

—⁓—

Subj: L-House?
Date: 04/18/2002 8:23:24 AM Central Daylight Time
From: HotGirl11@mail.com (Karen)
To: DirkDolls (group)

What gives on the Love Shack?

We can't get a straight answer about the sign in Lara's yard. The real estate people won't let us in to see it. They say we have to be "serious buyers only". And there's no key anywhere so no one can sneak us in. I guess Lara is meeting everyone who sees it.

She has to be bluffing. There's no way she'd sell her house. Half the stuff she did was house stuff. She's just putting this sign out there to get Dirk's attention.

Subj: Re: L-House?
Date: 04/18/2002 10:06:17 AM Central Daylight Time
From: LipsToLuv@mail.com
To: DirkDolls (group)

I heard it's for real. That she's for real selling it.

I bet Dirk is moving her out to a private island to get her away from all the stress of her fame here. Maybe one in Paris, where he'll have her closer.

Subj: Re: L-House?
Date: 04/18/2002 10:26:32 AM Central Daylight Time
From: HotBabe@mail.com
To: DirkDolls (group)

Say it ain't so! She keeps getting all this stuff! It is so unfair!

What are we going to do with Dirk's girlfriend gone? Before Lara came, all we had was Dirk coming and going from his Mom's or that other place. We hardly had anything to do at all. It'll be back to that. Boring.

What are we going to do for fun?

—៷៷៷—

"*You're* overdressed." Blair looked Michelle up and down, then turned back to the mirror. Her pink fake-satin robe hung open, revealing her nude tanned body.

Michelle's blue jeans did look rough amid the silks and feathers in this familiar dressing room. She walked over to the open closet door and picked up a corner of a feather cape. "I don't go on tonight," she said. "Not 'til Saturday, for that matter. If you want out of any dances, give me a call."

Blair glanced over at her and raised her eyebrows, then eyed herself in the mirror again. She had several quarter-sized glow-in-the-dark stars glued onto her body. She pressed another one onto the top of her left breast as she spoke. "You here begging dances? Times must be rough. I'm not having any trouble getting work."

She met Michelle's eyes and added, "And neither is Delta!" She laughed.

"Well, Rocko and I have an agreement." Michelle fiddled with the cape's feathers as she spoke, avoiding looking at Blair. "He thought I was working too hard and wants to keep me fresh."

Blair's laugh was loud and harsh. "I'm sure! Well, I hope you're getting your beauty sleep, but I don't have any extra dances for you. I'm looking into buying a house, so need the cash. Uh, Rocko and I have an agreement, too. That he'll make me filthy rich!" She hefted up each breast and pressed stars under them.

"I'm not here looking for work! I'm doing okay. I thought you might have some information, is all." Michelle had thought hard about how to get on Blair's good side. It seemed a lost cause. Blair knew she called her "Big Blair" behind her back, and she was being a bitch about how Michelle had treated Delta. And some other people. But she had to try; it was down to this, sucking up to Big Blair.

Blair was silent as she glued a star on her upper thigh.

Michelle continued. "Do you happen to have Shirl's number?"

"Yeah, and I know you do, too."

"The number's changed. I called it and it's out of service. Do you have the new one?"

Blair didn't look up. She pressed more stars against her skin as she spoke. "Nope. No new number."

Michelle didn't believe her. "I need to talk to her about something. She wouldn't mind if you gave it to me. She told me to call her once Lara left, and she'd fix me up with some people."

Blair stopped and stared steady at her, then looked away. "Really, I don't have it. There's no reason I'd lie to you about that. I don't care what any of the Shirls are doing with themselves or who has their numbers.

Whatever they're doing, I can be pretty sure they're all lying about it."

Michelle was finding it harder to breathe. All her plans were falling apart. If she didn't get out to L.A., what was she going to do? She was almost ruined in Granville. Rocko was cutting her hours *and* taking out money for her boob job. She'd thought it was a gift, a bonus, and here he was charging her! There were other strip clubs in Granville, but only whores worked in those dives.

She needed Shirl's help, like she promised her. She couldn't go out to California by herself.

Blair noticed her stress and smirked. "Ah. The queen has met her match. Shirl has set you up, used you, and disappeared. Michelle, I'll try to be nice and not laugh at you. Right now, though, I need to practice some moves, if you'd clear some space for me in here."

Blair went to the door and opened it.

Michelle scowled at her and marched out.

—∿∿—

Lara packed her bags, got in her car, and moved on out to the next town. She chose Peoria, where she had friends and could afford a decent house. Her first day looking, she found a pretty two-story painted the same cheerful yellow as her house in Granville. It was a good enough place to be, especially given she didn't want to exist anyplace at all.

She took care of one last errand before she moved. She called Dirk Durmont's lawyer. In her heart of hearts she knew Dirk knew what had happened to her—because of him—but she wanted to make it clear.

The lawyer's assistant had asked Lara's name and what she wanted, then put her on hold. A few minutes later she returned and said the lawyer was out but that she could leave a message. Lara didn't believe he wasn't there, but her only option was to speak to his machine. She sat through a brief recorded intro, then began to leave her simple message.

To her horror, emotion overwhelmed her. She sobbed as she choked out her phone number, then hung up and sank to the floor, crying in embarrassment and desperation. He wasn't going to help her. No one was. There wasn't anyone anywhere who would help her.

CHAPTER LAST

The water drops formed into shapes like silver ladybugs and crawled forward, nudged by the air. Delta giggled as one took flight off the shiny red hood. She pushed the gas pedal harder, speeding along the highway until all the transparent beads were gone.

Rocko's guys had told her that to keep her new car nice, she should spray-wash it every week and visit the expensive hand-washers every month. A clean car was a happy car. And she should take it into the shop every six months, whether it was broken down or not.

She squirmed down lower in her seat as she entered Rockton. Immediately she was behind a line of cars making its way toward the fishing resorts. She leaned her head out the window and wished everyone would hurry; she had places to be. Like a parade, they passed the giant ice cream cone on the right, then the coffee cup on the left, and then stopped at a light near Rockton High.

As her car idled, Delta looked toward the windows of the old school. A couple of kids stared back and she knew they wished they were her. Here she was, driving a fancy new car, decked out in a new dress. She wasn't comfortable in the long plain dress, which hit mid-calf above boring shoes. "Sage linen" was the color listed on the tag. The shoes were beige pumps with medium heels thick as the wooden blocks she played with as a kid. Reeza had helped her pick the dress out. It was different, for sure. Its buttons ran to her neck, which left no place for her boobs to show at all. Lara would like it. But mostly, as Reeza said when she saw it, "This is something your Gramma would like."

The Dirk Dolls would know if Lara ever wore something like this. But they'd said she wasn't going in to work anymore in her new city, so it'd be hard to know where she'd be wearing it. She was staying in her house a lot now. No one knew what she was doing in there. She'd been to a couple of gyms working out, but never for long. The Dolls in Lara's new town were bored silly with her not being out to follow around. Grocery shopping, taking walks—without the big dog Buckley—hanging around with church people. That's all she did.

This was almost a church-going getup, except Delta had insisted on the nail polish being Raspberry Passion. And she and Reeza had talked about the dress being useful later if they cut it real short. But Delta had already decided that if Gramma liked it she'd keep it just like it was.

The traffic crawled along and soon she'd be coming to the street that wound up the hill to the right. That old street would first pass the big red McNought house and two blocks farther would be the narrow lane with the little white house.

Suddenly Delta turned opposite, careening to the left up a curving road. At the intersection at the top of the hill, she stopped to quiz out which direction. The times she'd been this way, she wasn't the one driving. She chose a left turn and several blocks later was rolling through the "new" part of town, a neighborhood of two-story brown and beige homes. Which one was Michelle's? What gave it away was the shabby grass, worn away in some patches and overgrown in others. No one in that family ever did do yard work.

Delta was shy to stop right in front, so she drove down a few houses before she pulled over. She sat a minute, thinking.

Michelle wasn't home, that was for sure. Delta didn't know where she was, but she knew Michelle would be sleeping in the gutters of Granville before she ever came back to live in Rockton. She'd moved out of the apartment building when Rocko ran out of dances for her. Someone said she was dancing at Lively Lady. Delta wasn't sure where she was living, but she knew it wasn't California.

How long had they been out of Rockton? She counted back in summers but couldn't believe the number, so she counted again. Three? There was that summer after they graduated when they'd all moved to Granville, except Stacy and Brittany. That was "one." Then there was the next summer when so many people were running after Lara. Two. Then last summer, Michelle moved out and life took off to busy times. Three. And here it was almost summer again, and three years since they graduated. She couldn't believe the number.

It seemed so long since they were good Dirk Dolls. Did they get too busy to keep up with him? Stacy was still in nursing school, so she was busy and doing okay. Brit was working in a nice spa in L.A., building a name and a list, she'd said. She was still with Jake and doing real fine. Delta had been out there on business a few times and looked them up. But she didn't have to sleep on their sofa; she always had a room at a slick hotel where Rocko had his parties. And Michelle. She was probably doing every man who was good for something and doing okay.

And here Delta was, traveling the country, driving a new car, and wearing a dress that she could buy for no reason but to please her Gramma. She hadn't met Dirk Durmont yet, had she? Seems she'd forgotten to try. It didn't matter so much now, especially since that Tony kept showing up. He treated her like she was some fancy piece of china that should be kept safe someplace, too fine and special for this hard world. He wasn't famous or the tallest of the men, but to her he was looking more like a movie star all the time.

Delta looked back again at Michelle's house, then turned the ignition and drove on. She had places to be. For an instant, she thought of taking a quick trip into the hills, to the trailer. But there was no sense in stirring up sorrows that were best left to lie in the dust. She wasn't worried about seeing her Pa. Gramma had schemed up a way to send him some place to "get him some help." But the absence of her brother would make her too sad. If she went up that road, she'd see Mark in the clothesline pole, and in the fist-dents on the metal walls, and likely there'd be some old car or bike of his rusting around. But the old Mark was dead and gone and in his place was some bad thing. He didn't come by much anymore and when he did he needed money. He was in deep trouble and that crazy animal look on him never went away. The last time he'd dropped by the apartment, he'd railed on steady about Lara ruining him. Whatever drug he was on, it was eating him alive, from the inside of his brain to the ends of his falling-out hair. It was too great a sadness to see.

Delta pulled back out onto the highway, traveled to the next street, and this time turned right. She hadn't seen Gramma since that night at Rocko's when she'd come in and surprised Delta. That was a memory she still had to trick her head away from, it made her feel so sorrowful.

But today she didn't feel sad, or afraid. That bad day was gone because her Gramma had wrote her a letter.

She wrote her a letter that made Delta cry like some broken baby doll every time she read it over. Gramma wrote that she'd always love her and it was wrong to judge her so hard about things that were God's business. She said a bit about Reeza, too, as if she knew her. Delta found out from Reeza that they'd become regular phone buddies, what with Gramma calling and keeping tabs on her.

Then Gramma invited her to a tea party.

She said they'd "sup" in the fine remodeled dining room of the

McNought Mansion under a crystal chandelier she and her church friends—now fixing up houses as the Purpose-Driven Painters—had hung. She'd asked Delta to call if she could make it. Delta wanted to go, but couldn't make herself pick up the phone, knowing she'd start boo-hooing as soon as she heard Gramma's voice. Finally Reeza told her to write a little postcard because that's what they did in the olden days of tea parties. So that's what she did. She wrote that she was "most pleased to attend" and would do so.

The house loomed on the right and Delta stopped in the road. It was so grand! Had it always looked so pretty or was it the work of the church ladies? Even the red brick walls looked cleaner against the green lawn and new flowering bushes. She eyed the long driveway that curved up to the front door. That was where the fancy ladies used to go in while Gramma watched them from the upper window. Those rich types used to drive up to the house for nice dinners dressed in their expensive clothes.

Delta looked down at her dress. She suddenly jerked the new red car through the iron gate. Relishing her new fanciness, she rolled toward the entrance.

The house and the shiny-fresh door were coming up close when Delta hit the brake, stopping short.

She cursed the silly tears that filled her eyes. 'Cause there was Gramma, standing at that upstairs window, wiggling her fingers in a wave.

Yep, that was Loopy alright. Michelle stood in the dressing room doorway watching Alice smooth makeup over a faint scar running up one leg.

"Too bad about your leg. But seems you're doing okay after that jumping incident."

Alice's eyes were strange as ever as she stared up at Michelle.

"There was no 'jumping incident.' But yeah, I'm doing fine. You?"

Michelle walked in and plopped down on a dirty sofa. The stench of cum was suddenly strong and she jumped up and looked at the cushions. Stains darkened the center; she sat again and pushed herself into a corner at one end. Working on looking cool again, she took a deep breath and faked a smile at Alice. "I'm doing fine, thank you very much. I knew you at Rocko's. I see you got wise too, and decided to dump that cheating creep."

"You talking about Rocko?" She looked surprised. "He was good to me. But yeah, I'm dancing here now. It's okay. Good money, just uneven. Some nights there's a bunch comes over when Rocko's is too crowded. They tip good."

Michelle lit a cigarette and puffed a few times. She had to get out of this dive *and* this city! This was L-whore's fault, her being in this dump and not with Dirk. "You and I have something else in common." Alice stopped and met her eyes. Michelle went on, watching her face. "As I remember, we both want Dirk Durmont. And we both hate Lara McKeon."

She got the reaction she expected. At the sound of Dirk's name, Alice's face lit up, then when she mentioned L-whore, it got stormy and hateful. Like she expected, and hoped. This crazy chick could be useful.

The sound of a toilet flushing on the other side of the wall interrupted them.

When it quieted, she continued. "Maybe things haven't gone too good lately, but I know what we can do to fix that." And Michelle leaned in to whisper to her new friend.

After Michelle left, Alice turned to the mirror and picked up a blusher brush. She remembered Michelle. She was that shapeless hill-girl, but she'd gotten new boobs somewhere along the line. And Alice knew that no one in this business left Rocko unless *he* dumped *them*. He'd been good to Alice—in spite of the trouble—and she hated anyone bad-mouthing him. But this hill-girl was like that, she recalled. Mean, and thinking no one knew it. She had been running around with that sweet Baby Doll back then. Baby Doll Delta. Delta must have dumped her, too.

But Michelle had some good ideas on ways to get Dirk's attention. So for that, this top-heavy hill-girl could be useful.

───※───

Lara's world had been bizarre so long, it was hard to recognize what was truly strange. She pulled her mind back to the kitchen as her mother spoke.

"They call out my name. I hear them at night. They even broke in when Danielle was here. She told me the next day, 'Your ghosts were back last night. They were calling for *me* this time.'"

Lara looked again at the back door. A chair had been pulled away from the table and braced against the doorknob. She got up from the table and gripped the knob.

"It's fixed now," Mom continued. "The lock wasn't working right, but Lynn fixed it."

Lara searched her memory. She'd heard about these women before, and told her mother her suspicions. Suspicions nothing! The fact was that the Dirk-obsessed nuts were harassing her mother now! It sounded as if they were getting bolder. She knew they'd have a vacuum in their lives when she left, but she thought they'd go after Dirk's family. Except, of course, he had security all over his own family by now. These criminals searched out the vulnerable people.

So now her mother slept with a chair jammed against the back door.

Lara sighed and listened to her mother's story. The women would creep into the backyard, complaining about the neighbor's barking dogs waking everyone up. They commented about her movements, tracking her as she went through the house. They were stupidly loud, so that Mom heard. Lara tried to picture which particular yellow-haired women they were.

It'd been a year since she'd moved away from Granville. She had traveled back today with gifts for her niece, born only weeks earlier. The timing let her catch a book group meeting. Her kind friends had agreed on a "membership in absentia" for her and they exchanged emails of book choices and opinions. Occasionally Lara came to town to see them, and stayed overnight at her mother's. Her visits were as brief as possible, and she went no where but her friend's house and her mother's. The less exposure to Granville, the better. To Lara, the town had become a cesspool.

This trip had been especially sad. She was homesick for the old Granville, the city she'd once considered her "hometown." The dinner at her friend's lovely house had deepened her sense of loss. Would she ever recover a life, or at the least a home?

Life in Peoria had been a mixed experience.

She'd made a list of the good things. 1) Her friends in Illinois were a good support system and she socialized as often as she wanted to. 2) Her pretty little house had a low mortgage, so she could get by with working little and writing much. It stood next to an historic district of beautiful homes through which she took long walks. 3) She'd prayed to meet some good people and found the soup kitchen of Mother Teresa's Missionaries of Charity. She was now a committed volunteer for this group of holy women.

She didn't bother with a list of the bad things. Blond women still trailed her through stores and libraries. Men followed her though grocery stores, stopping and standing behind her when she turned her back to them, or blocking her with a cart flung across the aisle. Her visits to gyms were frustrated by people crowding her, staring and sometimes giggling.

She was writing a second novel now, one about her incredible experiences in Granville. It was far from a healing experience; she had sobbed through much of the first draft.

But she had a new strength. She saw the rudies, and she ignored them. She did not engage, she walked away—from them, but not from whatever task she was doing.

"Some things are missing." Her mother continued, describing a pack of batteries that she and Diane had seen the day before it vanished. "And glasses from the china cabinet are gone." She opened the cupboard door and handled one, a wistful expression on her face. "I always take these out for holidays, and now some are missing."

Lara rose and walked to the cabinet. One shelf was so jammed with densely crowded glasses that the sudden gap at the front seemed to hold the ghosts of three tumblers. She took one out and studied it. It had been present at family gatherings for so many years that it felt familiar in her hand. Simple, straight, decorated with a picture of a country village—three buildings and a small pink pig.

"A set of keys is gone, too."

Lara shuddered.

These women were crazy. What would it come to? They had never understood that Lara wasn't Dirk Durmont. They wouldn't know the difference between stealing a pack of batteries, a drinking glass, a set of keys— or a baby.

She sat again and looked at her mother. Their faces wore the same sick expression.

Lara spoke. "I know they're the same women who were stalking me, Mom. They don't have anything to do with themselves now, so they're bothering you."

Good God, when would it all end?

What was she going to do? The familiar black sorrow began to cloud her thoughts.

But suddenly, a rush, a surge of light like that from the full moon in Mexico, filled her. And in the instant it takes a small bell to chime, she remembered. She saw headlights stopping a knife, visits from dolphins, pretty houses falling into her choosey hands, kind friends, and the Missionaries of Charity. She remembered and she knew.

She knew what she had in front of her to do. She would: 1) have the locks on her mother's doors changed and 2) finish her book.

And after that, she knew what she would do. She would wait, in confidence. Confident, because as she waited, God would send her a new idea, another plan.

She knew He would, because she trusted.